PRAISE FOR KATEE ROBERT

"Thriller fans will enjoy the action and suspense."
—*Publishers Weekly*, on *The Devil's Daughter*

"This cross-genre mystery/romance is fast-paced and suspenseful, with zesty dialogue and likable characters."
—*Kirkus Reviews*, on *The Devil's Daughter*

"Robert shows off her impressive versatility in this fast paced and inventive new Hidden Sins series."
—*RT Book Reviews*, on *The Devil's Daughter*

"Robert easily pulls off the modern marriage-of-convenience trop . . . This is a compulsively readable book! It's more than just sexy times, too, though those are plentiful and hot! . . . An excellent start to a new series."
—*RT Book Reviews*, on *The Marriage Contract*

"*The Marriage Contract* by Katee Robert is dark, dirty, and dead sexy. I want a Teague O'Malley of my very own!"
—Tiffany Reisz, author of the Original Sinners series

"A definite roller coaster of intrigue, drama, pain, heartache, romance, and more. The steamy parts were super steamy, the dramatic parts delivered with a perfect amount of flair."
—*A Love Affair With Books*, on *The Marriage Contract*

T0051083

THE
HUNTING
GROUNDS

ALSO BY
KATEE ROBERT

The Hidden Sins Series

The Devil's Daughter

The O'Malleys Series

The Marriage Contract
The Wedding Pact
An Indecent Proposal
Forbidden Promises
Undercover Attraction

The Foolproof Love Series

A Foolproof Love
Fool Me Once
A Fool for You

Out of Uniform Series

In Bed with Mr. Wrong
His to Keep
Falling for His Best Friend
His Lover to Protect
His to Take

Serve Series

Mistaken by Fate
Betting on Fate
Protecting Fate

Come Undone Series

Wrong Bed, Right Guy
Chasing Mrs. Right
Two Wrongs, One Right
Seducing Mr. Right
Seducing the Bridesmaid
Meeting His Match

THE HUNTING GROUNDS

KATEE ROBERT

Montlake
Romance

Published by Montlake Romance, Seattle

www.apub.com

Amazon, the Amazon logo, and Montlake Romance are trademarks of Amazon.com, Inc., or its affiliates.

ISBN-13: 9781503946705
ISBN-10: 1503946703

Cover design by Mecob Design

Printed in the United States of America

To Connor—
I think we can both agree that this book just proves why
being an inside kid is the best!

CHAPTER ONE

Saturday, June 17
12:03 p.m.

"Someone just reported a body being found out at the Kootenai Lakes campground."

Startled, Maggie Gaines jumped to her feet and snatched the radio from the desk. She knew that voice. David Downey was one of their new seasonal rangers who had been brought on for the summer, and she'd last seen him this morning when he left the Goat Haunt ranger station with a group of tourists. The kid was young, but in the couple of weeks she'd worked with him, he'd remained calm and unruffled even when dealing with the most difficult of tourists.

To have him sounding this panicked made her skin crawl.

She held the radio up, trying to think—to keep the past from creeping in. *A body.* "Are we going to need a team to retrieve it?"

This wouldn't be the first time a body had been found in Glacier National Park, and it wouldn't be the last, but they still maintained one of the lowest death counts of the national parks. Maggie wasn't too keen on seeing that change.

She also wasn't thrilled by the fact that *she* was going to have to deal with this one.

"Maggie, it's not a fall."

Right. She should have realized that. Kootenai Lakes didn't offer a lot of places to fall from, even if that was the leading cause of death in this park—historically, at least.

"They said they found her *strung up.*"

Her stomach dropped. Maggie braced her hands on the desk as the world took a slow turn around her. *Protocol. Stick with protocol.* She took a deep breath that did nothing to calm her racing thoughts. "You haven't seen the body?"

"No. The couple who found her are freaking out, and freaking the rest of the group out. The husband is having chest pains, so I'm sticking here to monitor the situation."

"Good." At least David was keeping his head. But then, he'd worked in the Grand Canyon last season, so he'd likely seen worse than a potential heart attack. "I'm coming."

A previously healthy heart didn't mean a damn thing when it came to hiking, especially with the elevation changes that came from hiking south out of Goat Haunt. The 220-foot vertical gain wasn't as severe as many of the other hikes in the park, but it was a lot for someone not used to it.

She looked up to find Ava Boyle already handing her one of the packs they kept stocked. "You sure you don't want me to call in someone else?" Ava had grown up just outside the park on the Blackfeet Reservation. A few inches taller than Maggie, she kept her long black hair back in a serviceable braid, as usual. She'd been hired the year before Maggie, and as two of the only women park rangers, they'd ended up rooming together. It was hard to live day in and day out with someone without ending up fast friends or bitter enemies.

Luckily, they fell into the former category.

"No, I'll do it. I've been cooped up here for days." She tried really hard to sound in control, but her voice wavered.

"Maggie, with your history—"

"I'm fine." She managed to fake a smile, even though she suspected Ava saw right through it. "You know as well as I do that my history has nothing to do with this body. I've been a ranger longer than I was with the Feds, so I'd like to think I'm more than capable of hiking out there and figuring out what's going on." She thought she did a good job of sounding reasonable. Better than good.

Ava gave her a long look. She didn't have to say anything—it was all there in her ink-dark eyes for Maggie to see. *You don't sound okay.* But she just nodded. "Then let's go. The sooner we get up there, the sooner we get this over with."

They grabbed the equipment necessary to retrieve a body—something Maggie had been naive enough to hope she'd never have to do in this job capacity—and headed for Kootenai Lakes campground. It was just under three miles, and Maggie almost welcomed the struggle of having to keep up with Ava's longer legs and legendary stamina. As rangers, they had to be in pretty good shape, and as women, they had to work twice as hard as the men to prove to themselves and their coworkers that they weren't getting special treatment. But Ava was in another realm entirely.

Even the faint, burning protest of her legs and the harsh inhales of cool air into her lungs did nothing to distract her from David's words. *Strung up.*

There were a lot of ways a person could die in Glacier, at least in theory. Fall, grizzly attack, exposure. *Strung up* did not fit in with any of those possibilities.

Strung up sounded a whole lot like murder.

Stop it.

She hitched her pack higher onto her back. There was another option besides murder, and it was far more likely. Suicide. Kootenai Lakes got a lot of tourist traffic, even this early in the season, and there were quite a few studies out about how national parks had more than their fair share of suicides. But, again, Glacier's number was minuscule compared to the others. They didn't even hit the top five in deaths and rescue-mission numbers on an annual basis.

That doesn't mean anything, and you know it.

All the numbers in the world didn't change the fact that they were hiking up to retrieve a body. Projecting all sorts of wild theories was something she knew better than to indulge in.

She would have remembered issuing a permit to a lone hiker. It was possible that whoever the woman was had hiked up from the Many Glacier ranger station. Or even from a different entry point. People did all sorts of crazy stuff when it came to parks, though it seemed weird that a suicide would travel that far and then hang herself.

Stop guessing. You won't know until you see the body.

They made good time, reaching the campground far faster than she was prepared for. Ava made a beeline for David's distinctive park ranger uniform. They were ungodly ugly—green pants and a khaki shirt—but it made them easy to pick out of a crowd.

The relief on his face relit the flicker of unease that she'd been doing a damn good job of ignoring on the trip up there. David straightened. "I'm glad you guys are here."

Ava didn't smile, but she managed to radiate calm all the same as she sank onto her heels next to the man sitting on the ground. "I'm Ranger Ava Boyle. Can you tell me how you're feeling, sir?" Ava shot her a look, and they'd worked together long enough that Maggie understood the silent command.

Figure out what the hell is going on while I deal with the tourists.

Maggie drew David aside, watching the people milling about as she did. The group had ten adults and a kid, and they were gathered in small groups, talking in hushed voices. She spoke low so her voice wouldn't carry. "How many people saw the body?"

"Just the couple Ava is talking to."

"Do you have a good bead on the location?" She really, really didn't want to be the one to cut down the body, but Ava's skills lay in dealing with scared people.

Maggie didn't do people. Not well. She could fake it for the tours that her job required because she loved the park, but her patience was always too limited, her temper too close to the surface. It had been a relief for everyone when she started being scheduled for more back-country work.

"Yeah. It's the southernmost lake on the northwest edge."

It wouldn't take them long to get there and assess the situation. She took a fortifying breath. They were wasting daylight, and she didn't relish the thought of hauling a body back to the ranger station in the dark. "Let's get to it, then."

She could do this. It wasn't a usual part of her job, but it *was* part of her job. Park rangers were a strange kind of catchall. If it happened in the park, it was their jurisdiction. Because of the nature of Glacier, they didn't see as much of the drug trafficking or other crazy stuff that some of the parks did, but weird shit still went on in these woods.

The hair along the nape of her neck rose as they skirted first one lake and then the other. She kept an eye out for moose, because while they might look like big cows with awesome antlers, they had nasty tempers and were too fast to evade if they got it into their heads that they wanted to trample a person. Behind her, David huffed and puffed a little. Maggie shot a glance over her shoulder. "Problems keeping up?"

"Nope." He set his jaw and picked up his pace until he was nearly on her heels. She liked the man's stubbornness, but he had to learn to ask for help if he needed it.

Not something she needed to worry about now.

"What do you know about the body? You said it was strung up." The more information she had going into this, the better it would be. Maggie hadn't been in the BAU—Behavioral Analysis Unit—for going on seven years, but apparently some habits died hard. It didn't make a bit of sense. She'd been a Fed for less than a year. She'd been a park ranger for almost six.

But she still found herself falling back into the old mind-set.

David dodged a rock and hurried up until he was even with her. "They weren't super clear. They said they thought it was a woman, but there was a lot of blood, and she was hanging from a tree."

Maggie's mind worked on the possibilities the same way she worked on her puzzles during her downtime. Hanging from a tree likely meant suicide. Blood, though? "Could be one of the cougars got to her." The big cats sometimes hauled their kills into trees, so it wouldn't necessarily be deterred by a hanging body if the woman had been there long enough.

"It'd have to be that. Bears aren't going to manage it—or even want to bother."

No, they wouldn't. They moved through the trees on a little path that was barely a path. Most people were content to stick around the campsite at Kootenai Lakes, but there would always be those who wanted a little more privacy, and there were enough hikers these days to beat down a regular path. Her feet tried to slow, but she forced herself to keep her pace quick. *Losing daylight, Gaines.*

"Could be a gunshot."

She frowned. "You think someone went to the trouble to shoot themselves before they hung themselves?"

"Stranger things, right?"

It was something of a motto when it came to Maggie. A person saw enough weird shit and they stopped doubting that people would find a variety of ways to get themselves into trouble, despite all warnings to the contrary. It was like some tourists left their common sense at home when they went on vacation. "Yeah."

She pushed through the break in the trees that led to the last lake. Maggie stopped short, wrinkling her nose as a breeze kicked a very distinct stench into her face. It smelled like a slaughterhouse.

That should have warned her.

She caught sight of a dark red against the greens and browns she was expecting to see. *What the—?* She moved forward, frowning. It didn't make sense . . . until it did. "Shit."

David gagged, but she didn't spare him a glance. "Hold it together, kid."

"I'm twenty-fucking-five, Maggie. You're not that much older than me."

Thank God poking his pride worked. I can't have him losing it right now. "You're younger and less experienced. That makes you a kid where I'm concerned." She kept her tone bland even though her heart-beat sounded like a herd of stampeding horses in her head. *This is so, so bad.*

Forcing herself to walk closer, she stopped just outside the circle of carnage. Thanks to her grandfather, Maggie had hunted on and off since she was a kid. It was one of the many ways her parents felt that she'd failed them—hunting wasn't highbrow enough for their tastes. As a result, she knew what field dressing looked like, though her experience started and ended with animals.

Not humans.

This was no suicide, unless the woman had somehow managed to hang herself from her ankles and then split herself open from groin to chest. Maggie took a careful breath, but there was no decay, just shit and blood. She couldn't know without getting closer, but this kill looked recent—within the last day or two.

Probably more recent, since the innards hadn't been scavenged by animals. "Fuck," she breathed.

"I think I'm—"

"You puke, you do it somewhere else. You hear me, David?" She rubbed a hand over her face, feeling a full decade older than her twenty-nine years. "*Fuck.* We need to call in . . ." Her mind blanked. National parks were on federal land, which meant the state cops might get some say, but this wasn't a drunk and disorderly or any of the normal reasons she'd stick someone in a cell to cool their heels.

This was murder.

◆　◆　◆

Saturday, June 17
9:30 p.m.

Vic Sutherland stared out the windshield as he drove into Kalispell. The sky wasn't completely dark despite the hour, and he barely noticed the majesty of the mountains and the sprawling green forests that surrounded the city. If it could be called a city. With a population resting just over twenty-two thousand, it was really more of a big small town. That didn't change the fact that it was one of the largest settlements on the west side of Montana.

None of which really mattered.

What mattered was the body waiting in the morgue, found by park rangers. He should be focusing on the victim, contemplating what he knew about the crime scene and what little evidence had been found. That was the way he liked to operate—familiarizing himself with the case before he ever set foot in the place he was headed.

The case was different, though.

Not because of the location of the body found. Not because of the method of murder—a murder that matched two others he'd been investigating. The unfortunate truth was that he'd seen worse than what was done to those victims—at least as far as the preliminary report went.

No, the main reason the case was different was because he knew one of the park rangers who had found and transported the body back to civilization.

Maggie Gaines.

He hadn't seen her in something like seven years—not since their first and last case as partners. There had been a whole hell of a lot of changes in his life since then. Promotions, a new partner, divorce, a few notorious cases—though he did his damnedest to stay out of the spotlight—and another new partner. When Maggie had left, he'd respected her need to put as much distance between herself and the FBI as possible, and he'd even managed not to take it personally most days.

He hadn't expected to ever see her again.

He pulled into the parking lot and stopped in a spot next to the only other car there—a serviceable truck that looked like it never got stuck, no matter how vicious the winters became. Everything about this damn state was harsh. He liked it well enough in the fall and now in the spring, but a winter holed up here sounded like the worst kind of hell.

He'd never seen the appeal of the national parks. Oh, they were beautiful, but he'd spent enough of his time in the Navy living out of a pack that he had no desire to do it recreationally. Sleeping on the ground and potentially no longer being at the top of the food chain made his skin crawl.

And there was more than wildlife to worry about out here.

He climbed out of his rented 4Runner—the only rental-car choice that would fit his six-foot-four-inch frame comfortably—and headed for the building. Despite the fact that it was well into June now, the wind snapping at his face held a hint of winter's cold. The park kept quite a few glaciers year-round, though the exact number escaped him, which meant that even in the height of summer, there was snow and freezing water to deal with even on the well-traveled trails. The victim had been found close to one of the main campgrounds, but that didn't mean that was where she had initially been attacked.

Part of him tried to wonder how Maggie was dealing with it, but he shut it down. He was here to work, and letting himself get distracted—even by Maggie—was inexcusable.

The dead woman needed justice. She had to come first.

After? Well, he had no reason to think Maggie would be happy to see him, and every reason to assume she'd be ready to slam the nearest door in his face once this case reached a satisfactory resolution.

You're doing it again. Stop. Focus.

The morgue was like many others he'd visited over the years—never enough windows, everything made of easy-to-hose-down materials, and a lingering scent of decay. Mixed with the sterile smell of bleach, it created an aroma he would never mistake for anything else.

He knocked on the door as he pushed it open, startling the woman standing over the body. She jumped, cursed, and then cursed again. Vic stopped, not wanting to spook her further. He was used to it, to some extent—he was tall enough that he loomed when he wasn't paying attention. He tried to pay attention—especially around women. "Sorry. I'm Agent Sutherland. We spoke briefly on the phone earlier."

"I was expecting you." She managed a smile and took off her glasses to clean them. Dr. Katherine Huxley was a nice-looking woman somewhere in her midthirties, her dark hair pulled back from her face and her smile easy despite the unease that lingered in her brown eyes. "It's fine. Working a case like this makes me a bit jumpy, is all." She motioned to the body on the table in front of her.

He took that as an invitation and moved closer. He'd seen this before, twice now, in different parks. It didn't make it any easier to see the third time around. "She's been—"

"Field dressed. Yes."

He'd grown up in Philly and had bolted to join the Navy the first chance he got. It had been his only ticket out of the city, and he'd signed up because of the lure of free college, not realizing what he was getting himself into until it was too late. Even with what he'd done and seen while in the service—and since—these recent killings set his teeth on edge. People were not animals, no matter how monstrous they acted from time to time. Most of the victims he'd seen over the years had been hunted, but that word meant something different than what had happened to this woman.

"Was that the cause of death?" He tried to imagine the fear she must have felt to be strung up by her ankles, and had to shut it down. *Just get the facts. Deal with the profile later.*

"No." Dr. Huxley exhaled carefully like she wanted to curse again. She pointed to the chest, just above the heart. "See this?"

He recognized the wound only because he'd seen it before. "Arrow."

"How did you know? Never mind, forget I asked." Dr. Huxley ran her gloved finger along the edge of the wound. "Judging from the damage and the trajectory, I can give you my best guess that this wasn't a crossbow—it was a compound bow. The wound runs at a slight inversion, so whoever shot her was higher than she was."

"Taller or on high ground—or both." He straightened, his suspicions confirmed. This woman was just like the other two. The only difference was the location. The unknown subject—the unsub—was park hopping. If his past was anything to go by, he wouldn't hit Glacier again, but Vic still had to collect every bit of evidence he could while it was still relatively fresh.

That started with the body itself. "So she was shot with an arrow, strung up, and then field dressed." Like someone would do with wild game during hunting season.

"That about sums it up. I'm still working on getting through the autopsy, though. I'll forward you any further findings."

"Thank you. My partner will be checking in tomorrow." He checked his watch. It was too late to drive into Glacier, though his muscles had twisted enough that he knew sleep wasn't in his future. It would be better to stay overnight in Kalispell and then head in to the main station tomorrow. From what he understood, Maggie was north at the Goat Haunt ranger station, along with the other rangers who'd found the body. He had to talk to them, to figure out what they knew about the victim and if they could identify her.

Maggie was one of the rangers who'd hauled the body back to the ranger station. There would be no avoiding talking to her. In all honesty, it gave him the perfect excuse to see her again.

Even if it took a serial killer to make it happen.

The rate of escalation was happening too fast. Some unsubs took years between kills, and this marked three in less than nine months. The cooling-off period was shrinking rapidly as he worked himself into a frenzy. In the evolution of a killer, that meant a higher chance of being caught as he unraveled—but it also meant more victims in the process.

Vic headed for his rental, his skin crawling with the knowledge that this woman wouldn't be the unsub's last victim. And the next victim would be coming sooner rather than later.

CHAPTER TWO

Sunday, June 18
11:12 a.m.

Maggie looked around the small group of hikers who had just dis-
embarked the Waterton Lake ferry from the Canadian border. She'd
agreed to stick around Goat Haunt all day and check paperwork. No,
not agreed. The truth was that she'd shamelessly begged her boss, Wyatt
Thornton, not to force her to take any time off. The thought of sitting
in her room with scenes of that woman's corpse flashing through her
mind was too much to bear. She loved this park. She didn't want to fear
it—or the human predator who might still be somewhere within it.

Wyatt gave her a choice—a day off or paperwork duty. She'd chosen
the latter.

There were only two groups of people milling around, waiting for
her to get to them. She dealt with the first group—a couple and their
friend on a day hike to Kootenai Lakes—and then moved on to the
second group. They were five—three women and two men—and she
put their ages around midtwenties.

The tallest man, a big blond who could have passed for a linebacker, raked his blue gaze over her. "You're awfully pretty to be a park ranger."

The woman at his side—short, Hispanic, and pretty in a porcelain-doll sort of way—rolled her eyes. "Give it a rest, Josh. She's not interested."

"How do you know she's not interested? Don't be a bitch, Lauren." The look he shot her was filled with barely concealed disgust, but he covered it quickly, offering Maggie a brilliant smile.

The smile didn't seem to fool Lauren for a second. She shook her head. "Can't block something that's not going to happen in the first place."

This is why I hate dealing with tourists. She managed a tight smile, even as the temptation rose to march into the woods and never come out again. The world might be getting smaller each year, but that truth didn't apply to places like Glacier. With limited cell service, no Wi-Fi outside a few select locations, and more places to hide than a person could find in a lifetime, it was exactly the kind of private place that soothed her soul.

That soothing feeling didn't extend to tourists who thought they were smoother than they actually were.

A second woman approached, shooting Josh a sharp look. "Stop it, both of you." The smile she turned on Maggie was downright dazzling. "Sorry about them. We don't get together too often these days, and when we do, it's like all those years between now and high school never happened. I'm Madison."

Maggie didn't comment on the fact that there couldn't be *too* many years since they'd all graduated, based on the look of them. This woman, in particular, was small and fresh-faced enough to pass for eighteen. Maggie accepted the paperwork and glanced over it. "Where are you all headed?" Their pass was for ten days in the park, which meant their destination could be literally anywhere.

Lauren slid past Josh to stand next to Madison. She was taller than Madison, but they could have been sisters or maybe cousins. They were both Hispanic, and similar enough in coloring—black hair, warm brown skin, brown eyes—but that's where the similarities ended. Lauren's long black hair was curlier than her friend's, and she had the look of a woman who spent a whole lot more time outside than Madison, her skin a couple of shades darker. Even their posture gave the sense of polar opposites—Madison's open and welcoming, Lauren's closed off, whether from shyness or a general dislike of strangers.

Lauren cleared her throat. "We're hiking down to Many Glacier, north to Elizabeth Lake, circling down to Helen Lake, and then back north to Goat Haunt."

"Ambitious." But she was still relieved that they seemed to plan to stick to the regular trails. It wasn't a guarantee that they'd stay out of trouble, but it lessened their chances of getting hopelessly lost. "Any of you familiar with the park?"

"Oh, yeah." Madison's smile brightened, if that was even possible. "We grew up over in Kalispell, and we've hiked here nearly every summer since we were, like, twelve."

"Until you got all fancy and ran away to the big city." Lauren's joke fell flat, but Madison didn't seem to notice.

Laughing, she said, "Yeah, yeah, I've heard it all before. But I'm back for this trip, so that's something."

Their being relatively familiar with the park didn't mean they wouldn't do something stupid like lean over a slippery edge to get a picture of a waterfall or try to pet a moose, but it significantly raised the odds. The strange undertones to their friendship weren't Maggie's problem, though she kept an eye on Josh where he'd moved a bit away from the group to glare at the girls.

Maggie finally nodded. "Check in at the Many Glacier ranger station and let them know where you're headed and if your plans change." If something *did* go wrong, the rangers had a better chance of pinpointing their rescue efforts if they knew the hikers' destination. The park might seem small in relation to the state, but it was plenty big enough that there were still people missing from decades ago—and even ones who'd disappeared as recently as five years ago.

Maggie handed the papers back. "Be careful. At least a few of your party should have bear spray."

"We all do. You can never be too careful. Thanks, Ranger!" She turned, gave Josh a playful shove, and then darted back to where the other woman and man waited. As Josh and Lauren followed her, Maggie hesitated, wondering if she should warn them about the murder.

A onetime thing. That's what the brass said.

She wasn't sure she believed it.

It didn't really matter *what* she believed, though. Since they had no reason to believe that anyone else was in danger from this killer, they had to treat it the same way cops treated normal homicide investigations— delivering information on a need-to-know basis only.

She watched them follow the trail that would lead them to Kootenai Lakes and beyond, and then checked her watch. Only a couple of hours left before the next ferry. She'd have to work to keep herself occupied in the meantime.

Anything to avoid thinking too hard about the dead woman.

Sunday, June 18
3:20 p.m.

Vic stocked up on gear before he drove into the park. If his instincts were right, he was looking at multiple nights spent in the outdoors, and that meant he had to be prepared for any eventuality. He needed to talk to the rangers who had found the body and actually *see* the place where the woman was found. Pictures could only tell so much, no matter how graphic.

He parked at the rangers' headquarters and headed inside. It was like any other government building he'd come across in his travels—nondescript and sturdy. A man approached—a ranger, judging from his uniform—and Vic took him in with a glance. Midfifties, excellent shape, and kind eyes, though the man was currently glaring at him. "Took you long enough. Wyatt Thornton, park manager."

He didn't take it personally. Death made monsters of them all. Vic nodded. "Vic Sutherland, BAU. I'm going to need to talk to the rangers who found the body."

"I suspect you'll want a look at the site where the body was found, too."

"Yes, sir." He kept his tone respectful. It wasted everyone's time to get into pissing contests with local law enforcement. National parks were a special kind of animal because they were federal land, and the park rangers handled most of the crimes that happened in the territory. When they needed the big guns, they called in the Feds. Whoever handled this area normally, they obviously had a decent enough relationship with the rangers that Wyatt wasn't going into this expecting a confrontation.

Which wasn't to say he looked happy to see Vic, but no one could blame him for that. Murder was messy business, and this particular murder was messier than most.

The whole thing made Vic so damn tired. He'd been doing this for more than a decade, and though each case revealed new and depraved depths that humans could descend to, some days he felt like he was simply going through the motions.

Learn about the murder. Travel to the murder site. Investigate to the best of his ability. Either catch that particular unsub or don't. Fly back to Quantico.

The only thing *truly* different this time was Maggie.

Wyatt huffed out a breath, snapping Vic back to the present to find the ranger watching him closely. "Unless you're keen to spend a few days on the trail, we'll need to fly in."

"We can't waste any more time. Let's take the chopper." The Goat Haunt ranger station was at the very northern edge of the park—and the country—and the closest road was the one running just outside the building where he now stood. He'd done some quick calculations, and while someone could probably hike from here to Goat Haunt in a day if they pushed themselves hard . . . There were elevation changes to take into account, too.

No, a chopper could get them there long before they had to worry about nightfall.

Wyatt nodded like he'd expected the answer. "You got questions, I might be able to give you some answers while we wait."

He had a lot of questions, and the condition of the body only created more. Dr. Huxley had e-mailed over her findings this morning, and he'd read through the information while he downed his coffee. The woman—whoever she was—hadn't been dead long before she was found. Less than a day, in fact.

Since she was naked, and no clothing had been found at the scene, *who* she was presented the biggest mystery, second to who had killed her. Most crimes were solved by looking at the victims rather than searching blindly for the killer. He hadn't had any luck with the last two murders, even knowing who the victims were, but there was always the chance that this one would highlight the connection. "Do you have any leads on her identity?"

"No." Wyatt sounded like the answer was personally offensive. "We get hikers who come through without permits sometimes, but that close to Goat Haunt, it's not common. When it happens, they avoid the ranger station. If she *did* have a permit, she didn't come through via the ferry on her own, and none of the rangers who have seen her recognized her." He cursed. "Though with her being in the condition she was found in, that's not a big surprise."

"Have you contacted the other stations to question the rangers there?"

"Of course." Wyatt's shoulders dropped a fraction of an inch. "It might be well into summer in the rest of the country, but we're barely into the beginning of our season here. There haven't been enough hikers coming through for a single woman hiking to be forgotten."

"Is that normal for a woman to be hiking alone?"

"We don't make a habit of encouraging anyone to hike alone. This trail is relatively well traveled, but that doesn't mean there aren't troubles to get into. Hikers have a nasty habit of peering too close to waterfalls or leaning too far over edges. The rocks are surprisingly slippery in the rivers and streams, and the rock itself isn't the granite you find in other mountain ranges in these parts. It's sedimented, and so pieces break off without warning. We do what we can to maintain the trails and remind hikers not to be idiots, but we can't stop them from coming into the park if they have permits." Wyatt made a sound suspiciously like a growl and muttered, "Even in the middle of July and August, my people would have noted a lone hiker—woman or man—and passed along the information. Hiking alone is a goddamn fool decision."

Hiking in pairs was recommended across the board—the buddy system was there for a reason. Vic didn't think this hiker had gone out alone, though. What were the odds that she'd fallen into the unsub's hands by chance?

Impossible, or next to.

Murder was often a crime of opportunity, but whoever shot that woman with two arrows had taken the time to treat her as if she were nothing more than meat. *Didn't go so far as to eat her, though.* All her organs had been present and accounted for, which either meant the unsub had been interrupted before he could finish or—more likely, since he hadn't eaten the other two—he was more interested in marking her as *meat* without actually treating her as such.

"Did you search the area around the body for her clothing?"

"I was more concerned with getting her out of the park before a grizzly or one of the cats came around for an easy meal." Wyatt obviously found his question irritating, as if he was leveling an accusation at the man himself. Vic had run into Wyatt's kind before. He wasn't a bad man—on the contrary, he was a good one. He considered the people around him to be under his care, and he took it personally when they went and got themselves killed.

The question was more formality than anything else. The unsub had come prepared, and if the clothes weren't on the woman, they probably weren't in the immediate area. *But we can't know that for sure until we search the area.*

"When's the last time there was a murder in the park?" Vic asked.

"Back in 2013, when that fool girl went and killed her husband. The Newlywed Murders, I think the newspapers called it." Wyatt snorted. "More like natural consequences. She pushed him off a cliff and then all but admitted her guilt by being the one to find him when our people weren't moving fast enough. Girl wasn't right in her head."

And pushing a new husband off a cliff was a far cry from what had been done to that woman occupying a slab in the morgue.

Wyatt's radio chirped and he gave a nod, almost to himself. "Chopper is here." He eyed the pack Vic had set by his feet. "Looks like you came prepared. You hike often?"

"No." Not since he left the SEALs. "I can hold my own, though."

The ranger snorted again. "Heard that more times than I can count, usually before the so-called expert goes and gets in over their head. I'll get you to Goat Haunt, and then my girl Maggie will act as your guide." He gave Vic a long look. "She used to be a suit like you. Might push some buttons for her, so don't take her shitty attitude personally. Murder makes everyone cranky, I imagine."

Murder—and the fact that there wasn't a scenario out there where Maggie was happy to see him. *Lock it down. The case matters, not your history.* He nodded. "Let's go."

The sooner he got out there, the sooner he dealt with this case, the sooner he got back the hell out of Maggie's life like she'd always wanted.

CHAPTER THREE

Sunday, June 18
4:46 p.m.

Madison Garcia was already starting to regret agreeing to this trip. It had been five years since she and her former friends had taken their last trip into the park—before she'd moved away to college and put all that ugliness out of her mind—and time had softened the memory and heightened her nostalgia.

She loved Glacier. She always had. Seattle was wonderful, but the beauty of the Sound couldn't compete with the siren call of this park. Even the San Juan Islands that were barely occupied still had a feel of civilization. She couldn't quite put her finger on it, but being back in Montana—in the park—brought the stark differences that much more into contrast.

Here, she was as close to at peace as a person could get. "I missed this place."

Ashleigh Marcinko, her best friend since they were in first grade, rolled her blue eyes. "I don't know why you love it so much. There isn't a Starbucks for miles and miles, and the only available men around are these two idiots." She jerked her thumb at the duo in question.

As expected, Josh Conlon couldn't let that stand. "Aw, honey, don't tell me you're not interested. You were happy enough to fuck me against every available surface for two years. What's once or twice more for old times' sake?"

"Engaged, asshole. Don't be a hater." Ashleigh held up her left hand and pointed to the massive rock on her ring finger, and then dropped all fingers except her middle one.

"As if that would stop you."

Madison sighed and looked to Ethan, Josh's brother. He gave her a small smile, and that was almost enough to make all the crap worth it. It was her fault, after all. He was the one who'd suggested a hiking trip in the park, and she'd gotten spooked—even though they'd known each other since kindergarten and had been meeting up whenever he made it into Seattle, a ten-day hike together seemed like a huge step.

So, being the chickenshit that she was, she'd invited their old friends to tag along. She and Ashleigh were just as close as ever, but Lauren and Josh had faded away almost as soon as she left town. And she couldn't blame anyone for that distance except herself.

Now she was starting to remember why.

She should have known that getting her best friend and Josh in the same zip code was just asking for trouble. Considering how their relationship ended, she'd considered leaving Josh completely out of the invitation . . . but Ethan was trying to repair his relationship with his twin, and that meant she had to deal with him.

And by inviting him, she'd been forced to invite Lauren as well. So here they were, one big dysfunctional group of friends.

Madison forced a smile and tried to put a positive spin on it. "Guys, come on. It's too great a day for you to be sniping back and forth." She still didn't know why Ashleigh had even agreed to come on this trip. Her friend hated the outdoors, hated hiking, hated anything that reminded her too much of Kalispell.

Most of all, she hated Josh.

"I'll *behave* if that jackass does."

Madison shot a pleading look over her shoulder at Josh. He glared at a spot between Ashleigh's shoulder blades but gave a short nod. Asking for more from either of them would be a lesson in frustration, so Madison turned back to the path and picked up her pace. Lauren remained farther ahead, seeming totally lost in thought.

Madison knew better.

She caught up to her and forced herself not to let her smile dim. Lauren had dated Ethan for a little while when they were in high school, and despite how things fell out, Madison still wanted to . . . Actually, she didn't know. Five years was enough time that getting Lauren's okay for making her relationship with Ethan official seemed silly. It wasn't like they'd gotten engaged and Madison ran off with him a couple of days later. Things had just sort of . . . worked out.

Her smile faltered, but she fought to keep it bright. "I'm so looking forward to this trip."

"I know." Lauren shook her head. "You've said so half a dozen times." She hesitated. "Thanks for inviting me. I know things got weird there for a while."

Weird was an understatement. She did her best not to think too hard about that. "Yeah, well, you and Josh are together, and Ashleigh's moved on, and—"

"You and Ethan are dating." Lauren snorted. "Funny how things work out, huh?"

"Yeah. Funny." She didn't find anything funny about the way Ethan made her stomach erupt in butterflies just by being in the same room. He'd grown up. They'd *all* grown up.

She took a deep breath of the crisp mountain air and forced herself to release the stress that had been plaguing her for weeks. Her job, her family, what she was going to do when she and Ethan finally figured out what they were and what their plans were—all her worries seemed small and mundane here. It was just her, her friends, and the park.

Madison hefted her pack higher onto her back, her legs already burning from the climb. In the past, they'd started their hikes farther south, and it was a whole hell of a lot easier to hike down twenty-four hundred feet of elevation change than it was to hike up it. *Totally worth it.* She dug her water from the side pouch in her pack and took a long drink. "How are things with you and Josh?" She hadn't missed the heated look he sent Ashleigh, which seemed out of place since he and Lauren were together now—*had* been together since the summer after high school.

Lauren gave her a sweet smile. "Fine." Her friend didn't look much older than she had at eighteen, her big brown eyes and smooth brown skin just the same as when they were thirteen. She turned to look up the path. "It's good that we brought ice axes. There's a snow warning on a couple parts of the trail."

Nice change of subject.

Madison let it go. It wasn't her place to meddle, and she had enough worries of her own. It had been a few years since she'd hiked a trail that required the ability to self-arrest—to use an ice ax to stop herself from falling if she slipped on the snow—but she'd come prepared. "It will be okay. We've done it before."

"Yeah." Lauren's mouth twisted, the only sign that she wasn't perfectly happy with their current situation. "Things are a lot different now." She shot a look back down the trail. "A lot is different than I thought it would be."

"Me, too." She glanced to where Ashleigh was trudging along, her blonde head bowed and her shoulders set in a rigid stance that only seemed to appear around her ex. Josh had the same look on his face, though at least he'd stopped glaring at Ashleigh and was now talking in low tones to his brother, Ethan. Ethan just nodded without saying anything back.

He looked so perfectly in his element out here, his broad shoulders filling out his long-sleeved T-shirt, his strength readily apparent by how easily he made the climb, his focus laserlike on Josh. He must have sensed her watching him, because he looked up and gave her that sweet smile that had her grinning back like an idiot. *God, I like him so much.*

"You two are just too precious."

Madison shook her head and resumed her climb. It was a good thing she wasn't asking for Lauren's blessing, because that snide tone just about guaranteed that she wouldn't get it. "Things change, Lauren. That's life. You and Ethan didn't work out—and I think we both know why—so you don't get to be rude about my being interested in him." As soon as the words were out of her mouth, she knew she should have kept silent. They had nine days left in this trip, and antagonizing Lauren was a surefire way to get Josh riled up, and then Ashleigh would take it over the top, and it'd be a complete shitshow.

Maybe Ethan and I can just break off from the rest of the group.

She knew better. Ethan wasn't a coward who wanted to avoid this, and that meant she couldn't be, either.

They hadn't even been hiking a full day, and everyone was already questioning their decision to come on this trip, herself included. Well, too bad. They were here, and they were going to make the best of it. Madison would keep a positive attitude if it killed her.

◆ ◆ ◆

Sunday, June 18
6:05 p.m.

Vic thought he was prepared. He wasn't the type of man to spend too much effort worrying about what could possibly happen—it made more sense to deal with what *did* happen. He knew seeing Maggie again after all this time would be a shock, but they'd been partners for twelve months at best. There was no reason to think he couldn't roll with this development the same way he rolled with every other.

Then he arrived at the Goat Haunt ranger station. He followed Wyatt out of the chopper, using a hand to shield his face from the wind the blades created. The ranger station was set against Upper Waterton Lake, and with the mountains in the background, it could have been a scene out of a painting.

All of that paled in comparison to Maggie.

She looked good. Better than good. During her time as his partner, she'd been too thin, running on too little sleep and too much coffee, and her health had suffered as a result. Obviously being a park ranger agreed with her. The unfortunate uniform did nothing to hide how her curves had filled out, her body honed from the many hours of hauling around a pack similar to the one he now carried. Her hair was longer, too, the dark locks pulled back into a braid that hit just past her shoulders.

But she was still Maggie.

Even in the bright sunlight, he could see the way her dark eyes flashed as her shock wore off. And her nose, the only feature of hers that could never be termed *pretty*, was the same—long and slightly crooked from where it'd been broken in the FBI academy.

Maggie shook off her paralysis faster than he did. She frowned. "What are you doing here, Vic?"

"Agent Sutherland's here for the murder." Wyatt stepped forward, breaking what remained of the spell cast between them.

Rationally, Vic knew it had lasted seconds at most, but it felt like a small eternity. He struggled to put the past in the appropriate box to deal with when they weren't on a case. *When we aren't on a case, I'll leave* . . . He shut the thought down. He had a duty to the victims, and letting himself get distracted by Maggie wasn't going to find the unsub.

Even if Maggie was a bright, shining star in the midst of darkness.

He moved closer and slid off his pack. "Where's the best place to talk?"

For a second, it looked like Maggie would pepper him with more questions, but she finally nodded. "This way."

Wyatt cleared his throat. "You do what needs to be done, Maggie. I'm headed back to headquarters to see if I can nail down who this girl was." He shot Vic a look. "I'm sure you have a partner arriving at some point."

It wasn't a question, but Vic nodded all the same. "He'll be here by the end of the day." Twelve months ago, it would have been Eden Collins. He didn't have it in him to begrudge her her happiness, but working with her replacement irritated the hell out of him. Tucker Kendrick was a good agent, but he was a pain in the ass, and his sense of humor left something to be desired.

"Excuse us." Wyatt pulled Maggie to the side, just out of earshot.

In an effort to give them more privacy, Vic wandered closer to the lake's edge. Even the small group of people milling around the picnic tables while they waited for the ferry couldn't combat the devastating beauty of the view.

I can see why Maggie chose this job.

He shook the thought off and turned to the west, studying the mountains. If someone was an experienced hiker, they could enter the park at any point and hike off-trail to reach the point where there would be victims to choose from. It didn't mesh, though. There were too many things left to chance—the finding of an appropriate victim being one of them. While it was possible the unsub had stalked the woman long before she came to the park, that didn't line up in his head, either. There was something *off* about this case, though he couldn't put his finger on what it was.

"Hey, Vic."

All his thoughts dried up as he turned to face her. He tried to focus on the case, but all he could see was her. "You look good, Maggie."

She raised her eyebrows. "You do, too. How's Janelle?"

He tensed, waiting for the pain to lance through him at the thought of his ex like it had the first year after they divorced, but it was a wound that had long since healed. He dragged his gaze away from Maggie to look back at the mountains. "We divorced five years ago. I'm single now."

"I'm sorry. Was it—"

"No." Even after all this time, he knew what she was going to say—how her mind worked. "She was angry about the kiss, but it wasn't the final straw." That came later. He hadn't thought about his ex-wife in a long time. Their marriage had gone down in flames, and she'd never let him forget that it was his fault.

It had nothing to do with Maggie. Not really. Him losing his damn mind in that moment when he kissed her all those years ago was a symptom of the problem, not the problem itself. He'd married Janelle because it seemed like it was the thing a normal, well-adjusted person was supposed to do once they hit twenty-five. His own parents had divorced before he was born, and he'd been raised by his mother in Philly. A part of him had craved the normalcy that came with following what society declared was the usual sequence of events.

He'd met Janelle at a coffee shop he'd frequented while he was in the FBI academy. She was on her way to law school, and it had seemed like they'd fit, so he'd pulled the trigger.

It wasn't until the first year of their marriage that he realized what a terrible mistake he'd made. She wanted more than he could give—wanted him to be the traditional guy he'd sought to emulate.

Normal men weren't so comfortable around murder. They didn't travel across the country seeking out monsters. They played golf and aimed for jobs in upper-middle management.

No, his marriage falling apart had had nothing to do with Maggie and everything to do with the ways he and Janelle had failed to adapt when dreams crashed into reality.

It wasn't something he'd thought about much in the last five years.

That, more than anything, allowed him to set it all aside and focus on what really mattered—the murder. He jerked his chin at the surrounding mountains. "How do you keep people from crossing the border?"

"Motion cameras, kind of like the ones hunters use." She took the change of subject without a hiccup. "Have you talked to Kat—Dr. Huxley?"

"Yeah." Of course she knew the medical examiner—and apparently she knew Dr. Huxley well enough to be on a first-name basis. He forced himself to focus. "Though before we get into what she found, I want your impression of things."

She jerked back. "What?"

"Maggie, you were BAU."

"For a year."

He shook his head. "You had the training. It might be a while ago, but that sort of thing sticks—and it's more than either of the other rangers on the scene can say. I'll talk to the kid when we're through, but I want you to walk me through it."

She chewed at her bottom lip, an old habit of hers. "It'd be easier to walk you through it if we were at the scene. You're going to want to head up there anyway, so we might as well save it until then."

He considered arguing, but she was right—he wanted to see the spot where the body had been found. Vic glanced at the sky. "It's three miles from here?"

"Approximately. Though the elevation change will slow us down." She shot a look at the pack by his feet. "We can wait for morning. It's a day trip at best, and we're starting late."

More wasted time. The clock ticked away in his head, counting down until when they lost the unsub again. Vic had arrived within hours of the first two murders, and he'd worked both cases until he could actually feel them go cold around him. The more time they gave the unsub, the higher the likelihood of him slipping through Vic's grasp again.

He couldn't let this bastard get away a third time. He refused to.

CHAPTER FOUR

Sunday, June 18
6:20 p.m.

"If we go out tonight, we can overnight at the campsite near the crime scene and then hike back first thing in the morning."

Maggie knew he was going to say it even before the words left his mouth. Vic Sutherland might present a laid-back persona to the world, but that surface hid a drive and restlessness that used to rival hers. He looked . . . good. He'd always been attractive in a nontraditional sort of way—his features a little too craggy, his pale eyes too unnerving against his black hair and dusky skin, the movements of his big body always perfectly controlled. She'd forgotten how tall he was. It was such a silly thing to focus on, in the face of everything going on, but at five ten, she'd gotten used to looking everyone in the eye.

Vic towered over her.

She very carefully didn't think about the fact that he was no longer married. It didn't change anything. She wasn't the same kid with stars in her eyes that she'd been after graduating from the FBI academy. She'd seen enough of the world to leave her bruised, and though her parents had pressured her to come home afterward and fall into line like a good little child, she'd gone searching again. She'd found something in the FBI, and even if she hadn't been able to cut it, she couldn't trade her dreams in for a job as a lawyer or doctor or, heaven forbid, a *housewife* to a lawyer or doctor. She would have wilted away to nothing in those roles.

It was only when she found the park rangers that she'd achieved something resembling peace.

She should have known the monsters would follow her. It took them seven years, but they managed all the same.

She didn't say any of that, though. If he could focus on the case, then she'd be damned before she did anything else. "We can get up there before dark and take a look. It would give you a chance to let it sit and then take a second look in the morning if you need to."

Vic liked to mull things over, to prod and push until facts shifted into place in his head. Unfortunately, he wouldn't get that opportunity this time around. The fact that the weather had held this long was a small miracle. Storms along the Continental Divide were a regular occurrence, and sometimes downright violent. Even without taking the isolated location into account, it was only a matter of time before one of those storms rolled through and eliminated anything worth finding.

He watched her as if he could divine her thoughts. "Okay."

She hated the way her cheeks heated. She had more control than this. He was attractive and they had something of a history, sure, but he hadn't tracked her down because he missed her so much. Even if he had . . .

Stop it.

She grabbed the backpack she'd packed before guiding the day trip today. "I just need to throw a few extra things in here."

"I have a tent."

She stopped short. "Great." Maggie forced her feet back into motion. She methodically refilled her supplies from the ranger station and then headed back out. *This is about the case. Remember that. Damn it,* remember *that.* "Let's go." She knew she was being short with him, but he'd had time to come to terms with the fact they were going to be face-to-face again.

Maggie hadn't.

She kept her pace slow, even though all she wanted to do was charge onto the path and get this investigation over with as soon as possible. Professional. She could be professional. It didn't matter that the last time she'd seen Vic she'd had a total breakdown, had ended up needing him to comfort her, and then had lost her mind and kissed him. Her partner. Her *married* partner.

At that point, she'd already planned on getting the hell out of the FBI. But after embarrassing herself so thoroughly, she'd cut all ties with Vic and everyone else in the BAU.

Maggie stopped short and spun. "What is the BAU doing here?"

Vic, damn him, just raised his eyebrows. "I got called in."

"Don't try that bullshit with me. I know how the system works. We have a murder, they send in the local Feds. That means it's either Jake or Tessa. *Not* the BAU." The FBI's Behavioral Analysis Unit had been set up as a support system for law enforcement dealing with the worst kind of criminals imaginable. Serial killers, specifically—whether they crossed state lines or not. All local law enforcement had to do was call in for assistance and the head of the BSU, Britton Washburne, would send a team to create a profile and offer an outside opinion.

They wouldn't be called in for a single body, no matter how horrible the murder was.

She narrowed her eyes as a chill raced down her spine. "What do you know?"

He hesitated, as if debating whether to lie. Finally, he sighed. "Keep going. I'll fill you in."

Standing there, a hundred yards from the trailhead, and demanding answers was childish—especially when they were wasting precious daylight. She nodded and started walking again, painfully aware of the man at her back. "Tell me."

It took another hundred yards before he spoke. "This is the third murder in a national park in the last year."

Third.

Three meant serial killer. Three in a year was a *lot*. "What about before then?"

"Nothing. Some parks have more deaths than others, and some of those are even murders, but nothing that bears any similarities to this."

Each serial killer was different, but some had cooling-off periods that numbered in the years when they first started. To go from nothing to three kills in a year was unusual in the extreme. "What parks?"

"Grand Teton and Mount Rainier."

Different parks for different kills. If this was a hunter, it made sense to stick to one territory, but at the same time, if it was a hiker who was familiar with the parks in the Northwest, then maybe that offered more opportunity . . . The whole thing made her head hurt. She hadn't thought like this—like an agent—in almost a decade. She was out of practice.

So she went with what she knew—the parks. "I worked a season in Mount Rainier. That's a quiet park. The storms coming off the coast cause the most problems, but even then, there are rarely deaths as a result."

"I know." Another silence, and she could almost hear him debating how much to share. Again.

"You might as well tell me. Though, from the little you've shared, it sounds like your unsub hits a park, kills their victim, and then moves on."

"That's been the case previously, yes."

She heard what he wasn't saying. "But you don't think it is this time. Why?"

"I think the unsub was testing out how they felt about killing with the two previous victims. The first one—female, Caucasian, midthirties—was shot with a bow from the back. The unsub strung her up but didn't go through with the field dressing. There was a small cut in the groin area, but that was it."

"Chickened out."

"That's my take."

No matter what fiction would have people believe, it took a special kind of monster to kill another human being in cold blood. Most murders were perpetuated by those closest to the victim, and they were driven by emotion. Love, hate, jealousy, fear. Stranger-on-stranger murder was significantly rarer, and serial killing was rarer yet. Maggie ducked under a low-hanging branch. The fact that there were hesitation marks in the cuts seemed to indicate that that woman was the first victim—rather than the first victim they'd found. "The second victim?"

"Grand Teton. It was a man this time—also Caucasian, midtwenties—and whatever held the unsub back with the first victim, they went all the way through with the field dressing this time."

Maybe because it was a man, maybe there were other factors. Escalating was normal. It was likely that during the cooling-down period, while the unsub fantasized over and over again about the kill, he or she had worked themselves up into a frenzy. In an effort to re-create that feeling of bliss, they'd taken their plans all the way this time. "How long between murders?"

"Nine months. Three months between the Grand Teton one and this one."

She shot him a look over her shoulder. "Any connection between the two victims?" They wouldn't know if there were connections between those two and the third until they figured out who the hell she was.

"No. The man was hiking alone—something he did regularly. The woman had been with a group of friends and split off to head back to the trailhead because she had work later that day. She was also an experienced hiker, though she didn't go out as often as the man did. Both were reported missing within twenty-four hours, and both were found near designated campsites."

She mulled that over as she climbed, her legs burning from the second time up this trail in a day. Maggie had hiked longer distances over worse terrain, and there were a few times she'd sprinted the majority of the trip from Goat Haunt to Kootenai Lake, though excepting the murder, it'd been a while since they'd run into an emergency needing that kind of speed.

A killer who hunted lone hikers usually meant a crime of opportunity, but there was a lot of prep that went into hunting, let alone hunting a person. This wasn't some random person who woke up one day and thought it'd be a great idea to hunt humans. This was someone who'd hunted most of their life. Unfortunately, in Montana, that didn't narrow down the field of suspects much—especially if this person was killing strangers.

She dug her water out and took a long drink. "I'm sure you've already thought of this, but you're looking for someone with extensive hunting and backcountry experience. No one is going to be able to haul a compound bow in through the normal trails—not without a ranger or some other hiker seeing it. Even with an overnight pack, it'd be nearly impossible to hide it." A compound bow case was made to fit the bow itself, since the bow didn't collapse. A hiker's backpack was big, but it wouldn't fit inside. Someone would notice. "Depending on what time of day they were killed and where, exactly, this person also stayed at least one night in the park and might have a camp set up somewhere off the main trails."

"How do you track that sort of thing?"

Squatters were always something of a problem, simply because there was so much ground to cover and no effective way to do it if they weren't on the trails. "We have backcountry rangers like me. We monitor the less-traveled trails for potential issues—rock slides, avalanches, anything that isn't as it should be—and keep an eye out for anyone who's where they're not supposed to be."

"We checked park permits against the two parks, but no one popped as being in both during the time frame."

Whoever this guy was, he was too smart to slip up like that. She frowned. "The unsub would cover their tracks on that, but I'd bet he or she applied for permits while they were casing the park." She used the turn in the trail to look behind her, noting the way his lips twitched. "But you already thought of that, didn't you?"

"There's over fifty people who applied for permits in both parks in the last year, and that number doubles if you go back two years."

And there was no telling how long the unsub had spent planning this. There could have been many trips to all three parks over the course of several years. Lots of avid hikers in this area of the country hit all three parks—in addition to Yellowstone. It would be like hunting for a needle in the haystack. "There's something you're not telling me."

He didn't bother to deny it. "It's not based in fact. I just have a feeling that this woman won't be the last in Glacier."

She'd learned to trust Vic's feelings when they were partners. He wasn't much older than she was—a mere five years—but between his time in the SEALs and his years in the BAU, he had finely honed instincts. People tended to doubt the woo-woo aspect of a cop having a sixth sense, but she'd seen it in action. "Then I guess we need to find out who the hell this woman was and figure out who might be next."

Her mind went to the group of midtwenties kids she'd met earlier, but she shook it off. They were a group of five, and none of them had any plans on hiking to the trailhead to go to work. They wouldn't venture out on their own, so the unsub had no reason to track them.

With there being only one murder, no matter how terrible, the park wouldn't be issuing any kind of warning or closing any trails. The unsub had a pattern of killing once and leaving the park behind, so there was no reason to think that creating a panic by announcing that there was a serial killer in Glacier was worth the trouble.

She still wished she'd taken the time to warn them.

◆ ◆ ◆

Sunday, June 18
7:31 p.m.

Vic tried to pay attention to his surroundings. It was possible—probable, even—that the unsub had hiked this very trail at some point. It was more likely that he or she had hiked in from one of the less-traveled trails, but it still paid to take in the area around them.

One never knew who could be watching.

But his gaze kept tracking back to Maggie. She moved with purpose up the trail, undeterred by the steep climb and barely breathing hard. She wore pants and utilitarian boots, and her pack blocked most of his view, except for the back of her head.

He should stop staring. Things were already awkward between them without that kiss suddenly feeling like it was yesterday instead of seven years ago. If he concentrated, he could still feel her in his arms, taste her on his lips. It shouldn't have been the defining moment of their time together as partners, but he couldn't set it aside. "I took advantage." He didn't realize he'd intended to speak until the words were out of his mouth.

"That's not what it was."

It said something that she answered without asking him to clarify. He should have been the solid presence for her to break against during that case, and he'd betrayed that. "I was the senior partner. I shouldn't have let it get that far."

She stopped and turned to face him. With incline in the path beneath their feet, she could look him directly in his eyes. "I was an adult. I kissed you, knowing you were married and that it was inappropriate. So if you're so determined to start aiming the blame somewhere, aim it at me." She sighed. "Vic, it was one kiss, and you stopped it almost as soon as it started. I'm embarrassed I even went there. *I* was inappropriate. Can we just forget it happened and move on?"

That was the problem. He'd never forgotten. He'd tried. Fuck, he'd done his best to exorcise the memory of her in the years since he'd seen her. So much shit had been packed into that single year—his marriage reaching the breaking point, a case that would give even the most jaded agent nightmares, a new partner that he should have protected but who had burned out instead.

Now's not the time.

It might *never* be the time.

But it sure as hell wasn't appropriate to start this conversation when they were on their way to a crime scene. So he nodded. "We'll talk about it later."

She frowned. "That's not what I said."

"That's what I'm offering." He wasn't willing to let a chance with Maggie—a *real* chance—slip through his fingers. It didn't matter that the circumstances were less than ideal.

"I don't understand you." She turned without another word and kept going.

Vic didn't speak for the rest of the hike. He'd already crossed the line as it was. He wouldn't keep pushing Maggie. Now that he had plans to talk to her later, he was better able to focus on what they were walking into.

Kootenai campground was tucked just inside the tree line. Maggie didn't pause at any of the designated tent spots, continuing on to the lake's edge. Vic stopped short, the sheer beauty of the place washing over him.

From the clear, untouched lake, the forest and mountains rose up to snowcapped peaks. He'd seen the park from the helicopter and through the drive on Going-to-the-Sun Road, but it was something else altogether to be in the middle of it, knowing that you were no longer at the top of the food chain. "How many people are injured and killed by wildlife in this park a year?"

"Usually none." Maggie's gaze was on the mountains across from them. "We have more grizzlies than there were a few decades ago, but our rangers do our best to educate people on how to handle them, and ensure that they have bear spray when they're going to certain parts of the park during certain times of the year."

"And the other animals?" Grizzlies were what Glacier was known for, but that didn't mean they were the only ones to be on the lookout for.

"Moose are mean, but usually keep their distance unless they're feeling threatened. Same with the others. Mountain lions are ambush predators, but they're cowards at heart. They might go after a lone hiker and stalk them for miles, but they will usually stay away from groups." She hesitated. "That's the key word there—*usually*. Any animal is dangerous if cornered or with its young, and we're in *their* territory. But as long as people are respectful of that and take precautions, deaths are the exception to the rule."

It sounded like a rote lecture, and he had to wonder how often she'd given it. Vic nodded at the blur almost in the middle of the mountains, too regular to be natural. "What's that?"

"Porcupine Lookout. It's kind of a bitch to get to, but the view is totally worth it. Only one trail in and one out."

He noted that. There would be a lot of places like that in the park—places off the beaten trail that an avid hiker could get to for a spectacular view. That wasn't where they were headed, though. "Where was the body found?"

"This way."

He'd half expected it to be near the lake itself, but Maggie led him along the shoreline and then into the woods themselves. They passed

40

several more lakes before she finally stopped at one that was just a fraction of the size of the largest.

There was still evidence of blood on the dirt beneath two trees, though the ground had been disturbed by some animal. He circled the small clearing slowly, letting his impressions roll over him.

The two trees were equal distance apart, and both had marks high enough on them to require either a person well over his six foot four inches, or climbing. "Lot of trouble to get to that." He pointed to where the ropes were still knotted.

"Not really." She set her pack down, rolled her shoulders, and nimbly scaled the tree. Maggie braced herself between a branch and the trunk and held up her hands. "The unsub has probably practiced the knots—they didn't slip when he put weight on them—and he chose these trees for their position relative to each other and the fact that they're easily scalable."

"He."

She rolled her eyes, the worry that had lurked there since he'd arrived retreating. "Don't take the instructor tone with me. You know as well as I do that, historically, the vast majority of serial killers caught are men, and that women, while more than capable of murder, tend to use different methods than men do." She made a face. "Though you also know my thoughts on that."

Yeah, he did. Back when she'd been fresh from the academy, Maggie had spun her theories that they only found male serial killers because that was all they expected to find. If a person was looking for evidence to support a theory they believed was a truth, they would ignore any indication that didn't support their conclusion.

She had a point, but the number of female serial killers caught was still a fraction of the males.

Then again, a year ago, he'd assisted on a case involving just that, so she was right—ruling out one gender seemed foolish in the extreme. "We'll use *he* to simplify things, but I promise to keep an open mind."

"How big was the man killed in Rainier?"

"One hundred fifty pounds, tops." He followed her train of thought and nodded. "Not impossible for a strong woman to string up in this manner, but it would be challenging."

"Moving deadweight around is challenging no matter which way you swing it—unless you're the Hulk." She shimmied down the tree and carefully stepped around a patch of dried blood. "Did they take the rope in?"

"It appears to be generic mountaineering rope, which can be found in any outdoors-type store."

She propped her hands on her hips and glared at the remnants of the rope tied to the trees. "It would have been really convenient if it was some kind of special rope only sold in one store, huh?"

"Unfortunately, that sort of thing only happens on television."

"I know."

Vic did another circuit of the area. He was no tracker, able to determine how many people had entered a clearing or divine any information about them, but even he could see the broken branches and flattened greenery leading to the west. "This wouldn't have been made by one of your rangers or the tourists."

She walked over. "The tourists came in from the east, the same direction we did. They took one look at the body and basically fled screaming. David and Ava were here with me, but all we did was cut down the body and transport it back to the station." Her face went a little pale, and he didn't imagine that was a trip she was keen to remember anytime soon. She rallied. "This is too uniform to be an animal, but I'd expect better of our unsub." He started to speak, but she murmured, as if to herself, "But then, it's hard to be stealthy when hauling around a dead body."

Maggie hadn't lost her instincts. That much was clear.

He glanced at the sky, taking in the first streaks of purple. "Do we follow it or come back in the morning?" He didn't like the idea of leaving a lead dangling, but he liked the idea of being stranded in the middle of Glacier in the dark even less. There were no city lights to break the night here, and the stars, while beautiful, weren't adequate to keep them from stepping wrong and hurting themselves—or worse.

She looked like she wanted to chase down the trail as much as he did, but she shook her head. "We camp. In another hour, we won't be able to follow the trail anyways, and we might destroy evidence trekking back if we're not careful. Better to start at dawn, when we have plenty of time."

"Good."

He turned and looked out over the lake. While smaller than the first one, it was still plenty large and created an unobstructed view of the entire shoreline. The walk here from the campgrounds hadn't taken all that long, and the trail was worn down enough to suggest that plenty of people had made the same exploration. "How many people come through this park a year?"

"A little over two million. A good portion of those will go through this park once and never come back, but there are people who come every year—multiple times a season."

They'd considered that after the first death. "We looked at seasonal and temp workers, but nothing is popping. The seasonal rangers sometimes jump parks, which complicates matters further."

"You think it's a park ranger?" There wasn't shock or horror in her voice, just a true curiosity.

Vic finally moved away from the view and started back toward the campground. "Do *you* think it could be a ranger?" He genuinely wanted to know what she thought—but he also wanted to know how well her training had held up. It had been a long time since she was an agent, and though she'd had the makings of a good one, she'd left the BAU before that had been realized.

"Sure. I mean, I instinctively want to say no, because I'm at least on speaking terms with all the regular rangers here and most of the seasonal ones, but it's possible. Anything is possible."

He let her chew on that as they hiked back. No one had arrived since they left, and so they had the campground to themselves. Though it meant they didn't have to watch their words, it still made him a little uncomfortable.

It was more than the unsub potentially being close enough to be a threat.

It was the fact that the last time he and Maggie were alone, she'd been in his arms. Even with the case hanging over their heads, the memory stood between them almost like a living thing.

So much for not being distracted.

◆ ◆ ◆

Sunday, June 18
9:45 p.m.

Maggie had been so focused on getting to the scene where they found the body as well as thinking about the past bearing down on her that she hadn't really thought about the overnight accommodations. But as she set up the tent, she couldn't ignore the truth any longer.

She and Vic were going to sleep in the same tent.

The thrill that went through her at the thought had no place in a murder investigation—or a national park. *Maybe I should just set up my sleeping bag by the fire.* It wouldn't be quite as secure as the tent, but she wasn't going to get any sleep lying a few scant inches from the man who'd occupied more than his fair share of her thoughts over the years. Here he was, still larger than life and still too handsome—and now single.

Stop it.

Think of the case. Think of the murderer who might, even now, be stalking the woods around us.

Maggie caught a whiff of wood smoke and turned to find that Vic already had a fire burning. "Handy."

"You aren't the only one with outdoors skills." His brows slanted down. "Though I'm out of practice."

That obviously bothered him. When they were partners, she'd assumed the way he acted was because he was the senior partner who intended to show her the ropes. In hindsight, it was more than that. It was one of the fundamental things that made up his personality.

He protected. He led. He took care of those around him.

It had to be killing him a little bit to be so out of his element in their current situation.

"You're still faster than most people." She dragged her pack over to the fire and dug through it. They'd refilled their water before coming back to the campground, so now it was a matter of figuring out food. "Do you want beef ravioli or chicken noodle?"

"Maggie."

She glanced up to find his pale eyes laughing at her. "What?"

"You didn't really think I'd come out here without my own MREs, did you?"

Well, now that he mentioned it, she felt a little silly assuming that he'd act the same as the Fed had the only other time she'd played guide. *That* idiot had hiked behind her, complaining the whole way about his shoes pinching, and had forgotten to pack anything except a single bottle of water. No water purifier. No bear spray. No MREs. Not even a damn protein bar. By the end of that day, she'd been ready to wring his neck.

So now she always packed double the food she'd personally need if something went wrong. It was a pain to add more weight to her pack, but it was better than having to sacrifice much-needed calories because some tourist hadn't planned effectively.

But Vic was no tourist.

To cover up how flustered that realization made her, she said, "What have you got? Want to trade?"

45

His smile reached his lips. "I'll take that beef ravioli if you want some spicy turkey chili."

"Deal." She passed it over, and they went about preparing their food. With MREs, it was easy—they were self-heating, so it was a matter of engaging it and letting it do its thing. Some park rangers packed in other stuff, but she preferred the MREs. Easy to cook, easy to clean up, easy to pack in and out.

They ate in silence, and she went back to mulling over everything he'd told her. A serial killer. In her park. Oh, she knew Glacier wasn't actually *hers*, but she claimed it all the same. To know there could be someone hunting innocent people out here in the woods made her skin crawl. There was no telling when the unsub would strike again—or whom. Depending on the timeline and the path he took, he could hike well over twelve miles a day, traveling anywhere in the park within a few short days. They didn't know his plan, didn't know his timeline, didn't know *anything* that would catch him before he killed again.

Get ahold of yourself.

"I left the FBI because I didn't want to deal with this kind of thing anymore." She didn't realize she was going to speak until the words were pouring out of her. "Maybe you're wrong. Maybe he'll move on like he has the last two times." They had absolutely no indication that the unsub would stay in the park, aside from his shrinking cooling-down period. If he followed the previous pattern, he'd halve the time between murders—which meant they had another six weeks or so before someone would be in danger again.

In theory.

"Maybe." There was no censure there, no judgment.

She felt the sting anyway. Maggie looked up, finding him watching her. All the old insecurities she'd fought so long and hard to get past rose up in a wave that threatened to pull her under. "I couldn't cut it. You don't need to say it—we both know it's the truth. It took all of one case to break me. It was pathetic."

"Maggie, stop."

She realized she was breathing hard and cursed herself all over again for her weakness. She had failed so spectacularly at being an FBI agent, but up until this point, she'd been a pretty damn good park ranger. Having the two meet in such an unexpected way sent her right back to that feeling of helpless fury she couldn't escape seven years ago. "See. I'm not cut out for it."

"For fuck's sake, Maggie, that case messed up everyone. No one keeps their head on straight when kids are involved. You were twenty-one, and it was your *first* case. You were allowed to be shaken up seeing that shit. I understand why you left the BAU—I never thought less of you for that decision. No one did. But this self-pity act isn't you."

"How do you know what is or isn't me anymore? We haven't seen each other in seven years." Some days she was so *sure* she knew who she was. Others . . . not so much. She had been mostly written off as a lost cause by her parents after that fateful Thanksgiving seven years ago. They'd thought her leaving the FBI was a sign that she was finally seeing the light and deciding to follow along with *their* plans. The only thing she'd wanted was a safe place to recover from her burnout . . . The fight had been loud and angry, and she'd barely spoken to them since.

And, aside from a few misogynistic assholes in the park rangers, she'd more than proven herself ages ago professionally.

That was the problem. She might have proved herself to other people, but there was still a nagging little voice inside her that assured her she'd never be good enough.

He didn't look away. "I know enough."

She started to tell him that he was wrong, but a sound cut through the night. Maggie shot to her feet, spinning to face the lake. The fire made her night-blind, and she took several steps away from it, squinting. She felt Vic next to her, so close his shoulder brushed hers. He had his gun out, and he was staring at the same spot she was. "That wasn't any animal I know."

"You're right. That wasn't an animal. That was a human screaming."

CHAPTER FIVE

Five years ago, July

"I'm not ready to tell them." Madison double-checked her pack for the sixth time in ten minutes, her nervousness demanding she do something with her hands. She'd effectively put off this conversation for a couple of weeks—longer, really, when she added in the time since she'd gotten her college acceptance letter.

"Mads, you don't have to apologize for wanting to get the hell out of here."

She finally put her pack on the ground and straightened. Ashleigh leaned against the door frame of her closet, her arms crossed and her eyes bright. Her grip on her elbows was white-knuckled, and Madison felt sick when she thought about why. "You have a reason to leave— several reasons. It's different for me."

"Your mom and dad are good people. Mine aren't. That isn't what this is about." Ashleigh pushed off the wall. "Look, they already told you they support you. *I* support you, even if I'm cranky for selfish reasons that we aren't going to the same college—at least we'll be in the same city. Even if you decided to go to New York or, hell, London, I would still be supporting you. It's about *you*. It's not about them." She jerked her thumb at the window.

It didn't matter that they'd had a variation of this same conversation at least once a week for the last month. Madison still felt sick over the thought of leaving.

No, not over leaving—just over leaving *her friends*.

Over leaving her family in Montana, which had been the only home she'd ever known.

Over leaving Glacier, which was almost the hardest part. She knew there were other parks, and that Seattle and the Sound were beautiful and she'd never lack for outdoor activities to keep her occupied . . . but it wasn't the same.

Admitting to the others that she'd been accepted into Seattle Pacific University meant she was one step closer to actually leaving after summer was over, and she just flat-out wasn't ready.

Ashleigh narrowed her eyes. "You aren't thinking about changing your mind, are you?" They'd been best friends since Ashleigh's family had moved to Kalispell when they were both in first grade. They'd bonded over their shared love of pink and mutual dislike of gross boys . . . and the rest was history.

Am I thinking of changing my mind? Madison didn't know.

That was a lie. She did know. She was just too cowardly to face it.

But her best friend was still waiting for an answer, so she forced a smile. "No, I'm still going. But just let me have this trip, okay? I promise I'll tell them after we get back."

One last trip where everything was perfect—before it all changed.

They'd graduated three weeks ago, and Lauren and Ethan had been talking about the trip they'd put together for months previous. They'd hiked through Glacier on overnight trips, weekend trips, and spring-break trips, but this was different. This time, they were all adults.

Whatever the hell that meant.

The future stretched before her, terrifying in its possibilities. She didn't know if she'd stay in Seattle forever, but even her parents were in agreement—a partial scholarship to SPU was a dream come true. A good school was now affordable. She could always move back after college, but if she didn't leave now, she might *never* leave.

And that was more terrifying than anything else.

At least until she thought about facing down Ethan, Josh, and Lauren.

Madison took a deep breath and straightened. "Promise, Ashleigh. Promise you won't tell them until I'm ready."

For a second, it looked like Ashleigh might argue, but she finally sighed and lifted her hands in surrender. "I promise. But it's just going to get harder to pull the trigger the longer you let it go. It's better to rip off the Band-Aid now and get it over with."

"Like you have with Josh?" That was petty, and she regretted the words as soon as they left her mouth.

Ashleigh just shrugged. "What can I say? I'm a coward. Maybe we can just text them after we hit the town limits and call it a day."

She laughed even as she shook her head. "We can't." No matter how attractive that solution sounded. She didn't like confrontation, and ever since they were in grade school, their friends had had a plan. The plan itself had changed over the years—superheroes, secret agents, park rangers—but it had one constant: them, together.

And now she and Ashleigh were breaking rank.

A horn honked outside, and the tension between her shoulder blades ratcheted up. "That'll be the twins and Lauren."

Ashleigh closed her eyes, and when she opened them, she was herself again. "We can get through a five-day trip. We've done it before."

"Yep." She secretly hoped that being in Glacier would soothe her like nothing else seemed to, but it might be a long shot. "Ready?"

"As ready as I'll ever be." She laughed. "And, hell, worst case, they freak out, we freak out, and we move away and just never come back. Easy, peasy."

Ashleigh was right. The worst case was that they severed friendships that had been years in the making . . .

God, that sounded seriously crappy.

It was different for Ashleigh. She'd been born and spent her first seven years in Seattle. As a result, she'd never felt at home in Kalispell, and she'd had a countdown to college—and leaving—on her wall since they were in sixth grade. There had never been a single doubt in her mind that she was destined for somewhere else—*anywhere* else.

She'd never understood that Madison loved their town. The decision to leave was one Madison had waffled over for long enough to drive herself nuts, and now that the time was coming to actually pull the trigger on it, she kept finding herself wondering if maybe it'd be better to stay. She could keep her job at the general store and fall back on . . .

But that was the problem. She didn't want to *fall back* on a plan. If she ended up back in Kalispell, she wanted it to be her choice to come back, not the result of her being too afraid to take a risk.

Madison took a long breath, held it, and exhaled. "They'll be mad, but we'll get through it. We've gotten through everything else." In the years since first grade, they'd had fights and dramas and high points that made the bad look small by comparison. Not even junior high or high school could drive a true wedge between them—though things had gotten a little strained when Josh and Ashleigh started dating two years ago.

The truth was that her friends being mad at her was a crutch she'd been using to convince herself that maybe staying wasn't the worst thing in the world.

She had to make this decision for *her*.

She *had* made this decision for her.

Her friends might see it as a betrayal, but they would get over it. It was just college.

It wasn't the end of the world.

◆ ◆ ◆

Sunday, June 18
10:59 p.m.

"Wyatt? Wyatt, come in." Maggie had been trying to radio him for fifteen minutes. Reception was spotty in these mountains at best, so her phone was next to useless. She adjusted the frequency and tried again. "Wyatt, we need you."

Finally, *finally*, an answer came through. "Maggie? What's going on?"

"I think someone is being attacked."

Silence, only broken by the crackle of the radio. Vic sat next to her, a respectable distance away, a rock in the midst of what was becoming a seriously shitty situation. Finally, Wyatt said, "You *think?*"

She realized what it sounded like. First-year rangers often got spooked in the park at night. A whole wide world spread out beyond the faint light of their campfire, and that bone-deep terror of the darkness became something real and overwhelming for some people. She'd felt the same the first couple of summers she worked here, though she'd never admitted it because she knew how it would look—that she was a woman who couldn't handle her job. Wyatt might not think she was a hysterical female—especially almost six years into the job—but some of the other rangers were less than pleased to have her on staff, so she always had to be stronger, better, less afraid. Jumping at strange sounds and flickering shadows wasn't the way to do that.

She was used to it now. She'd learned when to keep her head down and her mouth shut—and when to snap back.

Snapping back now, when she was on the verge of losing control, was a mistake. Maggie swallowed her instinctive sarcastic reply. "We heard screams farther up the trail. Hard to pinpoint, but they were possibly coming from Porcupine Lookout."

His sigh almost blended in with the static. "Maggie, you know very well I can't authorize a helicopter or search-and-rescue team on the basis that you *think* you heard screams. There are a lot of animals out there that can sound like a human."

She knew that and resented that he was implying that she didn't. But Maggie also recognized a losing battle when she saw one. Wyatt was a good ranger and a good boss, but he would always put the bottom line first. And the bottom line was that, without evidence that something had actually gone wrong, he wasn't going to call in expensive resources.

"I'm going after them." Whoever *they* were. It could be the group she'd interacted with earlier today, or it could be someone hiking north from Many Glacier. It didn't matter. What mattered was figuring out who was hurt and helping them.

"No, you're not. Not tonight." More static. "Take the Fed south along Mountain Trail to the Loop. I'll have someone meet you there with a car. It will only add half a day to your trip, and you can investigate on your way."

"But . . ."

"That's an order, Maggie."

He was her boss, not her commanding officer, but he had a point. The park was tricky to navigate in the middle of the day. Even knowing it as well as she did, charging out there at night was the very height of stupidity. She tried to take a deep breath and acknowledge that. It took several breaths before she got control of her anger. "In the morning, then."

"Report when you have something."

She set the radio down even though she wanted to throw it into the darkness. That was a childish response, and she wasn't going to cut off her nose to spite her face. That didn't stop the frustration from nearly overwhelming her. "Damn it."

"He's right," Vic said. "If we can't follow a trail from the murder site into the woods in the dark, we shouldn't be running into an unknown situation."

She hated how calm he was. It reminded her of their time as partners, when she was constantly on the verge of freaking out, and he was totally and completely unperturbed. "Someone could be dying out there."

"If they are, they're already dead."

She stopped short and turned to face him. "How can you say that? We could—"

Vic's face showed nothing, though she could see a shadow of the frustration she felt in his pale eyes. "Maggie, you said this could be coming from Porcupine Lookout. How long would it take us to get there?"

"In the dark? Hours." Realization crept over her, and she sagged. "The person would be dead by the time we got there."

"Yes."

She faced the night again. Somewhere out there, a person could be fleeing for their life, and there wasn't a damn thing she could do about it. Frustration and fear combined, melting away in the face of her fury. "I'm going to find whoever is doing this in my park, and they're going to see justice."

"I know."

She caught movement out of the corner of her eye, as if he'd reached for her, but the touch never came. Instead, Vic turned back toward the fire. "Do you want first watch or second?"

Watch. Because whoever was out there in the darkness, hunting, could potentially come for them next. She shivered. "I'll take first." She didn't know if she could sleep at all, so there was no point in wasting both their time by being awake.

Vic gave her a long look, but he didn't argue. She watched him settle into the sleeping bag and close his eyes. Within two minutes, his breathing evened out and his body relaxed completely. She'd never been able to master that particular skill—to shut off her brain and fall into unconsciousness at the flick of a switch. If old habits held, he'd be able to burst back into wakefulness without the webs of sleep clinging to him, so she took a seat across the fire from him and settled in to wait.

Time passed, and she tensed with every rustle in the shadows around the campground. There was going to be no sleep for her tonight, even though she knew she needed it. The adrenaline rush she'd gotten after hearing the screams faded away, leaving her tired and cranky, and she only got more tired and cranky as the night went on. Her mind wouldn't stop, though. She reviewed the pieces of information—the few that they had—over and over again, trying to see them in a new light.

Hunting people wasn't a novel concept. It'd existed for time unknown, though modern civilization frowned on that sort of activity. But the BAU wouldn't exist if human predators didn't. They specialized in bringing down the monsters lurking inside the most unassuming of people. Because that's exactly what those serial killers and rapists were—predators.

Most of them didn't hunt in quite so literal a sense. It was easier to pick victims in suburban areas and cities, to stalk their victims as they went about their lives, and to attack at a time of the unsub's choosing. Organized killers usually liked things planned down to the smallest detail, even when they were first starting out.

This unsub left so much open to chance. There was no way to divine the habits of the victim, because the unsub would have to hunt them over the course of multiple hikes, and, even then, things constantly changed in these parks. A rock slide or avalanche could put a trail out of commission and force a different route—the same with animals and weather. This unsub couldn't just follow the victim into the park. Bows—hunting weapons of any kind—were illegal, and any ranger worth their salt would catch and detain the person carrying it. To bring it in without risking notice, the unsub had to hike in without using a trailhead or try to time it to when a ranger wouldn't be around. *Risky.*

Maybe he gets off on the challenge.

If that was the case, she had to wonder how many potential victims had just missed death because of circumstances beyond the unsub's control.

Maggie counted down the minutes until dawn put enough light in the sky to see the trail. She wasn't an FBI agent anymore. It wasn't her job to figure out how the unsub's brain worked or what he would do next. All she was responsible for was guiding Vic around the park without getting him killed or injured or doing something to jeopardize the rangers' relationship with the Feds.

That was it.

She'd do well to remember that.

She chewed her nutrition bar methodically and shoved the wrapper into her pack. It might as well have been sawdust for all she tasted it, but passing out because she hadn't taken in enough calories wasn't an option. Neither was being too weak to help if her worst fears were realized. She checked the time. "Vic."

He opened his eyes and instantly frowned. "You should have woken me."

"I know." Too late to worry about it now. If they got through the day, she'd let him take first watch. *You're already planning on another night in the park. Pessimistic much?* "Let's get moving."

"Maggie."

She turned away from the concern in his voice. She didn't want his pity now any more than she had when they were partners. "I'm fine—but whoever we heard screaming last night isn't. How long do you need?"

"Five minutes. I can eat while we walk."

It took her a good five minutes to get herself in order, too, and then she and Vic dismantled the tent as if they'd done it a thousand times before. She didn't look directly at him. What was there to say? Part of her wanted to reassure him that, no matter what they found on the trail, she wouldn't have a meltdown. She was stronger than she used to be. She wasn't the weak link anymore. The rest of her didn't feel like she owed him a damn explanation.

They started south up the trail without a word. Usually the rhythmic movements of hiking and the calm of the park brought her peace. There was none to be found that morning. She forced herself to a slower pace that wouldn't burn her and Vic out, but all she wanted to do was run full tilt up the trail.

"How sure are you that the screams came from this lookout?"

She didn't look back but turned her head to the side so he'd be able to hear her. She wished she had a nice, easy answer for him, but the truth was more important than her pride. "Not sure enough."

◆ ◆ ◆

Monday, June 19
6:10 a.m.

Vic was furious with himself. He should have known better than to let Maggie take first watch. He'd never had the particular skill of being able to set an internal clock and wake himself up, otherwise he would have put a stop to that shit last night. The worst part was that he wasn't even surprised. This case would bother a normal person, even if they didn't have her knowledge concerning the monsters in human skin. Maggie knew all too well what people were capable of.

She'd be tired today, wired from the hunt, and as a result she'd be a liability.

He couldn't tell her that without pissing her off, which would push her closer to the edge and make her more likely to do something foolish if they ran into trouble. He had missed his mark with this case already. He searched the trees around them as he considered her response. "The mountains make the acoustics problematic."

"Yes."

He wished he'd spent more time studying a map of the trails, but beyond the most popular ones, he didn't have a clear view of the park in his head. "Tell me about Porcupine Lookout."

"It breaks from this trail a mile and a half from Kootenai Lake and then rises five miles to the lookout point. There's a little over twenty-six hundred feet of elevation change from the trail break to the end."

He considered that. Distances seemed to be deceptive in Glacier, because five miles was a cakewalk, but five miles with a three-thousand-foot elevation change was something else altogether. He did some quick calculations. "That's a day hike from Kootenai Lake for most people."

"Yes."

If he hadn't known how twisted up she was about being forced to sit on her hands while someone might be dying, her terse answers more than broadcast that. Vic wanted to shake her. There wasn't a damn thing they could have done, and rushing off to get themselves killed wouldn't have accomplished anything. It was shitty to have to wait for daylight, but it was the right call.

Instead, he said, "Is there a camping spot up there?"

"There's a place where rangers can stay, though it's a rarely used one." She missed a step. "There's no way that scream came from Porcupine Lookout."

He'd started to think the same thing. Even if someone camped up there, it didn't seem like an ideal spot for their unsub to hunt. Lookouts were, by nature, limited in the number of ways in and out. Their guy liked to stalk and hunt his prey, and it was damn near impossible up on the ridge of a mountain.

"There's two fords this time of year, and then a switchback trail that's pretty gnarly and covered in overgrowth for the first half or so." She shook her head. "There's no way someone would choose that route if they were running for their life. They wouldn't be able to *find* it in the dark. Shit. I should have thought of that."

"You should have slept." The words came out harsher than he intended, but once they drifted in the air between them, there was no going back. "Playing the martyr is going to get someone killed. You're an experienced ranger—you know how easy it is to die in this park."

She stopped and spun to face him. "Sorry that I can't just shut my emotions off like a robot the same way you can, Vic. Someone is out there, dead or dying, and maybe you could sleep like a baby, but that wasn't an option for me."

It was a complaint he'd heard before. Too controlled. Too locked down. Too robotic. His own mother had called him a freak because of it. The SEALs had seen it as an asset and used him ruthlessly as a result. Janelle had launched accusation after accusation, pulling shitty stunts to try to provoke a response and then using his lack of one as evidence to prove her point.

To have those same complaints coming from *Maggie* put them on another level entirely. If he hadn't already been angry, he could have bitten back the words, but she had always gotten under his skin like no other. "It's called being a professional. You should try it sometime."

He regretted the words instantly, but there was no taking them back.

She jerked back as if he'd struck her and narrowed her dark eyes. "So the truth comes out. It only took seven years."

"We don't have time for this." No matter what he said right now, it'd be the wrong thing, and he was too angry to carefully consider his words—which would likely be yet another misstep. There was no winning, because she'd already decided to take out her frustration on him.

Normally, that wouldn't bother him so much, but he thought better of Maggie. Or, rather, he was letting his past feelings cloud his current situation.

Her mouth twisted. "Fine." She charged up the trail. "Since searching the entire park is damn near impossible, we should follow the trail and see if anything stands out." She shifted her pack higher on her shoulders. "I'd like to check on the hikers I saw yesterday, though they should be almost a full day ahead of us."

He glared at the back of her head, more irritated than he should be that she'd taken the change of subject in stride without arguing further, even though that was exactly what he'd asked for.

Vic tried to focus on the case instead, though he hadn't expected this turn of events. They were supposed to spend today searching the area surrounding where the body was found, but here they were, hiking farther into the park and farther away from anything resembling civilization—and calling the Goat Haunt ranger station civilization was a stretch.

His partner, Tucker Kendrick, would have landed not too long ago after taking a red-eye flight from Quantico, and he'd be expecting an update from Vic as soon as he got to the park. He had no doubt Tucker would think this was a wild goose chase . . . and Vic wasn't sure he would be wrong.

But he'd heard that scream, same as Maggie.

There was no way that had been an animal.

It took what he clocked as nearly half a mile to get himself back under control, and even then, he could feel the anger broiling beneath the surface. It wouldn't be an issue if his guide was anyone other than Maggie, and that fact should be enough to keep him in line.

It wasn't.

He exhaled harshly. "I'm sure those hikers are fine."

"You're patronizing me."

Just like that, his mouth got away from him again. "Christ, Maggie, if you're going to take everything I say wrong, then maybe we should get someone else in here."

"Too late. I'm all you have, and you're just going to have to deal with it." She sighed, her pace slowing to something resembling reasonable. "But I'm sorry all the same. As usual, you're right. I'm sure they have nothing to do with what we heard."

He opened his mouth, reconsidered, and shut it. Better that they keep hiking in silence than for him to stick his foot in it. Again. Vic surveyed the trees around them, all too aware that they could be being watched, and it would be nearly impossible to know.

That's how he tracks them. Probably sets up some sort of stand near a trail and sits like a spider in his web and waits for his victim—somewhere he can see the trail with ease.

It would be simple enough to shoot his victim right there, but he likes the hunt too much. He does something to push them to flee so he can chase them. It's probably his favorite part, and a confirmation that he is superior in every way to his prey.

He'd visited the sites of both the other murders—or where their bodies were found—and neither of the other parks felt like this one. Rainier was a quick hop from half a dozen towns, and two hours' drive from Seattle. Grand Teton was wilder, but the body hadn't been left more than seven miles from the trailhead. He was painfully aware that they were far enough from any kind of backup that they were on their own. "You radio Wyatt?"

"Shit." She grabbed her radio and fiddled with the dials. "Wyatt? Wyatt, come in."

"He's not here."

Vic didn't recognize the voice, but Maggie obviously did. She frowned. "Ava, what's going on? I thought he was in the station."

"He's waiting for a chopper. There's another Fed at headquarters, says he's your Fed's partner."

She met Vic's gaze. "He's not my anything."

Ava ignored that. "Yeah, well, Wyatt said to radio if you find anything, but otherwise to get your ass to the Loop once the job's done. We just need about an hour's notice to get someone there in time to meet you."

"Got it." She stashed the radio back in her pack. "So much for that."

"He's going to meet Tucker."

"Your partner."

"Yeah." He waited, half expecting some other kind of outburst, but she just nodded. "Okay."

Time passed, and he let it go without comment. The trail got steeper and then dropped off sharply into a little valley. Even with a murderer on the loose and all the underlying crap going on with Maggie, he still stopped periodically and just took it all in. He could see why people came here and braved the overnight conditions. In a world where everyone was hyperconnected, in this park, he felt small again. A small moving piece against a massive world.

An individual.

At the bottom of the decline, they hit a creek. Maggie skirted the edge of it. "The rocks are slippery. Be careful."

Since he had no intention of taking a dip in the freezing water, he stepped where she stepped as they hopscotched rocks to the other side. The sun was well beyond the tops of the surrounding mountains now, but the spot where they stopped still stood in shadow. He eyed the tops of the trees. "Not very warm for June."

"Nope." She took a swig of her water. "We highly recommend that any hikers who come along certain trails carry ice picks and know how use them to self-arrest if they fall, especially this early in the season. We won't have to worry about that, because we're not going far enough into the park. I hope."

But he wasn't listening. Vic turned a slow circle, the hair along the nape of his neck standing on end. His hand drifted to his service weapon, but he didn't draw it yet. He turned again, trying to figure out what had put his instincts on high alert.

There.

He kept his voice low and calm, designed to carry to Maggie and no farther. "There's something in those bushes." In the gaps between the leaves, something flesh-colored could just be seen.

Not flesh-colored. Actual flesh.

She followed his gaze and whispered a curse. "Stay here."

"The hell I will."

She glared even as she grabbed her bear spray with steady hands. "Trust me, Vic. I wasn't joking when I was saying this is bear country. If that's what I think it is, then we need to make sure there's not a predator lurking. Just . . . don't make any sudden movements or try to play the hero."

He watched her stomp toward the bushes, making enough noise for three people. *So she doesn't surprise any animals close by.* He'd read somewhere that bear attacks were usually for two reasons—a mother bear protecting her cubs from a perceived threat, or a surprised and scared bear reacting out of instinct.

Understanding the reason behind a bear attack wasn't going to do anything to make dealing with a potentially furious animal easier.

Maggie stopped short when she reached the bushes. "Fuck."

Vic was at her side in an instant, and he only barely contained his own curse. A woman's body lay behind the bushes.

Or what was left of her.

CHAPTER SIX

Monday, June 19
7:48 a.m.

Maggie threw her hand out as Vic started to take a step forward. "Wait."
She was half-surprised when he obeyed, and a small, treacherous part
of her luxuriated in how good his chest felt through the thin fabric of
his shirt. Setting that aside was the only course of action, especially
considering the body. If she didn't miss her guess, it had been partially
eaten. *Fuck again.* She didn't want to go closer, didn't want to see a
human turned to meat in such detail, but there was no other option.
"I'm going to get a better look."

"Our guy didn't do this."

"Not all of it." She waded through the bushes and crouched
next to the body. Vic's presence at her back comforted her despite
the circumstances. She didn't have to worry about something—or
someone—getting the drop on her while he was standing guard.

"Bear?"

"That seems most likely. The cats don't mind already-dead bodies, but they tend to stash them in trees—or at least move them." She

pulled out a pair of gloves from the side pouch on her pack. They were thicker than latex, but they wouldn't leave behind residue the same way her cloth ones would. The animal had already screwed up the chance of getting an untouched body to forensics, but she wouldn't muddy the waters further if she could help it. *Does the probability of animals getting at the bodies contribute to the unsub hunting here?*

If it does, then why leave them so close to well-traveled places, where they're bound to be found within a short window?

Vic's jeans brushed her back, his voice coming from directly over her head. "This is our guy."

She touched the two arrows protruding from the woman's back. Those, at least, hadn't been disrupted by the animal. Seen from behind, the woman looked almost normal, her dark, curly hair in a disarray, her clothes mostly intact. From the front . . . there wasn't much left of her. "They'll need some kind of way to collaborate her identity, but I think this girl was in the group I met yesterday." *Lauren.* That had been her name. Whatever tension there'd been between her and the other girl— the one with the permits—would never be resolved. The unsub had made sure of that. Maggie could perfectly picture the way the girl's big, dark eyes had watched everyone around her, seeming to miss nothing.

She wouldn't be watching anything again.

"He didn't finish what he started, like with the others."

Vic's voice snapped her out of the sorrow she felt for this near-stranger. She sat back on her heels and looked around. "We aren't far off the trail. She was coming from Fifty Mountain, and coming fast if she started after they set up camp." She frowned. "But where are the rest of them? If we only have one unsub, taking on a group of five people is insane. Most of that group seemed to know the park well enough that they wouldn't be taking stupid risks like wandering off alone." The buddy system was king in this world, and she would have bet good money that Lauren and the others knew and practiced it.

She frowned harder. "No way would they let this girl head back for the ranger station without someone else coming with her."

"Which provokes the question—why *is* she alone?" Vic moved around the body, staying a careful distance away, until he came to the stop where the woman had obviously crashed through the undergrowth. She'd been moving roughly parallel to the path, which made sense if she was running and couldn't see well in the dark. He bent over and looked up the way her trail led. "Rough shot in the dark, let alone to hit her twice."

"Maybe he has night-vision goggles."

"Maybe . . ." He shook his head. "I don't think so. This guy gets off on the hunt—on being better than his victims—and I have the feeling he'd see technology like night vision as cheating."

She was inclined to agree, though she didn't like thinking about it. This woman—a girl, really, since she was barely old enough to drink—had experienced the kind of terror they should have left behind centuries ago. "Why her? Why now?" There had only been a couple of days since the last murder. Even with the unsub's cooling-off period getting shorter, a leap from months to mere days was unprecedented.

Unless.

She shot to her feet. "She's the one he was waiting for." But this girl hadn't been alone. "The group is what he was waiting for—what he was working himself up to. The others might have been practice."

"That's a significant number of conclusions you just jumped to."

Maggie rocked back on her heels, but she lifted her chin. "It's the only thing that makes sense."

"Wrong. It does make sense, but focusing on that means you're going to miss evidence because you're only looking for clues that support the result you decided on."

She felt like she was back in the academy again, and she wasn't too fond of Vic lecturing her like he was one of her instructors. Even if he was right. So she moved a little back from the body and yanked her radio out of her pack. It took ten minutes to get a response to her call and another ten to get confirmation that there was a chopper on the way. There was no way the pilot could land anywhere near their location. There were maneuvers that could be done if an injured person was in need of rescue, but they were dangerous, and no one was willing to risk their life for a dead body just to save a few hours.

The chopper would land near Kootenai Lakes, and a pair of rangers would hike to their location with a stretcher to haul the body back to be transported out of the park. They'd also check in with Maggie and Vic, collect their report, and get the information back to Wyatt.

Best-case scenario—which wasn't saying much—this girl had wandered away from her group for reasons unknown and been killed by the unsub.

Worst case . . .

Maggie's gaze drifted back to the corpse despite her best intentions. In the worst-case scenario, there were four other bodies waiting to be found, all riddled with arrows.

If they didn't find the hikers alive, Wyatt would have to authorize a search-and-rescue team to start combing the trails. They had an idea of where the hikers were headed, which was more information than they had in a lot of SAR missions. In most missing-person cases in Glacier, they found the person or group with little difficulty, discovering that they'd wandered off the path or taken a trail beyond their hiking abilities and gotten stranded.

This wouldn't be one of those cases.

She shook her head. "Hunting five people with a bow is madness. Even in the dark, all it takes is one or two of them to figure out where the arrows are coming from, and it's over. Even an experienced bowman can only reload so fast."

"Hmm?" Vic was still peering up the trail. "Well, the unsub shows some familiarity with a knife, though dressing a kill and fighting for one's life are two very different things." He didn't seem the least bit affected by the woman lying dead at his feet.

Even though she knew better, she couldn't help resenting him a little for his cool exterior.

Maggie had seen death, both in her limited time as an FBI agent and during her years as a park ranger. Whether human or animal, the stench remained the same—shit and raw meat and blood all mixed into an odor she wished she could forget. It didn't matter that this girl hadn't been dead long enough to start decaying—death *stank*. Knowing that this body had started human and had been turned into so much meat made her sick to her stomach.

She turned away, needing a second to get herself under control. "Do you need to call your partner?"

"Actually, I do."

"Might as well if you can get service. We have time." She kept staring into the forest around them, comforting herself with the fact that she was watching for bears. The burning in her eyes and throat gave lie to that.

Her park had been tainted. They said one never escaped the sins of their past, but she hadn't realized she'd bring that truth with her when she made her home in Montana. *Mom and Dad will trip all over themselves to say, "I told you so."* It wasn't a charitable thought, no matter how true it was. Rationally, she knew that these murders would have happened whether or not she was working here.

But there was nothing rational about her emotional reaction. She kept looking at Lauren's body, thinking about the fact that she hadn't warned them. She'd *known* there was danger in Glacier, and she hadn't said a damn thing.

If she'd warned them, would this girl be dead right now?

◆ ◆ ◆

Monday, June 19
8:14 a.m.

Vic pulled out his satellite phone and checked to make sure he had enough service to call out, keeping one eye on Maggie. Her shoulders were too tight, her speech stilted. *Blaming herself.* Their earlier argument meant nothing in the face of the scene before them. Private issues would wait—the unsub obviously wouldn't.

Tucker answered immediately. "You know, when you said you'd meet me out here, I didn't realize that meant you'd spirit the lovely Ranger Gaines away before I had a chance to see if the reality lives up to legend."

"Give it a rest, Tucker." Vic knew there was no malicious intent behind his new partner's words. Tucker's attitude was an asset most of the time—he had the ability to put people at ease, which had never been a skill Vic possessed—but sometimes it grated. Times like these made him miss Eden and her blunt manner.

But she had to go and fall in love and be happy.

"Can't help it. Not even going to try." Tucker immediately sobered. "They said you found another body."

"We did."

"Two in a week is escalating—a lot—and he didn't jump parks this time. His timeline is moving faster than we anticipated."

"Tell me something I don't know." Vic moved several feet farther along the trail the victim had broken on what appeared to be a wild sprint down the incline.

"We don't have an ID on the body in the morgue yet, but I spoke with the lovely sounding Dr. Huxley as soon as I landed. She's running the prints, so we should have some kind of answer soon if the woman is in the system. Dr. Huxley thinks she looks familiar, but that just means that she might have come in contact with her at one point—or

69

that she might look like someone she came in contact with. So no point getting excited yet."

If the first dead hiker was local, it was entirely possible that the medical examiner *had* come in contact with her at some point. "Let me know when you find something."

"Will do. Tell me about the new one."

Personal issues aside, Tucker had a keen mind and an excellent record. People felt comfortable around him, so they talked to him. Usually they didn't realize they were hanging themselves out to dry until it was too late.

Vic eyed the sky. It was still early yet, but it would take hours for the retrieval team to arrive. "She's part of a five-person group who hiked through Goat Haunt yesterday morning, all originally local to Kalispell. She was found alone, and some kind of predator got to her overnight." He walked a little farther, stopping when a glint of dark red spattered over the dirt caught his eye. Vic leaned down to look at the ground. *Blood.* "Looks like she might have managed to keep running even with two arrows in her back."

"He didn't track her down to finish the job."

"Nope." Could mean any number of things. Maybe the unsub had been hunting her and was scared away by the predator finding the body. The universe wasn't kind enough to have the unsub fall down a ravine, but it *was* a possibility. That was the problem—there were too many possibilities and not enough concrete facts.

"Do you want to call in a report to Britton, or should I?"

At the mention of the head of the BAU, Vic turned back to the scene, taking in the woman's body and where Maggie stood with her arms wrapped around herself, her foot tapping furiously. Every thirty seconds, her attention jumped to the body and away, as if she couldn't help looking but hated doing it. He wanted to go to her, but she wouldn't take his help now any more than she would have before—offering would just piss her off more.

Though if she was angry, at least she wouldn't be freaking out anymore.

"I'll call." Britton would want an update—both on the case and on his former agent. Not that one ever managed to be a former anything to Vic's boss. The man was as meddlesome as he was brilliant, and he had no problem pulling strings to accomplish what he wanted. He'd been responsible for Vic's last partner, Eden, getting a spot in the local office without so much as a hiccup.

It didn't hurt that she was a damn good Fed and had connections to a local cult that made her worth her weight in gold.

"Vic."

He hesitated, not liking the sudden seriousness in his partner's voice. "What?"

"Be careful. This guy knows his way around the wilderness. I know you were some kind of international badass in the Navy, but that was more than a decade ago. Don't get yourself shot and strung up."

"Careful, Tucker, or I might actually think you care."

"Training a new partner is a pain in the ass." Tucker was Vic's age, so he'd had his fair share of partner changes—and that was one area where they saw eye to eye. Settling in with a new partner, figuring out how their mind worked and how to complement each other, took time and work. He might not always like Tucker, but the man was a good agent and an asset to the BAU.

"Agreed." Vic snorted and hung up. He raised his voice enough to catch Maggie's attention. "You good? I need to make one more call."

"Yeah." He could actually see her swallow hard. "I mean, no. I'm not good. There's nothing good about this situation. But I'm holding it together, and I'll continue to hold it together. Just don't wander too far, because there's a decent chance whatever predator got to her will come back at some point for another meal."

His skin crawled at the idea of facing down a bear, but he gave a short nod and moved a little farther away. Maggie wouldn't appreciate yet another reminder of the life she'd left behind when she quit the FBI.

As expected, Britton answered almost immediately. "Washburne."

"It's Vic. I have an update." Not every Fed who'd run the BAU liked to keep such close contact with their teams, but Britton wasn't like most of the corporate jackasses. He'd worked his way up from the bottom, which meant he had a very specific set of skills. He knew that fresh eyes were an asset with some cases—and that this job had a higher rate of burnout than most. And, most shocking of all, he actually cared about his people. So Vic didn't chafe too much at the request to keep him updated.

Most of the time.

"Another victim?"

He didn't ask how Britton had guessed. He wouldn't be calling for anything other than a game changer, and the man knew it. "Different this time. This one was part of a group, and the timing means that she couldn't have been like the second one. She had no reason to leave the campsite before morning. It looks like the unsub shot her, and she managed to get away long enough that he didn't have a chance to finish his ritual. A predator got to the body—probably a bear—so we can't confirm ID, but Maggie thinks she was one of five hikers who left Goat Haunt yesterday."

"How's Maggie these days?"

Vic took a few more steps farther into the trees and lowered his voice. "Seems fine. She likes this park ranger shit, and she's good at it, though her FBI training hasn't completely worn off." He glanced at her. "Still touchy, and she's got more of a temper on her than she used to."

"Hmm." Just that.

"What's that supposed to mean?"

"Just that she's not the only one who's touchy in the current situation." There was censure in the other man's voice, but he moved briskly on before Vic could respond. "If the unsub is escalating, you need to be extra alert. We can't guarantee that the rules from the first three murders will hold true. You're going deeper into the park to track the other four hikers."

It wasn't a question, but he answered it all the same. "Yeah. If they're fine, that means the victim took off by herself for reasons unknown—and that the unsub isn't deviating as much as we feared. He might think he's the ultimate hunter, but taking down a bear with a bow is a whole hell of a lot trickier than murdering a person. Could be that's what happened." But he didn't think so. Even if there was a bear, the woman had still run for some distance after she'd been shot. She couldn't have been moving fast—not injured and not in through this terrain in the dark. They'd still have to backtrack to find out how far she made it, but there wasn't a single damn reason for the unsub not to finish the kill.

It didn't make sense.

Unless he'd already moved on to the next victim . . .

CHAPTER SEVEN

Monday, June 19
11:35 a.m.

It seemed to take forever for the other rangers to arrive with the stretcher to extract the body. Maggie used every ounce of her willpower not to pace. She wanted to cover the body, but she knew what Vic would say if she suggested it—that it was a waste of time and resources. All they had that would cover a body was the tent or a sleeping bag, both of which they needed if they were going to track down the rest of this girl's party.

The sound of footsteps across the creek brought her head up. She moved to the edge of the running water and waited. It didn't take long for two people to appear, and Maggie relaxed a little when she recognized David and Ava. It made sense that they'd sent those two—Ava had medic training and seniority, and David wanted a permanent position in Glacier, which meant it was trial by fire for him as far as Wyatt was concerned.

They made their way across the creek, holding an empty stretcher between them. From the way David's shoulders were slightly bowed and he wouldn't quite look directly at Ava, he'd offered to carry the stretcher and she'd told him where to stick it. Ava wouldn't put up with that shit any more than Maggie would, and it wouldn't occur to her that he was offering because he was a genuinely nice guy—not because he was a dick who didn't think she could handle it.

"David, stand right there and try not to screw anything up." Ava set down her side of the stretcher and nodded in greeting. "Hell of a way to start the season, huh?"

"You can say that again." She took a deep breath. "It's going to be tricky getting her back to the chopper. We can't cut the arrows out of her back without screwing up evidence even more than it already is, and I think a bear got to her front."

David went pale beneath his tan. "Shit."

"Pretty much."

Ava didn't so much as blink. "No time like the present."

In the years Maggie had known her, she'd never seen anything get under Ava's skin. The woman had a wicked sense of humor, and she was more than a little bit of an adrenaline junkie, but she could set all that aside when the situation called for it. Honestly, Maggie was kind of surprised she hadn't transferred out to Grand Canyon or Teton. Glacier wasn't the wild ride that some of the other parks could claim for their rangers, and the sometimes-sedate pace didn't seem to mesh well with Ava most of the time.

There was nothing sedate about the events of this week.

She turned to face the body. It didn't matter how long she and Vic had been here, it was still a shock to see. Her attention kept coming back to the girl's curly, dark hair. It seemed such a strange thing to draw her, but with the damage done to the body, it was the only thing that was *Lauren* anymore.

Maggie swallowed past the lump in her throat. "You brought the camera?"

"Yeah." Ava held it up. "You going to do it? Or is the Fed?"

"I will." Vic strode down from where he'd been wandering through the trees in widening arcs since he'd finished his calls. She knew what he was doing—making sure they didn't miss something—but that didn't stop her from nearly jumping out of her skin every time he made a sound.

Ava passed over the camera and crouched down to look at the body. "Definitely a bear." She sighed. "Wyatt's not going to like this."

No, he wouldn't. It was entirely likely the bear would move on with its life and never bother humans again . . . but if it got a taste for human flesh, it could pose a very real danger for the hikers that traveled along this trail. It was plain bad luck that the girl had died so close to such a popular trail, because there would be people hiking up and down it most days for the next few months. "He'll have to be the one to make that call."

Maggie had never aspired to being in charge, one of the many things her parents had never forgiven her for. Ambition was the heart and soul of the Gaines family and had been for generations. Her paternal grandfather had made partner in his law firm before he was thirty-five, and her father had followed in his footsteps. Even her mother had an MBA from Harvard, though she'd turned all that ambition into being the perfect wife once she and Maggie's father got married.

If only she'd put half as much effort into being a good mother.

No, Maggie mostly just wanted to be left alone—and situations like this just drove that reality home. Either Wyatt would take a risk with people's lives by hoping this situation was a one-off, or he'd have to put a kill order out on the bear who'd eaten part of the victim. Neither option was a good one.

An unfortunate side effect when people and nature came in such close contact. As a park ranger, it was her job to protect nature from people and people from nature, and most of the time, she was successful.

Ava frowned at the body. "Is he eating them?"

It took Maggie a few seconds to jump topics with her. "They don't think so."

"Good." She nodded. "Good. That's a kind of evil that you don't want to be messing with."

Since Maggie couldn't imagine an evil much worse than hunting a defenseless and terrified person through the dark, she kept her mouth shut. Ava was right. Eating the victim would be much, much worse. She shuddered.

"How're the pictures coming, Vic?" she asked. The sooner they got the body on its way out of the park, the sooner she and Vic could keep moving and leave this place behind.

She'd never be able to hike this trail without thinking about finding the body—without picturing the woman lying on the ground and dying. Maggie's stomach lurched. *Oh, God. Please tell me she was dead when the bear found her.*

Vic snapped one last picture and stood. "I'm good. Mind if I keep this until we get back?"

"Sure." Ava shrugged. "It's Wyatt's." She shot a look at David. "You good?"

"Yeah." He looked green, but his hands were mostly steady as he laid a body bag next to the dead girl and helped Ava shift her into it. A few minutes later, it was zipped up to the arrows and strapped to the stretcher. David shuddered. "So glad we don't have to do this shit often."

"Grow a pair, Downey. You want to be a full-time ranger, that means sometimes you're on body retrieval—and believe me, the corpses are rarely pretty." Ava turned to Maggie. "You watch your back, you hear me? I like your contrary ass, and I'm going to be seriously pissed if you get yourself murdered by some psychopath."

"I'll do my best to stay among the living." She hadn't really thought about it too much when she'd first agreed to this, but it was becoming all too clear that she might actually come face-to-face with this unsub at some point. If he was condensing his cooling-off period this much, he wasn't going to stop. He'd track each of those other four kids, and then he'd keep going until someone stopped him.

Until *they* stopped him.

There was no one else. Even though Wyatt needed to authorize a search party, the SAR people were trained in rescue—not self-defense. They'd be out in the park and potentially putting themselves in the line of fire.

Stop.

Maggie took a deep breath. *One thing at a time. Figure out where the other four hikers are. Then you can freak out as necessary.* She rubbed a hand over her eyes, exhaustion starting to weigh on her. "I'll try," she said again.

Ava's gaze flicked over her shoulder to where Maggie could feel Vic standing. "You, too, Fed." Then she motioned to David, and they lifted the stretcher. They crossed the creek and marched down the trail toward where the helicopter would be waiting for them at Kootenai Lake.

Maggie watched them until they were out of sight and then rolled her shoulders. "We need to get moving. There are a couple spots before Fifty Mountain where we could camp in a pinch, but it'd be better to just bust ass and make it."

"Agreed," said Vic.

He didn't have to say that they might not be getting much sleep—again—depending on what they found. She was afraid there were more dead bodies in her future.

Better to be the one finding the dead bodies than one who turned up dead.

◆ ◆ ◆

Monday, June 19
12:51 p.m.

Vic couldn't shake the feeling that he was being stalked. It started about a mile after they left the creek and only seemed to get worse the longer they hiked. He had to force himself to keep his eyes on Maggie, because otherwise he was in danger of looking over his shoulder every three seconds. He wouldn't see anything. Even if it was the unsub, the guy was too good at what he did to be observed.

If it *wasn't* the unsub . . .

He picked up his pace, skirting the edge of the path to walk next to Maggie. "We're being followed."

She didn't so much as miss a step or look at him. "You think it's our guy?"

"Hard to say."

Maggie pressed her lips into a thin line. "On one hand, if it is him, we don't want to spook him. Getting him close is worth the risk of an arrow in the back—especially since I'd bet my best pair of boots that he gives some kind of warning before he attacks. That fucker likes the chase too much to settle for a sneak attack."

Her logic was sound, and it fit the working profile he'd put together for the unsub. "Still a risk."

"Yeah. Especially since, if it isn't him, it's one of the cats." Maggie finally looked at him, her dark eyes serious but nowhere near as panicked as a normal person would be if they discovered they were prey. "And if *that's* the case and if we ignore it, we won't see it coming until it's too late. They're dogged. They'll stalk their prey across miles before a kill if it's necessary."

He finally glanced back down the trail. As expected, it was empty. There wasn't some convenient sign shouting **BEWARE MOUNTAIN LION**. Fuck. Tucker was right. He was out of practice in a big way. "Not a bear?"

"No. They'll bum-rush you or attack if startled, but they don't do the silent-stalking thing." She rubbed the back of her hand across her mouth. "Having both a cat and a bear in such close proximity is a real bitch."

"Especially since there's a third predator to consider." He moved closer and touched her elbow. It should have been innocent contact, but the touch sparked a slow heat that rolled through him.

Inappropriate.

Just plain wrong.

But no matter how many times he thought the words, his body wasn't getting the memo. Vic stepped closer yet, until they were nearly chest to chest. "They cover dealing with mountain lions in that ranger training of yours?"

She raised her eyebrows. "Pretty sure it was in the handbook."

He could barely draw a full breath for wanting her. *My problem. Not hers.* Vic took a measured step back, and then another. "We'll have to hedge our bets and hope we aren't scaring off the unsub."

"We wouldn't scare him off. He's not the type. If anything, it'd just add spice to his hunt. Just stay here. This shouldn't take long."

"Wait." He started to grab her and aborted the move halfway through. Vic didn't *grab* women, no matter how crazy they were determined to act. "You can't honestly think I'm going to stand here while you bolt off into danger." It had been bad enough when he'd had to watch her march forward to find the body and a theoretical bear.

To do it again?

Out of the question.

Maggie gave him a look like he was an idiot. "You might have been the more experienced partner when I was in the BAU, but this is *my* wheelhouse. I've spent almost six years working here, first as a seasonal ranger and then full-time. When it comes to these trails and the wildlife, *I* am the more experienced one. I'm not going to let you get yourself hurt or killed just to assuage your manly pride." She didn't give him a chance to argue, turning on her heel and heading back down the trail.

"Hey! Hey, cat!" she yelled, waving her arms and charging forward.

Vic took a step before he caught himself. As much as he hated it, she was right. Maggie was more qualified when it came to dealing with this shit than he was. He might be able to theoretically call on his SEAL training to live off the land indefinitely or kill a man in a dozen ways without a weapon, but he didn't know the first thing about facing down a hungry mountain lion or bear.

Fuck.

Something made a noise that sounded a whole lot like a scream, and then Maggie took a menacing step forward, her arms still waving. It should have looked ridiculous, but all he could imagine was a cat leaping out of the trees and onto her back. She wasn't petite, but she didn't have claws or teeth to defend herself. All she had was some goddamn bear spray, and that was no guarantee against a mountain lion. It might scare it off, or it might piss it off enough to drive it to attack.

Vic touched the butt of his gun, tracking her movements and searching the forest around her. Every instinct demanded he protect her, but that wasn't in the cards for their situation. If he wanted to protect her, he should have insisted she accompany the other female ranger back with the body and taken that guy as his guide. He'd actually considered it while she was talking with the woman—Ava—but he hadn't been able to make himself speak.

He was too fucking selfish.

He'd *always* been too fucking selfish when it came to Maggie.

Her shoulders dropped, and he heard her sigh across the distance. "It was a cat. He backed off, but I suspect we haven't seen the last of him."

"Because mountain lions can be dogged in pursuit of prey."

"He can be taught." She moved back to him, never quite presenting her back to the spot where she'd seen the cat.

He kept his eyes peeled, but it all looked like trees.

Something like panic rose, a trapped bird fluttering in his chest. He didn't know how to do this. He'd spent the last ten years in control. He might not choose his cases, but he'd worked his way up to being one of the best in their department because nothing put him off his game.

The triggers that other agents had just didn't apply. Vic had considered that an asset.

It never occurred to him that it would make him soft.

"I can't protect you."

She stopped short, a line appearing between her brows. "I can protect myself."

"That's not the point." He couldn't tear his gaze from the trees, certain that the second he did, there'd be an attack. Even if there was, he might not be able to react in time. She could be hurt because he was out of his element.

"Vic." The quiet strength in her voice drew him to her face. She didn't look annoyed or amused. Her expression was full of understanding. Maggie smiled. "It sucks realizing you're not at the top of the food chain, doesn't it?"

"That's not what this is about."

"That's exactly what this is about. You're a control freak, and you're just starting to realize you can't control this park or anything in it." Maggie chuckled. "Congratulations—at least you're smart enough to recognize that fact. Too many people come out here thinking they can control it. You can't dominate nature, not in its rawest form—and Glacier is nothing if not raw. Trying to control it is a good way to get yourself killed."

Vic stared at her, feeling like an idiot. "I'm not a control freak." He might keep himself removed from everything around him, but that was just being a good FBI agent. *Except I was like that before I was an agent.*

He knew what a shrink would say—the one time he'd been involved in a shooting of a suspect, Britton had ordered him to see the department psychologist. Vic was used to doing the profiling, so having someone try to crawl around inside his head hadn't appealed to him. He'd gotten through it because it was required to get back to the job, had listened while the woman told him that his coldness was a result of his childhood spent without the true safety that children needed to flourish, and then he'd said all the right words to get her to give him a pass.

It wasn't like she was telling him anything he didn't already know.

He knew damn well that all the men, and moving without notice, during his formative years created a bone-deep desire for stability. When he enlisted in the Navy, he'd thought there was nothing more stable than the military. In some ways, he was right . . . in others, not so much. But he'd learned to love the balance—both in the SEALs and in the BAU. A good team led by a strong leader against the worst the world had to offer. He didn't need a PhD in psychology to put two and two together to get four.

This was different.

This felt like Maggie had just flayed him alive and peeled back his skin to expose throbbing nerves to the daylight.

"You're the biggest control freak I've ever known, and that's saying something. You just hide it better than most. People think because you're a big, quiet guy, you're laid-back. You're not."

None of his other partners had ever bothered to figure that aspect out. They did their job, he did his, and most of them ended up friends to one degree or another. He'd never consciously held people at arm's length, but it was just the way he operated. "It won't affect my ability to do my job."

"I didn't say it would." Maggie pushed a stray hair out of her face and eyed the sky. "We need to get moving. We have a long climb ahead of us, and the altitude change can be killer if we're not careful."

And that was that.

She started off without looking to see if he was following. He shook his head. *Just when I thought I had everyone's number down, she goes and changes it up on me.*

He wasn't sure what it said about him that he actually kind of liked it.

Five years ago, July

Madison watched her friends' faces in the flickering firelight. Ashleigh sat next to Josh, though there was a careful distance between them that wasn't there normally. From the tight set of his shoulders and the meanness in his eyes, Madison knew what was coming. Josh had always had a vicious streak when things didn't go his way. He rarely turned it on her or the others in their circle, but she'd seen it in action enough times to be wary of it.

Would she and Ashleigh even be considered part of the circle anymore if they left?

Would there even *be* a circle with just the Conlon twins and Lauren?

Ethan had his arm draped over Lauren's shoulders as they lounged against a fallen log on the other side of the fire. Madison had always found it strange that they were together. They were both so reserved, and they seemed to get even more so when they were together. One night not too long ago, Ashleigh had jokingly asked Lauren if they even talked when they were alone, and Lauren had snapped back harshly enough that she'd set them all back.

All Madison wanted was for her friends to be happy, but right now it felt like what she'd *thought* was happy was a fracturing thing that covered up . . .

She didn't know what it covered up. But she didn't like looking up and realizing that her idyllic teenage years maybe weren't as great as she thought. *Let it go. You're overthinking because you feel guilty. That's all. There's nothing to worry about.*

Lauren met her gaze over the fire. "I needed this so bad."

They all had. The tension that had ridden them all individually when they got into Josh's SUV faded as soon as they lost sight of the trailhead. It always happened like that. With the mountains the only thing hemming them in and the sky seeming endless, there wasn't a single worry that could cling in the face of Glacier.

Even her worry couldn't hold up against that feeling.

Madison tilted her head back, taking in the stars above them. It was a clear night, and it promised to be good weather all week. "Me, too."

"You know what *I* need?"

She didn't have to look to know what Josh meant. Ashleigh's bitter laugh confirmed it. "Not going to happen, Josh."

"Why the fuck not?"

The tone of his voice brought her head up. She jolted straight at the fury on Josh's face. "Guys——"

But Ashleigh was having none of it. She shook her head, looking disgusted. "It might shock you, but I have no desire to go out into the woods and have you fuck me against a tree."

"Since when?" His voice rose, becoming almost a roar. "Since you've been fucking that piece-of-shit lawyer in Washington?"

Madison froze, still in the process of shooting to her feet. "Josh, what the hell are you talking about? Knock it off. We're having a good time." And there was no way Ashleigh was sleeping with someone else. She wasn't a cheater, and even if she was, she would have told Madison about it. They told each other everything, and this was too big of a bombshell for her not to have known about it if it were true.

Except the look on her best friend's face wasn't one of righteous fury that a baseless accusation like that deserved.

It was one of guilt.

Madison slowly straightened. "Ash?"

"Look, I don't want to talk about it, okay?" She glared at Josh. "And what the hell is wrong with you? If you knew, you should have talked to me about it instead of bringing all of them into our shit." Her wave encompassed everyone—even Madison.

Josh stood slowly, menacingly. "You're nothing but a whore."

"Sure. Yep. A whore. Whatever you have to tell yourself, because *you're* as innocent as a virgin. *Right.*"

Madison caught Lauren's gaze, her friend's expression reflecting the misery and discomfort she felt at having to witness what should have been a private fight. She glanced at the spot where Ethan had been sitting, but he'd melted into the shadows, obviously preferring the dark forest to the scene playing out around the fire. Right now, she'd have given anything to join him and avoid the coming confrontation.

Ashleigh wasn't done. She stood, getting in Josh's face. "Did you really think I'd be satisfied in this shitty little town with a shitty boyfriend who only wants to talk about hunting and fishing and his shitty truck? Please."

Josh clenched his fists, and Madison started forward, recognizing the warning sign for what it was. No matter how bad their fights had been in the past, he'd never hit Ashleigh—that she knew of.

She was starting to realize she didn't know nearly as much about her friends as she'd thought.

"Guys, stop." She wedged herself between them. "Now isn't the time for this."

Help came in the form of Lauren, grabbing Josh's arm and pulling him away from the fire. At first he resisted, but then he finally shot Ashleigh one last look of loathing before he let Lauren tow him in the direction Madison hoped Ethan had gone.

Madison took one breath, and then another, and then she spun on Ashleigh. "What the hell was that?"

"I'm sorry, Mads." Ashleigh's blue eyes filled with tears, which scared Madison almost as much as the fight had. "I couldn't do it anymore. I couldn't do *any* of this anymore."

"It's okay." It wasn't, though. Her one last escape from reality was now ruined. There was no way Josh would let this go for the next four days, and that meant the rest of them would have to play referee to make sure things didn't get out of hand instead of enjoying their trip like they'd planned.

She didn't have the heart to say that aloud, though. Ashleigh had never loved this place the way Madison did, and she wouldn't understand. All it would do was potentially cause another fight, and that was the last thing she wanted.

Still, she couldn't help saying one last thing. "You should have told me. I thought we told each other everything."

Ashleigh's smile was both bitter and condescending. "Mads, you know better. We all have secrets—even you."

Especially me.

CHAPTER EIGHT

It was too quiet.

Maggie searched the area. The Fifty Mountain campsites were a couple of hundred yards up the trail, but they should have been able to see people by this point. *Not if the kids kept hiking like they were supposed to.*

She'd spent most of the hike up here from the creek trying to convince herself that it was just coincidence that they'd found a dead girl who seemed to have come from this site—from this group. She didn't want it to be Lauren. She didn't want any of the others to be hurt, either. If the victim didn't belong to the hiking group, then there was nothing to fear.

She didn't believe that anymore.

Even without seeing the dead girl's face, Maggie had recognized her hair. What were the odds that someone with the exact same build and hair was hiking in the same area and had ended up dead?

Astronomical.

"Vic."

Instantly, he was at her side. Things had been tense since the cougar made an appearance, and she hadn't felt much like chatting even without the ever-present threat of attack. They didn't know what they were walking into with this campsite.

They *still* didn't know what they were walking into.

His knuckles brushed hers, a contact so slight it might have been an accident if he was anyone else. But she hadn't been lying when she called him a control freak. For such a big man—*because* he was such a big man—he was overly careful with how he moved, and she'd never seen him touch someone unintentionally.

Pack it away.

It was harder to do the longer they spent together. Twenty-four hours didn't seem like it should be long enough to unravel seven years of doing her damnedest to forget Vic Sutherland, but it was becoming increasingly clear that she'd never be able to put the past in the past.

Not when it came to him.

She made it up to the ridge of the hill, still surrounded by the eerie silence. People sometimes thought nature was silent, but there were a thousand sounds that accompanied a walk through the woods. Even in a meadow like Fifty Mountain, there were insect noises and the rustling of animals and the cry of birds in the surrounding area.

There was none of that now.

The wind died down, as if the entire world held its breath to see what they'd find at the campsite. She almost reached for Vic before she caught herself taking him up on an offer he hadn't made. Instead, she strode forward, needing to see, to get this over with, to *know*. Not knowing was worse than anything she'd find.

Except she was wrong.

All the campsites were empty except for one. And that one . . . it looked like a hurricane had gone through it. She stopped short, trying to take in as much as possible, looking for some indication that this wasn't exactly what it looked like. "Shit." The three two-person tents stood untouched, a bastion of normalcy against the shredded backpacks and scattered fire pit. She reached for her bear spray before she had finished the thought, even though all evidence pointed to the animal being long gone.

Fifty Mountain was an area known for bears. There were procedures to store food and anything that could tempt the animals to get over their instinctive fear of humans, but it didn't look like the group had gotten that far. Maggie took a deep breath. "Draw your gun, but don't shoot unless we're in immediate danger." The bear was probably gone . . . but it wasn't a risk worth taking.

Not to mention that the unsub could be involved in this somehow. She hadn't forgotten the girl's body at the bottom of the trail, two pristine arrows impaled in her back.

She walked a half circle around the camp, keeping well away from the tree line it was backed up against, Vic on her heels. She readjusted her grip on the bear spray. "I don't see anyone."

"I don't, either."

They could be in the tents, but that seemed a foolhardy hope. Still, she had to investigate before she radioed back. *Nothing but bad news for Wyatt today.* She picked her way across the campsite, taking in the slash marks that definitely indicated a bear, and crouched to unzip the first tent.

It was just as pristine on the inside as the outside, two sleeping bags laid out on either side. Maggie moved on to the next tent before she could think too hard on that.

This one obviously belonged to one of the men—a pile of dirty clothes in the center gave the whole space a messy look, like a teenage boy's room. Maybe that was just television skewing her perspective, though. It wasn't like she had any siblings of her own to verify that knowledge with.

The third tent stood out from the others because the sleeping bag was a two-person one, and it had been thrown back as if someone jumped from it in a hurry. That tent alone hadn't been zipped up, either, though the bear hadn't bothered it. Probably because it'd been too busy ripping apart a trio of packs near where the fire pit had been. She recognized the distinctive patterns on two of them—they belonged to Lauren and the man Maggie had met, Josh.

Vic poked through the carnage, his gaze flicking to the trees every few seconds. "Looks like they had their food packed correctly—at least from what I can tell."

"They did." The problem was that not everyone who hiked these trails did. In an area with a high bear population, all it took was a handful of mistakes and bears started looking at campsites as a place for some easy and tasty grub.

And then accidents happened.

She stood and looked around. "Maybe a bear scared the group away from the camp, but that doesn't explain why they haven't come back." She held up a hand when Vic opened his mouth. "Yes, I'm aware that if one fell victim to the unsub, the others could have, too, but unless he's got some kind of superpowers, he couldn't take out five people together at once. Even if he could, there would be *some* kind of evidence here. Blood, at least, if no bodies."

"Radio it in and then we'll have a look around."

Maggie sighed, knowing she was going to ruin Wyatt's day even more so than finding a second body had. It took her a few minutes to get a response, and she laid out the facts as she knew them. Four missing campers, part of the same hiking party as the girl she and Vic had found this morning, signs of a bear coming through their site—though impossible to say if it was the same bear that had helped itself to the body.

What a shitshow.

Wyatt cursed long and hard, and her stomach soured at the sound. The man didn't curse, at least not around her. She'd known the situation was bad, of course, but hearing her boss so far out of his element suddenly brought it all home. He gave one last heartfelt *fuck* and sighed. "I'll get a call in to SAR. See what you can find out by the time they get there, and then get back to headquarters."

She froze. She'd known he was going to call in search and rescue—she'd counted on it, but she hadn't expected him to drag her back to headquarters. "But, Wyatt—"

"You were only supposed to be out there for an overnighter, and you're going on two. That Fed of yours isn't any more prepared than the one back here is. If we find something else, then you can head back out there as guide. It's not negotiable, so don't even bother arguing."

She gripped the radio tighter, bitterness leaking into her tone despite her best efforts. "You wouldn't make this call if I were a man."

"Wrong. Get that chip off your shoulder, Gaines. The chopper will be there as soon as I can get a team off the ground." And then he was gone, effectively getting the last word.

That wasn't what it was about. She *knew* that wasn't what it was about. Wyatt had more important things on his mind than her hurt pride, and she should, too. Letting her issues get the best of her wasn't the way to prove that she was the seasoned and capable ranger she knew she was. *Get it together.*

She shoved the radio into her pack. "Let's take a look around the perimeter in ever-widening circles and see if we find anything so we'll have a direction to point the team in when they get here."

"Maggie—"

"No." She shook her head. "I don't want to talk about it." If she could just keep moving, she could work off some of the furious energy coursing through her. It wasn't Wyatt's fault, and it wasn't Vic's fault, but she was in danger of taking out her temper on both of them if she didn't get better control of herself.

"Too fucking bad."

She didn't see him move, but he was suddenly in front of her, taking up too much space. How the man managed to suck the air out of the entire park was beyond her. Maggie glared, more than happy to take her irritation of being sidelined out on him. "Get out of my way."

"He's making the right call."

Vic *would* think that. He was even more overprotective than Wyatt, though she'd never had him try to sideline her like this. *Maybe because he never got the chance. I was gone just outside of a year. Not that long at all.*

Even if it had felt like forever while she was in the midst of it.

She clenched her fists. "I can handle it. You don't get to hold that case over my head for the rest of my life. I've *been* handling things since I left the BAU, and I'll continue to handle things long after you've flitted off to your next case."

His dark eyebrows rose. "Mmm-hmm."

"What?" she snapped.

"Were you going to actually listen to me? Or do you want to rant some more?" He sounded so calm and collected that she wanted to hit him, and *that* gave her pause.

I don't hit someone because they're being aggravating. What the hell is wrong with me?

Maggie took a slow breath, and then another. She was so incredibly tired. She wanted to go to sleep and wake up to realize this had all been some twisted nightmare, but that wasn't how the world worked. Reality was ugly and harsh and far more inventive than any horror fiction she'd ever come across. She couldn't make herself meet Vic's knowing eyes, but he obviously wasn't going to move until they addressed this. "I chose to leave this behind when I left the BAU."

"I know."

"This . . . this bastard has come into my safe place and made it unsafe." Saying the words aloud brought home how childish she was acting. *There is no safe place. There never was.* It felt a whole lot like someone had just crapped all over her dreams, but she wasn't off enough to say *that* out loud. She scrubbed a hand over her face. "I'm sorry. I was out of line." Which meant Wyatt was right—she needed to sleep and reset before she kept going on this.

Because she *would* keep going on this. Letting some other park ranger take over for her was admitting defeat. She'd done that once before, had abandoned a case that was her responsibility. Vic and his new partner had caught the man responsible for those deaths, but she'd never quite forgiven herself for not being strong enough to see it through.

Sometimes seeing it through meant knowing when to take a step back.

◆ ◆ ◆

Monday, June 19
2:08 p.m.

Vic watched Maggie's face closely. He was waiting for the explosion, or that's what he told himself as his gaze traced the lines of her face. Her nose had always screamed that she was a strong character, but it was her lips that caught and held his attention. Her pronounced Cupid's bow was feminine, and her full bottom lip seemed designed to nip.

He took a hurried step back. What the fuck was he doing, thinking about Maggie's lips when they were in the middle of a crime scene? He'd made a comment about her losing control, but he was the one in danger of crossing the line yet again. "Maggie—"

"You're right." She turned away. "I'm freaking out, though whether it's the circumstances or the lack of sleep or some combination is up for grabs. The end result is the same—I'm acting like an idiot."

"It's a shitty situation. Anyone would break a little under this kind of stress." And it was going to get worse before it got better. *If* it got better.

She shot him a look. "Anyone except you, apparently."

If she was brave enough to face down her unprofessional behavior, then he could do the same. If she was anyone else, he wouldn't bother, but she wasn't anyone else—she was Maggie. "You were right before. I'm not handling being out of control right now. This case was already touchy before running into you again, and now that it's escalating, I'm . . ." He lifted his hands and let them drop. "I'm out of my element, and it makes me want to control things all the more."

"I'm glad we got this mini therapy session out of the way." She rolled her shoulders, closed her eyes, and took a deep breath. When she opened them again, she smiled. "I don't know about you, but I feel loads better. So let's get back to doing our jobs before one of us says something to ruin it."

Since he couldn't argue that, he surveyed the campsite again. It still seemed to defy explanation that the unsub had hunted down all five of the hikers, especially if he had to chase the victim they'd found down the trail several miles. It was easier to hike down than up, for sure, but he'd still have to make it back here to track the other four, who seemed to have scattered to the wind. In a place like this, that would take longer than twenty-four hours, as long as none of the hikers tried to come back for their stuff.

But someone would. It was human nature. The trap so many victims fell into was distrusting their instincts. People tended to write things off with the most benign explanations. They weren't being stalked—they were being paranoid. People didn't *really* kill other people—until they did.

As a result, victims rarely knew they were in danger until it was too late.

◆ ◆ ◆

Monday, June 19
2:30 p.m.

They found nothing on the first circuit. Maggie huffed in frustration. "The area is trampled, but we haven't had any kind of weather lately that would reset it. There have been half a dozen groups through in the last week."

"Is Wyatt going to close the trail?" That wasn't Vic's call, though he knew what call he'd make if it *was* within his control—especially now that they knew there would be more victims before—if—the unsub jumped parks again. Hikers presented more potential victims, and that wasn't a good thing for anyone but the unsub.

Not that they could stop someone if they were determined to be in the area. There were too many ways in and around any blockade they could set up. He clenched his jaw.

She stopped short. "There's something . . . Damn it."

He strode to her side, instantly seeing what held her attention. "Definitely complicated." Vic squeezed her hand before he could remember why he wasn't supposed to touch her, and then picked his way through the dense trees to the scene that looked nearly identical to the one that had brought him to Glacier in the first place.

A naked man hung from two trees, gutted the same way the other victims had been. The blood on the ground was dried and nearly black because of it. *Long since dried.* "This didn't happen last night."

"He's not one of the group." Maggie pointed to the ground at their feet. He moved aside and, sure enough, there were boot prints that didn't belong to either of them. Maybe that was why Lauren had been flying down the trail toward the ranger station—to report this.

But that still didn't explain why she'd been alone.

"What time do you think they got up here?"

"Probably well before dark. It can be a rough hike from Goat Haunt, and there are a dozen things that could slow them down, but since the days are so long, there would have been plenty of daylight left."

Made sense. He and Maggie still had hours of daylight left, even with having to wait for the body retrieval at the ford. "So they get here and set up their tents first."

"Tents are a pain in the ass to deal with in the dark. They had enough people to have someone holding the light, but it's easier for everyone to get them done first." She looked back toward the camp. "But they didn't have time to store their food, so they couldn't have been here long—especially considering this." She pointed at the dead body. "It would have taken Lauren hours to get to the spot where we found her, even going downhill. It muddies up the timeline a bit, but Kat should be able to tell us more."

He nodded at the scene. "This would be unsettling to come across in the dark. How many groups do you think have come through here in the last weeks? Six?"

"Something like that. The last one was three days ago. They hiked north from Many Glacier and then took the ferry into Canada. The weather report wasn't looking good, so we had a couple groups decide to go different routes. This one isn't particularly challenging, but there are a few snowpacks along the way, and things can get dicey in a hurry. Only the most avid hikers don't find those kind of conditions to be deal breakers."

"Even without the official time of death, that puts this body at less than three days out." They'd found the woman by Kootenai Lake two days ago, and it was enough of a coincidence that he suspected they were connected in some way. *But why kill them so far apart?* If they *were* connected and the unsub had separated and hunted them individually . . .

It didn't line up.

He'd have to wait for ID and confirmation one way or another, but if they had hiked into Glacier together, he'd bet the man was killed before the woman. Easier to subdue a woman than a man, and she hadn't been kept alive long enough to show signs of dehydration and malnourishment—but he'd still talk to Dr. Huxley about that once they knew more information.

If the woman *had* been kept alive, it meant the unsub had somewhere to keep her—somewhere that might have more structure than the camp theory they'd been working with.

He looked around, mentally calculating the distance to the campground. "Strange that the bear didn't touch this guy."

Maggie straightened slowly, the line between her brows appearing. "Yeah. It is."

He surveyed the campsite with new eyes. "What are the odds that a bear would come through and not touch a nice supply of meat that's nowhere near far enough off the ground to deter it?"

"Not good. Strictly speaking, bears aren't total scavengers, but there are tons in the immediate area. For none of them to have touched him defies the laws of probability."

He stalked back to the tents, crouching down and examining the blatant bear paw print. Now that he was looking at it, it seemed too perfect. Vic wasn't a tracker by any means, but as Maggie said—the odds were astronomical that a bear had torn through here and managed to leave one perfect paw print. He frowned. "Easy enough to tear apart the backpacks with a knife, scatter shit around to look like it's been gone through. Hell, maybe the unsub *did* go through it."

"And he just hauls around a bear-paw mold?" She bent over next to him, her ponytail swinging over her shoulder. "He hasn't done anything like this with any of the other murders, right?"

"No. We never found where he killed them or stashed their stuff. It's possible that he took a trophy and destroyed the rest, but there's no way to tell for sure, since we don't have their clothing or gear to create a list to compare it to." Vic straightened. "Everything about this is different. He's never left us anything to find other than the bodies themselves—and he's never gone after a group. Even if you assume that the bear getting to Lauren before he did wasn't part of his plan, he's deviating across the board now." He turned to the tent with the missing packs. "What if the unsub was waiting for this group, specifically?"

"But unless he's connected with them, how would he know that they were coming here? I mean . . . I guess the same way he would know about the others. But five people? I know we keep saying it, but that's because stalking a group is a huge undertaking, especially when they're all able-bodied and have at least some outdoors experience." She propped her hands on her hips. "That's just crazy."

"Not if he specifically planned for it." He waved away the question written all over her face. "We don't know enough, so we're making wild speculations. First, we work the scene, and we talk to Dr. Huxley and see if she's able to shine some light on at least a few of our questions. Then we see where we end up."

"All that takes time." Her voice reflected the frustration lancing through him.

Too much time.

They were *so close*. The unsub had been in this place less than twenty-four hours ago. He'd possibly even stood exactly where Vic did now. He was hunting these kids somewhere in the park at this very moment, and there wasn't a damn thing they could do to stop him. Not yet. "Let's see what we can find before the SAR team shows up." They'd have to share a ride back to the headquarters with a body, but he'd had worse experiences.

Two hours later, they didn't have a damn thing to show for their investigating. *That, at least, is consistent with the other murders.* This guy was good. Vic hated to admit it, but he'd obviously planned these killings down to the barest detail, and as a result, he'd left little behind for them to find. There were no dead bodies lying in wait, but there were no convenient clues to the unsub's identity and plan, either.

He'd just made Maggie sit down and eat something when the sound of helicopter blades cut through the area. She started to stand, but he put a hand on her shoulder. "We have time."

"Not enough."

Never enough. He watched the handful of people climb out of the helicopter and mentally compiled a list of things he had to do before he could get back into the park. Making sure Maggie got some sleep topped the list, though he knew she wasn't his responsibility, and she damn sure shouldn't be his priority.

Having her here, so close he was literally touching her, had skewed his priorities so much, he didn't know which way was up. Part of him was tempted to talk to Wyatt and request a new guide so that he could keep her safe, but the rest of him was more concerned with maximizing the time he had with her. *Selfish.*

He didn't care.

He'd told her they had time, but he was a goddamn liar. The truth was that there wasn't enough time in the world for them. At some point, they'd be saying good-bye once and for all. That should bring him peace—she was obviously happy in her new life, or at least happi*er* than she'd been as a federal agent. Doing anything to jeopardize that was a dick move. He was better than that. She deserved better than that.

He just needed to get a damn hold of his control before he did something stupid like try to convince her to give them a shot.

CHAPTER NINE

Monday, June 19
5:56 p.m.

Sharing a helicopter ride with a corpse wasn't the worst thing Maggie had ever done, but it definitely ranked. By the time they made it back to headquarters, she wanted nothing more than a shower and twelve hours of sleep. It wasn't in the cards, though. First, she had to brief Wyatt. She'd already passed on what little information she had to the initial SAR team, but there would be more people joining them before too long, and at this point, time was of the essence.

Sleep could wait.

So could a shower.

She very pointedly tried not to smell herself as she sank into the uncomfortable chair next to Vic's. Wyatt looked more tired than she'd ever seen him, big bags beneath his eyes and the lines on his face deeper than they were yesterday. He pinched the bridge of his nose, not looking at either of them. "Three bodies. With another four missing, only two of whom *might* have gear to survive more than a night or two."

It sounded bad when he said it like that—because it *was* bad. Exposure was a very real risk. The days might be in the seventies, but nights easily got down into the low forties, and that wasn't even taking into account the misery waiting for them if it rained—which it was forecast to do. Rain wouldn't make or break someone who was prepared, but it would make the risk of suffering from exposure skyrocket. Not to mention creating slippery surfaces and decreasing visibility, both of which upped the chance of a fall.

The chance of finding those hikers alive dropped with every hour they stayed lost.

She should be out there looking. Maggie rocked forward in her chair to say exactly that, but Wyatt spoke first. He pinned her with a look. "You stick with the Fed. I don't have time to bring anyone else up to speed, and I need every man on deck for this search that I can manage. You focus on that goddamn killer and leave the missing hikers to us."

She bit her words back before she asked if he was keeping Ava out of the search, too. He and Vic were right—she *did* have a chip on her shoulder. Every time they tried to protect her, it shined the light on her deep and dark suspicion that she wasn't good enough—would never be good enough.

That's your issue. Not theirs.

Maggie straightened and did her best to control her expression. "The killer and the missing hikers are connected."

He shook his head slowly. "That doesn't change a thing, and you know it. We have to process this like a normal SAR, because if there's a chance of getting those kids back alive, that's what it will take."

"With all due respect, sir." Vic spoke up for the first time since they'd sat down, startling Maggie. He leaned forward. "This unsub has been hunting people in national parks for months now. He's escalating as we speak. I don't think you should pull your people back, because you're right—those hikers need to be found, and the faster the better—but they need to be aware that there is more at risk than the usual things they could encounter out there."

Wyatt's bushy brows lowered. "And, with all due respect, Agent Sutherland, I'm well aware that we have some nut job hunting folks in my park—as are my rangers."

Vic's mouth tightened, but he nodded. "Then I need to brief my partner and schedule a talk with the medical examiner. I'd like to be back in the park by tomorrow afternoon at the latest."

"No can do."

Vic went still. "Excuse me?"

"You see, you make a good point about us providing this sicko with more people to kill. My rangers are familiar with the area and will know to report back anything unusual. You aren't, and from what I understand, you don't have more outdoors skills than your average joe—which makes you a liability."

"He was a SEAL," Maggie blurted. Embarrassment heated her skin as they both turned to look at her, but she refused to back down. "Don't shelve us, Wyatt. Vic has been on this case from the beginning, and he knows this unsub. It's a mistake to keep him back." To keep *them* back. She didn't say it, but the speculation in her boss's eyes told her that he heard it all the same.

Vic rose. "Thank you for your time and assistance. Keep us updated?" He held out his hand, effectively ending the conversation.

He could have fought Wyatt. Control of the case was a flexible thing because of the murderers happening in a national park, and BAU was only brought in on cases to assist—not run them—but Vic was a Fed and, as such, he could have thrown his weight around and forced Wyatt to change his mind.

She couldn't be sure if he hadn't done so because he agreed with Wyatt or if it was politics.

Maggie hated politics—doubly so when there were lives on the line.

Wyatt shook Vic's hand, looking like he'd just eaten something sour. "We'll find the hikers, and you'll find your guy."

He didn't sound like he believed that any more than she was starting to.

Maggie walked out of the office, practically weaving on her feet. Skipping sleep last night had been beyond stupid, and she was going to pay for it now. It was probably too much to hope for a full night without anyone calling in an emergency, especially when there was an SAR team on the ground.

First, though, she needed a shower and a warm meal. If she concentrated, she could almost feel the scalding water hitting her skin. *Heaven.*

"Maggie."

She stopped short, almost having forgotten Vic was there. No, that was a lie. She could never forget Vic, not when he was standing mere feet away. It had been easier to ignore the way his presence affected her when they were on the trail. The park tended to overwhelm everything else, and it gave her plenty to focus on besides Vic.

Labeling the ranger station as civilization was a stretch by any definition of the word, but the immediate danger to them had passed, which opened the door for her to . . . notice Vic.

More than notice him.

Resisting the childish urge to flee into the encroaching night, she faced him. "Yes?"

"What's your number?" When she blinked, he kept going. "We need to see Dr. Huxley tomorrow, and as charming as I find this park, searching for you for hours doesn't hold much appeal."

She blinked again. "You don't need me with you to see Kat." She hadn't seen her friend in a couple of weeks since she'd been working from Goat Haunt. But Maggie had wanted to go have a drink with her—not meet her in their official capacities. Call her crazy, but it wasn't quite the same thing.

"Not officially, but you're the only person who saw all three of the scenes before anyone tampered with them. And as much as you hate to admit it, you have the same training I do. You might see something I miss."

"We've had this conversation." She didn't want to get sucked back into the BAU, no matter how freakishly tempting she found Vic Sutherland.

He's not married anymore.

Maggie dug her nails into her palm. It was exhaustion making her thoughts crazy. They'd shared one kiss a lifetime ago, when they were in the middle of a horrific serial-killer case and running on fumes. As she was evincing at this exact moment, sleep deprivation played hell on her decision-making abilities. She refused to let it get the best of her again.

"Wyatt all but gave you an order. You can try to slide out of it, but he'll agree with me."

She glared, all her good feelings disappearing. "That's a dick move."

"I don't have time to dance around your feelings right now." He scrubbed a hand over his face. "I need your eyes and your brain on this, Maggie, but I'm not going to drag you kicking and screaming along with me."

He made her sound like a child . . . probably because she was acting childish. She sighed. "I hate you a little bit right now."

"I know." He didn't sound too worried about it, but then why would he be? She'd never been able to maintain distance where Vic was concerned. It had started with her stupid crush on him when she was fresh out of the academy and had been assigned to the fabled Vic Sutherland as a partner, and solidified with that ill-advised kiss. She would have thought she'd learned from those mistakes, but apparently if she wasn't careful, she was doomed to repeat them.

She rattled off her number and started for the ranger cabins that were tucked well away from the headquarters building She'd roomed with Ava since she was hired, but Ava would be out with the SAR team, which meant she'd have the place to herself. "I'll see you in the morning." Shower, food, sleep. That's all she could deal with right now. Vic would have to wait.

◆ ◆ ◆

Monday, June 19
8:25 p.m.

Vic slid into the booth across from Tucker Kendrick. The redhead barely looked up from his three plates. "Three bodies—five when we count the first two. Five is a lot of bodies, Sutherland."

"Yeah." He accepted coffee from the waitress and ordered the one meal guaranteed to be safe at any diner in the States—burger and fries. "There are going to be more before the week's out, though it's up in the air whether the park gets them or the unsub does."

"I think we both know that bastard isn't going to let nature cheat him out of his kills." Tucker pushed a thin folder across the table with one hand while he stuffed a fry in his mouth. "ID on the girl they found by the lake."

Vic scanned the details. Jennifer Haglund, twenty-six. As was often the case, she was much prettier in life than she'd been in death, her eyes shining with happiness in the photo pinned to the first page of the file. The scanned copy of her driver's license put her as living in Whitefish— close enough to Kalispell to be considered a local—and married. He flipped through the other papers. "What's her husband look like?"

"If I were a betting man, I'd bet Bill Haglund looked a whole lot like that stiff you brought in with you."

"What I want to know is how their times of death line up."

Tucker narrowed his eyes. "If taking down a couple was him escalating, that adds a whole lot of complications to his process."

"Yep." He flipped the file closed as the waitress approached with coffee. He put her as somewhere in her thirties—though she could be a tired late twenties—and the look she gave Tucker was as blatant an invitation as such things came. "Anything else for you two?"

Tucker gave her one of his slow southern smiles, and Vic almost rolled his eyes. He dialed up the drawl, too. "My partner would love some cherry pie if you have it once he's done with his burger."

"Your . . . partner." She blushed, and then blushed a deeper red when Tucker didn't jump to correct her.

Vic opened the file again as the flustered waitress backed away, waiting until she'd moved behind the counter to say, "You could have corrected that assumption." They didn't get it often, but every once in a while someone would mistake business partner for domestic partner and assume they were lovers. Tucker never played it up, but he never rushed to correct them, either.

"Maybe I'm harboring a serious unrequited hard-on for you, Sutherland."

"You're not." Tucker was as straight as they came, and Vic had initially thought that he let people think the wrong thing just to be a dick. Six months later, he knew better. Tucker was a looker. He attracted female attention wherever they went, whether because of the red hair, the accent, or something else altogether, and Vic hadn't missed that it was almost always in small towns that he let women think he and Vic were lovers.

Made it a lot easier to turn down offers if they didn't come in the first place.

Even made investigating easier in some cases, because it put them firmly in the nonthreatening category when it came to interviewing women.

An interesting little insight to his partner that had created plenty of questions as a result—questions he hadn't asked. They had time.

Pushing too soon was a mistake. They had to have at least some trust between them, even if they were never going to be friends.

So he hadn't asked.

Vic found what he was looking for—the scrawled report by one of the park rangers he'd met on the trail—David. "Quite the hike they had planned. North from the Loop, then west to Two Ocean Glacier, and north to Brown Pass, before circling back." The ranger had noted that they'd been to the park several times a year for nearly a decade, and seemed well prepared for the trip. They weren't supposed to be back for a few days yet, which explained why no one had reported them missing. "What do we know about this couple?"

"Not much more than what's in the report. I've only talked to her family, but they're as average as they come. She teaches high school, and he works the pipeline in Alaska. Both were born in Kalispell and never quite left, his job aside. They spend the weeks he's home in the summer hiking, and have since they started dating five years ago. Solid middle-class folks—no kids, no crazy outstanding debt beyond the house they purchased last year, and no readily apparent skeletons hiding in their closet."

"No, there wouldn't be. It's the park that connects them, not their history." Vic sat back, smiling in thanks as the waitress—Judy, by her name tag—set his food in front of him. He let the expression drop the second she turned away. "Damn it, I'm making assumptions."

"You're tired." Tucker's blue eyes narrowed. "And you've been wrangling things on two fronts. Britton says you used to be partners with Ranger Gaines, and being a smart man, I put two and two together to make four. She's the one who burned out during the Drover case, isn't she?"

"She's not up for discussion." Britton should know better than to gossip like some kind of high school kid.

"Uh-huh." Tucker took a drink of the Mountain Dew bottle that he'd no doubt hauled into this place since he didn't drink coffee. His face turned as serious as it ever got. "The Drover case was bad—one of the worst I've ever seen. What the hell was Britton thinking, putting a baby Fed on it?"

"You know as well as I do that Britton has his own reasons for doing the shit he does." But Vic had wondered the same thing. The FBI academy could only prepare students so much. Getting out in the field was a different world altogether. Nothing was in theory and the danger was all too real. There wasn't such a thing as starter cases, but the Drover case had been in another world.

He and Maggie had come in after the third death—all preteen girls—and there had been four more deaths in the year they were on the case. It was after the seventh that she broke down, and it had taken two more murders before he and his new partner finally found the unsub—a lab tech whom he and Maggie had interacted with countless times during the course of the investigation.

Even after all these years, it made him sick to his stomach to know that they'd been so close, and that bastard had still pulled one over on them.

Tucker snorted. "Finish your food and get back to your hotel room. I'm pretty sure you just fell asleep while sitting up." He wrinkled his nose. "A shower should probably be on the to-do list, too."

The knowledge on his partner's face gave the lie to his words. Tucker had been around long enough to know that some cases stuck with a person. Vic had failed six girls, and he'd never get the image of them out of his head.

It was a fitting sort of penance.

He pushed his plate away. "We're meeting the medical examiner tomorrow at nine."

"See you there."

Vic strode to the counter and paid for their meals and then left without another word. There were too many things demanding his attention, and he wasn't used to feeling conflicted like this on a case.

Normally, he had no problem focusing on what mattered and setting aside the rest for a more convenient time. It was one of the things his wife had always despised about him—and one that she had cited as their reason for divorcing. Their marriage was constantly one of the things set aside, and there was never a convenient time to deal with it.

Part of him wished he could set Maggie aside so easily. If their time in the park was any indication, she wasn't going anywhere. It wasn't her fault—he was the one who kept getting distracted and moving his priorities out of order. He wanted her safe, but she was right—she was more than capable of taking care of herself.

Fuck if that helped him feel better about the whole situation.

He made it back to his hotel room in record time and showered as quickly as humanly possible. He needed to review the file one more time and then pass out for a few hours. *He* hadn't missed much sleep last night, but the hiking had still taken more out of him than he'd realized. After drying off, Vic's gaze fell on his phone. Maggie's number was now in the contacts folder. It would be easy to dial it, just to check on her.

Except it was late, and she hadn't asked him to babysit her.

He'd gone years without seeing her, and now that they were in the same general area, it was like they were two magnets that could barely resist the pull. He wanted to hear her voice, to sit her down and share a meal that wasn't military issue, to actually *talk*.

His phone rang, which startled him so much he almost dropped it. Vic stared at the screen for several precious seconds, wondering if he was more tired than he'd thought, because it sure as fuck looked like Maggie was calling him. "Sutherland."

"It's me."

He sat on the edge of the bed, suddenly painfully aware that he wore only a towel. It shouldn't matter. She couldn't see him, didn't know what he was or wasn't wearing, but it *did* matter. "Hey, Maggie."

"I have to apologize." He could almost feel her soft sigh. "You were right, and I was acting like a stubborn kid. This whole thing—the murders in the park and having to deal with my past and you—has got me all twisted up."

Maybe it was the events of the last two days, but he was so goddamn tired of doing the noble thing. He never put himself or his personal shit before a case. Not once.

He'd never wanted to before.

"I twist you up?"

"As if you didn't know. I had something of a crush on you when we were partners—which I'm sure you knew after I threw myself at you—and apparently I didn't outgrow it as much as I thought."

The dimness of the room evoked an intimacy he didn't deserve. Was Maggie sitting in her bedroom in low light, too? He liked the picture that made. "You have nothing to apologize for."

"I've been making an ass of myself since you stepped off that helicopter." She shifted, the sound painfully loud in the near silence. "And I'm doing it again, apparently. My whole point was that I'm sorry and I'll be professional from now on. You don't have to worry about any breakdowns or hissy fits."

It he was smart, he'd take her apology for what it was and allow it to move them back to solid ground. There were lives on the line, and a condensed timeline that was only going to get more condensed with each body that popped up.

But when Vic spoke, he didn't move them back to firm ground. He threw them right over the edge of the cliff. "Fuck being professional. I want you, Maggie. Not the former FBI agent. Not the park ranger. I want *you*."

CHAPTER TEN

Monday, June 19
9:39 p.m.

Maggie clutched her sheet to her chest, trying to convince herself that she'd heard Vic wrong. She played back his words in her head, but they didn't make any more sense the second time. "I'm sorry, what?"

"It's about damn time for the truth between us. I want you, Maggie. I have ever since we became partners, despite there being a whole hell of a lot of reasons for me to keep my hands off you."

She looked around her darkened bedroom wildly. There was a camera set up somewhere, recording this. There *had* to be. It was the only explanation why Vic's low voice was in her ear, telling her things she'd almost given up fantasizing about. "But . . . you were married."

"I haven't been married in a very long time."

"But the case—" Her voice broke, and she had to stop and clear her throat. "Vic, what are you saying?"

"I'm saying that if you tell me you aren't interested, this is it. We'll pretend this conversation never happened. I'll pick you up tomorrow at seven thirty, and we'll move on with both the case and our lives."

She wetted her lips. "And if I say I'm interested?"

"Then I'll still pick you up tomorrow at seven thirty so we can visit Dr. Huxley." He kept talking before disappointment could take root. "But tomorrow night, we'll go find somewhere to eat—just the two of us. We won't talk about the case, and we won't talk about our past. And at the end of that date—because make no mistake, it will be a date—I will kiss you, and this time it won't be something that can get swept under the rug as a mistake."

She couldn't quite draw a full breath. "That sounds nice."

"It may be a lot of things, but nice won't number among them." He exhaled as if releasing the same tension twisting its way up her spine. "Good night, Maggie. Get some sleep tonight—you need it."

"Good night, Vic." She hung up before she could do something truly insane—like invite him over now. Maggie plugged her phone in and then double-checked to make sure it was charging before she wiggled down to cuddle up under her covers. She closed her eyes, but her mind wouldn't stop whirling. How did Vic think she was going to get any sleep after dropping that verbal bomb on her?

A date.

Being a park ranger didn't leave a ton of time to pursue relationships— unless it was with other rangers. It had taken all of a week before Maggie decided that wasn't a path she was going to take. It was hard enough getting the other rangers to take her seriously without sleeping with one of them— the park rangers and FBI were a lot alike when it came to that sort of thing. It was a slippery slope, and she had no intention of taking any part in it.

She'd tried online dating about a year ago. For two weeks, during which she'd been sent three unsolicited dick pictures, been called a bitch by two dates—one when she wouldn't sleep with him on the first date, and the other when she had to cancel because of work—and the single guy she'd managed to go on three dates with had been so uninspiring in the bedroom that she'd written the whole experience off as a loss.

Dating Vic was something else altogether.

◆ ◆ ◆

Tuesday, June 20
6:45 a.m.

Maggie's alarm went off, shooting her into awareness. She sat up, frowning at the pale light steaming through her window. "I fell asleep. No way." She must have been even more tired than she realized, because she'd been sure she was destined for another all-nighter, mentally circling around the idea of dating Vic. "Stupid. So stupid." She should be worried about what the unsub was up to while she'd been out cold—and if any of those hikers were still alive.

No. She couldn't think like that. There had to be hope. There *had* to be.

Her phone rang, and she cursed as she scrambled for it. "What?"

"I'm running early." Vic sounded far too awake and put together for the hour.

She peered at her clock. "It's not even seven."

"I know. Can you be ready in fifteen?"

Maggie was already moving, jumping out of bed and stripping on her way to the shower. "You know, being early is only a virtue after noon."

"I have coffee."

"Key is on top of the door frame. I'll be ready shortly." She dropped her phone at the edge of the sink and twisted the handle to get the shower going. There wasn't time to wait for it to heat up, and the freezing spray of water had her cursing again. It was almost enough to distract her from the fact that Vic was on his way there right *now*. If she lingered in the shower . . .

"He wanted a date, he's going to get a damn date." Saying the words out loud didn't do much to dispel the image of him walking into the bathroom, his pale eyes going hot at the sight of her through the clear plastic curtain. He'd cross the room, yank the flimsy barrier aside and . . .

She started. "What am I doing? *Move.*" She had to get through today without the world falling apart before she could worry about the date with Vic tonight—or about what might come after. There wasn't anything standing between them anymore—nothing to keep them from doing anything and everything that two people did when they were attracted to each other.

Desire rolled in a tidal wave that made her knees weak. She shut off the water before she could give in to the temptation to touch herself. There wasn't time, and it wasn't like before—there was a very real and very tangible possibility that *Vic* would be touching her before too long, and it felt a little like robbing him of that if she jumped the gun.

Though she was pretty sure wanting him had curdled her brain at this point, because that last thought didn't make a lick of sense.

Maggie dried off and grabbed her uniform. Not for the first time, she wished it was more comfortable and in line with what was required for long days spent hiking and dealing with all sorts of weather, but it was the uniform rangers had worn basically since the beginning of park rangers. In the grand scheme of things, it wasn't *that* big of a deal. She dried her hair enough that it wouldn't leave a wet spot on her shirt and then braided it out of her face.

Maggie wasn't beautiful. Her features were too strong to be termed beautiful, much to her mother's chagrin. Even before her nose had become crooked from getting broken, it had been too big, too prominent. So much so that her mother had offered to get her a nose job for her sweet sixteen.

Sweet sixteen, indeed.

It was right around then that she'd decided to stop bending over backward to try to please her parents and start focusing on what pleased *her*—being capable. She was smart and had skills that many people didn't possess. She even had the respect of most of her coworkers and her boss, which wasn't something to be taken lightly.

But today, with Vic showing up shortly, she spent a useless moment wishing she'd paid attention when her mother tried to teach her about makeup or doing her hair in anything other than serviceable styles. "Stop it. He knows you. Out of all those idiot dates you've been out with in the last few years, this man isn't going to expect anything of you but the truth." Hell if that wasn't terrifying in a totally different way.

The sound of the front door opening spurred her into movement. She cast one last look at the mirror and chuckled softly. Makeup. What in God's name was she thinking?

She found Vic in her tiny kitchen, setting coffee on the counter. His head nearly brushed the ceiling, and his eyebrows raised as he looked around. She knew what he saw. The cabin was barely up to code—the walls didn't do much to keep out either the cold or the heat—and the furniture she and Ava had bought was secondhand because neither of them spent enough time here to justify more expensive options.

They kept the kitchen in closer to working order out of necessity, but the counter was scarred from whoever lived there before them, and the cabinets had seen better days. The fridge was a blast from the seventies, but it worked, which was more than she could say for the microwave.

Maggie cleared her throat. "It's not fancy, but the government doesn't exactly blow big money on ranger housing."

He looked at her, and she forgot what she'd been about to say. Vic stalked toward her, his huge strides eating up the distance in two steps, and then he was there, his chest brushing hers with each breath. He cupped her jaw with one massive hand. "I told myself I'd be professional until tonight."

She licked her lips, devastatingly aware of the way he tracked the move. "How's that working out for you?"

"It's not." He kissed her. It wasn't like the last time, hurried and so full of guilt that she could taste it. No, Vic kissed her like he was memorizing every second of the experience. She opened for him, sliding her hands up his chest, drunk on the fact that she was touching him. That she was *allowed* to touch him. The second her tongue touched his, a shudder worked its way through his body, and he lifted her, walking them backward until he had her pinned between his body and the flimsy living-room wall. He used his hand on her face to angle her mouth to allow him deeper, even as his big body wedged between her legs. His free hand was everywhere, stroking up the outside of her thigh, over her ass, dipping beneath her shirt.

Vic dragged his mouth along her jaw and down her neck, and she let loose a breathless laugh. "We're going to break a hole in my wall." She didn't even care. Maybe she'd frame the damn thing. It'd be proof that this happened, long after he'd gone.

He exhaled harshly, his body so close she could feel exactly how much he wanted her. Maggie shifted, biting her lip at the feel of his hard length. She wanted. God, she wanted. "Vic—"

"Give me a second."

A small, purely feminine part of her was pleased that he was so close to losing control. It made her want to arch and kiss him again, to see if he'd throw caution to the wind and follow through on the promises their bodies were making to each other.

But then she caught sight of the digital clock on the oven over his shoulder. If they kept this up, they'd be late, and there were more important things than the hollow ache between her thighs. They'd waited this long. They could wait a bit longer. So she held still and didn't protest as Vic's hands came to her hips and he lowered her to the ground. He stepped back, but not far enough to require him to stop touching her.

His pale eyes flamed with a hot light. "I changed my mind."

"About what?" She couldn't look away.

"We're not ending tonight with just a kiss."

CHAPTER ELEVEN

Five years ago, July

Madison fought her growing unease. After Ashleigh and Josh's fight, the tension had become unbearable. They'd hiked all day yesterday, but this morning they'd decided to write the trip off as a loss and turn around. Better that than to risk tempers fraying further and worse fights breaking out.

The group had split in two, leaving her in the middle. There was no pleasing anyone. Either she spent too much time at Ashleigh's side, which earned her nasty looks from the Conlon twins, or she walked with Lauren, feeling her best friend's glare between her shoulder blades the entire time.

By afternoon, they'd reached Fifty Mountain, which was where they'd camp overnight. It was one of Madison's favorite spots, a place where Highline Trail and Mountain Trail converged, which meant they usually ran into another group of hikers. Sharing a fire with strangers was their way of carving out a little piece of immortality. They'd never see the people again, but there would always be the shared memory.

Like the doctor who'd been so terrified of bears that he'd jumped at every sound in the darkness but, when he'd finally relaxed, had told the most wonderful stories of his time spent in Africa working for Doctors Without Borders.

Or the pair of brothers they'd met late last fall, who had spent the last six months hiking the Continental Divide trail, all the way up from New Mexico's southernmost border. The stories they'd told about those months awakened a yearning unlike anything she'd known. It was *that* conversation that had finally spurred Madison to do what she'd been so afraid of up until senior year—leave Kalispell.

There was an entire world out there. Montana was only a tiny piece of it—a wonderful, glorious piece, but a piece nonetheless.

Disappointment clogged her throat as they reached the campsite, only to find it empty of anyone but their group. There would be no sharing the fire tonight or wonderful conversations. She was left with only her warring friends for company.

Which meant she had to do something to at least temporarily mend the bridges. Otherwise, they'd spend the remaining four days of their trip in hell, and she'd like to think that none of them wanted that.

"This is bullshit," Ashleigh muttered.

Madison thought so, too, but she doubted it was for the same reason. She focused on getting her tent put up, all too aware that she'd have Ashleigh sharing it despite her friend having planned on sharing with Josh.

She glanced over to check the progress of the others. Ethan was gone, but she'd expected as much. He'd already set up Lauren's tent, but he didn't sleep in there unless the weather drove him to it, preferring the open sky above him. He'd been like that ever since she could remember. When they'd play in the woods behind the Conlon home, Ethan would lead them deeper than she'd have ever dared go by herself. The things he showed her always made it worth it—a brand-new nest of baby birds, a fox, once even a bear, though they'd stayed far away from that one.

He didn't like the campgrounds or well-trodden trails that much. He'd disappear for long stretches during their hikes, exploring different parts of the park and meeting up with them around nightfall. She'd even come out here with him alone a couple of times. Ethan didn't feel the need to fill up the silence, and she'd enjoyed being able to appreciate the park without having to divert her attention to her hiking partner.

And then there was Josh, who had disappeared while she was distracted, leaving only Ashleigh at the camp with her.

She sighed and rubbed her hand over her chest. She desperately didn't want to hunt Josh down and risk him turning that anger on her, but there was no way Ashleigh would be the one to do it. Just as well, since after that fight she didn't completely trust him not to do something they'd all regret. She'd never feared him before, but there was something like it wrapping around her chest, growing tighter with every heartbeat.

Silly. It's just Josh.

"I'm going for a walk."

Ashleigh snorted. "We just spent the entire day walking."

And if I don't do something to chill the hell out, I might scream. She didn't say it. She couldn't. Ashleigh might not always understand her, but she *was* her best friend. "Just for a few minutes. Lauren went to check out that huckleberry patch just south of here. I'll check in on her." A flimsy excuse as such things went, but she needed the break.

There were plenty of bears in the Fifty Mountain area, but they mostly left humans alone unless someone was stupid enough to leave food out—or they were startled. Lauren knew what she was doing, but Ashleigh couldn't argue with her wanting to check on their friend. "I'll be back soon."

She escaped before Ashleigh could say anything else.

The quiet washed over Madison as soon as she slipped through the trees. She instinctively used the skills her father had taught her to move soundlessly through the forest. He'd been taking her hunting since she was a little girl, carrying her in one of those kid backpack things when she was too small to keep up. When she was older, there had been the lessons and gun-safety courses and, finally, their hunting trips. The last two years, they'd only gone on one annual trip instead of one for each hunting season, her job preventing her from taking too much time off.

She missed those trips—they were yet another thing that caused the guilt to drive home, no matter how often he told her that he supported the move.

A faint groan had her turning toward it cautiously. *That didn't sound like an animal.* Madison went still, listening hard. There it was again, low and pained. She picked up her pace, still moving silently. If it *was* an animal, she didn't want to scare it.

She peeked around a tree and froze, her mind frantically trying to come up with a reasonable explanation for the scene in front of her.

There wasn't one.

Josh's pants were around his thighs, his bare ass too pale from lack of sun, the muscles flexing with each thrust. Lauren had no pants on at all, her legs wrapped around his waist, her fingers gripping his shoulders tight enough to whiten her knuckles. She moaned, low and restrained— the sound Madison had heard.

They were . . .

But . . .

She must have made some sound, because Lauren's eyes shot open, and her jaw dropped. She slapped Josh's shoulder. "Let me down."

"Almost . . ." He realized something was wrong and turned, going still when his blue gaze met Madison's. "Mads, I can explain."

There was only one explanation, and from the ease with which they touched each other, this wasn't the first time this had happened. Madison shook her head, backing up. "How could you?"

"For fuck's sake—"

"Josh, shut up." Lauren slid out of his arms and held out a hand. "Please, Mads. Please don't tell Ethan."

Her stomach lurched. Had they been doing this since before Ashleigh had cheated? She shook her head again, the taste on her tongue bitter. The breeze changed, bringing with it the scent of sex, and it was everything she could do not to puke. "I can't believe you—either of you."

Josh opened his mouth, but Madison slashed her hand through the air. "I don't even know you right now. Don't you *dare* ask me to keep this secret. Just . . . don't." She turned and stomped away, wishing she could leave the memory behind as easily.

She'd known Josh and Ashleigh and Lauren the majority of her life. Before this trip, she would have bet everything she owned that none of them would ever cheat. And they all had.

And to do this to Ethan . . . He was the only innocent in the whole situation, and it made her sick to think that he had no idea that his twin was having sex with his girlfriend.

What other secrets did her friends have that she didn't know about?

Madison moved faster until she was almost running. She didn't want to know. It was better to remember them as she thought she knew them than to deal with the fact that she didn't actually know them at all.

For the first time since she got her acceptance letter from SPU, she was actually looking forward to leaving Kalispell behind.

The faster I get out of here, the better.

Before I find out any other ugly truths about the people I care about.

◆ ◆ ◆

Tuesday, June 20
8:12 a.m.

Vic barely looked at Maggie as they drove into Kalispell. He could feel her there, a grand total of twelve inches away, and it was everything he could do not to pull the car off onto one of the little side roads and give her what they both wanted. Her taste still clung to his lips, and it was driving him crazy.

Maggie, apparently, didn't have the same issue. "I was thinking about the unsub—and the group of hikers. If this guy is really connected with those kids in some way, then we need to know more about them."

That, at least, gave him something to focus on. He reached between the seats and grabbed the file he'd put together last night. "Here."

"Two steps ahead of me. Of course." She snorted and flipped through the file.

"You keep calling them kids. They're, what, ten years younger than you? Not that much difference."

She didn't look up from the file. "I'm five years younger than you, and I distinctly remember you calling me 'kid' half a dozen times before I lost my shit when we were partners."

"Point taken." He let her read in peace. He hadn't been lying yesterday when he said he valued her input. She'd been a great partner during the Drover case. Kids being hurt fucked with everyone, and getting *so* close to catching the killer time and time again, only to miss and have to wait for another victim . . . It had been one of the worst years of his life.

He couldn't blame that solely on the case. There had been so much background shit going on with his marriage reaching the breaking point and his attraction to Maggie flaring into being.

Some nights he lay awake and wondered if his distraction with personal matters had been the reason Sean Drover slipped through their fingers repeatedly.

Ultimately, they'd caught the killer. Not soon enough for the victims' families, but he wouldn't hurt another little girl. The Drover case was one of those that seemed designed as a reminder that the BAU was not all-knowing, and sometimes they were outmatched despite the resources they had at their disposal.

He set it aside. It was harder to pack away his need for Maggie. Kissing her like that had been a mistake. It wasn't her fault. The blame lay solely on Vic. He was the one who'd crossed the line last night and then stampeded over it again the first chance he got this morning.

She closed the file as they hit the city limits and tapped the folder against her knee. "They're local, and they've been friends for years, and every single one of them has a background in hunting and fishing and basically every outdoor activity. Normally, I'd say that's what you get when you have folk from Montana, but when you pair it up with this case, it's suspicious, to say the least."

"We found one of the girls—at least, allegedly. We'll have to wait for Dr. Huxley to confirm, but I think it's safe to say that it's not the whole group killing these hikers."

Maggie made a face. "Can you imagine? They'd be like a pack of wolves, herding their prey through their territory, amping up its fear until they put it out of its misery. I can't imagine much more terrifying than that."

He couldn't, either. Fleeing from a single predator was nightmare enough. Being herded by a pack? He shook his head. "It's one guy— or one woman. Everything in the profile points in the direction of a thrill-seeking hunter who's upped his game to the most dangerous prey. Judging from the victims piling up in Glacier, I'd say we're on his home turf, and this is what he's been training for."

"The normal course of escalation would be to jump to two people— which it looks like he did with the couple from Whitefish. But two are difficult enough to handle without them getting the upper hand. Even if they were the easiest victims in the world, jumping to *five* people is insane. This guy isn't insane—not beyond the typical sociopathic tendencies." She tapped the folder faster. "So why this group?"

"He's got to have some kind of connection to them—a personal one."

Maggie raised her eyebrows. "It reads a little cold for revenge. And isn't that something like out of a horror movie? They bully this guy years ago in high school, and now he's constructed this elaborate plan to make them pay. If that's his motivation, wouldn't it be easier to break into their houses and put a bullet in their brains?"

"This guy doesn't want easy." He pulled into the parking lot and shut off the engine. "Their being local opens up more possibilities than it removes. If it was a seasonal worker killing tourists, that would be easier to track than someone who has a personal vendetta but was just practicing until now."

"There are only so many people in Kalispell." She sighed. "But you're right. We don't have twenty thousand seasonal workers, so that at least would have shrunk the pool of suspects. Right now, we can't even restrict it to someone who graduated when these kids did, because it could be literally anyone they met before they went their separate ways—or since, because the only two people who *didn't* stay in town are Madison and Ashleigh. This sucks."

"It does." He finally had control of himself enough to turn and look at her. The full night of sleep had done her good. Maggie looked . . . brighter. It might be his desire for her coloring his perception, but Vic didn't think so. "You ready for this?"

"The morgue doesn't bother me the way it used to." She climbed out of the car before he could pursue that topic of discussion. It drove home a point that had been hovering at the edge of his mind for the last couple of days.

He might have known Maggie seven years ago, but he didn't know her anymore.

Which wasn't to say that she was a stranger. She wasn't. No matter how much they'd both changed in the last near-decade, he knew her on a level that he didn't share with anyone else. It didn't make a damn bit of sense, but times like this really brought that knowledge to the forefront.

They strode into the morgue together, and Maggie walked like she knew where they were headed. It made sense. She was on a first-name basis with Dr. Huxley—something that only came after quite a bit of time spent together.

"Kat?" Maggie knocked on the door as she opened it.

Dr. Huxley looked up from the body she'd been leaning over with a smile. "Maggie. I'd say it's nice to see you, but it seems you have a problem of the worst sort out at the park."

"You can say that again." She walked into the room and motioned to Vic. "You've met Agent Sutherland?"

"He stopped by earlier." The medical examiner gave a half-hearted smile. "It seems your killer hasn't decided to change his ways."

"It would seem so."

Maggie moved to the body they'd found first. "Wyatt is dragging his heels about sending me back into the park right now, but if we end up with enough info, that might be right where we're headed." The comfortable way she spoke translated into a history between these two women. Vic wasn't sure where it ended—if they just chatted when Maggie was in here for work or if they socialized—but it was obvious they were fond of each other.

Dr. Huxley gave her a look. "If I were you, I'd stay the hell out of that damn park." She waved at the two bodies. "This guy's on a spree. He's not going to stop, is he? If he was, you wouldn't be needing to go back."

Vic shifted, drawing her attention to him. She flushed, instantly looking embarrassed. "Sorry, Agent Sutherland. As you might have noticed, things tend to be informal in Kalispell. We're more small town than big city, especially when you work for government in any kind of official capacity."

"It's okay, Kat." Maggie nudged him with her elbow as if telling him to tone it down. He thought he'd been pretty damn toned down, but everything about him was off right now. Part of it was the case, and part of it was the temptation Maggie offered just by standing there.

Get ahold of yourself.

Easier said than done. To distract himself, he moved to the woman's body. "We thought it was a bear that got to her."

"It was. Or at least the jaw measurements line up." Dr. Huxley switched gears effortlessly, once again the unflappable woman he'd met the first time. "Mountain lions and bears have different teeth, and the way they go at prey is different." She pressed her lips together, something like pity blossoming in her brown eyes. "She didn't die from the arrows. She was weakened from blood loss and might have died of it, given enough time—or she might have made it to the ranger station."

Even though he suddenly very much did not want to know the answer, Vic asked, "What was the cause of death?"

"Blood loss from a torn femoral artery." The medical examiner pointed to the savaged legs and torso. "I don't know if she was conscious for it. There aren't any defensive wounds, and she didn't curl into a ball or try to get away. From what I can tell, she just . . . lay there as the bear attacked."

Maggie made a pained noise. "I hope to God she had passed out at that point." She patted her hip like she'd forgotten she didn't have her radio on her. "Shit. That means we have a bear to track in the midst of this cluster."

"I'm sorry, Maggie."

"It's not your fault. It's this damn hunter. Who knows if that bear would have hurt this girl if she wasn't bleeding because she'd been shot twice by a sociopath?" She shook her head. "What else have you got?"

"We had to use dental records to identify her because of the damage done to her face and hands, and there not being conveniently placed tattoos." Dr. Huxley moved to a file set on the counter, well out of range of anything she'd have done to the bodies. "Your partner, Agent Kendrick, sent over the information about who you think this girl was. I made some calls, and though we'll have to go through official channels to confirm it, I happen to share a dentist with the woman." She shuddered. "Though that's a whole different type of eerie if I think too hard about it. He confirmed that what was left of her teeth *could* match Lauren Rosario's records, but that doesn't mean a whole lot since we don't have a complete set. Without her prints on record, we're left to a DNA test to be sure, and that will be weeks before we get a conclusive answer."

"How likely is it that there were two girls matching the same physical description on that trail at the same time?" Maggie shook her head. "While it's possible it's not Lauren, realistically, that's the only person it could be."

Vic was inclined to agree. The most obvious answer usually *was* the truth. "We'll know for sure once we compare the DNA to her parents." There wasn't much more to do before then. He nodded at the arrows on the tray next to the bodies. "Are the arrows the same as the first victim?"

"Yes. I did some checking on the brand." She flushed. "I know that's your job, but this whole situation bothers me. I know you hear this kind of thing on a regular basis, but this doesn't happen here. We're not exactly the smallest town ever, but we had one murder last year. *One.* And now I have three bodies in as many days, so you can understand why I'd like to do my part to make sure this monster is put behind bars."

Maggie instantly went to her and took her gloved hand. "It's okay, Kat. I understand. This case is hitting me a lot harder than I expected, too. You helped us by picking up a piece of work that we didn't have to. What did you find?"

Vic let her handle the conversation because he didn't think Dr. Huxley would take any comforting words he said to heart. He was used to his size and looks intimidating the people around him—especially women. Most of the time, he did his damnedest to tone down the factors that created an instinctive wariness, but it was still better for Maggie—someone the medical examiner knew and trusted—to tell her that she wasn't in the wrong.

Truth be told, they could use every bit of help they could get.

Though, technically, he couldn't remove Dr. Huxley—or *anyone*—from the suspect list, his instincts said she was so low on the list of possible unsubs that she might as well not be on the list at all. He'd still verify the information she passed on.

"They're Bloodsport Evidence." Dr. Huxley paled as she spoke, which was saying something, because the woman looked like she didn't get much sun to begin with. "Obviously, that goes without saying, since the name is plastered on the arrow itself, but this particular arrow is expensive—almost one hundred dollars for a bundle—and it's supposed to give extra penetration to the hit. While that makes sense when someone is hunting a deer or an elk, it seems a strange choice for hunting people." She motioned to her body. "The average person has a whole lot less bulk than even a small deer. If this guy is close enough, he'd run the risk of shooting right through his victim."

And yet he hadn't appeared to do that—not with the victims in Glacier, and not with the two previous. Vic moved closer to the man on the slab and studied him. "You hunt, Dr. Huxley?"

"God, no." She laughed nervously. "It might seem strange considering the work I do, but I can't get over the idea of taking something's life, even for food."

"Kat's a vegetarian."

"I don't eat meat, but my entire family lives in Kalispell and in the surrounding area, and nearly every single one of them hunts on a regular basis. We all got the safety training growing up and were forced along for at least one season of turkey hunting." Dr. Huxley made a face. "Suffice to say if I hadn't been planning on never eating meat again, picking out pellets from a turkey that my cousin had shot would be enough to make that decision for me."

He could imagine. "What can you tell me about this guy?" He pointed to the other victim.

She blushed again. "I'm sorry. I'm prattling on like I'm Sherlock Holmes." She gave herself a shake and moved to the other side of the slab. "This man has been dead longer than the others—approximately ninety-six hours. He was killed the same way the first woman was—two shots to the back, the first of which pierced his lung. He didn't last long after that. The killer removed the arrows like he did with the other woman."

Vic did some quick math in his head. "Ninety-six hours puts his death as the first."

"Yes." Dr. Huxley looked at the body. "There were something like twelve to eighteen hours between his death and the first victim."

Further proof that his theory about the Haglunds was correct. Vic crossed his arms over his chest, thinking hard. Why two victims? That was the part that stuck out to him. If the unsub had been planning for the group of now-missing hikers, he only needed one body to scatter them. However he chose his victims, it shouldn't have been too hard to pick a single person. Less challenging. Less chance of something going wrong before the main event.

Dr. Huxley continued, "The field dressing is postmortem, and some of the organs are missing, but from the evidence of tearing, it looks like scavengers rather than our guy." She moved to the man's face. Or what remained of it. "Birds got to his eyes, though—I'd say crows, but that's just a guess."

"Why did they go for the eyeballs and leave the rest?"

"You'll never believe this." She touched the side of the corpse's face with a gloved hand. "Honey."

Maggie made a choking sound. "He smeared honey on a dead body's face knowing it would draw animals."

"That's new." Vic stared at the body. "Jennifer Haglund was killed later, but he didn't do that to her."

"Maybe he was interrupted?" Maggie shook her head. "No, that's not what happened. He plans things out too well—at least up until Lauren's death. He leaves them at well-traveled places, knowing they'll be found before scavengers can get to his handiwork. This guy wants an audience."

"Jennifer Haglund was nearly identical to the second body." Except for the fact that her death was completely unnecessary to his plans. That's what bothered Vic the most. Every other death had been carefully planned, excepting the mistake with the bear and Lauren. "Bill Haglund's death wasn't, even though he was killed before his wife."

Whitefish wasn't that far from Kalispell. If they were right about the unsub being local, it was likely that he'd had interactions with all the Glacier victims at one point or another.

Bill Haglund had done something extra to earn the unsub's ire.

"Think it's symbolic?" Maggie had regained control of herself, and her face was set in a careful mask that said she was thinking fast and trying to keep her emotions from interfering. "An eye for an eye and all that?"

"Then why not take the eyes himself?" Dr. Huxley had her arms wrapped around herself. "This guy kills people. Why leave things to chance when he could prove that point and ensure it's done right?"

A piece snapped into place in Vic's head. "He doesn't have the stomach for it." When both women gave him an incredulous look, he held up his hands. "Bear with me. Yes, he's hunting them, shoring up their fear and probably enjoying the hell out of being the biggest, baddest predator in the area, but if his arrows don't hit something vital on the first go, he runs them into the ground. It would be easier to walk up to the injured person and slit their throat."

"That's what they do with a deer that's down but not dead yet." The medical examiner looked a little green. "It's bloody and terrible, but ultimately a mercy."

"Our guy doesn't do that. He waits until they're dead."

"If he's so squeamish, why bother with the field dressing at all?" Maggie snapped her fingers as soon as the last word was out of her mouth. "To put them in their place. The unsub is the ultimate predator, like you said, and so shooting them isn't enough. He's got to string them up and mark them as prey for everyone to see."

"Be a lot different gutting a dead man than gutting a live one. There's blood, for sure, but it's just so much meat. Easier to forget the person was actually a person."

"But if you want to make a point—say, taking the eyes of some poor bastard who pissed you off something fierce—that's a little different." Maggie moved to Vic's side, staring down at the dead man. "Hands and face are the two main things that mark us as people—as human. Harder to mess with the face than it would be to take a knife to the belly."

Dr. Huxley made a sound, drawing his attention. "What?"

She waved a hand at both of them. "I can tell that you were partners once upon a time. You're nearly finishing each other's sentences. It's kind of crazy."

"Jeez, Kat. Way to make me feel like a circus-sideshow freak." Maggie laughed, but it fell flat in this room of cold metal and corpses. "Let us know if you find anything else?"

"Will do. And Maggie?" Dr. Huxley waited for her to turn back. "Be careful."

CHAPTER TWELVE

Tuesday, June 20
9:13 a.m.

Maggie huffed out a sigh of frustration when they got into Vic's car. "Knowing that this guy doesn't like getting his hands dirty, so to speak, doesn't do a damn thing to help us figure out who he is or catch him." She ran her hands through her hair, but all that did was make the chemical smell still lingering in her nose worse. Her chest tried to close up, her mind flailing to find an answer to a question that never should have been put into being.

She closed her eyes, inhaling deeply through her nose, filling her lungs to capacity before exhaling. The scent didn't disappear, but her mind stopped its frantic circling. By the third breath, she felt something resembling calm. "It's one step closer, which is better than what we had before."

"Yes." Vic's voice was mild, and when she opened her eyes, it was to find him watching her with interest. He gave a half smile. "Yoga?"

"At least once a week—more if I can swing it." She had a class that hiked into various parts of Glacier before doing the actual exercises, so they could be as close to nature as possible. She liked the peace it brought, liked the ability to be with people without them needing to fill the silence, just plain liked it.

Vic put the car into drive and headed out of the parking lot. A few minutes later, she realized where he was headed. "I'm not really hungry."

"Neither am I, but Tucker likes the place, and we could both use a meal."

She'd known he had a partner, of course. The BAU could send out a single agent in a pinch, but Britton had always liked to keep his people in pairs. She didn't imagine that had changed much in the intervening years. People worked better when they had someone like-minded to bounce ideas off, like she and Vic had done in the morgue.

She hadn't realized how much she missed it.

It doesn't matter. That part of your life is over—by your choice.

It didn't make the loss any less potent.

She recognized Vic's partner the second they walked through the door of the diner. He was dressed in jeans, a henley, and a generic coat, which should have meant he'd blend in with the locals, but there was a stillness about him that said he saw everything in the room and had filed it away for later use. The fact that he was attractive and had hair a startling shade of red only added to the picture.

"Tucker is a good agent." Vic touched her elbow, and she watched his partner note the move.

"Okay." Interesting that *that* was the first thing he pointed out about his partner. She was curious, and not a little jealous. This man got to work with Vic daily and had the comfort of knowing that his association wouldn't end when the case did.

But she couldn't think about that right now.

He rose as they reached the table and offered a hand. "Tucker Kendrick. You must be Maggie Gaines."

"I wish I could say whatever you've heard is false, but I'm sure it's all too true." She slid into the booth. Her heart lodged itself in her throat as Vic scooted in next to her, his thigh pressing against hers. He spread his arm over the back of the seat, not touching her, but she could feel the heat of him all the same.

"Hmm." Tucker raised his eyebrows but didn't say anything else.

The tension radiating from Vic's body wasn't something she would have noticed if she wasn't touching him. Vic gave him a significant look. "Let's focus on the case."

For a long moment, it seemed like Tucker would push the issue—and she knew exactly what the issue was. *Me.* Vic might not have shouted his interest in her from the rooftops, but Tucker was trained to watch people and see beneath the surface. Even if he wasn't, Vic hadn't exactly been subtle.

She could set things straight. It wouldn't take much—a sarcastic comment and some distance between her and the man sitting next to her.

Maggie didn't do it.

They weren't breaking any rules by going on a date. It might be seen as a distraction—and it was—but there wasn't much to be done about that. More than anything else, she refused to give up the chance to see if this thing between her and Vic was actually *something.*

I already know the answer to that.

They didn't say anything until the waitress, a teenager named Becky, brought them coffee and took their order. Both Tucker and Vic loaded up on bacon and sausage, but she went with an omelet. She couldn't stomach meat yet. After this case, she might have to take a page from Kat's book and go vegetarian.

Vic's thumb brushed her shoulder, almost imperceptibly. "We're going back into the park the first chance we get. I need you to start putting things together on this end. The unsub orchestrated the husband's face getting mutilated, though he didn't do it himself."

Tucker's blue eyes narrowed. "Pretty damn personal to go for the face. Wonder if he backtracked to check out his handiwork after it was done."

This, at least, Maggie had some authority to speak up about. "Almost impossible to track that, with the disturbances in the area from the animals—and it looks like two of our hikers found the body before they scattered. Wyatt should know more when we check in, but the whole scene was contaminated—all of them seem to be."

Vic tapped one finger on the table. "What if the married couple isn't connected to the missing hikers?"

"What?" She twisted to look at him. From his pensive expression, this was something he'd been chewing on for a while now. "Why kill both of them, then?"

"You mentioned eye for an eye. That's one reason to go for the eyes of a victim. There's another option, though."

Tucker hissed out a breath. "He saw something he shouldn't have."

"Yes." Vic nodded.

Maggie pressed her lips together and looked at the murders of the Haglunds in a different light. They were locals and avid hikers. In the report, David said they were hiking a loop on some of the primitive trails to hit the glaciers that West Glacier got its name from. "We've theorized that the unsub has some sort of camp set up. The Haglunds' planned path took them close to Fifty Mountain, and then they veered west. It could be that they stumbled on that camp."

"Would he really risk camping on one of these so-called primitive trails?"

She shook her head. "Probably not. But it wouldn't take much—the Haglunds seeing something that caught their attention and going to investigate. Some sections of the trail they were on are so high, you can see for miles around." She'd done the same thing in the past.

"That changes things—and nothing at all." Vic caught her look. "We can guess that they weren't far off Fifty Mountain when they found him—if that's what happened—because of where the bodies were found. Even if he was capable of herding a victim to his chosen location, their time of deaths were too close together for him to have done it twice."

That made sense. She followed his line of thought. "All it really means is that there might not be an apparent connection between them and the missing hikers." It was a piece of the puzzle, but it wasn't ultimately helpful.

And she still had to talk to her boss about the bear. Knowing the bear killed Lauren Rosario, rather than found her dead body, changed things. The fact that Lauren had been injured to the point of death was irrelevant. No matter how discreet Kat was, this information would have to be reported, and, as a result, it would get out. If they didn't take decisive action, the local media would have a heyday. There was nothing people liked to read about more than killer animals, and the park had been fighting for years to keep the grizzly population growing. If some of those assholes had their way, they'd exterminate the entire species.

All of it meant that when a bear killed a person, certain measures had to be taken, and they had to be taken quickly.

It was a goddamn tragedy, as far as she was concerned—yet another blame to lay at the feet of the unsub.

"Maggie?"

She looked up to realize both men were staring at her. Obviously they'd said something that she missed. "I'm sorry, I was thinking about the bear."

Tucker blinked. "You're going to have to elaborate."

"Lauren Rosario's cause of death was blood loss from a severed femoral artery—severed by a bear's bite." She spoke quietly and clearly, hating saying the words aloud as much as she hated thinking them. More, really, because it made this whole nightmare that much more real.

Tucker shook his head, still looking shocked. "That's a seriously shitty way to go."

"Yes."

Vic cleared his throat. "It doesn't change anything. She was hit twice by the unsub, and if the bear hadn't gotten to her, he would have. Find the connection, Tucker. Line it up, nice and neat, so when we bring this guy in, any jury they come up with will convict him."

Maggie wanted to say that if—*when*—they found this person, then of course a jury would find him guilty, but she knew better. Innocent until proven guilty. Even if they caught him in the act of killing a person, there was room for doubt about a number of things, mainly his state of mind. Juries didn't go for insanity pleas as much as they used to, but that was generally because there was concrete evidence of premeditation. That's what they needed to ensure the unsub was put behind bars for good.

"I'll start with the missing hikers and go from there." Tucker drained his Coke. "You're going to want to update Britton before you head back into the boonies again." He stood. "Nice meeting you, Ranger Gaines." And then he was gone.

She watched him get into his rental car and then turned to Vic. "He seems nice."

"He's charming." Vic said the word like it was a bad thing. But then, he would think that. He was someone who valued deeds over words, so a partner who oozed charm on command would drive him batty.

She shook her head. "What was Britton thinking putting the two of you together?"

"I'm sure he's trying to teach one of us a lesson, though whether that's Tucker or me is up for grabs."

Becky reappeared with their food, looking crestfallen when she realized Tucker was gone. Maggie started eating, only belatedly realizing that Vic probably should have moved to the other side of the booth. "I know we have plans tonight and Wyatt wants us to take another night before going back into the park."

"I'm sensing a *but* coming."

Because there was. She took a bite of her omelet, chewed, and swallowed. "But every hour counts right now. The more feet on the ground, the better."

She thought he'd argue, but he just took several more bites before responding. "Let's talk to Wyatt and then we'll see where we end up."

Though she wanted to argue that there wasn't time for that, the reality was that they couldn't get transport back to Fifty Mountain without Wyatt's permission, not unless they hiked in themselves, which would waste even more time than being forced to wait for morning. She bounced her foot, irritated by the delay. "There's got to be something to find. I know it. If we were just *there* . . ."

◆ ◆ ◆

Tuesday, June 20
11:30 a.m.

Vic didn't want to go back into the park, where Maggie would be in danger again. He wanted to pack her up and take her to a hotel and lock themselves in for a few weeks. By the time they surfaced, this would all be over and they could move on with life as normal. It was a childish desire, and unforgivably selfish in the mix. If he wanted to, he could send Tucker into Glacier in his place and take over pulling at the strings connecting the victims to see what fell out, but Maggie would be going back into the park regardless. It was her job, and his wanting to protect her wasn't going to be enough to convince her to stay out of it.

Hell, she might lose her job even if she was willing to listen, and it was readily apparent that she loved her job, the last few days excepting. He couldn't ask that of her.

They drove back to the ranger headquarters, each lost in their own world. He didn't tell her what he was thinking, because it wouldn't do a damn bit of good. She was right—there needed to be more boots on the ground, and they needed to do their part.

That didn't mean he had to like it.

"Stop brooding."

Vic looked over as he parked. "I'm not brooding."

"Yes, you are. You're thinking awfully hard over there about something that isn't making you happy." She hesitated, indecision written across her face. "Do we have to have another talk about my capabilities? Or are you regretting crossing the line with the kissing and talk of dates?"

"Never." He reached over and took her hand, the only move he'd allow himself. Her calluses were a match for his, her nails unpainted, the skin on the back of her hand soft and sun kissed. "I should have found you after my divorce."

"No." She covered his hand with her other one. "No, it wasn't right before, and that would have affected everything. Maybe it's not right now and this is all a lost cause, but if we're going to do this, it's not going to be with the shadow of your ex hanging over us—or with the shadow of that case."

"Do I have to tell you again that you were perfectly justified in walking away?"

Her smile was sad. "We all have our demons to answer to. I don't want this to turn into another one."

"It won't." He didn't know what he could say to wipe that look off her face, and kissing her here, in front of her place of work, wasn't an option. He wasn't so far gone as to forget that. So Vic just squeezed her hand and reached for his door. "I'm being overprotective. Someone whose opinion I value told me that I need to knock that shit off, but it's harder than I anticipated."

"Packing me away won't solve any of these problems, and it won't bring you peace. You'll still spend every waking second wondering what I'm up to and if I'm okay." Maggie motioned to the park as a whole.

"Statistically, I'm more likely to be run down by a drunk driver than get hurt here."

"Statistics don't mean a damn thing when there's a killer on the loose." It didn't take much to superimpose her face over the victim's, to see her skin gone pale with death, the two arrows protruding from her back, the lingering fear in her eyes despite the very thing that made her *Maggie* being gone.

He went cold at the image. "I won't let him touch you."

"I know." She rounded the car, and this time her smile was a whole lot warmer. "And right back atcha. We'll watch each other's backs."

There really wasn't much more to say than that. He'd do his best to make sure she emerged from this case unscathed, and she'd do the same for him—as if they were still partners, though the new awareness simmering between them was something that could explode when he least expected it. Even now, knowing better, he wanted to reach for her, to press her against the side of his rental, to kiss her until neither of them cared about the case or the unsub or the missing hikers. Vic cleared his throat. "We should get moving."

"Agreed." But she reached up and pressed her hand to his chest. "Promise me that even if we don't manage it today, we'll find time for that date."

"I promise."

The wind chose that moment to kick up, and he held up a hand to shield his face. In the last few minutes, clouds had appeared to blot out the sun, the sky turning from a happy blue to something significantly more sinister. If he were a superstitious man, he'd take that as an ill omen. "Weather changes fast up here."

"Hmm? Yeah." She cast a suspicious look at the clouds. "It's the Continental Divide. We're a bit west of it right now, but when you get the wet climate of the west part of the park colliding with the more arid of the east, microbursts are the least of your worries." She pressed her lips together. "This spells trouble for those missing hikers—and for our team out there. Rain masks the trails, and there's a very real risk of exposure."

The chances of their getting back the four remaining hikers unscathed decreased by the hour. "Let's get in there and talk to Wyatt and see where they're at with things."

"Okay." She led the way, marching through the doors and back to Wyatt's tiny office. He was on the phone when they came through the door, and held up a finger requesting silence. He didn't say much beyond "Yes, sir" and "No, sir." Which meant he was getting his ass reamed by a superior over their current situation.

Vic's suspicion was confirmed when Wyatt hung up the phone and turned to Maggie. "What have you got?"

"Only bad news. The male victim was killed before the female we found at Kootenai Lake, which we suspected." She hesitated and then lifted her chin, looking like she was about to step into the ring. "And it was a bear who got to the other female—and it got to her before she died."

"Shit." Wyatt pressed his hands to his face for a long moment and then dropped them onto his desk. "I'll take someone and go after the bear myself, though we're going to have a hell of a time tracking it with this bitch coming at us fast." He waved at the window.

From the shocked look on Maggie's face, Vic would bet the other man didn't swear all that often. Not surprising that this situation was bringing out the worst in him—it would bring out the worst in all of them before it was over. She recovered faster than her boss did. "We need to get back out there."

"Impossible."

"But, sir—"

Wyatt pointed again at the window. "We need more manpower—but no one is going to be flying in this until it's over. The teams are going to have to hunker down where they can, and we'll just have to pray for the missing hikers."

"Prayers aren't going to do a damn thing, and you know it."

He raised a bushy eyebrow. "Neither is getting you, your agent, and a pilot killed because I made the wrong call." He leveled a look at Vic. "You're not saying much."

"This is your wheelhouse. I'd like an updated report, if possible, before we head out." He ignored Maggie's staring daggers at him.

If anything, Wyatt's eyebrows rose higher. None of that leaked into his voice, though. "Found three different trails leading from Fifty Mountain. One headed south toward Many Glacier, and they're sticking to the path from all appearances. Hard to say how many of the hikers there are or what condition they're in."

Sticking to the trail was the worst thing they could do, even if it made the going faster. Vic straightened. "Could they reach the Many Glacier ranger station by today?"

Wyatt nodded. "Barring disaster or injury, it's easily a day's hike."

Vic glanced at his watch. "From all accounts, those hikers have been missing going on thirty-six hours now. Shouldn't that mean that whoever is headed south would have reached the station by now?"

"Hard to say," Wyatt said.

"Not hard to say." Maggie crossed her arms over her chest. "Did they find sign of injury? Blood? Anything?"

"No—nothing amiss other than the body you found."

Which meant that either the party on the trail had gotten lost or met with something terrible. Vic sighed. He needed coffee and to get moving. It was the only solution, because if he held still for too long, he'd crash. When he was in his twenties, going for days on end with minimum sleep was barely a hiccup, but these days, the frenetic cases took a lot more out of him. The hike combined with tossing and turning in an uncomfortable hotel bed while thinking of Maggie hadn't done him any favors.

He pinched the bridge of his nose and pushed his tiredness away. "And the other trails?" Maybe if the unsub had started tracking the easiest prey—the ones who kept to the trail—the others had escaped his hunting them.

For now, at least.

"One leads west, though the pair of rangers there are having a hell of a time tracking whoever it is. They keep zigzagging across Kootenai Creek," Wyatt said.

"Dangerous," Maggie murmured. "But smart if they think they're being hunted."

"It's *our* people hunting them."

"Maybe they don't know that." There wasn't an easy answer there. If those hikers saw Bill Haglund's body and thought his killer was after them, they weren't just going to trust some stranger who appeared in the woods. "Are the SAR folk wearing some kind of uniform?"

"Some are."

Which meant some weren't—all the more reason for whoever it was to be cautious. "Damn."

"Final trail leads east, but it went cold a few hundred feet in." Wyatt sat back in his chair. "I have rangers coming up from Many Glacier, but the majority of our folk are after the other two sets of people. There isn't an easy answer here, and I don't like that this group split. They'd have had a better chance if they stuck together."

Or they would have made a bigger target for the unsub. "Are you still doing flyovers?" Vic asked.

"We were before the storm made it too dangerous." As if on cue, thunder boomed, nearly making the room shake.

Vic nodded, because there wasn't anything else to do. Wyatt was right about hauling them out into the park being too dangerous right now. There were no new crime scenes to work or bodies to examine, so he would just be another set of boots on the ground. Not a bad thing, but also not where his area of expertise ran. "When's the weather supposed to break?"

"Late tonight." Wyatt stood as well. "We should be able to get you out early tomorrow—and hopefully I'll have some good news by then."

None of them commented on the fact that good news seemed to be in short supply with this case, or the very real danger the rescuers were in, both from the unsub and from the storm itself.

Vic followed Maggie out of Wyatt's office. The rest of the building was nearly empty, only a single ranger working the radio and the phone. He nodded to Maggie, and she nodded back, but she didn't stop to chat. The rain started to fall as they walked through the door, heavy sheets that obscured anything farther than ten feet away. He stopped just beneath the overhang. "Could be that the storm will slow him down the same way it'll slow down the rest of them."

"Maybe." She didn't ask whom he meant. There was only one *he* right now. "Or it could be that he's better prepared than both the rescuers and missing hikers are."

"Say he's as experienced as he seems—what would someone who's not a murderer do in this situation?"

"Find shelter and ride it out. The rock out here isn't granite—it's sedimented—so it can crumble beneath a person even if it looks solid. The rain makes that far more likely. Not to mention the potential for flash floods and slippery rocks and . . ." She nodded, her dark eyes losing some of their fury. "I see your point. He's in this for his kills, but he's not going to risk his life for it." Maggie looked to the sky, now a gray so dark it was nearly black. "Storm like this, you can walk right by a person and not realize they're there. Unsub probably knows that. If he has some kind of permanent shelter close by—and if he killed the Haglunds for the reason you suspect, that supports this theory—he'll be there. He doesn't, he's probably capable enough to find a hidey-hole until the worst of it passes."

Which meant they'd all been granted something of a reprieve. Everyone who could find shelter would do so until the storm passed, so they might as well head back to Kalispell and help out with Tucker's part of the investigation. "Only one real downside to this."

"The missing hikers." She nodded, her quick mind already grasping where he was headed. "Right now, they're in a lot more danger from the park than from the unsub."

CHAPTER THIRTEEN

Tuesday, June 20
12:50 p.m.

Maggie and Vic met his partner in a little subdivision in Kalispell and divvied up the missing hikers. They would talk to the families and see what they could find out. Tucker seemed unsteady for the first time since she'd met him, his face too pale, his mouth tight and not even attempting a smile.

While Vic looked over the addresses, she shifted closer. "Are you okay?"

"Yeah." He looked back at the house at the end of the street—the one belonging to Lauren Rosario's family. "Just never gets easier, you know? Local Feds handled having her parents identify the body—she's definitely wearing Lauren's clothing—and providing DNA samples to verify, but they're still in shock and just starting to grieve." His mouth tightened. "She's got three little brothers—youngest is ten. She went to school in town, was engaged to a local guy—another one of the missing hikers, Joshua Conlon. Things were kind of rocky there, though her family didn't want to come out and say it. She was just a normal twenty-three-year-old. Knowing she's dead, let alone that she went out like that . . ." He shook his head. "Not right."

"We'll get her justice." Vic spoke without looking up.

"Doesn't bring her back, does it? Doesn't make it so her parents never lost a child or those boys never lost their big sister. Justice is a sad substitute for a loved one." Tucker gave himself a shake and turned a surprisingly steady smile on Maggie. "I'm fine. This shit just messes with my head, but I'll be back to my charming self before you know it. Which ones are you taking?"

"Madison and the brothers."

Tucker nodded. "Works for me. Ashleigh Marcinko's family lives a ways out of town, so it'll be a jaunt to get to them." He hesitated. "At least there's some hope for the others." He said it like he didn't quite believe it.

That was fine. She wasn't sure anyone quite believed that those kids would make it out alive at this point. It didn't matter. They couldn't afford to doubt. Until they saw bodies, they had to operate like there *was* hope.

She flipped through the information while they drove to the house Madison Garcia grew up in. Tucker had added to the file since yesterday. The Hispanic girl—woman, really, since she was old enough to drink—had graduated valedictorian from high school and immediately moved to Seattle. She'd finished college at SPU with minimal student loans and worked her way up from an unpaid internship to a pretty decent job with excellent employment benefits. For all accounts, she lived a relatively quiet life in the city with her best friend—Ashleigh—and stayed out of trouble. "Nothing popping here."

"That's because it's focusing on the now, not whatever it is that links her to the unsub." Vic took a turn, bringing them off the beaten track to a row of tiny houses.

They were old and shabby, but obviously well loved in spite of that. There was a bright box of flowers in the window of the home they pulled up in front of, and Maggie had the sudden urge to beg Vic to stay in the car and keep driving. "I don't want to be the one who breaks the news to them."

"There isn't any news yet. Madison's party of hikers has gone missing, and we're looking at any helpful information we can find."

She turned to him. "You're not going to tell them about the unsub?"

"What good would it do? They're going to panic." He shut off the engine. "We need information—something they're less likely to give us if they're worried about their daughter being murdered."

"Their daughter *is* in danger of being murdered."

"Which is why we need the information." The expression on his face held none of the warmth she'd become accustomed to seeing. "Can you handle this? Or do you want me to drop you with the high school teachers to see what they have to say?"

She started to snap back but forced herself to stop and think. She was angry and frustrated and wanted to shred something, but she wasn't in danger of breaking. "I'm fine. Or as fine as I can be given the circumstances."

"If you're sure."

"I am." She wanted to be there, both for the missing hikers and for him. She wouldn't falter again. She wouldn't let herself. Maggie climbed out of the car before she could talk herself out of it and started for the door.

Vic caught up before she hit the front porch. "I'll take lead."

"Of course." She would have thought that went without saying. She was just a park ranger. He was the FBI agent. "I'll keep my mouth shut and observe."

He nodded, but she could tell his mind was already on the people who lived in the house in front of them. Maggie tried to look over it with a critical eye, but she kept coming back to the flower box. No matter the state of the house, those flowers represented a kind of hope that came from making the best of any situation. Happy people decorated their homes with flowers and put in the work to keep them alive. She turned and looked back down the short walkway. The grass in the yard was sparse but well maintained, and someone had taken the time to sweep the dirt from the walkway into the street.

Happy. Definitely happy.

Only one way to tell for sure, and that meant knocking on the door and throwing a bucketful of bad news onto these people.

Vic knocked before she could think better of it, which was just as well. The woman who answered was pretty in a very down-home sort of way. She wore jeans that were broken in and a button-up cotton shirt that covered her from neck to wrists. Her thick dark hair was pulled back into a low ponytail that spoke of something done on the fly to keep it from her face while she worked.

She looked just like her daughter.

They had the same strong jaw, direct brown eyes, and warm brown skin, and there was a level of confidence in the way they held themselves. *Madison is going to need that confidence and a whole hell of a lot of strength to get through this.*

The woman frowned. "Something I can help you with?"

"Mrs. Garcia?"

"Yes." Worry appeared on her face for the first time. "It's not Peter, is it?"

Vic didn't hesitate. "As far as I can tell, your husband is just fine."

"Thank God." She sagged against the door frame. "That last heart attack took more years off *my* life than it did his, and do you think he slowed down a hair?" Maggie saw the exact moment the truth hit. Ruth Garcia shot straight. "If you're not here because of Peter, you're here because of Madison."

Maggie stepped forward, bringing the woman's attention to her. "Can we talk inside?"

"Yes, of course. I'm being a terrible hostess." She stepped back in, her gaze jumping between them. This wasn't the type of woman to panic unnecessarily, but they were here because of her only daughter—her only child. There was a level of fear there that nothing they could say would fix.

And they were about to make it a whole hell of a lot worse.

She led them into a small living room with a well-loved recliner and sofa that had been re-covered in a cheery floral print sometime in the last few years. "Now, please tell me what's going on."

"Madison went hiking with a group of friends a few days ago. Did she tell you what her plans were?"

"Sure." The wariness didn't leave Ruth's eyes. "They drove up through Canada, because Madison and Ethan wanted to start the trip with the ferry ride. They were planning on going down through Many Glacier to hike their favorite loop. I told her to keep her phone on, but ever since she moved to Seattle after high school, she likes to disconnect as much as possible when she's in the park."

"Madison and Ethan Conlon planned the trip?"

Ruth nodded, a small smile pulling at the edges of her lips. "Never would have guessed on things falling out like that. He's always been such a quiet boy, and he dated one of Madison's friends in high school—Lauren—but they somehow ran into each other about a year back."

Vic leaned forward. "They're dating."

"It's not 'official.'" She made air quotes with her fingers. "Madison is determined not to rush into anything, and he seems to be on the same page, but all this talk of official and not official is silly to me. Life is too short, you know?"

"Yes."

And life had already been cut short for one of their friends. The same friend who had dated Ethan in high school. Maggie shot Vic a look, and he gave an almost imperceptible nod. "Were Ethan and Lauren serious when they were teenagers?"

"As serious as anyone is at that age, I suppose." She shrugged. "It's a small high school, and most of the kids have known one another since they started kindergarten. We don't get much in the way of new blood around here. Everyone seemed to date everyone over the course of four years. If I'm remembering correctly, Lauren and Ethan weren't together long after graduation, but I couldn't tell you specifically when it ended."

"Does Madison come back to Kalispell often so she can hike?" Maggie shot Vic a sharp glance, wondering where he was going with this line of questioning.

"She and her father have gone out once or twice in the last five years. She comes home for Thanksgiving and Christmas, but no one in their right mind goes hiking out there during those months."

"She and her father go out?" Vic asked.

"Yes, Ashleigh came back with her on those trips home to visit her parents, but that girl hates the outdoors." She shrugged. "Whatever fight happened on that last trip, Madison hasn't hiked with her other friends again—until now."

She frowned at Maggie, seeming to take in her uniform for the first time. "Did something happen to her? She's an experienced hiker. She's been in that park in every season, and I won't pretend that I don't know that accidents happen, but she was prepared." Ruth's hands crept to her mouth, her eyes wide. "Tell me what's going on right this instant."

Maggie kept her mouth shut, allowing Vic to take the lead. He didn't disappoint. He leaned forward again, his elbows on his knees, his tone easy and meant to convey support. "There's a situation in the park, and Madison is involved."

Ruth narrowed her eyes, and her hand dropped to her lap. "A situation. They aren't lost, but something happened." Anger appeared in the line of her mouth and the set of her shoulders. "It's that little shit Joshua Conlon, isn't it?"

"Why would you think that?"

"Because he has been nothing but trouble from the time he hit grade school. Oh, my daughter and he were friends, make no mistake, and I tolerated him because he never turned that trouble on her, but that doesn't change the truth." She paused but pushed on, face resolute. "He's the reason Madison left two months early for college."

That was news. Maggie leaned forward. "He hurt her?"

"No, nothing like that." Ruth looked troubled. "There was a fight—a verbal one. He and Ashleigh broke up on that last trip after they graduated, and no one would confirm what exactly happened. Since he hadn't hurt my girl, I had no reason to step in."

"Do you know what the fight was about?" Vic asked.

"I can take a few guesses."

When neither of them said anything, a clear invitation to elaborate, she gave a tight smile. "Ashleigh went and moved in with a brand-new boyfriend that same summer. Big step, moving in together, and Madison let it slip that Ashleigh hadn't exactly been the best kind of girlfriend to Josh, if you get my drift."

Meaning she'd cheated on him.

Ruth continued. "And that Josh barely waited for the girls to leave town limits before taking up with Lauren. So I firmly believe that those sins went both ways. And then there were the fights—he's been brawling since he was old enough to walk."

Cheating *and* a temper to match . . .

People had killed—and been killed—over less, though waiting well over five years to do it seemed a stretch. *Stop making assumptions. What do we know for a fact?*

Things changed for those kids during that last trip into Glacier—which meant that there was a good chance the triggering event had happened during the same time.

Maggie tried to process that, but her mind kept coming up against one possibility she'd never even considered before now. *Surely not . . . no way is the unsub one of these missing hikers.*

Except . . . what if he was?

While she was chewing that over, Vic hadn't missed a beat. "Do you think Joshua would harm Madison or any of the others on that hike?"

"I wouldn't put anything past him." She sighed. "But I'm biased, I suppose. Ethan isn't so bad, but Josh and the rest of his family have been no friend to mine over the years. That boy is made in the image of his father—and I believe they both have a bit of a drinking problem. Mark Conlon has gotten into it with my Peter more than a few times over the years down at the bar." She sighed. "And, to be honest, it's hard not to blame Josh instead of Ashleigh for my Madison leaving Kalispell like the hounds of hell were on her heels." She seemed to realize what that sounded like, because she straightened. "We are proud of our girl. I went to college, but I stuck close to home. She got an opportunity, and even if that meant she was leaving for a few years, that was worth it for her to be happy. Her daddy and I are proud of her."

"You have every reason to be proud," Maggie said, but her mind was still circling the revelation that things hadn't been completely friendly among friends. She'd caught some of that tension that first day when she'd met them, but she hadn't put much thought into it. Get enough people together, and having *no* tension was the surprise.

But tension was different from being actually afraid of a person.

If Madison really was that afraid of Joshua Conlon, why would she come back and agree to go on a multiday hike with him? For that matter, why would Ashleigh, who had apparently cheated on him? Not to mention the strangeness of adding Lauren to the mix. It was possible that everyone had gotten over whatever broke up those two relationships in high school, but it was equally possible that someone was harboring the kind of jealousy and rage that could potentially evolve into murder.

But there was murder, and then there was *this*.

If Vic had made the jump with her, he gave no indication for Ruth to pick up on. "Madison and the other members of her hiking party are missing. The circumstances surrounding why that's the case are murky at this point, but it appears that they set off in different directions unexpectedly." He held up a hand when Ruth would have spoken. "Search and rescue is already working the area and tracking them. The storm is going to complicate matters, but they're doing the best they can."

"It doesn't make sense." She shook her head. "Madison has been hunting since she could walk. She knows that park as well as any of you ranger folk do, no disrespect. I don't see how she could possibly be lost."

Maggie understood that Vic didn't want to advertise that not only were the hikers lost but they were being hunted, but she could handle this aspect. "I've worked in Glacier for seven years now, and even though I know parts of it like the back of my hand, there are times when things happen beyond my control. It's more likely than you'd think."

Ruth stared at her hands. "It could very well be that she's not lost but that she's ended up in a spot where she has to take an alternate route back to the nearest ranger station."

It became readily apparent that this woman wouldn't believe that anything truly bad could put her daughter at a disadvantage. Maggie and Vic shared a look, and then he changed tactics. "Tell me about Madison's forestry skills. You said she spent a lot of time hunting?"

"Her and her daddy went out every year." Pride crept into her tone, though she still didn't look up. "She's good with a rifle—a crack shot, really—and he taught her bow hunting when she was in high school to give her a bit of a challenge."

Bow hunting. Maggie straightened. "She as good with a bow as she was with a rifle?"

"Lord, no. She said she didn't like the feel of it, so that only lasted a year." Ruth shrugged. "She promised my husband they'd go out again next year, said she'd have more time now that she's not in school anymore. She's even considering moving home if things get serious with her and Ethan." Her lower lip quivered. "Madison and her daddy would go out for a solid week and camp. She's more than capable of feeding and defending herself and anyone else she's with in a pinch."

If she was capable of all that, she was more than capable of potentially evading the unsub for long enough that SAR could find her.

Unfortunately, it meant she was more than capable of *being* the unsub, too.

◆ ◆ ◆

Tuesday, June 20
1:34 p.m.

They didn't get anything else out of Ruth Garcia, though she promised to call if she thought of something that might be helpful. Vic didn't expect her to. She was worried about her daughter, and rightfully so. But the line of questioning had opened up something he'd had eating away at the back of his mind. It was possible that the unsub was some heretofore undiscovered person who happened to have a connection with the missing hikers, and that he had infiltrated the park by hiking in off the grid . . . but it was also possible that the unsub had walked into Glacier in the most blatant way possible.

Hiding in plain sight.

They didn't have evidence to back it up. At this point, it was barely a hunch. But he'd keep the potential in mind going forward, because it would complicate things to an infinite degree—and it would mean that any of the hikers they recovered alive couldn't be trusted.

He drove to the Conlon house in silence, and though he could see Maggie practically brimming with questions, she kept them to herself. Joshua and Ethan Conlon had grown up about a mile from Madison, but in a significantly nicer neighborhood. It was solid middle class, though the houses were a good thirty years old and starting to show wear and tear. The driveway was pitted—a combination of not being sealed correctly when it was put in and the harsh Montana winters—and the yard was slightly overgrown. It might be a larger house than the one they'd just left, but the Garcia place was a home, and this was just a structure that housed people.

He'd learned to tell the difference over the years.

The man who opened the door was balding, a little red around the face from a life spent drinking, and dressed in jeans and a faded shirt beneath the flannel that seemed to be ever present in this area of the world. Since he'd experienced firsthand how cold Montana nights got, even in June, Vic understood.

"I don't need to buy anything, and I already found Jesus." He started to shut the door.

"Mr. Conlon?"

Watery blue eyes blinked at him, as if taking him in for the first time. "You the five-oh?"

Vic registered Maggie sliding a little farther behind him. He almost turned and looked at her, but there was something about the man that was setting off all sorts of alarm bells. Though he'd played coy with Mrs. Garcia, doing so with this man might get him drawn on. "Your sons, Ethan and Joshua, went on a camping trip a few days ago. Something went amiss, and they're currently missing."

Conlon didn't relax. "They're big boys, and they know their way around these parts. They'll be fine."

Vic waited, but there didn't seem to be more coming. He affected a casual stance. "You don't seem that worried."

"Why would I be? When those boys were growing up, they'd spend half the summers out in the forests, living like little savages. Didn't stop when they graduated, either. They spent last summer at some survival-camp shit in Colorado. There ain't nothing Glacier can throw at them that they haven't seen before. You tell them to call their old man when they finally show up, you hear?"

"You happen to know anyone by the names of Bill and Jennifer Haglund?" He brought them up on a whim. Mrs. Garcia hadn't recognized the names other than being vaguely familiar, but if they could pin down the connection between the Haglunds and the missing kids, they might start to get somewhere.

He was still surprised when Conlon's eyes narrowed. "What are you wanting with my nephew and his wife?"

"Bill Haglund is your nephew."

Even though he didn't phrase it as a question, Conlon still answered. "My sister's kid. He grew up a couple blocks over. Answer the fucking question."

There was no way around it—and it'd be public knowledge shortly. The local sheriff had already sent his folk to talk to the victims' parents, so Conlon would hear before too long as it was. "Bill and Jennifer Haglund were killed over the weekend in Glacier."

Vic didn't get another word out before Conlon shut the door in his face. He blinked, surprised for the second time in as many minutes. He'd expected the man to curse at him or threaten him or maybe even show a glimmer of humanity. Apparently that was hoping for too much. "Well—"

"Not here." Maggie grabbed his hand and towed him down the walkway to the rental. It wasn't until they were pulling away from the house that she relaxed.

Another surprise. He kept his tone even and his eyes on the road, wanting to put her at ease even though he needed answers. "Want to tell me what that was about?"

"There's a group of locals who have this whole conspiracy theory that park rangers are out to get them. We're the ultimate buzzkill, because we expect them to actually follow the laws. I didn't put it together, which I should have, but Mark Conlon is one of the biggest loudmouths in the area. He hates us—hates us even more because Wyatt dumped his brother in jail when they caught him poaching."

It made sense that she wanted to minimize any chance of the guy throwing a huge bitch fit, but that didn't cover the fact that there'd been fear in her eyes just then. "There's more."

She gave a half smile. "Isn't there always? He made some threats—some pretty serious threats. I don't think he'll go out of his way to come into the park to carry them out, but I wouldn't put it past him when I'm standing on his doorstep."

"I wouldn't let anyone hurt you." He knew exactly how ineffectual the words were, and he still said them because they were the damn truth.

"If he and his brothers get together, you wouldn't have much choice." She shook her head. "It's neither here nor there. I'm sorry I didn't tell you before we went in there. I was letting you take the lead, but I still should have given you a heads-up. He didn't bother to recognize the uniform, or pretended he didn't because you were there. But you add in the information he passed us—along with the talk with Ruth Garcia—and we're looking at a picture much different than we thought."

"I think I underestimated how many people in this town have the ability to walk into the woods and not come out again for weeks—and how interconnected the relationships would be." Bill Haglund was cousin to the Conlon twins. Another connection, though Vic still held to his original theory that the man and his wife had been at the wrong place at the wrong time. It seemed absurd that his being related to the Conlon twins had no bearing on his and his wife's deaths, though, so Vic wasn't prepared to discount the possibility that he was wrong.

He'd been wrong before.

If Mark Conlon had been anyone else, he would have questioned further. As it was, Vic couldn't even begin to guess if the man's attitude was because he was hiding something or just a general distrust for the government.

"There's a difference between hunting recreationally—and using it as an excuse to leave life behind and spend a few days drunk off your ass—and what we're talking about with the Conlon twins and Madison. Most locals can hunt, but it's more of a conditional thing. They get up early, they head out to the stands they have set up, and they spend the day out there. Not everyone takes it to the lengths where you're becoming one with the forest," Maggie said.

That made sense. Vic tapped his finger on the steering wheel. "The unsub falls into the latter category. It'd be almost impossible to track who has those abilities if they don't broadcast it, even with a narrowed-down population, but it's something."

That was the problem, though. All they had were a bunch of disconnected puzzle pieces. He knew from experience that if they managed to close the case, they'd have the gift of hindsight to put everything in its place.

There was no telling if they'd put things together fast enough to help the innocents among the missing hikers. Those kids wouldn't realize that one of their own had potentially turned against them. They'd see a friendly face and have just enough time to experience hope before things went to hell in a handbasket.

CHAPTER FOURTEEN

Five years ago, July

Madison didn't realize that she had no intention of going back to camp yet until darkness fell with her still in the forest. She blinked in the low light, part of her wondering how it'd gotten so dark so quickly. But she knew better. Once the sun made contact with the top of the mountains, everything went fast.

That didn't change the fact that she was going to have to be careful making her way back to Fifty Mountain if she didn't want to get hopelessly lost. She hadn't brought her pack, though she still wore her lightweight jacket.

Compared with what waited for her at their camp, getting lost would almost be a relief.

She knew she was being hypocritical, but she couldn't help it. *Her* secret wasn't poisoning and hurting those around her . . . was it?

No. It wasn't even in the same league. There might be hurt feelings when Lauren and Josh and Ethan found out that she was planning on leaving town, but it wasn't like she was burning bridges. That's exactly what Lauren and Josh were doing.

Relationships came and went. Friendship was supposed to be forever.

There would be no coming back from this once Ashleigh and Ethan knew. Ethan and Josh might be okay in a couple of years, if only because they couldn't avoid each other indefinitely since they were twins. But everyone else?

There was no escaping it. Lauren and Josh had ruined *everything*.

"Mads."

She jumped half a foot and bit down a curse before realizing she had no reason not to curse. She wasn't hunting or camping with her parents. So she gritted her teeth and forced the word out. *"Fuck."*

"Mads?"

She turned, wishing it was anyone else who had come to find her. "Ethan, what are you doing here?" He moved between two trees, his broad shoulders scraping against the bark. Josh was big, but Ethan had always been more giant than man. In grade school, he'd been teased for being too quiet—too *weird*—until he came back in the fall of seventh grade six inches taller than anyone in their class. No one had dared provoke him after that.

Not that he'd done much to deserve the reputation he'd acquired. Josh was the one with the hair trigger. Ethan only got into fights because he couldn't stand to let his brother go it alone.

And Josh had repaid his loyalty by sleeping with Ethan's girlfriend.

Fury rose, smothering her lingering guilt and leaving only ash in its wake. She was so freaking tired. For the first time, knowing she was leaving town before summer ended was a relief instead of a burden.

"You're going the wrong way." He jerked a thumb over his shoulder. "Camp is back there."

"Maybe I'm not going back to camp." She wanted to tell him, to take his hand and lead him away from camp and just . . . go. It made her sick to her stomach thinking of Ethan left alone in Kalispell while Lauren and Josh screwed around behind his back.

"Really?" Interest lit his dark eyes. "Where are you going?"

Nowhere. Everywhere. Anywhere that wasn't there.

She swallowed hard and managed a smile. "No, you're right. We should both be heading back." If she was smart, she'd keep her mouth shut, ride out the rest of the trip, and get the hell away from everyone. But if there was an innocent in this mess, it was Ethan, and Madison had never been the type of person to sit silently when she saw something wrong. "Ethan . . ."

His expression immediately closed. "Yeah?"

He was giving her a chance to back out of whatever she was about to say, but she'd already decided on her path. Madison looked away, realized what a cowardly move it was, and met his gaze. "Your brother and Lauren . . . I saw them . . ."

"I know."

"*What?* If you knew, why . . ." She sounded so bitter, but she couldn't stop. Madison pointed back the way she'd come. "How long has this been going on?"

"More than once, if that's what you're asking."

"How long have you known?"

"Since the first time." He finally looked away. "I can't give Lauren what she needs. I tried. It didn't work."

She grabbed his arm, turning him to face her. "Don't you dare. This isn't your fault. If things weren't working out, then she should have ended the relationship. That's how it's supposed to go. She's not supposed to fuck your brother." She flinched. "I'm sorry. I'm making this worse, aren't I?"

"No." He covered her hand with his and then let it fall away. "You're trying to help."

Which wasn't the same as saying that she was actually helping. She ran her hands through her hair. "It's not fair. They shouldn't be doing that to you."

"What about Ashleigh?"

"Ashleigh can take care of herself." She wasn't lacking in guilt, either. "What are you going to do?"

"Leave."

Of them all, Ethan loved this place even more than she did. If she'd been forced to choose one of her friends who'd leave Kalispell behind—besides Ashleigh—he would have been at the bottom of the list. But that was before the truths this trip revealed. "Where will you go?"

"I enlisted in the Army." He shrugged when her eyes went wide. "My grades aren't good enough to get into college. Even if they were, that's not what I want."

"What *do* you want?"

He looked at her for a long moment, and she found herself holding her breath, though she couldn't admit why. Finally Ethan gave a half smile. "To get out of here. To be free. To create enough time and space for me to figure out what I really do want."

She released her pent-up breath. "That sounds like why I'm leaving."

"College?"

"Yeah. In Seattle."

She'd been so worried about what kind of reaction he and the others would have, but he just nodded as if it was something he'd suspected all along. "You'll be happy there."

"I hope so." She hesitated. "When are you going to tell Josh and Lauren?" She wasn't sure what she was asking. When he'd tell them he knew what they'd been doing. When he'd tell them that he was leaving. Maybe both.

All the warmth left his face, making her feel like she was looking at a stranger. "I'm not."

◆ ◆ ◆

Tuesday, June 20
3:00 p.m.

Vic's phone rang as they walked out of the high school. He recognized the number instantly. "Give me a second?"

"Tell Britton I said hi." Maggie's smile was almost wistful as she accepted the keys from him and walked to the rental car.

Well, hell. Vic was feeling pretty damn wistful right now, too. He answered before the emotion could get the best of him. "Sutherland."

"I have something for you."

That was new. Normally, Britton called for reports and used those short conversations as a way to let his agents off-load frustrations and get a new perspective. It had bugged the shit out of Vic originally, because he took it as criticism of his ability to do the job right. Now he saw it for the benefit it was. When an agent was in the middle of a case—especially a case that stretched on for months—they often lost the ability to see the forest for the trees.

Even considering that, two calls in as many days was unusual.

He stopped walking and checked to ensure no one was within eavesdropping range. "We've had some developments as well."

"Ethan Conlon was in the Army—a Ranger."

Vic stopped short. "There's nothing in the files about him having served."

"He was in for four years, as best I can tell. Dishonorably discharged, though someone rather high up the line has ensured that it doesn't pop in normal background checks."

That was hard to do, and a waste of time. It was easier to mask what a soldier did during their time enlisted than it was to mask the enlistment itself. Why bother? "Either he did something very, very bad, or he was the tool of someone who did the same."

"I'm inclined to agree. The discharge came a little over a year ago, so he's still fresh. It's something to take into account—both for the case and for the safety of you and the search-and-rescue folk."

Because an Army Ranger was a whole different story than your average lost hiker. Though Vic was starting to get the feeling that none of the lost hikers were exactly what they seemed. "It's possible—probable, even, at this point—that the unsub is one of the missing hikers. With the exception of Ashleigh Marcinko, they're all more than capable of hunting in the same way he's been hunting."

"Careful with your pronouns, Vic."

He exhaled. "Yeah, I know. The profile leans male, but there are no guarantees, and after how things fell out with the case in Clear Springs, I'm not willing to make assumptions anymore. Easier to just stick a *he* on there when we're talking, though."

"Just ensure that it's not coloring your view of things. This case reads strange to me. Hunting is a traditionally masculine hobby, though that may be overgeneralizing it."

"There's something off about this one." It wasn't until he spoke that he realized what had been bothering him. "There's no frenzy, and even though the unsub gets up close and personal with the bodies, the killing blow is delivered from a distance. That should make the whole thing methodical, but there are breaks in the pattern. The unsub smeared honey on the last male victim's eyes postmortem."

"A significant amount of anger there."

"Yeah, but also squeamish." He shook his head. "There's something there, some piece that we're missing. Bill Haglund was the Conlon twins' cousin, but I have a hunch he wasn't killed because of that connection. I think he saw something he wasn't supposed to." Though that didn't explain why Jennifer Haglund didn't have the same thing done to her.

"Time will tell."

That was the problem—they didn't have enough time. Vic looked up at the sky. It was still raining, the overcast giving the afternoon the feel of pending night. "You got anything else for me?"

"Be careful, Vic. This case is becoming complicated for a variety of reasons, and I don't see it untangling itself before the end."

On that, they could agree. "We'll find this guy." The question was whether they could find him before he did any more damage. "We'll keep an eye on any of the hikers we find—make sure it's not the unsub in sheep's clothing." They wouldn't be able to tell just by looking at them. This guy had managed to pass well enough not to be caught up until this point, but he'd only been at it for a year. "There had to be a trigger. Something happened to push the unsub over the edge—from fantasizing about killing people to actually killing them. Normally, given the evidence of the other two murders in the other parks, I'd assume there were kills we never found—or at least some kind of criminal history."

"But?"

"But it doesn't feel right for me. Something about this group makes me think this is personal. This is skewing almost into spree-killing territory. If it wasn't for the exact same MO being in all the murders, I'd almost think we had two separate killers."

"Is that likely?"

Vic considered it. "No. Not with the timeline. It's *possible*, but I think calling it probable would be stretching the definition to the breaking point."

"I tend to agree." Britton sighed. "This one is going to get messy. When are you heading back into the park?"

"I was aiming for tomorrow, but I think it'd be wiser to stay in town and continue this avenue of investigation until either the hikers or another body is found. Tucker is with the local Feds, digging deeper into the hikers' background—they'll need to talk to locals who graduated with them and see if that offers any insight—and we still need to get a warrant to dig into the financial background of the hikers to see if there's any record of any of them buying the weapons the unsub uses. It's a long shot, but it needs to be done. I want this guy buttoned up and gift wrapped for the lawyers, and short of finding him in the act of murdering someone, that's going to be impossible unless we have the evidence to back it up." The rain chose that moment to pick up, and he headed for the car. "I'll keep you updated."

"See that you do."

And that was that.

He was so focused on getting the rental going and the defroster up and running that it took Vic a few precious minutes to realize Maggie hadn't said anything. He found her arms crossed, her gaze straight ahead, though it was pretty obvious that her mind was elsewhere. "Something wrong?"

"Hmm? No, not exactly." She shrugged. "I just didn't expect to miss it."

Even though he knew what she was talking about, he still asked. "It?"

"This. The investigating. Pitting ourselves against the worst humanity has to offer. The whole team atmosphere that Britton has cultivated. It's not comfortable being in this position where I feel like I'm back, but not really back." She ran her hands through her hair, dislodging her hair tie. "It's fine. I'm fine."

Maybe it was time to finally clear the air. Vic had always trod cautiously when it came to Maggie. Not because she was sensitive and fragile—the exact opposite—but because when he was around her, *he* was likely to react before thinking.

He wanted to comfort her, to make her happy, even if what he really should be doing was spitting hard truth. "I said it before, but that doesn't make it less true. That Drover case would have broken any new agent. I've been doing this damn near nine years, and cases involving kids still have me questioning everything about this world and what good we're actually doing."

"I thought I wanted kids."

For a second, he was sure he must have misheard her, but of course he hadn't. Vic reached across the console and took her hand before he could think of a reason not to. "Maggie—"

"Knowing what's out there . . . that's something I can't unknow. How can I bring a kid into this world knowing they might end up prey to one of the monsters? It's wrong and it's selfish, and I won't do it."

She was breaking his heart. He squeezed her hand. "Maggie, the BAU spends all its time hunting monsters, which gives us a disproportionate reality about how many of them there actually are."

"Really? Because I think you have pretty damn good job security. Almost nine years as a federal agent, and have you ever shown up for work and *not* had a case demanding your attention?"

She had him there, but she was also missing the point. "If you don't want children, there's nothing wrong with that. But don't let fear dictate your decision."

"Do *you* want kids?"

He started to jerk back and caught himself.

Not soon enough, because she gave him a sad smile. "Didn't think so."

"Now wait a damn minute. You know the divorce rates in any law-enforcement–type job are significantly higher than those of civilians. I'm a statistic now. I'd have to be in a rock-solid relationship to even consider it, and that hasn't happened yet."

"You were married."

"And you know what my marriage was like—through no fault of Janelle's. We just didn't fit, and neither did our vision for what our relationship should be like." He hated thinking about how he'd failed his ex. He hadn't set out to end up divorced when he proposed all those years ago, but time had a way of changing people, and he and Janelle had changed in separate ways. Instead of their experiences forging them tighter together, they'd cleaved them apart.

For a long time, he'd taken full blame for things ending. It was only in the last two years that he'd realized Janelle had as much a hand in their divorce as he did. She'd gone into their relationship expecting to be able to mold him into the husband she'd always wanted. He could have tried harder, true, but people didn't change. Not really. If he'd tried, he would have failed, and the final implosion of their marriage would have been far uglier as a result.

"Even with the right person . . ." He took a deep breath. "I'm gone more often than I'm home. It'd come down to a choice between my family and the BAU."

"Exactly." She carefully extracted her hand from his. "It's okay, Vic. You don't have to explain it to me—and you're not going to change my mind. I love Glacier, and I love being a park ranger, but sometimes I catch myself wondering if I could be doing more good if I was back in the FBI."

He flipped the windshield wipers onto a higher speed and turned onto the street. "No one can decide that except you."

"Thanks, Obi-Wan." But some of the darkness left her tone. "But enough about me. We have plenty to worry about otherwise. The school was a dead end."

"Yeah." The principal had held the position for more than a decade, and the man claimed to remember clearly every one of the missing hikers—and the Haglunds. According to him and every teacher they could track down who had worked at the school at the time, the entire group of kids had been those type of people who seemed to get along well enough with everyone. The Conlon twins—Joshua, specifically—got into a bit of trouble with fighting, and Ashleigh had been caught bringing vodka to school in a water bottle on two occasions, but there weren't any giant red flags. And if the unsub wasn't one of the hikers, they were still no closer to answers, because it didn't appear that anyone had trouble of the variety that would cause five years of pent-up rage.

"Could be love." When Maggie just stared, he realized he'd spoken aloud. "I was thinking of motive."

"I gathered that you weren't professing it to me." She laughed, the sound forced.

Vic checked the clock. "You know what? Let's put this on hold. I'll drop you off at home, meet up with Tucker for a few, and then swing back to take you to dinner."

The break was what they needed right now. They could keep beating away at the case, but the facts weren't going to magically reform themselves into an answer. More information was needed, and until they had that, they were stuck.

And he wanted time without having to share her with the case.

He flat-out wanted *her*.

◆ ◆ ◆

Tuesday, June 20
5:49 p.m.

Maggie showered and changed into jeans and a tank top as soon as she got home, forcing herself to slow down and take her time. Then she made a sandwich, even though the last thing she felt like doing was eating. Even after all that, she still had ages until Vic was supposed to show up, which left her with nothing to do but pace and flip-flop over whether she was really willing to go on a date without dressing up a bit, or if she should just call the whole thing off. Desperate for a distraction, she called Wyatt.

"Good lord, Maggie, when I told you to take the night off, I meant actually take the night off. Do you know what time it is?"

The clock said it was twenty to seven, which was still a reasonable hour to be making phone calls. She frowned. "Have you slept since this started?"

"When would I have the time to sleep?" He seemed to realize he was in danger of yelling at her, because when he spoke again, he'd tempered his tone. "Is there a reason for this call?"

Now that she had him on the phone, she felt kind of silly. "I was just checking in to see if there were any developments."

"If something had happened that required your presence, you would have heard about it." There was background noise that sounded a lot like him knocking things around on his desk. "The search parties are still fine, though Jerry got a nasty cut on his shoulder that he's going to have to get looked at when he's back. No one has found anything, and what little signs there were are gone with the storm. Our people are camping out tonight, and then I'm sending a secondary team out tomorrow—which I'd like you to be part of, FBI agent tagging along or no."

"I'll be there."

"Good. Enjoy your night off and show up ready to spend a few days out there. The weather is supposed to clear for the next four days at least, so we need to make headway before then."

The longer those hikers were missing, the less likely they were to be found alive. The unsub had nothing to do with those odds—the weather and exposure and half a dozen other things could kill a person in Glacier. She hung up, not sure if she should feel disheartened that no one had been found yet or grateful that she'd be back in the park and doing something that would keep her moving and her mind off all the things that had been twisting her up since Vic rolled back into her life.

Maggie checked the clock—a grand total of five minutes had passed. She paced from one side of her tiny place to the other. Too much time across the board. So she did the only thing she could think to do. She called Ava.

"Why are you calling me? You actually have a night off, and you're wasting both our time right now." She could almost hear the frown in

Ava's voice. "Unless you're calling to gloat, in which case I might have to kill you and bury your body in the park."

"That joke isn't nearly as funny now as it was two weeks ago."

Ava chuckled. "I know." A creak sounded over the line, confirming that she was in the minuscule office they mostly used to store paperwork that hadn't made its way into the digital age yet. "So if you're not gloating and you're not calling to try to get me to convince Wyatt to let you back early—which I won't, by the way—then why *are* you calling?"

Now that she had her friend on the phone, she barely had the courage to admit what a mess she was. "I don't know how to do this."

"This? Or *him*? Because if I have to explain how tab A goes into slot B, I think we might need to have a completely different talk."

"Ava, be serious."

"I *am* being serious." She could almost see her friend roll her eyes. "Let me guess—and correct me if I'm wrong. Hot Fed finally got the balls to ask you out, and now you're a picture of Catholic guilt because you think you should be killing yourself to close this case and not jumping at the chance to jump Hot Fed."

"I'm not Catholic."

"You might as well be." Ava snorted. "Bet you five bucks you already called Wyatt just in case you missed something or he changed his mind about flying you in in the dark."

"Shut up." Her skin flared hot, and she didn't need to look in a mirror to know she was blushing. After living together for three years, she and Ava knew each other better than most married couples, but that didn't mean she liked being called on it. Maggie took half a second to consider ending the call, but she'd just go back to driving herself nuts. "What am I supposed to do on this date?"

"What normal people do on dates—eat somewhere they have cloth napkins, drink something fruity, and have a conversation that doesn't revolve around murder. Bonus points if you manage to skip talking about work, too."

"You're not helping."

"Wrong. I'm helping. You're just being difficult." Ava sighed. "Look, this is your what-if guy. Missing a chance to find out the answer to that because you feel guilty over something outside your control is just downright stupid. You're not stupid, Maggie. Stubborn to a clinical degree, yes. Stupid, no."

"Gee, thanks."

"You're welcome." Ava didn't bother to be sarcastic. "Now, you're wasting both our time. Hang up and pour yourself a shot of that vodka I stashed in the freezer. Breathe. Relax. Actually try to enjoy this break and see where it goes with Hot Fed."

Maggie opened the freezer and snagged the promised bottle of vodka. "You make it sound so reasonable when you say it like that." She didn't bother with a shot glass, pinning the phone between her ear and shoulder while she unscrewed the cap and took a healthy swig. She closed it before she could drink more. One was enough.

"Because it *is* reasonable."

A knocking on her flimsy front door had her turning toward the sound. "He's early. No surprise there."

"Go get him, tiger."

CHAPTER FIFTEEN

Tuesday, June 20
6:51 p.m.

Maggie opened the door, her breath stalling in her throat at the sight of Vic standing under her eave. He'd found time to change into a different pair of jeans and a black henley shirt that hugged his chest and shoulders. Apparently she was right on target in her jeans and tank top, because the look he gave her as his eyes swept over her from boots to head made her entire body perk up and take notice. "You look good, Maggie."

"Do you—" Her voice broke, and she had to clear her throat. "Do you want to come in?"

"Yes. But I won't." He gave a half smile. "I promised you a date, and if I come in, leaving is going to be the last thing on either of our minds."

It struck her that Vic had been driving this thing between them from the start. She'd been a more than willing passenger, but she'd been passive to a criminal degree. *No longer.* Maggie took a step back, and then another, painfully aware of the way he watched her every move. "You know, I'm not really hungry."

Vic's fists clenched. "Maggie, you're playing havoc with my control."

"Don't you ever get tired of being in control of everything?" She reached her arms over her head and pulled her shirt off, leaving her in jeans and her bra. "We don't need a date, Vic. Even with seven years of distance between us, I know you. A couple hours' worth of small talk isn't going to make a difference when you've seen me at my worst. If you still want me after that, then I don't want to waste any more time."

He stepped into the house and kicked the door shut behind him. "I'll always want you, Maggie." Vic stalked toward her, his long striding eating up the distance so fast her heart lodged in her throat. "Always. Endlessly." And then he was on her, his hands sliding around her waist and jerking her against his body, his mouth taking hers as if it had been his all along.

This time, Maggie didn't wait for him to drive things. She traced the seam of his lips with her tongue, delving inside when he opened for her. Vic tasted like the peppermints he liked to eat when he was thinking hard on a case. She slid her hands down his chest and back up again. He was so damn big. Big and strong and careful with her in spite of it.

She wanted . . .

Him.

She wanted him.

She broke the kiss long enough to peel his shirt off and let loose a laugh when he undid the back of her bra with a smooth move. "You learned that in high school, didn't you?"

"Guilty." His voice went deeper. "Never been so grateful for the girl who took pity on me and showed me how it was done." Vic lifted her effortlessly, pinning her against the wall, kissing his way down her neck to her breasts without missing a beat. "You are so damn beautiful." His whiskers rasped over her skin, making her shiver.

She arched her back in a silent offering that he took full advantage of. It was like a fever dream she never wanted to wake up from. Vic was here, his hands on her body, his mouth tracing tantalizing patterns from one nipple to the other. The temptation to close her eyes was almost too much, but she didn't want to miss a thing.

Not when the one thing she'd always wanted—and always denied herself—was finally within her grasp.

There was nothing standing between them now. They had no reason to stop.

Vic lifted her higher, the wall sliding along her bare back, and licked a line from her belly button to the top of her jeans. "How likely are we to actually knock a hole in your wall?"

She choked. "Pretty likely."

"Thought so." He let her slide back down his body until their hips lined up. "Where's your bed?"

"Door at the end of the hall." Maggie laughed when he started in that direction. "You can let me down. I'm more than capable of walking."

"You won't be when I get through with you."

She blinked. "You know, the times I pictured what it would be like to go to bed with you never included you being this . . ." She picked and discarded several word choices before settling on "possessive."

The grin he gave her was the personification of said word. "You've spent a lot of time thinking about us."

"Well . . . yeah." There was no point in denying it. She clung to him as he walked them to the bed. "Don't try to say you haven't."

"I wouldn't dream of it." He laid her on the bed and settled his weight between her thighs. "I've spent more nights than I can count thinking about what it would mean to have you like this. To be with you like this."

He moved away long enough to peel her jeans off and strip her out of her underwear and bra. Maggie propped herself up on her elbows and watched, his movements no less sexy for their efficiency. The body he revealed was one she'd pictured time and time again, but her imagination hadn't done it justice. In normal cases, Vic was in the gym during his downtime because the physical activity helped him put things together. Apparently that was a habit he still had, because his body was *cut.* "Jeez, Vic."

He stopped, his hands on the button of his jeans. "Second thoughts?"

"No. *God, no.*" She sat up fully. "I'm just admiring the goods."

His eyes darkened. "You're not the only one." He left his jeans on and took the single step that brought him to the edge of the bed. "Fuck, Maggie." He leaned down and ran his hand from her throat, between her breasts, and over her stomach, stopping just short of where she already ached for him. "I don't have words to describe your body."

She followed his hand as he did another circuit, stroking her in a way that would be almost innocent if not for the fact she was naked and the look in his eyes was consuming her. Her body was her body. She knew she was supposed to hate it because she wasn't a size six or under, but her body was strong and tough and had never failed her. She could hike a dozen miles in a day without failing. She could climb and rappel and carry someone for a not-inconsiderable distance.

The one guy she'd been with in her failed dating experiment hadn't liked that she could break him "in half" if she wanted to.

Vic was looking at her like he wanted to push them both to their physical limits, until they were so exhausted they couldn't move.

She wasn't sure her crappy little place wouldn't be rubble around them by the time they were finished, but she grabbed his hand and pressed it between her thighs. "Stop teasing me."

"I'm just getting started." He went to his knees at the edge of the bed, hauling her a few precious inches closer, so that it was only his grip keeping her from sliding to the ground. His breath ghosted across her sensitive skin, followed by his whiskers scraping over her inner thighs. She tensed, holding her breath.

He didn't make her wait this time. His mouth found her, his tongue delving and exploring until she was sure the top of her head would explode. *"Vic."*

His growl vibrated against her clit, but he didn't pick up his pace or stop that slow, torturous exploration that pushed her, second by second, closer to the edge. She gripped her sheets on either side of her hips, trying to arch against his mouth, but he held her immobile.

So close . . .

He lifted his head. "Not yet, Maggie."

She cried out at the loss. "Please. Don't leave me like this." But he was already moving, slipping off his jeans and grabbing something out of the pocket. She heard the crinkle of what had damn well better be a condom wrapper seconds before he slipped an arm under the small of her back, crawling onto the bed and taking her with him.

"When you come, it's going to be with me inside you." He kissed her. She could taste herself on his lips, and with his mouth exploring hers the same way he'd explored the other part of her body, she completely forgave him for leaving her teetering on the brink.

She forgot why she'd been frustrated the second he guided his cock to her entrance. Vic braced his hands on either side of her head and lifted himself enough to see her eyes. "You sure about this?"

"Yes." She didn't wait for him to ask again—because he was going to. Instead, she looped her leg around his waist and arched up, sheathing him deep inside her. He went still, his forehead resting against hers. She found herself holding her breath again. Now was the time when he'd say something about this being a mistake, about her pushing them too hard.

But he didn't say a single thing.

Vic kissed her, long and deep. And then he moved. Each stroke was a long, sensuous slide, his big body pinning her in place so all she could do was take it.

Her climax rolled over her in a wave. She cried out his name as she came, and buried her face in his neck. Maggie was vaguely aware of his pumping becoming faster, harder, but she just clung to him, trying to remember how to breathe.

Vic came with a curse, driving into her one last time. She kissed his neck—the only part of him she could reach without moving. "Damn, Vic."

He pulled out of her and tucked her so that her back was against his chest. She had a moment of confusion, but then his hand was between her thighs again. "I've waited seven years for this. Once isn't going to be enough."

She spread her legs wider and looped one over his so that she was completely open to him. It was easier to focus on what he was doing to her physically than to deal with his words. "Randy bastard, aren't you?"

He laughed hoarsely. "I might not be twenty-five anymore, but I'm nowhere near done with you, Maggie."

◆ ◆ ◆

Wednesday, June 21
5:38 a.m.

Vic woke early, as he often did, but that was the only thing normal about the current situation. He rolled over and watched Maggie sleep for a few minutes. Her hair was a tangle over the pillow, and her face was completely relaxed for the first time since he'd met her. He ran a hand over her arm, tugging the sheet down as he did.

"Coffee." Maggie spoke without opening her eyes.

"I thought you were asleep."

"I am asleep, and I will be until coffee." She smiled and burrowed deeper beneath the sheet, looking too damn cute for words.

Vic rolled out of bed and padded down the hall to the kitchen. It took a little riffling through the cupboards to find where she kept everything, but since the space was small, he had a pot of coffee going before too long. The laws of the universe meant that balance must be had, so he made the coffee strong because there was no possibility that shit *wouldn't* hit the fan.

He had a cup in each hand and had just reached the doorway when a phone went off. "Mine or yours?"

"Mine." She reached for her nightstand, her eyes still closed, and dragged the phone to her ear. "Yeah? Wyatt?" She sat up, instantly alert, and shoved her hair out of her face. "When did they find him? Any sign of the others?" She listened, nodding. "Okay, we'll be there in fifteen. Yeah." Her gaze met Vic's, and there was nothing but bad news there. "I'll call Agent Sutherland."

As if on cue, his phone started ringing. He set the coffee on the dresser so he could answer. "Sutherland."

"Where are you? I just went to your hotel room, and you didn't answer."

It would just figure that Tucker actually sought him out the one time he wasn't readily available. "I'm out. What's going on?"

"They found another body. Too early to tell more than the bare facts, but basic description matches Joshua Conlon. Guess that means we can knock him off the suspect list, too."

"Guess so." Vic pointed to the coffee cup when Maggie started to stand. She shot him a look but accepted it and took a long sip despite its temperature. "You get anything more since we talked last?"

"No. I think you're onto something with one of the hikers being the unsub. Everyone I talked to yesterday who graduated with them said what we already know—they were friends, Joshua Conlon had a temper, but no one had the kind of lasting problem with another that would spawn something like that." There was traffic in the background.

"Unless something changed and you want me to be the one to check out the crime scene, I'll head into the local Feds' office and get started on the financials of the hikers left alive."

"I'm going back in."

"Thought so. I'll handle the morgue this afternoon once the body is recovered."

That made sense. There was a decent chance that going in for the body would end up like the last time, with several days spent hiking through the park in search of more evidence. The investigation couldn't be put on hold because he wasn't there to micromanage. It still took more effort than it should have for him to say, "You deal with things on this end and we'll meet in the middle once I get back."

"Watch your back in there."

"Will do." He hung up. It had taken nearly a year, but it was starting to feel like he and Tucker were hitting their stride. *Probably took so long because we're both old, stubborn bastards.*

Maggie set her cup down. "Guessing you just got the same call I did."

"New body, probably Joshua Conlon, though we'll have to see him to know for sure." Unless a bear got to him. "I didn't get details about his exact location."

"I did." She stood and stretched, giving him the view of a lifetime. If it weren't for the pressing nature of their calls, he'd tell the whole world to go to hell and take her back to bed for another twenty-four hours or so. It wasn't an option. It might not be an option again before this case ran its course.

Vic met her at the corner of the mattress and pulled her into his arms. "Promise me something."

"We really don't have time for this." But she leaned into him all the same.

All they'd ever had was borrowed time. He sifted his fingers through her hair, tilting her head back so she looked him in the eyes. "I'm not going to insult you by telling you to be careful."

"Good."

He tugged gently on her hair. "If you have a shot at this guy, take it."

Maggie's eyes went wide. "You can't be saying what I think you're saying."

He didn't even know what he was trying to accomplish with this, but the thought of her falling victim to their hunter made him sick to his stomach. "I don't mean murder the unsub in cold blood—but if it's you or him, don't hesitate. I just found you again. I don't want to lose you."

"I'm trying really hard to be charmed by your overprotectiveness instead of annoyed." She pushed up on her toes to kiss him. "I'm not going to sacrifice myself, but we're going out there to look at this body and find these kids. That's it. Whatever you think in your worst-case scenario, he's not going to show himself. The unsub is on a mission— and the search-and-rescue people might be a pain to get around, but I don't think he'll go after them unless he's forced to."

That was the problem, though. It might not take much for the unsub to feel threatened. They had more people out in the park than he was used to, and that was a threat in the making. All it would take was for one of the pairs of people to stumble on him, and they might have more victims on their hands. There wasn't anything else to do. He'd warned Wyatt, and short of trying to radio every person individually . . . But even that wouldn't make a difference, because they couldn't anticipate where the unsub would strike next.

Except . . .

"You've got that look in your eye. What are you thinking?"

He pressed a quick kiss to Maggie's forehead. "I need to make a call. Can you be ready in fifteen?"

"Yes." She grabbed her cup of coffee and headed for the bathroom.

Vic spent half a second considering joining her in the shower before he set it aside. He called Tucker, already speaking the second his partner answered. "I think there's a link to the order of deaths."

Tucker was silent for half a beat. "If we set aside the murders in the other two parks—say they're practice and only connected because of opportunity—that leaves us with the four victims in Glacier. They all went to high school together, and even if they didn't necessarily move in the same circles, that school isn't big enough to pretend that they never ran into one another. Especially when you take into account that Bill Haglund and the Conlon twins were cousins. Doesn't mean they were close, but it means that they interacted on some level."

"Take the Haglunds out of it for now. I think they were first because they stumbled onto the unsub's camp—or permanent structure, if he has one." Vic paced into the kitchen and refilled his coffee mug. "Focusing on the other two—Lauren and Joshua. Something triggered the unsub, and that something is linked to the order of the deaths. I'm sure of it."

"Okay, I'll play."

"Ruth Garcia said that Josh and Lauren are together now—and that they were both dating other people in high school."

"Lauren with Ethan and Josh with Ashleigh."

"If I heard the undertones correctly, their relationship might have started before the other two ended."

"You really think someone is pissed off enough about that that they're going to start killing people five years later?" Tucker took a deep breath. "What am I saying? People have been killed for less. You thinking what I'm thinking?"

"Ethan Conlon is looking pretty damn good for this."

◆ ◆ ◆

Wednesday, June 21
9:17 a.m.

Maggie had never felt so conflicted in her life. On one hand, she'd just spent a glorious night with Vic. Having him touch her like that, make love to her while whispering things in her ears that she hadn't allowed herself to dream, was beyond . . . just beyond. Her body ached with what he'd done to her, and she cherished the feeling.

Because they wouldn't have the opportunity to do it again anytime soon.

She noted the markings the SAR people had left on the path and veered left, maneuvering over a fallen tree as she led Vic downhill to where the body had been found. *Four.* Four bodies in less than week was like something out of a nightmare. As much as she'd always wanted a chance to explore the what-if that had been left open-ended with Vic all those years ago, she hadn't wanted it at the expense of anyone's life.

Rationally, one had nothing to do with the other. The unsub still would be murdering these people even if it was a different FBI agent assigned to the case, or if she was working at a different park. Knowing that didn't help ease the irrational guilt wrapping itself around her throat.

"You've been quiet."

She didn't look over her shoulder, even though Vic's voice was close and she could feel him at her back. "Lots to think about."

"Regrets?"

It was just like him to sum up so much with a single word. She'd set the tone last night, and now he was giving her a way out. It made her lo—

No. No time for dancing along that line of insanity.

Maggie shook her head, still not looking at him. "No. I wish that different circumstances had brought you here, and I don't even know what to think of the future, but I don't regret last night at all."

She wasn't sure, but he might have exhaled in relief. "We can talk about the future after we catch this guy."

Which implied that there might actually *be* a future for them. She gritted her teeth, angry at herself for being so damn selfish. They were less than a mile from a man who had died cold and alone and probably terrified out of his mind—and she was preoccupied with her love life. She finally stopped and looked at Vic. He wore serviceable clothing, the same way he had the entire time he'd been in Montana, and looked at home in his pack and jacket.

She wanted to kiss him.

It was totally inappropriate.

Maggie scrubbed a hand over her face. "Right. We'll talk once the case is closed." She had to *focus*. It wasn't like her to let bullshit get in the way of her job, but then, nothing about Vic was bullshit—or simple.

"Maggie." He waited for her to look at him. "Make no mistake. There *will* be a future between us—unless you tell me that's not what you want. We've already wasted too much time dicking around. I'm not interested in wasting more."

It sure as hell sounded like he'd just declared his intentions. She opened her mouth, but he beat her to it. "Is that what you want?"

Maggie looked around. "I thought you wanted to have that conversation after the case was over? We're in the middle of it—literally."

"I changed my mind." He shrugged, not looking the least bit repentant. "We can talk details later. You know where I'm at with us. Give me the same courtesy."

She didn't know how he could talk so calmly when it felt like her heart was trying to beat its way out of her chest. She wanted so many things. She always had. Maggie had never been shy about shooting for the stars when she was younger, but after her career in the FBI blew up in her face, she'd gotten gun-shy. She couldn't help it. She'd overestimated her abilities there, and it was always in the back of her mind that she might do the same and get someone else killed.

And here Vic stood so calmly, asking her to put her heart and soul on the line and have faith that it wouldn't backfire in her face.

She wanted to turn and flee into the woods. To leave all this behind and maybe spend the rest of her life without talking to another person that she'd potentially disappoint. It was crazy and irrational and at least she was able to recognize that.

So she straightened her spine and took a leap of faith. "I want you, Vic. I don't know what a future would even look like, but I want to try."

"Good." There was that almost-silent exhale again, and it was *definitely* relief—as if he'd been holding his breath while waiting for her answer.

It struck Maggie that, as scared as she was, Vic had to be feeling something similar. They'd both been burned in the past in different ways, and that kind of pain left its mark.

Maybe it was a good thing that we had seven years to try to figure shit out separately before we ran into each other again.

She managed a smile. "Glad we got that sorted. What do you say we go track down a psycho hunter so we can get around to ironing out the rest of the details?"

"Sounds good to me."

She laughed, which was totally out of line considering the scene they were on their way to view. "Let's go, then." She turned and followed the directions Wyatt had given her during the debriefing. The body had been found in Kipp Creek, wedged between two large rocks. There were the expected two arrows sprouting from his chest, but that was the most that Wyatt knew. Since the body had just been found a few hours ago, the SAR folks had taken their pictures and were waiting for Vic and Maggie to get there before they figured out the best way to extract him.

The trees were so close that she had to slide through them sideways at some points, the underbrush overgrown to a degree that it almost required a machete. The place was primed for a fire. It had been a few decades since one hit this spot with any degree of severity, and the underbrush was out of control.

She heard voices before she saw anyone and used the sound to guide her to where two people stood next to the creek. David gave a weak smile when he saw her. He looked like he was about to pass out on the spot, but he squared his shoulders and nodded, silently telling her that he could handle it. If he didn't secure a full-time job in this park after handling this mess, she'd be really surprised. Most people would have faltered by now, but he was still plodding forward.

The other man was Brent Holland, one of the Flathead County SAR guys, who'd been on countless searches with Maggie since she'd started as a park ranger. He was a couple of inches shorter than she was, and slight, but her first season as a park ranger, he'd run her into the ground half a dozen times.

She could keep up now.

"Maggie Gaines. Long time, no see." He made a face. "Wish it could be in better circumstances."

"Yeah, well, we all wish for better circumstances."

"How about you let me take you out to drink ourselves stupid and banish this experience from the good old memory banks?" He gave her a winning smile that she'd seen work on quite a few women.

"How about not?" she responded automatically, pointedly not looking at David when he snorted. Brent was one of those guys who flirted as naturally as breathing, and when he was stressed, old habits were dialed up to eleven. "Brent, this is Agent Sutherland. He's here investigating the deaths."

"Not doing much of a job of it, is he?" Brent smiled as if he hadn't just insulted Vic. "Kidding. Just kidding."

She bit back a retort, mostly because if she wasn't intimately acquainted with Vic, she might be feeling the same. Having murders in the park offended her on a personal level, and the rest of the staff had to be feeling the same. A certain number of deaths were normal in places like the Grand Canyon or even Grand Teton, but Glacier wasn't those places. They prided themselves on the sheer number of visitors the park had without racking up hundreds of injuries or more than one or two deaths a year.

They weren't going to have that this year.

Brent looked between them, his brow furrowed. "The media get ahold of this yet?"

"They're going to." Vic chose that moment to break his silence, though she had a feeling he'd taken the man's measure in the few seconds they'd spent talking. He stopped next to her. "It's amazing that it's been kept as quiet as it has."

Brent shrugged. "Murder might be good for the asshole reporters, but it's bad for business across the board. Most people recognize that."

Maggie wasn't sure she agreed. All it took was one mauling from a surprised grizzly, and it seemed like everyone and their dog descended on the park to get statements and petition for the removal of the bears once and for all. The media didn't care that Glacier was one of the last bastions for the grizzly population in the United States. All they wanted was a good story and an interview to support it.

"The body?"

Brent seemed to realize that he was sitting here gabbing when he should be working, because he straightened, and his joking demeanor fell away. "Yeah, sorry. I was surprised to see Maggie, and it got me all discombobulated."

"Flatterer." She shook her head. "Wyatt was scarce on the details. David, fill us in?"

"Sure thing." He shot a look at Brent as he walked past the man and then picked his way down to the creek. It was a decent-size creek at this time of year, the snowmelt turning the water treacherous and running up the risk of slipping, drowning, and hypothermia even if a person managed to get out. Their victim hadn't had the chance.

"We are part of the group fanning out between the Continental Divide and Flattop Mountain. Trying to cover as much ground between the trail and the ridge while another team takes the other side. Spent most of last night tucked into a shelter that we threw up last minute in a close stand of trees, and started out at dawn. Found him a little over four hours ago. No way was he alive, but we checked all the same."

She saw what he meant when the body came into view. Some dead bodies looked like they could be sleeping until a person noticed certain details. This guy wasn't one of them. She recognized his face from the group of hikers and mentally matched his name to the one in the file Vic had compiled. "Joshua Conlon."

Vic nodded. "No need for dental records on this one." Not with his face more or less intact.

The same couldn't be said for the rest of him.

◆　◆　◆

Wednesday, June 21
9:45 a.m.

Vic moved past David and Maggie and crouched as close to the body as he could get without wading into the water. The two arrows sticking out of the victim's chest were to be expected. He leaned closer. The water had washed away most of the blood—and there had been a significant amount, judging from the shredded front of the man's shirt. He drew out a pair of gloves he'd stashed in his pocket and yanked one on. It took some balancing to be able to shift the shirt to the side, but he found what he'd suspected. "He was stabbed." He counted a dozen easily recognizable wounds, but the pattern was so frenetic, there might be double that. "The unsub is changing his MO."

"Or maybe he's getting to the victims he really cares about." Maggie sank down next to him, her gaze on the dead body. "Think about it.

He's escalating, and if you're right and he's purposefully picking the order of his victims within the group, that means he's working his way up to a grand finale, so to speak."

They'd have to wait for the autopsy to be sure, but Vic thought the stab wounds had happened while the victim was still alive, rather than postmortem like the field dressing. "Didn't mind getting his hands dirty with this one, did he?"

"Which makes you wonder what sets Joshua Conlon apart from the others."

"Explosive temper. One of the few in the group who seemed almost universally disliked."

Maggie sighed. "If he hadn't turned up dead, my money was on him being the unsub. Though that doesn't really line up with him killing Lauren first. I would have thought he'd work his way up to her since they were together."

"Together, but on the rocks. She dated Ethan back in high school and then switched him out for his twin. That's got to piss a guy off," Vic mused.

"Sure. But why wait this long? And if this has to do with some kind of fixation on her, why kill her first?"

"Following that line of thought, why save Ashleigh and Madison for last? For all accounts, Ashleigh and he haven't spoken since they were teenagers, and they weren't particularly close then."

"I think we might have to face the fact that using the male pronoun when we talk about the unsub might be dead wrong. Both Madison and Ashleigh have just as much motivation to kill Lauren and Joshua as Ethan does. Well, maybe not Madison, but it could just be that we haven't dug deep enough yet to find it." Maggie shook her head, her expression of frustration mirroring his. "We don't have enough information."

"You two are fucking creepy, you know that?"

191

Vic turned to find Brent watching them, his face pale beneath his tan. "It's normal for murder to bother you. It's nothing to be ashamed of."

"I'm fine."

He didn't look fine, but Vic chose not to mention it. Pride was a funny thing, and as much as the "creepy" comment irritated him, they had an investigation to run. He looked at the creek. It wasn't large, as such things went. It was possible that the water had shifted the body a bit, but it wouldn't have moved him far. The dense trees made a shot tricky, but their hunter had already proved himself more than capable of making difficult shots. Still . . . "Even if it wasn't night when he made that shot, it was in the rain."

Maggie followed his gaze. "High ground helps. Lost hikers tend to find water and follow it. Not always helpful in the park, because the Continental Divide means water runs in two different ways—three, technically—so it can confuse the issue. But the end result is that they're on lower ground than the area around it, which makes it easier to stalk them, and it's an easier shot. Unsub could have followed for as long as he wanted without being seen, if he was careful."

Why wait? He exhaled in frustration. They didn't *know* if he'd waited, and for all the talk of careful stalking, there had been nothing careful about the way this victim was stabbed to death. "The arrows slowed him down, weakened him."

"Easy picking for the unsub to swoop in with a knife." Maggie frowned. "Kind of like Lauren, when you think about it." She must have caught David's shocked expression, because she held up her hands. "I'm not saying he lured a bear there to finish the job. There are so many factors there that can't be accounted for, and this guy is too careful. I'm just saying that maybe it gave him an idea."

Vic tried to picture it. The hunt, the thrill beating through the unsub's blood, the surge of victory knowing his arrows struck true. Was there fear seeing the bear go after the girl? No . . . not fear. Not after the initial surprise. "It's the right way of things, nature taking its course. I bet he sees grizzlies as equal predators, or predators as equal in a general whole."

"That's pretty sick," Brent muttered.

Maggie glared. "Either be helpful or go get the stretcher ready. You're distracting."

David jumped into action. "We'll get the stretcher. Come on, Brent." He ushered the other man away, shooting a silent apology over his shoulder at them.

Maggie waited for them to move beyond eavesdropping range before she lowered her voice. "This stabbing wasn't about drawing in another predator. He wanted this kill for himself."

"Yes." It was personal, similar to Bill Haglund, but even more so, which stood up to his theory that Bill Haglund had done something to piss off the unsub but hadn't figured into the original plan. Vic sat back on his heels. "It's not normal for a woman to kill like this." When Maggie shot him a look, he amended, "You know what I mean—the hunting is hypermasculine."

"Traditionally, sure. But all the murders up to this point have been from a distance. The unsub field-dresses them, but it's postmortem. There's an emotional distance there that lends itself to the theory that the unsub is a woman." Maggie shrugged. "Or at least doesn't present evidence to the contrary."

"The unsub didn't field-dress Joshua," Vic said.

"No, he or she didn't. If our theory about one of the missing hikers being responsible is correct, there are only three options left—and two of them are women."

Which prompted the question—why? Vic turned again to look at the surrounding area. "I think time of death is going to be our answer." Too many kills in such a short time, too much to jam into a limited agenda. The clock started ticking the second the hikers scattered. It was only a matter of time before SAR found the survivors, one by one.

The unsub had to get to them first or miss the opportunity altogether. "Sloppy," he murmured.

"How do you figure?"

"If the hikers hadn't scattered, he wouldn't be pressed right now. Leaving Bill Haglund's body at Fifty Mountain pretty much guaranteed that he'd be putting himself on a tight timeline. There's a difference between a challenge and the nearly impossible situation he's in now."

"Unless . . ." She bit her bottom lip, but then charged on. "This is going to sound paranoid in the extreme, but what if he planned on it? What if he's . . . herding them? He would have had to do something like that if he's going after them in a particular order." She stood and waved to indicate the area. "Even in the rain, this is a prime spot for an ambush. If he had some way of guaranteeing at least one of them would head this way, then all he had to do was sit up there and wait." She narrowed her eyes. "In those conditions, range is going to be a little limited, and it'd be nearly impossible to cover up all traces with the wet ground. I bet if we search that ridge across the way, we'll find where he was."

"Let's do it." He raised his voice. "Brent. David. If you can handle extracting the body, we're going to do some investigating."

"Fucking finally."

Vic ignored that. "Lead the way, Maggie."

They started at the farthest point she'd estimated for range and worked their way along the ridge, searching for any sign of human disturbance. Fifteen minutes later, Vic saw it. "Here." He pointed to the turned-up earth. It wasn't much in the grand scheme of things, the slight imprint of a heel that wasn't distinct enough for even the best tech to get an accurate reading on shoe size. But it was enough to be out of place. He stood and frowned. "Trees are in the way."

"Only if you're six foot four." She stepped in front of him and raised her arms as if she was holding a bow. "I have a perfect view of the creek and the guys."

Vic bent a little to bring his head even with hers. There was a perfect shot. "So either a shorter guy or he knelt."

"Wouldn't want to kneel in that weather, but you can't rule it out. He'll have gear to keep the wet out." Her mouth thinned. "Better than what our victim had."

"What's next?"

"What do you mean?"

"Let's try out your theory. Logic has Joshua coming from that direction." He pointed upstream, north to where Fifty Mountain was. "So if he was guided here, I want to see how the unsub did it."

"Okay." She didn't hesitate, starting north, picking her way through the trees.

Vic followed in silence, doing his best to monitor the area around them. His gut instinct said the unsub had moved on to the next target, but he wasn't going to risk both himself and Maggie by assuming that there was no chance of them stumbling onto danger. Stranger things had happened.

He judged they'd been walking well over an hour before she stopped abruptly. "See that?"

"Where?" He followed where she pointed. "Fallen trees."

"Newly cut trees," she corrected. Maggie picked up her pace, and they worked their way to the trees. Sure enough, they'd been felled. They weren't uniform enough to provide a path, but if someone wasn't paying attention, it would create a funnel leading them south. Maggie propped her hands on her hips. "Downhill. You can see the creek from here, just barely. Might as well have hung a sign saying *This Way*."

"You were right."

She touched the nearest tree. "Hard to say when these went down, but if I had any guess, it wasn't in the last week or so. In reality, it could be longer."

A whole lot of planning had gone into this spree of killings. They'd known that. For all the random things like the bear attack and the frenzy of the stabbing, this was an organized killer. This had likely been years in the making, which threw out their theory of the triggering event starting around the first killing. "What the hell did these people do to piss this guy off so thoroughly?"

"As much as I hate the whole woman-scorned thing—or man scorned, for that matter—there's something to be said for taking your revenge cold."

Vic looked at the downed trees again. "If this is revenge, it's ice."

CHAPTER SIXTEEN

Wednesday, June 21
11:01 a.m.

Maggie paced around the open area that encompassed Fifty Mountain. "Okay, so let's say that the three trails our people found were intentionally made into paths, for lack of a better word, by our unsub."

"I think we can both agree that that isn't stretching the realm of possibility."

No, it wasn't. Not when there were newly felled trees that had led their latest victim to his death. It was still a theory until they could find more evidence, but that's what they were here to do. She'd already taken pictures of those trees. Now it was a matter of finding more. "Joshua's trail was to the southeast. Lauren ran down the *actual* trail. I don't see how the unsub could anticipate that, but it's possible that he herded them to where he wanted them on the first night. He would have been there to make sure they scattered like good little sheep, so he wouldn't have left anything to chance. Which means her trail won't fit the pattern."

"Agreed."

She knew they were on the same page, and he was letting her work her way through it aloud. "Joshua didn't make it very far in the amount of time he had. If he was as experienced a hiker as everyone claims, he should have been miles past the point where his body was found."

Vic had been thinking about that, too. They'd just spent an hour walking a distance that had apparently taken Joshua days. He closed his eyes for a few seconds, picturing the body. "Hard to say with the water—Dr. Huxley will be able to tell us for sure—but could be that he got hurt sometime in the initial panic. That would slow him down."

"True. Okay, let me think." She propped her hands on her hips. "Wyatt has two teams combing either side of the trail south, so whoever is on it will be found soon—hopefully. And hopefully alive."

"Then west it is."

"That's where Bill Haglund's body was found." She headed in that direction. "So how did he guarantee that the right people found the body and bolted west?"

"If he is part of the group, he could have guided conversation or asked someone to go check something out." He hesitated. "Timeline is kind of tight. Killing Bill, killing Jennifer, and then hiking out of the park and back in again. All of it takes time."

"Yes, but the unsub is obviously an experienced hiker. If Jennifer was killed roughly twelve to eighteen hours before the hikers came through on the ferry. If he hiked north from Kootenai Lakes and bypassed the ferry, he could have made it to the Waterton trailhead in Canada and driven down to Kalispell—and come back—in the window of time. Rangers on the Canadian side wouldn't have thought to worry about him if he had the correct paperwork."

"Which explains *that* timeline, but not what happened once they made camp here."

She nodded. "The place to stash food is in the opposite direction from the body—and they weren't there yet anyway, from the look of how we found the camp. There are some views this way, but nothing that should draw them so soon after setting up." Maggie turned another circle. "I guess it doesn't matter, but I think finding Bill's body was what caused the panic to begin with."

"So we start there."

As easy as that. She didn't know if she'd ever get used to Vic trusting her judgment on this case. Probably not. When they were partners, he'd been firmly in mentor mode. Every scene was a potential lesson, and every theory was one she had to walk through to show how she thought.

Now they felt like equals.

She pushed the thought away. There were more pressing issues.

They walked to where the body had been found. The storm yesterday had wiped away most of the evidence that anything had happened here. They'd helped remove the rope used to string up Bill Haglund, but it was climbing rope that could be found in nearly any store in this state. The unsub sure as hell knew how to cover his tracks, both literally and with his purchases.

"You know what I don't understand?" She caught sight of a fallen tree directly to the west and headed there. "Well, I guess you could make a long list of the things I don't understand when it comes to this case, but two things right this second. One, how did he know they'd go west instead of back to camp? Personally, I get startled by a dead body hanging from a tree, and the first thing I'm going to do is get back to my friends. Even someone without our training is going to recognize safety in numbers. Running into the forest in the dark seems seven different kinds of stupid."

She checked the tree—it looked identical to the ones they'd found near the head of Josh's trail. "And number two—why not lure these kids out here one at a time? Or in pairs, even. This whole 'having a group of five' blows my mind. It's risky to the point of stupidity, and that's not our guy."

"I don't know that anyone can answer that first question except the person or people who found the body." Vic pointed to another tree. This one was smaller and angled as if it had been brought down in a storm, but when she got closer, she saw hatchet marks.

She frowned. There were half a dozen other ones that she could see, though the unsub had been subtler this time. There was something . . . Maggie closed her eyes and brought up her mental map of the park. "He's herding them to Kootenai Creek."

"Another creek."

"We have a significant number of them in the park." She picked up her pace, keeping an eye on the trees. "But remember how I said that even inexperienced hikers instinctively head to water and follow it? A creek or river—or lake, even—is a guaranteed water source, which is something a person who's lost will be hesitant to leave behind." She shook her head. "He drove them to creeks so he could find them more easily again when he was ready."

"There's one exception."

"Yeah, there is." Whoever had made it onto the trail. The problem was that if they were on the trail, they should have made it to a ranger station or the road by now. It was only a single day's hike, and even though they'd closed the majority of this trail, *someone* would have seen them by now. Which meant they were either dead or they'd veered off the trail.

Or been driven off.

"I'm going to radio it in." She didn't wait for him to confirm before she pulled out her radio. For once, Wyatt wasn't waiting on the other end. It was Ava. "I have information that is hopefully going to be useful for the SAR people." *If* she was right. Maggie shut that doubt down real fast. It was a good theory, and all the evidence they'd found supported it.

"Girl, don't you ever sleep?"

Maggie laughed softly. "I had two glorious nights in my own bed."

"Lucky bitch," Ava said without heat. "Though I doubt you were sleeping last night, if you took my advice."

Vic raised his eyebrows, and Maggie blushed. "Shut up."

"Yeah, yeah. I kicked Wyatt out so he could snatch a few hours before he goes after that bear. What's up?"

"I think the hikers who headed west might be sticking close to Kootenai Creek."

"That's fine and dandy, but they've searched up and down that creek already."

Her optimism faltered. Damn, she'd thought for sure that would be a game changer. Maggie caught Vic's expectant look and tried to force herself to think. "It's been three days. They would have kept going, so they could have made it to the Waterton River by now. Honestly, I'd be surprised if they *hadn't*." The only problem with that realization was that the Waterton River formed a T with Kootenai Creek, so they could have gone either way.

But she was betting on south.

Natural ending points are Nahsukin Lake and Bench Lake," Ava said. Bench Lake had less cover if someone was hiding, but they didn't know if the lost hikers even knew they were being hunted.

Frustration rose, hot and thick in her throat, and it was all Maggie could do to speak past it. "Where do you want us?" They could hike north along the trail and veer west to hit Bench Lake today without a problem, even with the late start. But this wasn't her rodeo, and she'd do well to remember that.

"I have two SAR teams close to Nahsukin Lake, but you're my closest team to Bench Lake at this point. I can call in someone else from farther west, but it will take time for them to get there—that isn't me pressuring you, by the way. Let me know what your plan is."

Vic's stillness was of the predatory sort, so Maggie let go of the "Talk" button before responding to Ava. "What?"

He considered the campground around them. "Of the group, only Ashleigh is relatively inexperienced, so let's pretend for a second that she'd paired up. Logically, with only two trails, that means there's a group out there. Knowing what we know of the hikers, I'd lay money on Ashleigh and Madison being together, and Ethan Conlon being the other trail."

Maggie nodded. "That makes as much sense as anything." The theory that the simplest explanation was probably the most accurate likely held true here as well. Even if Madison and Ethan were dating, there was no guarantee that they'd be together—and if Ashleigh was alone, it was entirely possible that she'd fallen victim to the park before the unsub could get to her.

The unsub wouldn't want to be cheated out of his revenge.

If she isn't the unsub.

No matter which way she looked at it, it didn't overly affect their ability to search as well as they could. "What are you thinking?" Maggie asked.

"An experienced hiker might stick with water, but they're going to know that heading farther west into the park spells trouble. The closest ranger station is Goat Haunt. If they're being herded west and north, they're going to try to go back there," Vic said.

It made sense. It made a whole hell of a lot of sense. She nodded and pushed the "Call" button on the radio. "Ava, you there?"

"Ready and waiting."

"We're going to Bench Lake—or at least heading in that direction. I'll keep you updated if something changes."

"Okay. Stay safe, friend."

"You, too." Maggie packed away the radio and turned back toward Fifty Mountain. "We can get there faster by sticking to the trail. You up for a hike?"

"Always."

The same answer Vic had given her last night. She blushed just thinking about it and then called herself an idiot for blushing. She obviously wasn't above being stupid when it came to Vic. They had several hours' hiking in front of them, and she spent the first mile debating if she should bring up last night or the case again, or just let them both muse in silence.

Vic beat her to it, saving her from having to decide how she was going to break the silence. "You like being a park ranger."

It wasn't exactly a question, but she answered all the same. "I love it. Or, well, let me rephrase. I love the park. So much. After how things fell out with the BAU, I took some time off and ended up hiking the Loop through Glacier. It was the first time in months that I felt truly at peace, so becoming a park ranger seemed the next logical step."

"As easy as that."

She laughed. "Not that easy at all. There are a limited number of ranger jobs, and the competition is fierce. I worked my ass off to get a permanent position here." She made a face. "That said, I'm pretty sure the reason I got in so fast is because I'm a woman."

"Unfortunately, sexism runs rampant in most law-enforcement jobs."

It was one place where both the park ranger and the FBI were equal—how *un*equal the percentage of men to women were. "I do the job better than most, but Wyatt knows how much I hate the guided tours and dealing with people, so I tend toward the backcountry work."

"Until now."

"Until now." She didn't mind Vic's presence, though. If she was going to be honest with herself, she actually craved it. He didn't make the world feel like it was closing in on her until she couldn't breathe. With him at her side, the sky extended and the park sprawled out around them, still beautiful beyond belief.

If anything, Vic being here made it *more* beautiful.

Wednesday, June 21
1:12 p.m.

Bench Lake wasn't much to look at. It was beautiful in the same way that everything about Glacier seemed to be, but a small part of Vic had been hoping against hope that they'd find at least a few of the missing hikers here—alive. Apparently that wasn't to be the case.

If there were people here, they weren't in sight. He shrugged out of his pack, following Maggie's lead and stretching out muscles that had been tense for the entire hike. He'd never once stopped searching the surrounding area for signs of other people. No, not people—for the unsub.

The truth was, the unsub would see them long before they'd see him.

"What do you think?" He looked at Maggie, just like he'd been looking at her all day. The current situation might be holding the majority of his attention, but all it took was the line of her neck or the curve of her smile and he was right back there in her bed. It was distracting as hell. He didn't want to stop.

She pulled her hair off the back of her neck and fanned herself. The day had grown warm enough to actually fit the time of year. It might be nice if he wasn't so keenly aware of the cold night that was to follow—another night without the hikers found.

Maggie lifted a hand to shield her eyes from the sun. "No real way to tell if they've been here."

He'd never realized how much of search and rescue was guesswork. It was different than searching for a person in an urban setting—there were people to talk to in towns and cities, technology to rely upon. In the park, there wasn't a damn thing to draw on. "Don't you have some kind of tech to help with this?"

"Well, sure." She sighed. "There's this neat thing called a FLIR—forward-looking infrared tech—but it's nowhere near foolproof. They've tried it. They'll keep trying it."

"Forward-looking infrared tech." He'd never heard of it, which didn't mean a damn thing. "How is that different from normal infrared?"

"It has to do with the range, I think. I'm not exactly techy, but they used it with the helicopters to pick up heat signatures to help narrow down the search areas." Maggie rubbed a hand over her face. "Trust me, this isn't the SAR team's first rodeo. They know what they're doing, and they know Glacier." She hesitated. "But there are a lot of places a person can disappear to in here. It's happened before, and despite everyone's best efforts, they were never actually found."

It defied comprehension that a person could disappear so thoroughly. He'd never thought he was particularly married to technology. It was a tool like any other. But for it to so thoroughly fail them now was aggravating in the extreme. "So we just wander around and hope to stumble over them."

"They'll bring dogs in, if they haven't already." She made a face. "I'm not the one in charge of the search—Wyatt is. We're here for the unsub."

Which was a problem, because they needed the hikers to track down the unsub.

Frustration had him gritting his teeth, and he held up a hand. "I need a second."

"Sure." She picked a spot and sat. "Take a few."

Vic strode to the edge of the lake. He was so damn full of furious energy, and there wasn't a good place to burn it off. The lake was prettier up close, the water crystal clear in a way that made the whole thing look about two inches deep. He crouched and ran his fingers through the water. Ice-cold like all the water in Glacier seemed to be.

They would get through this. It wasn't the end. He'd had plenty of cases that had been filled to the brim with frustration without him losing his shit, and Maggie's presence here was no excuse. He rubbed a hand over his face to regain his train of thought. The lake sat in a natural valley surrounded by mountains on three sides, and the incline they'd just hiked down was the fourth side. It was a good place for an ambush, though it'd require the ability to shoot over long distances, because the tree line didn't extend anywhere close to the end of the lake. The small hairs on the back of his neck rose, the SEAL instincts that had never quite left him kicking to the forefront.

Someone is watching us.

*Or some*thing.

He searched the area for what felt like the twelfth time, trying to be casual about it. There was nothing readily apparent to cause the bells of alarm clanging inside his head. He stood slowly, still scanning. "Maggie."

"Yes, Vic?" She sounded exasperated.

He turned and froze. She still sat in the spot where he'd left her, but about twenty yards behind her, nearly blending in with the shadows cast between two trees, was a figure in a black jacket, the hood pulled up to shield his face.

And the compound bow in his hands was pointed directly at Maggie's back.

CHAPTER SEVENTEEN

Maggie saw true fear on Vic's face, even across the distance, and moved before her brain registered what she was going to do. She threw herself sideways, sharp pain sprouting deep roots in her back as she did. She tried to roll but didn't make it, the motion stopped halfway because of something long and straight sprouting from her back.

Arrow, her mind helpfully supplied. *You've been shot.*

She fought down the light-headedness that tried to take hold and pushed herself up. Vic went to his knees beside her, but she shoved him back. "The unsub. Get him. I'll call for help."

"But—"

"*Go.*"

For a moment she thought he wouldn't, but he finally gave a jerky nod. "Do *not* try to stand or move." And then he was gone, sprinting across the ground toward the trees faster than any man had right to.

That bastard *shot* her.

She gritted her teeth and started crawling to her pack. Even if Vic managed to catch the unsub, he'd have to drag him back here so they could cuff him. Normal laws being broken usually ended with the arresting park ranger marching the perpetrator out of the park on foot. That wasn't an option in this case.

And you're trying to distract yourself from the fact that it really fucking hurts to breathe.

A wave of dizziness rolled over her, and she shuddered before powering through it. They needed backup, and they needed it now. Unfortunately *now* didn't mean the same thing it did when ambulances and cars had easy access to the location. "Be a park ranger, I thought. It'll be a nice change of pace, I thought. No one will be shooting me, I thought." She let loose a slightly hysterical laugh. "Nice thought."

It took two tries to get her radio out of the pack, and her back felt distinctly wet by the time she succeeded. She raised her head to look at the trees, but there was nothing to see. Either the unsub had given Vic the slip or . . .

"No. We are not going there." Vic could take care of himself. He had damn well *better* take care of himself. She lifted the radio and then frowned. Did they even have a code for being shot with an arrow? *Oh my God, I'm getting loopy.* "Ava?"

Static was her only response. She rested her forehead on the ground and closed her eyes for the count of three. *"Ava."*

"Maggie?"

The mountains must be screwing up the connection. She forced her eyes open. "I've been shot. Bench Lake, east side." Not that there was much of an area to get lost on the tiny lake. Another hysterical laugh bubbled up, but she choked it off before it could pass her lips. "Unsub. Vic in pursuit."

"Shit, fuck, god*damn* it. Don't you dare die, Maggie. You hear me?"

She smiled and belatedly realized Ava couldn't see her. "Can't die. I owe you a drink."

"You're going to owe me a whole lot more than that when I get you out of this shit alive. Do *not* move. The medical chopper is on its way . . . now."

"That's good . . ." Black swept over her before she realized she was in danger of passing out. *Crap.*

◆ ◆ ◆

Wednesday, June 21
1:25 p.m.

Vic slid to a stop, breathing far too hard for the short distance he'd run. *Elevation.* Sure. That was it. He definitely wasn't having trouble keeping up because he'd left thirty in the rearview years ago, and panic was taking more of a toll than the sprint had. *Liar.*

He looked around, but the unsub had disappeared into the trees as if the bastard had never been there to begin with. He could keep charging forward, but if the hunter circled back . . .

Maggie was helpless.

He didn't hesitate. He just turned and sprinted back the way he'd come, finding a second wind that was driven solely by terror. If something happened to her while he was off chasing shadows in the trees, he'd never forgive himself.

He didn't see her when he burst from the edge of the forest, and panic made the entire afternoon go hazy. The arrow gave her position away, a small vertical shaft that shouldn't be able to stop someone as full of life as Maggie. Vic rushed to her side, his stomach dropping at the sight of her back bathed in red, showing through her lightweight jacket.

He wasn't a medic.

He'd never needed the training beyond basic first aid.

What the fuck was he thinking not getting that training?

He knew enough not to try to yank the arrow out, but beyond that, he was at a loss. Did he put pressure on the wound to stop the bleeding? Or would that move the arrow and potentially hurt her more?

He yanked his pack closer and brought out his satellite phone. There must have been a God in heaven smiling down at him, because it had service. He dialed from memory, put it on speaker, and set it carefully down where he wouldn't screw with it.

"Caroline Washburne."

He shouldn't be calling Britton's ex, but she was the only doctor he knew—even if it was distantly. "Caroline, it's Vic."

"What's happened? Is Britton okay?"

"He's fine." He didn't comment on the concern in her voice. He didn't have the necessary capacity to deal with it when Maggie was unconscious in front of him. "I have a woman here who has been injured. We're in a national park and she's called for medical assistance, but I don't know when it will be here, and she's unconscious."

Instantly, Caroline was all business. "Tell me."

"Arrow from a compound bow. Not exactly close range, but it's embedded . . ." He did some quick math. "A good two inches into her back."

"The location—be as precise as you can."

"Roughly the middle of the back—just to the right of the spine." He did a quick estimate. "T4 or maybe T5. Right between her shoulder blades."

"Okay, that's not bad. Or not as bad as it could be." Caroline took a deep breath. "Do *not* pull it out. Don't move her too much until the medical team gets there. If you can use a shirt or, better yet, bandages to slow the bleeding, that's ideal, but don't mess with that arrow, do you hear me?"

"I hear you." He was already grabbing his clean shirt from the pack and ripping it in half.

"You said you're in a park?"

"Glacier."

"Shit, Vic. Okay, keep it as clean as possible. They're going to pump her full of antibiotics as soon as she gets to the hospital, but that doesn't mean you need to be dragging her through the mud or any of that nonsense. Do *not* use any nearby water unless it's been filtered. Some of those creeks are chock-full of bacteria that will not do nice things to an open wound."

"Okay." He carefully pressed the shirt to either side of Maggie's wound. It wasn't easy with the slick fabric of her jacket, but he was afraid to move her too much. *More fabric to soak up the blood.* "Should she be bleeding like this?"

"Is it still pumping hard? Like it looks like it's severed something important?"

"I don't fucking know, Caroline. She's covered in blood."

There was no give in her tone. "Deep breath, Vic. I don't care if she's the love of your life, you *will* remain calm or you're going to distract the medics when they get there. Is the shirt you just put against the wound soaked?"

He checked. "Not all the way through."

"Good. That's good. Just keep her still, and keep the pressure on that wound, and do *not* remove or jostle the arrow."

"You said that already."

She huffed out a breath. "It's worth repeating. Those things tend to be designed to do more damage on the way out than they do on the way in. You could shred her if you try to do it yourself, and then you'd *really* have some bleeding on your hands."

Vic's vision grayed out for an alarming moment before he got himself under control. "Not helping, Caroline."

"Tell me what the hell is going on that you have a woman with an arrow wound in the middle of a national park."

"Is it really relevant?"

"Won't know until you tell me."

And so he laid it out for her. The bare basics of the case, the hikers they were out here trying to find, how he'd turned around and seen the unsub level that goddamn bow at Maggie's back. Somewhere around the part where he started back for her, he realized what Caroline had done. "You're distracting me."

"Yes. I am." She didn't sound the least bit repentant.

The sound of helicopter blades was the sweetest thing he'd ever heard. "The chopper's here. I've got to go."

"I know telling you to stay safe is a waste of breath, but at least give it a shot for me, okay?" She hesitated. "And tell Britton I said hi."

Before he could say anything in response, she hung up. Which was just as well, because the helicopter set down, the noise making it impossible to hold a conversation. It landed just far enough away that he was able to shield Maggie from the worst of the wind kicked up by the blades. By the time he looked up, a park ranger was sprinting across the distance between them.

It took Vic precious seconds to recognize the man sprinting toward them as that asshole Brent from earlier today. Brent went to his knees on the other side of Maggie. "You didn't take out the arrow. Good." He checked Vic's makeshift bandage and then took her pulse. "Okay, Maggie, hang on."

"Can you—"

"We'll talk later. Right now I'm going to go get a stretcher, and you're going to help me get her onto it and strapped down so she won't hurt herself." He shot a dirty look at the arrow. "That thing is potentially going to be a problem, but if we can get out of here without cutting it off, that would be best."

After that, it went quickly. Brent got Maggie strapped down with a strength that was surprising considering his small frame, and Vic helped him carry the stretcher to the helicopter. And then they were off, flying over the park for what felt like the millionth time. It wasn't. It wasn't the same as before, not with Maggie hurt and the unsub still free.

Call him crazy, but it hadn't been personal before. There'd been no doubt in his mind that the unsub was a killer who deserved to be brought to justice—preferably before he killed anyone else—but it was just a case.

It didn't feel like a case now.

◆ ◆ ◆

Wednesday, June 21
3:39 p.m.

Tucker met him at the hospital. Vic had ridden in the ambulance with Maggie, but the EMTs rushed her into the hospital as soon as they arrived, leaving him without updates or so much as a thread of hope. He'd trusted Caroline when she said Maggie would likely be fine, but Caroline wasn't here.

Tucker took in the blood still coating Vic's hands, and his blue eyes went wide. "Bathroom. Now." He didn't wait for a response, grabbing Vic's arm and dragging him into the nearest bathroom.

Vic could have broken the hold easily. But his partner didn't have that look in his eye because of a little blood. Tucker might not have a problem with Maggie, but she didn't mean anything special to him—not like she did to Vic. He wasn't going to get torn up over a near-stranger being shot.

Vic washed his hands while Tucker checked each of the stalls to ensure no one was going to be eavesdropping. He watched his partner in the mirror, it finally dawning on him that it wasn't *him* that was causing this reaction. "What's got you all worked up?"

"I'm being followed. I wasn't sure at first—this damn town is so small that you're bound to run into the same people just going about your business—but the same guy keeps popping up in my rearview and lurking on the streets in his beaten-up old Dodge whenever I leave the local Fed offices."

Vic's stomach lurched. What were the odds? "The same guy? Is the Dodge a faded blue with the passenger door rusted out?"

"How did you know?"

"That's the Conlon twins' dad's truck."

But Tucker was already shaking his head. "This guy isn't Mark Conlon. He's about twenty years too young, though he had a hat pulled down low so I couldn't get a good look at his face." His jaw clenched. "I'm trying not to make waves because I'm pretty sure the locals will close ranks the second I do, and all he has to do is claim that he's *not* following me and I don't have a damn case even if I was willing to push the issue—which I'm not. But it's eerie as fuck."

Vic headed out of the bathroom and strode to the nurses' station. The woman in charge was in her midfifties, her long dark hair liberally streaked with silver, and her inky eyes telegraphing that she didn't have time for whatever shit he was about to bring to her attention. He ignored the silent warning. "I came in with a woman who was shot with an arrow. Is there any way to get an update?"

"The doctors don't exactly phone down in the middle of surgery to give me a play-by-play." She sat back, frowning at his badge. "Fed?"

"Behavioral Analysis Unit."

"You're here for those missing hikers—and the ones who aren't missing anymore."

He wasn't sure if that would work for him or against him. Most people didn't care one way or another if the FBI showed up—not beyond a distant curiosity. Cops were different, but he wasn't talking to a cop. So he kept his tone low and respectful. "Yes, ma'am."

"Jennifer Haglund is my cousin." She made a face. "Was my cousin. We're all connected to one degree or another in this part of the world. You find whoever did this."

"I'll do my best." He'd given up promising things he couldn't guarantee years ago, but he wanted to promise *this*.

Because the line had blurred for him in that helicopter. He wasn't going to stop until the unsub was brought in or dead, and Vic knew which one of those options he'd prefer.

"Good." The nurse nodded. "Here's a little professional advice—go take a shower and change. She's not going to want to see you looking like that." She waved at his entire body. "Give me your number, and I'll call you as soon as she's able to have visitors."

As much as a superstitious part of him was convinced if he walked out of this hospital, Maggie would die, the nurse was right. He wasn't doing anything useful in the waiting room, and looking like he was now, he was liable to scare someone who came in. Washing his hands had taken care of some of the blood, but it still stained the front of his jeans and shirt.

He looked like a psychopath.

She must have seen his hesitation, because some of her sympathy fell away. "I don't feel like dealing with the hysterical on top of the injured. Consider it a favor to me. Now, write down your number and go clean yourself up."

Vic took a slow breath and released it. "Yeah, okay." He scrawled his number on the Post-it she provided and turned for the door.

Tucker beat him there. "I think that asshole is here."

Confronting the would-be stalker presented a number of problems, which was why Tucker hadn't done it yet, but Vic wasn't in the mood to play games. He stopped just outside the door and searched the parking lot. It wasn't hard. The hospital was built in a campus style, rather than housing every department in one building, so the various parking lots were on the small side, all interconnected with a set of narrow roads.

The pickup wasn't exactly covert, either. The blue was the same shade as thousands of other trucks on the road, but the rusted-out door set it apart. He judged the distance between them, working to keep the tension out of his body so he wouldn't telegraph his intentions. "You up for a round of questioning?"

"Jesus, Vic, are you sure?"

He wasn't about to admit how close to going off the rails he was. He kept thinking of Maggie—too pale, her blood staining both of them, that goddamn arrow in her back. It was possible that the guy following Tucker was just one of Mark Conlon's paranoid friends who had borrowed his truck. But Vic wasn't in the mood to give anyone the benefit of the doubt.

Not with Maggie hurt.

"We'll keep it legal." Barely. "Pursuing a lead."

For once, Tucker let his charismatic mask fall away. "You keep whatever is riding you locked up. If this guy is connected, we can't afford to blow the case because you have your panties in a wad."

"Fine."

The redhead waited another few seconds before he nodded. "It just so happens that the idiot parked one row down from my rental. Walk with me."

Vic kept his gaze on Tucker, though he watched the pickup out of the corner of his eye. "He take off when you get close before?"

"I haven't tried, but he doesn't bolt the second he sees me looking." Tucker rolled his eyes. "This guy could use some tips on effective stalking."

Or maybe he wasn't following Tucker for the reason they were both assuming. *Only one way to find out.* "A discussion for another day."

"For sure."

They turned as one and rushed the truck. The guy in the driver's seat jerked, frantically going for the ignition, but Vic yanked open the door and snatched the keys out of his hand. "Now, I think it's time we had a . . ." He blinked, wondering if he was seeing things. He knew that face. He had stared at it and four others more times than he cared to count when he flipped through the file he'd compiled for this case. "Ethan Conlon? What the fuck are you doing here?"

CHAPTER EIGHTEEN

Wednesday, June 21
5:03 p.m.

Vic stood outside the interview room, doing his damnedest not to grind his teeth. "You don't have jurisdiction."

"Wrong. You apprehended him in Kalispell, which makes it a Kalispell problem."

He'd realized his mistake of looping in the local police the second Officer Bob Jenkins stepped out of his cruiser and tried to take over the situation. But Vic didn't have a whole lot in the way of options. The murders took place on federal property, so they were within federal jurisdiction, which meant he was within his rights to drive Ethan Conlon out to park-ranger headquarters and question him there.

He had that right, but it would take time to get out there and time to get back when he got the call about Maggie. He didn't want to wait to see her once she was ready for visitors.

Dealing with Officer Jenkins had him reconsidering. "With all due respect—"

Officer Jenkins snorted. "People say that before they say something that isn't the least bit respectful. Spare me." The officer was a big man—as tall as Vic and built like a linebacker who had let himself go in recent years but still had more than enough strength to crush an opponent. His blond hair was both receding and thinning, and he kept it cropped short but hadn't gone so far as to shave it. It was the squinty brown eyes that irritated Vic the most. Those eyes spoke of a man who went on a power trip at the drop of a hat.

Or maybe he was tired and pissed and wanted to take it out on someone.

Tucker stepped in, all smiles and respect. "Officer Jenkins, we aren't questioning that. If you'd like to have one of your men in the room when we interview the suspect, you're more than welcome to, but as he's a suspect in our ongoing investigation—one with several people still unaccounted for—I'm afraid I'm going to have to insist that we handle the questioning."

Officer Jenkins chewed on that for a minute, his gaze narrowed on Vic. "This one looks unstable."

"Agent Sutherland is more than capable of doing his job." The edge to the words said Vic damn well better get ahold of himself.

Vic shook off his anger as best he could. "My partner is right. Unfortunately, this arguing over who gets first shot at him is wasting everyone's time—time we don't have. If he knows the location of any of the remaining two hikers, both locals, then we need to get that information as quickly as possible. They've already been out there four days."

Officer Bob's scowl cleared. "Four days. They have gear?"

"We think so, but we can't confirm it."

He shook his head. "It's been cold at night—colder than normal this time of year." He stepped back. "Take your crack at him. If you need us to hold him until other arrangements can be made, just let me know." He turned and strode away, leaving them staring after him.

Tucker whistled under his breath. "That was quite the about-face."

"It was the mention of locals missing that got him." Vic hated to have his instant dislike of the man questioned, but this he understood. "He's protective of the town—of the people." He turned to the door of the interview room. "Let's get this over with."

"Guess I don't have to ask who gets to play bad cop."

Vic ignored that and headed into the room. Ethan Conlon looked a whole lot like his photo, with his military-short dark hair and dark eyes. He was easily as tall as Vic and had enough muscle that he obviously spent quite a bit of time working on it. He'd acquired a scattering of cuts across his face and the back of his hands, and he had walked with a limp when they brought him into the station, likely from when they'd dragged him from the truck. To Vic's eye, the wounds were more likely to have been made by trees and bushes than fingernails, but the lab tech would know more once they swabbed him.

If they could.

Tucker took the chair directly across from Ethan, and Vic paced behind him, wound too tightly to sit still. "You made it back on your own."

He must have hiked down the trail itself to Going-to-the-Sun Road and managed his way from there. Vic crossed his arms over his chest. "Walk us through it."

Ethan didn't quite meet their eyes. "I heard that you found two people dead in the park. Was . . ." He stopped and had to visibly get control of himself. "Was Madison one of them?"

"Actually"—Tucker sounded almost apologetic, which nearly made Vic roll his eyes—"we need you to answer our questions before we answer yours."

His head jerked up, fury written all over his face. "Tell me!" The fire lasted half a second before he slumped. "I . . . I love her. Madison. I tried to find her, but she was gone by the time I circled back to the camp. They were all gone."

"So you went for help—except you didn't actually get help."

Ethan rubbed a hand over his face. "I couldn't tell the rangers. What did I know that they didn't? They'd already launched a search by the time I made it back to Going-to-the-Sun Road."

"How do you know that?" Vic took several steps, turned, and paced back to his original spot. It took a cold bastard to leave Madison behind if he loved her as much as he claimed to. But there were other factors to consider.

Ethan couldn't be in two places at once.

The man in question huffed out a breath. "I'm not an idiot, that's how. They don't have that kind of air traffic unless someone is missing." He glared. "I answered your questions. Answer mine."

"Hmm?" Tucker flipped through the file in front of him nonchalantly. "Oh, the dead part? Lauren Rosario and Joshua Conlon were both found dead. You know, in the time that you were conveniently missing."

"Josh." Ethan went so pale, Vic considered stepping forward to grab him if he passed out. "And Lauren. But that's impossible." He shook his head. "You're bullshitting me."

"Wrong." Tucker took two pictures from the file and slid them across the table. "You'll have to forgive the one of Lauren. We are having to identify her by DNA."

What little color was left drained out of Ethan's face, leaving him almost green. He took the time to look at the pictures, though, as if searching for the lie.

Vic stopped pacing and braced his hands on the table, intentionally using his size to loom. "Why don't you start by telling us what the hell happened out there?"

Ethan's shoulders dropped, and he stared at the table. "Mads and I planned the trip. We all used to be so close in high school before it all went to hell, and she missed Lauren. Missed Glacier." He shrugged. "It made her happy, so I helped put it together."

"You and Lauren dated in high school, right? Now she's with your twin." Tucker made a sympathetic noise. "That had to sting."

"Lauren is . . ." Ethan shook his head. "She and I weren't good for each other. I couldn't give her what she needed, and she thought she could find it with Josh. It was a long time ago."

Vic took another lap. "She the reason you joined the Army? You ran out of Kalispell like your ass was on fire after high school. We're smart men, Ethan. We can put two and two together. You broke up with her. You left. She immediately starts dating your twin."

"She was dating him before we broke up." Ethan leaned back, none of the expected anger on his face. "It hurt. Sure. It's shitty to be cheated on, and shittier yet when it's your twin. I wanted the hell out of here, so I left." Shadows flickered across his expression. "I saw enough during my time in the Army that it put things into perspective, okay? They were miserable together, and that's nothing more than they deserved."

"Convenient."

"What?" he snapped.

Tucker shrugged. "Just convenient that your ex sleeps with your twin, and then both your ex and your twin end up dead. You don't seem that torn up about Josh's death."

"We didn't talk for years after high school. Only started back up again last year, and even then, it was never going to be like before."

"That so?" Tucker tapped the file on the table a few times. "Word is that you two used to be damn near inseparable. You can't expect us to believe that you just up and left and stopped talking to him for years."

"You have siblings, Agent?"

"Sure. A couple sisters and a brother."

"If your brother slept with your girlfriend, would *you* want to talk to him?"

Vic couldn't argue with that logic. It was what had made Ethan so attractive as a suspect. The problem was that no matter what kind of motive they could attribute to him, he'd been *here* when the unsub shot

Maggie. That didn't mean he was innocent, but it meant that things might be more complicated than they'd expected.

Madison had just as much reason to kill as Ethan had. It was all conjecture at this point, but if Lauren had been willing to hop brothers once, she might be willing to do it again—especially if things weren't all rainbows and sunshine with Joshua. Vic couldn't see Madison being happy at the thought.

That was the problem. It was all conjecture at this point.

Serial-killer pairs were exceedingly rare. The odds he had of seeing two of them in two years were astronomical, but that didn't mean it *wasn't* what was happening. They couldn't afford to rule out any possibilities as long as someone was out there killing people.

"Ethan." Tucker was all sympathy and carefully veiled humor. "You might have made it out of Glacier all fine and dandy, but Madison and Ashleigh are still missing—something I think you know since you were stalking me."

His brows lowered. "I wasn't stalking you. I was trying to find out what happened."

Vic opened his mouth, but Tucker beat him there. He sighed and shook his head. "You've got to understand how this looks, Ethan."

"Yeah, I understand how it looks, which is why I didn't come to you earlier." He hesitated. "I was going to. But then I heard that someone had been killed—*four* people—and it looks—"

"It looks like you're the one who killed those people or that you're covering up for your girlfriend." That was a truth he had to deal with now. No matter which way they looked at it, if Ethan was here, then either Ashleigh or Madison was the unsub.

The latter seemed more likely at this point. He tried to picture the unsub, but the dark coat had hid any defining features, and he'd been too far away to even get a good read on a height. They could assume that the unsub was athletic—her speed had more than indicated that—but they'd already known that. She—because it *had* to be a she now—was hiking long distances, sometimes with a body in tow, and hadn't seemed to slow down in the least.

"I don't believe for a second that Madison wanted to get close to Lauren—the same Lauren who cheated on you and is shacking up with your brother." Vic crossed his arms over his chest. "No one would put themselves in that position, no matter how much time had passed, unless they had an ulterior motive."

Ethan narrowed his eyes. "Mads didn't have anything to do with any of this—and neither did I."

"Then why don't you answer our questions? Easy enough to clear things up, don't you think?" Tucker's smile was disarming. "No reason to waste everyone's time if you can prove it."

Vic's phone buzzed in his pocket. He turned away from the table so he could read the screen and saw it was a local number. "I've got to take this." Tucker made a noise of agreement, and he strode from the room, answering the phone as he did. "Agent Sutherland."

"This is Nurse Jones. I just wanted to let you know that Ranger Gaines is awake and asking for you."

"I'm on my way."

◆ ◆ ◆

Wednesday, June 21
6:16 p.m.

Maggie woke up in the hospital. Every breath burned, but she was alive, which was more than she could have hoped for when she passed out. What had happened? The last thing she remembered was radioing Ava for help and Vic tearing off into the trees after what must have been the unsub. She looked around the room, its pale-beige walls and nondescript furniture giving her no indication of what time it was.

Of what *day* it was.

She shifted and grimaced at the pain that shot through her. She hadn't expected Vic to be waiting at her bedside, but she couldn't help a stab of worry. Surely he'd come back with her . . . but what if he hadn't? What if the unsub had turned the tables on him? Vic was good—better than good—but whoever was responsible for these murders had years of training for this specific purpose. She wasn't sure how they'd match up, and now she couldn't get the image of Vic dead—shot, strung up, and cut apart—out of her head. "God."

A nurse popped in through the door, a young Native American woman in pink scrubs. She smiled when she saw Maggie, though the smile wavered almost instantly. "Don't move, please." She moved to the side of the bed at a speed that should have looked like rushing, but she managed to seem natural and unhurried. "It's good that you're awake."

"My partner." She stopped, realized that Vic wasn't her partner anymore. He wasn't her *anything* officially. They hadn't even had a chance to talk about the future, because the whole conversation had been put on hold while they pursued the investigation.

The nurse didn't seem to know that, though. "The big man who came in with you? Since he's not family, it's against policy to let him into your room until the doctor gives approval. He left his contact information, though, so we'll put in a call for him to come down now that you're able to have visitors."

Vic is okay.

The sheer relief the thought brought had her sagging into her pillow. She lifted a shaking hand to press it against her mouth, as if that would stem the questions that bubbled up. He hadn't caught the unsub. If he had, it wouldn't be as simple as dropping everything and running to her bedside, no matter what he might feel for her. Maggie closed her eyes and took several careful breaths. Her back ached, but it could have been so much worse. "What's the damage?"

"You'll be fine. You were shot with an arrow, and you lost enough blood that we gave you a transfusion, but you were lucky. There was no damage done that you won't heal from in a relatively short time."

She opened her eyes. "How short is a short time?"

The nurse—Colleen, her name tag said—gave her a knowing smile. "Lord, you park rangers are as bad as cops when you get hurt. There wasn't any damage done to your organs, and the arrow didn't pierce your lung—you are incredibly lucky on that note—so if you take a few days to rest up, you should be able to work a desk for another week or so and be back in Glacier not long after. I can print you out the specifics when we discharge you."

Too long. It was dumb to argue now, so she kept her mouth shut. She'd deal with the recovery time as needed. Right now, what she *needed* was to figure out what had happened after she passed out. Maggie licked her dry lips. "Okay."

Colleen straightened. "Let me grab you some water. How's your stomach feeling?"

She had to actually stop and consider it. "Woozy."

"We'll stick with saltines and see if that helps. If you can hold them down without too much trouble, I'll put in a food order for you. I'll be back shortly."

Maggie nodded and did her best to relax. Shot in the back. The unsub had been close enough to catch—maybe Vic would have if he hadn't stopped to check on her first. Guilt rose, thick and sour. She should have considered that an attack wouldn't have come from the lake, but from the tree line.

Hell, she should have considered that an attack could come at all.

For all her past training and so-called good instincts, it had never crossed her mind. She knew the unsub was out there, and she knew what he was capable of, but she'd still underestimated him—and wasted resources that should be focused on the remaining missing hikers in the process.

Maggie huffed out a breath. She couldn't do anything about it now. There was nothing *to* be done. They had to deal with it and move forward.

If she was even part of the case anymore. Stuck at a desk or the equivalent, she was less than worthless. Her entire job was the park. She wasn't a cop who could keep investigating even if she wasn't at full health. She *needed* to be able to do certain physical things in order to do her job.

Ava is never going to let me live this down.

Nurse Colleen brought back the promised water and crackers. After Maggie took a few small sips, there were the expected medical checks of blood pressure, listening to her lungs and heart, taking her pulse, and a humiliating trip—at least on Maggie's part—to the bathroom. Once they got her safely back into bed, Colleen smiled. "You'll be right as rain in no time. I'll be back shortly with something a little more substantial to eat. Try to rest . . . though I don't know why I bother even saying it." Her smile took some of the sting out of the words. "You can use the phone if you need to. Dial two to get an outside line." She closed the door softly behind her.

Maggie started to reach for the phone and paused. Her first instinct was to call Vic and make sure he was okay, to get an update. But should he really be her first call?

Then again, who else would she call? Her parents would use this as an excuse to say, "I told you so," or worse, to try to leverage it into convincing her to come home and *finally* fall into line like they'd always wanted—by marrying some doctor or lawyer, since, by their standards, she was far too old to go back to school. There was a reason they only spoke on birthdays and holidays. It made her tired just thinking about trying to deal with them—even if, miracle of miracles, they were actually concerned for her. It wasn't worth it. She was fine. She'd live to fight another day. She was never going to be the daughter they'd always wanted her to be—and they were never going to come to terms with that.

It was kind of pathetic that her list of people to call was so damn short. Kat would hear about this sooner rather than later, but she might not know yet. Ava, however, *did* know.

So it was Ava whom Maggie dialed. The park ranger answered almost immediately. "Hello?"

"It's me."

"*Thank fuck.*" She blew out a harsh breath. "You had me worried, Gaines. Seriously worried. The hospital wouldn't give us updates, and I know it's only been a couple hours, but . . . just don't do that shit again, okay?"

She smiled, able to picture the irritation on Ava's face perfectly. "I'll do my best."

"The park rangers are enough of a boys' club without you. If you were gone, I'd have to leave, too, because I'd kill all these idiots if left to my own devices. You rest and get better and then get your ass back in to work."

"Yes, ma'am." She laughed and it felt good. "You still at headquarters?"

"Yeah." Ava sighed. "Wyatt found the bear this morning. There was blood on its fur, but they're waiting for the autopsy results to confirm that it's the one that got that girl. He's handling it about as well as can be expected."

Which wasn't well at all. Wyatt never asked his rangers to do something he wouldn't do himself, but killing a bear because a human had been hurt took its toll. He loved the park more than anyone else Maggie had ever come across, and hurting any part of it hurt *him.*

Ava kept talking. "He's also pissed because he's having to pull the SAR people back in. There's a psychopath in the woods—which is something we did know, but knowing he's there and having him shoot one of our people are two different things."

She understood that rationally, but betrayal lay thick on her tongue. "What about the remaining hikers?"

"I don't know, Maggie. We'll keep up the aerial searches through the next couple days, but if they aren't able to signal one of the planes or helicopters, then there's a good chance they're beyond saving."

"Cold, Ava."

Ava hissed out a breath. "You think I don't know that? It sucks. We want to bring them home, in whatever form that takes, but getting more people hurt or killed to do it is out of the question. I'm with Wyatt on this." A pause as a guy in the background—probably Wyatt—said something Maggie couldn't quite make out, then Ava was back. "Wyatt said to take the rest of the week off. He does *not* want to see you in the park." Another pause. "It's paid leave."

That was a small miracle, but Maggie wasn't in the mood to be grateful. "This is a mistake."

"There's nothing that can be done about it now. Just hang in there and heal. I'm glad you're okay, Maggie." Ava hung up without saying good-bye, an annoying habit of hers.

Maggie dropped the phone into its cradle with a curse. Calling off the search. If those kids weren't dead already, they would be before the weekend was out. Whether the unsub got them or exposure did was up for grabs, but she wouldn't bet a single dollar on their survival without the SAR teams.

Admitting that Ava was right—if they weren't in the position to signal an aerial search, they probably were beyond saving—was harder.

She was still glaring into space when the door opened and Vic walked in. He'd changed since she'd seen him last, though he must have several of the exact same pair of jeans, because she couldn't differentiate between the ones he wore now and the ones he'd had on while they were hiking. Another henley fit him in a way that would have made her mouth water if she wasn't too busy grinding her teeth about the news.

Or the fact that, if Vic was here, he hadn't caught the unsub.

CHAPTER NINETEEN

Wednesday, June 21
6:40 p.m.

Vic couldn't make himself move away from the door. Maggie reclined against the pillows in the hospital bed, looking like she'd been through hell. She was too pale, the circles beneath her eyes making them look bruised, her hair lank and still filthy from hitting the ground as hard as she had.

She looked breakable, and he didn't know how to deal with that.

"Get over here and update me."

He blinked. *This* Maggie he knew. She couldn't be as bad as she looked if she was still able to bark at him like that. He breathed a small sigh of relief and crossed the room to grab the chair next to the bed. "You're okay."

She started to snap at him but made an obvious effort to rein it in. "Everything hurts and I'm furious that he got the drop on me, but I'm alive. I'll recover. I'm also on paid medical leave through the end of the week."

All of which went to explain the bad attitude. He'd be feeling the same if their positions were reversed. "Have you eaten anything yet?"

"No, the nurse is bringing something back for me when she gets a chance."

He eyed the empty packet of crackers on the bedside table. "Do you need anything else?"

"What I want is for you to stop treating me like a child and just update me." She made a face. "Please."

There was nothing for it. He hated giving her bad news, but he didn't have anything good to combat her pissy mood. So Vic sat back and gave it to her straight. "Tucker met me here when they brought you in, and part of updating me included informing me that someone had been following him for the last day or so in Mark Conlon's pickup truck."

"One of Mark's cop-hating friends?"

"That's what I assumed, but we cornered the guy, and it was none other than Ethan Conlon."

"*What?*" Maggie tried to sit up, but the IV tubing got tangled, and she had to settle for waving her free hand. "What the hell? He's out of the park? He's *been* out for long enough to figure out that Tucker is at least one of the investigating agents and follow him— and he never thought to, I don't know, give us a heads-up about his friends?"

"That's what it looks like. He says he doesn't trust law enforcement and was just trying to get information on Madison, but it rings false."

"I don't like going to the dentist, but I sure as shit will if I think something's wrong with my tooth."

Vic barked out a laugh. "The dentist, huh?"

"Mouth butchers, every one of them." She started to run her fingers through her hair, grimaced, and dropped her hand. "Does he know where the girls are?"

"He says not—he also says he hasn't seen Madison or Ashleigh since the night they scattered." He gave her a quick rundown of what he'd gotten out of Ethan before he'd left. Tucker would keep at the kid, but Vic wasn't optimistic at this point. "He's got an alibi for the final kill—and for the attack on you—and it's pretty damn unshakable. Even if Tucker can't place the exact time he first saw him, for him to have shot you, let alone killed Josh, would be—"

"Impossible. Unless he has a teleporter tucked away." She slumped back into the pillows, but her dark eyes were still watchful. "What's got that look on your face?"

"There's something off about his story." He couldn't put his finger on it. "He's worried about Madison and that feels genuine, but the guy has a significant amount of outdoors experience. He says he heard screaming the night they scattered and thought it was a bear. He had to have known that running off into the dark was more dangerous than any other option, short of running to confront the theoretical bear."

She narrowed her eyes. "There are a truly outstanding number of bears in that area of the park. If he's as experienced as his father makes it sound, he would have known the safest course of action is to climb a tree and wait it out. There are a whole lot in the way of options in trees between Fifty Mountain and the west entrance—I'm assuming that's where he came out of the park—but instead he hiked down to the road?"

"That's what it's looking like." He drummed his fingers on the arm of the chair. "That's what's bugging me. No one would expect him to run to save those girls, no matter how much he cares for Madison or how much shit I gave him over it. If he really thought it was a bear attack, why not do what you just said—climb a tree and wait for morning?" That would make sense. It would even make sense if he realized that the rest of the group had scattered in a panic and decided to hike out of the park. Did it make him an idiot for not reporting anything to the park rangers? Without a doubt. But it was a more plausible story than the one he'd put forth.

Not to mention shadowing Tucker.

He sat forward. "He knew at least two of them came back dead, and he had to know it was foul play or the Feds wouldn't be involved."

Maggie watched him closely. "You think he's connected to the killer. They're *all* connected to the killer, at least technically." She rubbed a hand over her face. "God, I need a shower and a gallon of coffee. My head is all fuzzy."

"That will happen when you've been shot." Just saying it had his chest tightening in fear as the scene from earlier played out in his mind. He'd actually thought for a short period of time that he might lose her. There'd be hell to pay for calling Caroline—if there was one thing Britton didn't budge on, it was his ex-wife—but Vic would do it again in a heartbeat. "You need to rest."

"What I *need* is to get out of this bed and get moving."

The door opened, and a nurse in pink scrubs came in with a tray of food. Every good nurse Vic had encountered over the years had perfected the no-nonsense attitude that managed to be firm and empathetic at the same time. This one was younger than most, barely out of school, if he didn't miss his guess, but she carried herself with confidence. For being so close to the Blackfeet reservation, Kalispell didn't have nearly as diverse a population as he would have expected, but the nurse was one of the few Native American people he'd come across since starting this investigation.

She nodded at him, but her focus was on her patient. "You know very well that you're going to have to stay overnight for observation. Don't make that face—if it was him in this bed, you'd be agreeing with me."

Maggie's gaze found him, and her lips twitched. "I suppose you're right."

"I am." The nurse set up the food on the table that would swing over Maggie's lap so she didn't have to strain herself, and then she took her vitals. "Looks good. Eat what you're hungry for, and see how you feel." She checked her watch. "The doctor will be in before the end of his shift. If you want to be difficult, you can be difficult with him."

This time, Maggie did smile. "I'll keep that in mind."

"See that you do. And you"—she pointed at Vic—"don't rile her up. She needs calm and rest, and getting her all excited or angry is going to potentially lengthen her healing process."

She was a good foot shorter than he was, but under that steely, dark gaze, he had a hard time not shifting his feet like he was back in grade school and had just been caught pulling on Rachel Westerman's pigtails. "Yes, ma'am."

With one last look at both of them, she walked out of the room and closed the door softly behind her.

Vic turned back to Maggie. "She's right. I shouldn't be talking about the case."

"Don't do that. Don't shut me out." She lifted the lid off the plate and set it aside. "My back hurts and I'm tired, but there's nothing wrong with my brain. If I'm stuck here overnight, you can't sit around and babysit me."

He knew what it cost her to say that instead of demanding he get the hell out of here and take her with him. As much as he wanted to do exactly that, he needed her healed and safe. It was a selfish need, and maybe not how he'd feel if it was Tucker in that bed instead of Maggie, but he didn't even try to fight it. Instead, he crossed to the bed and leaned down to press a soft kiss to her mouth. "I'll be back as soon as we figure out what we're doing with Ethan Conlon."

"He knows more than he's telling, but you're going to have to trick him into admitting it." She picked up half of her sandwich. "The girl-friend is the pressure point. If he cares about her as much as you think, it would have to be a difficult choice to leave her behind. He was following Tucker for more information, which he had to know was suspicious in the extreme. Hit that subject the right way and he'll react instinctively."

It was a good point—and one he might have gotten around to if he wasn't so damn worried about her. Vic stopped at the door and just took her in. She was alive. A little banged up, a lot tired, but she'd be fine before too long. "Get some rest."

"Pretty sure that nurse is going to sweep back in here with some excellent drugs that will knock me on my ass before too long." She shrugged. "I'll stay overnight. That's all I'm promising."

"That's all I'm asking." Trying to get her to slow down longer than that would require divine intervention. "Did they give you back your cell?"

"I think it's still in my pack."

The one he'd kept when she'd been admitted to the hospital. Vic nodded. "I'll go get it from the rental now."

"Just drop it at the nurses' station." She gave him a half smile. "If you come back up here, you're going to end up feeling guiltier, and then it'll slow you down when you should be back at the station questioning Ethan—I'm assuming he's at the police station."

"Yeah." He couldn't keep his grimace internal. "Officer Jenkins is a pain in the ass."

"He's territorial. He's not a bad guy." She shrugged. "Most of the cops around here are just as suspicious of big government as the rest of the population is. He's not going to welcome you with open arms, but he'll do his job."

It would have been really useful to have Maggie at his side to help him navigate the situation, but he'd been doing this shit for years without her. It shouldn't feel so damn wrong to walk out of the room and leave her behind.

But it did.

◆ ◆ ◆

Wednesday, June 21
7:32 p.m.

Vic met Tucker in the small room next to the interrogation room that Officer Jenkins had provided them. His partner's jaw was clenched and his blue eyes severe. "I can't get shit out of him."

He'd expected as much, but it didn't stop him from feeling guilty for walking out in the middle of the interview. "Maggie says that if he was telling the truth about the bear, an experienced outdoorsman would climb a tree and wait it out rather than run blindly into the night and risk getting himself killed."

"Makes sense."

Yeah, it did. Ethan struck him as stubborn, and he obviously had some shit in his past plaguing him, but he didn't appear to be dumb. "You want me to take another crack at him and then let him cool his heels for a bit while we figure out the next step?"

"By all means." Tucker waved him at the door, though he held up a piece of paper. "I wrote out all the times I saw him within the nearest half hour. Even if he had access to a helicopter to get him into the park with ease—and if it was feasible that no one would notice it—the timeline is too tight for him to be good for the most recent body. Or for Maggie being shot, for that matter."

Vic had already come to that realization, but he nodded all the same. "But it doesn't cover him for the others."

"A potential pair? It's a stretch, but I guess anything could happen." Tucker propped his feet on the table in the room—the only piece of furniture other than the chair he occupied. "Though serial-killing pairs—even spree-killing pairs—tend to have one dominant partner and one submissive one. I don't see Ethan submitting to anyone, not with that chip on his shoulder."

"Maybe. But he was in the Army, and they like to train their people to obey, so we can't rule anything out." Vic scrubbed a hand over his face, suddenly tired. It seemed the farther they got into this investigation, the more questions arose. Never any answers, just more questions. He needed to wrap this up and wrap it up now before anyone else was hurt.

Unfortunately, he could *want* to finish it, but that didn't mean it was going to happen. "I'll see what I can get out of him."

"Vic."

Something in Tucker's voice stopped him in his tracks. His partner sounded almost . . . guilty. He pinned him with a look. "What did you do?"

"Don't get pissy with me. You know how Britton likes to be kept in the loop." Tucker paused, seemed to realized that he was stalling, and rushed forward. "He's coming here."

"What?" Britton came into the field so rarely, Vic couldn't actually remember the last time it'd happened. "What did you say to bring him here?" He hadn't told Tucker about calling Caroline. There was no reason for him to know, and beyond that, she and Britton had been divorced well before Tucker joined the BAU. It would just confuse the issue.

He held up his hands. "I told him that Maggie got hurt. He wants to see for himself."

Vic relaxed, but only marginally. Maggie might not want to face Britton yet—ever—but there wasn't much either of them could do about it at this point. He'd tell Britton personally that he'd talked to Caroline and deal with any damage control as required. Not that his boss would do more than level a disappointed look at him, but Britton didn't need to raise his voice to bring his people to their knees. He didn't do it often, but the knowledge was there all the same.

Tucker gave him a significant look. "Have another pass at Ethan. We'll talk about this later."

There wasn't a damn thing to talk about. Britton was coming, end of story.

He had a suspect to interrogate—even if that suspect was looking less like a suspect and more like a material witness.

At least if they could get him to stop stonewalling them.

CHAPTER TWENTY

Wednesday, June 21
7:46 p.m.

Ethan looked like shit.

He had before, of course, but in the last couple of hours, he'd started to sweat, and there were wet spots at his armpits and down the center of his chest. Contrary to popular fiction, sweating didn't automatically make someone guilty, but the way the kid's eyes kept jumping to the door like he expected the unsub to burst through with his bow spoke volumes.

Vic casually flipped around the chair Tucker had occupied earlier and sat on it, draping his arms across the back. "You look scared, Ethan."

"Scared?" He lifted his chin, but his gaze shot to the door again. "Why would I be scared?"

Why, indeed? He kept his posture relaxed and his voice easygoing. Just making conversation. "You ever see a bear?" When Ethan didn't respond, Vic gave a rueful grin. "I've never seen one. I'm from back East—Philly. I spent some time in the Navy, but where they sent me there wasn't much in the way of bears. I hear Glacier is known for them."

Ethan crossed his arms over his chest. "There are a ton of bears out there. They mostly don't bother anyone, but sometimes people do dumb crap and get killed as a result."

Interesting that he immediately jumped to the bears' defense, but Vic had seen that kind of thing around here. People were protective of their land—their national park—and while that might not stop some of them from poaching, they weren't like city folk who thought that one bear attack meant the bears were coming for humanity as a general whole. He didn't look directly at the kid. "You were probably too young for the *Night of the Grizzlies* shit, huh?"

"For fuck's sake, I am so tired of tourists talking about that shit. It was decades ago, and it was *one* situation where people were acting like ignorant idiots. If those women had just climbed a tree like their friends . . ." He trailed off.

"Hmm. Climb a tree. That what you're supposed to do when there's a pissed-off bear in the area?" Vic propped his chin in one fist, all open curiosity. "That's interesting that you'd know that. Seems strange that you ran when there were so many trees around you could have climbed to get away from that bear that scared the shit out of Madison and Ashleigh." He leaned forward and lowered his voice. "Unless there wasn't a bear at all."

"Wait—"

He kept going. "Way I figure it, you saw something brutal out there that scared the shit out of you. Nothing wrong with that—I've seen some things since I got on this case that'll provide all sorts of nightmares later on. Difference between us is that I'm doing something to put the guilty party away, and you aren't doing fuck all."

"But—"

"Where's your girlfriend, Ethan? I figure this trip wasn't really Madison's idea. You had your own reasons for wanting your brother and ex-girlfriend in the park—and away from help. Did you convince Madison to play along? Maybe told her Lauren made a pass at you? That's something that would piss a woman off."

"That bitch *did* make a pass at me." He must have realized how much he'd just given away, because he sat back and raised his chin. "It was months ago, and it didn't get farther than her trying to kiss me before I shut it down. Madison didn't even know about it, because it meant nothing and I didn't want to upset her."

Several pieces clicked into place, all at once. "I figure she threatened to tell Madison about it. Things weren't going well with Josh. From what I hear, they were engaged, but things were rocky, and I bet Lauren looked at you and thought about picking up where you left off."

Ethan stared at a point over Vic's left shoulder. "Doesn't mean a damn thing. Madison wouldn't have believed her."

"Maybe, maybe not. But it comes right down to the real question here—did you do something wrong? Or are you just a coward who left his girlfriend behind to die so that he could get out?"

Ethan jerked back, his eyes too wide, his breath coming too quickly. "Shut your fucking mouth. I drew that bastard away to give Mads time to get free." He snapped his mouth shut, but it was too late.

Vic considered him for a long moment, watching him squirm. "You saw the killer."

"I didn't see much of anything. A guy in a dark coat with a bow. He shot at the girls and might have hit Ashleigh." Ethan lifted his chin. "I was a soldier. I know how to fight. I figured if he came after me, I had a better chance of defending myself. So I threw a few rocks, made sure I had his attention, and ran in the opposite direction of the others. I thought I could draw him south and then circle back to come up behind him."

"Didn't work out so well."

"No, it didn't. One second he was there, close enough behind me to worry me, and the next, he was gone."

"Why lie about this in the first place?"

He shook his head. "I know how it looks. I walked out of the park, and no one else has. I thought for sure Mads would make it to a ranger station, but she hasn't . . ." He stared at his hands. "I didn't hurt her. I would *never* hurt her."

Which wasn't to say he wouldn't hurt the rest of them.

It was possible that Joshua Conlon had been dead long enough for Ethan to have killed his brother and escaped the park, but that didn't answer the question of who had shot Maggie. They hadn't released any information about the deaths—not that they were the result of an arrow, and not that the unsub had been seen wearing dark gear with the hood up. Ethan might be telling the truth this time.

Or maybe he was lying to cover for Madison.

◆ ◆ ◆

Five years ago, July

Madison heard the arguing long before she and Ethan reached the camp. She picked up her pace, even though all she wanted to do was turn around and rush into the dark woods. Anything moving out there in the shadows was preferable to what lay in wait for her within the circle of the fire.

Only Ethan's solid presence at her back kept her moving.

Ashleigh had her hands clenched and was leaning in close, looking like she was three seconds from throwing her famous right hook to Josh's face. "I know for a fact your mama taught you to have respect for ladies."

"I do have respect for ladies." Josh raked a look over her that made Madison's skin crawl. "And this right here is no lady."

"You fucking asshole!"

"Enough!" Madison didn't realize she was going to speak until the word came out of her mouth as a shriek. "What is *wrong* with all of you? This isn't how we are. This isn't how we treat each other." She met each of their gazes in turn, her stomach twisting in knots as they broke eye contact, one by one. "We came on this trip so that we could get away from all the shit, and you've brought it with us. What the hell, guys?"

"We're not the only ones."

She leveled a warning look at her best friend. "Stop it."

Josh faced her, not even seeming to realize that he'd lined up with Ashleigh. "What's she talking about, Mads? You have some nasty little secret like the rest of us, don't you?" He raised his eyebrows. "Maybe you and Ethan were sneaking off to get some alone time in the forest, huh? How the mighty have fallen."

"What?" Lauren took two steps forward. "Ethan, what's he talking about?"

Ethan crossed his arms over his chest, not looking the least bit disturbed by the whole thing. "Glass houses, Lauren."

She drew herself up to her full five feet six inches. "What is *that* supposed to mean?" A vicious gleam flared to life in her eyes, all of it aimed directly at her boyfriend. "How long have you been fucking her? Don't even try to play innocent. I see the way you watch her when you think no one is looking."

How does he watch me? Madison didn't say the words. She couldn't.

The world was spiraling out of control around her, and she had no way to put on the brakes. Ashleigh watched the whole thing with something like amusement, probably because she loved drama as much as she loved anyone in this group. Josh still looked ready to throw a punch, and his slow grin was just as mean as ever. "You and Mads, huh? Someone finally cracked that safe."

Madison was pretty sure the top of her head was going to explode. "Shut the hell up *right now*. I'm not sleeping with Ethan. Unlike the rest of *you*, we have some honor." She didn't feel like mentioning that the possibility of something beyond friendship with Ethan hadn't occurred to her until today. It wouldn't have mattered. They were supposed to be this tight-knit group who put one another first.

Instead, they were a parasite eating itself from within.

"I cannot *wait* to get the hell out of here."

Lauren snorted. "Kalispell isn't that big. This will blow over, and we'll get back to normal before you know it."

She didn't get it. There was no normal after this. Everything that was supposed to hold them together was a lie. There would be no coming back from this.

Madison stared the other girl in her face. "I'm not staying in Kalispell, and I've never been so damn happy about it. I'm leaving for good."

"I'm leaving, too." Ethan spoke so quietly, if they hadn't all fallen silent, no one would have heard him.

Lauren turned to face him fully, her dark eyes wide. "What did you say?"

"I joined the Army, and I'm going to be a Ranger."

Ashleigh laughed, the sound low and mean. "Look at that, Josh. Everyone you love is leaving you. It's like fate or something."

He turned so fast no one had a chance of stopping him, backhanding her across the face. She hit the ground and then Ethan was there, stepping between them. "What are you doing? We don't hit women, Josh."

"That bitch is nothing to me." He looked at each of them in turn. "None of you fuckers are anything to me." And then he was gone, striding into the darkness.

Madison breathed a small sigh of relief once he disappeared from view. Only then did she move to Ashleigh's side, pointedly ignoring Lauren. "I made a mess of things."

Her best friend touched her mouth gingerly, remorse heavy in her expression. "I'm sorry, Mads. I know you wanted this trip to be perfect, and it's all gone to shit."

"It's fine." It wasn't, though. This trip had been their last chance to be together as friends the way they'd always been. Instead, it made her realize that even though she'd known her friends since they were in grade school, she didn't actually *know* them at all.

Maybe she never had.

◆ ◆ ◆

Thursday, June 22
4:38 p.m.

Maggie tried to keep herself occupied. She spent most of the day watching reruns, but even working as much as she did, she'd seen them all. Not to mention, every time she moved, she was reminded of the reason she was in the hospital to begin with.

When the door opened, she was pathetically grateful. Colleen telling her to stop being a problematic patient would be better than another hour spent alone. But it wasn't Colleen who walked into the room.

She stared, certain that the damn nurse had slipped something a little extra into her IV bag, because there was no way that Britton Washburne was standing in her room right now. She blinked and then blinked again but stopped short of pinching herself.

Britton had always been an attractive man. He was somewhere in his forties, though his black hair had more salt than pepper in it now. He kept his hair close cropped, and though he'd grown a beard in the last seven years, he kept it equally short. His skin was dark with cool undertones, and with his strong eyebrows, there was definitely an Idris Elba look about him.

She knew what she was doing—analyzing his appearance and comparing it to what she'd known when she was in the BAU—but she couldn't stop. If she stopped, she'd have to open her mouth and say something, and there wasn't a single thing she could say that wouldn't make her look like an asshole.

Why are you here? Here in Montana, here in my hospital room? Seven years and you didn't bother to check up on me, but now *you decide to rush over to see if I'm okay?*

She stubbornly kept silent, examining his perfectly polished black shoes, gray slacks that didn't have a single wrinkle in them, and pinstriped cream button-up shirt that complemented his dark skin perfectly. He'd obviously stopped somewhere after his flight, because not even Britton Washburne could fly without picking up a wrinkle or two. She might have believed such nonsense about her larger-than-life boss when she was with the BAU, but she didn't anymore. He might be brilliant, but he was still just a man.

The edges of his lips quirked up in something like a smile, silently acknowledging that she wouldn't break first. "You look well, Maggie."

"Funny you should say that." She sounded petulant and childish, and she tried to rein it in. One deep breath. Two. By the third, she'd gotten ahold of her anger. Mostly. "I didn't expect to see you here. I didn't think you went into the field often these days."

"I don't." He moved to the chair next to her bed and motioned to it, every move smooth to the point of elegance. "May I?"

"You're here. You might as well sit so you don't hover." Damn it, she still sounded like a spoiled child. "I'm sorry. I don't like being laid up, and you surprised me."

"You've never liked either."

She ignored that. "My point is that it's bringing out the worst in me, but that's not your fault. So I'm sorry for snapping at you."

He just looked at her with those unfathomable dark eyes. Despite herself, a little of her old hero worship rose, and with him sitting here, she could almost believe that everything would be okay. They'd catch the unsub and rescue the remaining missing hikers, and those left alive would move on with their lives with minimal trauma.

Maggie knew better.

She pressed her lips together but couldn't hold her silence. "Why are you here, Britton?"

"I was worried about you."

That wasn't the answer, and they both knew it. "I've been hurt plenty of times in the last seven years." Nothing like this, though. Breaking her arm in a fall in the park had been more a pain in the ass than anything else. She'd hiked her way out to Many Glacier and then argued with Ava about whether she could drive herself to the hospital. Or the time she sprained her ankle and didn't miss any work out of sheer stubbornness. None of those things would bring her old boss riding in like some kind of white knight. "Right now, I'm on paid medical leave, so I'm not worth a damn thing to the investigation."

He contemplated her just long enough for her to have to fight not to squirm. "Are you happy as a park ranger?"

"Yes." When his brows lowered, ever so slightly, she forced herself to be more honest. "I love parts of my job. I love the park. I feel like I can breathe there. I love what it represents."

"But."

"Yeah, but." She shrugged and winced when the move pulled at her back. "But the people suck. Not the park rangers—though some of them give the term *asshole* a new meaning. The tourists drive me batshit crazy."

"You've never been a big fan of people as a general whole." He sounded like he was musing aloud, but she still had to correct him.

"I like people just fine. I just don't have any faith in their ability to keep themselves from getting killed in the stupidest ways possible. It doesn't happen often in my park, but I cannot tell you how many times I've had to explain why feeding the bears is a bad idea, that standing underneath a waterfall is dangerous, or any number of things that should be common sense." Just talking about it made her tired. She loved her job most days, but it wore on her. She hadn't realized how much until recently, but sometimes that was how life worked.

Britton tapped his foot, and she found herself counting the soft sound of impact. When she got to ten, he went still. "When will you be discharged?"

"Bright and early tomorrow morning. They probably would have let me go tonight, but they don't trust me not to go running off and aggravate the wound."

This time he almost did smile. "Sounds like they have your number."

"Sounds like it."

He nodded almost to himself and stood. "I'll come by in the morning."

"You really don't—" She stopped, because there was no point in wasting her breath. Britton had his mind set on something, and he wouldn't be deterred. He also wasn't likely to share his plans until he was damn well good and ready. She'd forgotten how aggravating that little personality quirk of his was. "Fine."

"Get some rest, Maggie. We'll talk in the morning." He rose and walked out of the room, his stride so smooth it was almost a glide. When Maggie was a new agent, she'd had a theory that Britton had some kind of formal dance training in his past—no one moved that gracefully naturally—but she'd never been able to confirm it, and the one time she'd gotten the balls to ask him, he'd just given that half smile and changed the subject.

She settled back into her bed and stared blankly at the television. Why had he come? She knew obsessing about it wasn't going to give her any more answers than she'd had when he walked through the door, but she couldn't help it. Britton Washburne represented the career she'd gone into with stars in her eyes and then flamed out of so spectacularly she was pretty sure they were still telling stories about her in the academy, just like they had her predecessors. There were flameouts in every graduating class. It was just the way things went in a high-pressure job like working with the FBI.

Not that all jobs within the FBI were high pressure. There were plenty that were glorified desk jobs, but those weren't what Maggie had been aiming for when she graduated from the academy near the top of her class. Nothing less than the BAU would do.

She'd obviously overestimated her abilities.

◆ ◆ ◆

Thursday, June 22
5:10 p.m.

Vic left Ethan in the interview room and let Tucker convince him to eat something. He wasn't hungry, but going without the much-needed calories was a stupid thing to do. They chose a little chain restaurant not too far from either hospital or police station, and he ordered a steak as soon as the waiter appeared.

"Sleep wouldn't be a bad idea, either."

"Didn't ask you." He took a long drink of his water and considered if coffee at this hour was a good idea. They needed to release Ethan if they weren't going to arrest him—and since he had a solid alibi for at least one of the murders, they didn't even have a circumstantial case against him. He pinched the bridge of his nose, but no magical clarity appeared. "This case is a clusterfuck."

"Aren't they all?"

Vic opened his eyes long enough to glare. "You're not helping."

"Come on, you know I'm right. The locals don't call us in unless something has gone terribly wrong—usually in the form of three or more bodies appearing. I don't know about you, but I define murder in general as a clusterfuck, and the cases we cover are usually stranger on stranger, which makes things endlessly complicated."

"You're not telling me anything I don't already know." Vic switched to massaging his temples. Going back to see Maggie tonight was a shitty thing to do. As much as he wanted to see her—to reassure himself that she really was okay—she needed her rest, and she wasn't going to get that with him looming over her.

Tucker used his plastic straw to create a tiny whirlpool in his water cup. "My point is that this time, there *is* a connection. This isn't stranger on stranger. We have the name of the unsub even if we don't know which one of these kids he is yet."

"That doesn't change the fact that we don't *have* the unsub."

His partner shrugged. "I'm going with the glass half-full this time around, since you're such a fucking ray of sunshine. We'll get him—or her. We'll sit here, eat a very necessary meal, and not talk about the case. And then we'll go back and have another crack at Ethan before we take a break and catch some sleep."

"Easier said than done."

"Isn't it always?"

A shadow fell across their table, and he looked up, expecting the waiter, but it was Britton. Vic narrowed his eyes. "Do you have a tracking device on us?"

"That's unconstitutional."

Tucker snorted and scooted over so Britton could take a seat. "I texted him."

That made sense, but these days, he wouldn't put the former past Britton. Vic knew he was being uncharitable because he was tired and feeling guilty, but he didn't give a fuck. "What have we done to warrant a personal visit?"

Britton smiled at the waiter as the man hurried up with a third glass of water. He ordered without looking at the menu. Their boss was full of neat tricks like that, and Vic could never decide if it was because he was so anal that he had to have everything mapped out beforehand, or if he liked to feed into the legend that was Britton Washburne.

"Maggie might not be one of my agents anymore, but she used to be." He took a small sip of water. "And she was hurt assisting in a case that's being handled by the BAU. Why wouldn't I be here?"

Vic lifted his chin, ready to snap back, but he caught Tucker shaking his head and reconsidered. "I called Caroline."

Britton blinked, the only outward sign that he was surprised. "She has considerable knowledge in medical emergencies." Just that. Nothing more.

It made Vic feel like even more of a dick. "She talked me through it. She might have saved Maggie's life." At the bare minimum, she'd talked him through it so *he* didn't do something to kill Maggie by accident. He didn't say it, but the speculative look in Britton's eyes said that he was doing a piss-poor job of hiding how messed up this case was making him.

But Britton didn't let anything as mundane as personal bullshit get in the way of the job. Instead, he said, "You have a theory on who the unsub is. Let's hear it."

Even though Vic and Tucker had more or less decided to put the case on hold for the duration of the meal, Britton was a new person to bounce their ideas off. He had more than passing knowledge of where they were to date, though Vic hadn't called with an update today. Tucker obviously had.

Still, he and his partner took their boss through the most recent events—what they'd gotten out of Ethan.

And what they hadn't.

"We think he's covering for his girlfriend, Madison. I don't know what her motivation is, though the ex-girlfriend made a pass at him a few months ago—Lauren Rosario, the first victim. Lauren was also in a relationship with Joshua and had been since before they broke up back in high school. Great motivation for Ethan, but Dr. Huxley called with time of death on Josh, and it clears Ethan." Vic shook his head. "The motivation there is haphazard at best, but Madison does have the capabilities to be the unsub. She's been hunting with her dad since she was a child, and she's been trained to bow hunt as well."

"Hmm." The waiter appeared with their food, and Britton waited until he'd moved away from the table to continue. "From what I understand, every one of those hikers, with the possible exception of Ashleigh, has that same knowledge and interest."

"And therein lies the problem." Tucker took a bite of one of his fries and chewed. "The only thing that sets them apart from one another is their possible motivation for murdering their former—and in some cases, current—friends. They all have the means and skill set to be the unsub. But we're down to two options, if only from the process of elimination. We can't rule out Ashleigh completely, but Madison is the better bet."

"So the remaining potential victims are also potentially the unsub. It's quite the conundrum." Britton speared a slice of cucumber and took a bite.

They ate in silence for the next ten minutes, with the efficiency of folks who knew there might be some time before their next warm meal. Vic had just finished his food when his phone rang. He checked the number—local but not one he recognized. "Agent Sutherland."

"Hey, Vic, finally got some good news for you."

It took him a second to place the male voice. "Wyatt?"

"Yep." The man sounded tired, but happy. "One of our choppers was doing one last sweep of the area before nightfall and saw a fire. Long story short, we got the girls. They're a bit worse for wear, and Ashleigh has a nasty infection, but they're alive."

It took him precious moments to process the words. The case had been one piece of bad news after the next, so hearing something *good* set him back on his heels. "They're being taken to the local hospital?"

"They're in transit as we speak. Thought you'd like to know. I'm sure the doctors are going to want to get a good look at them before they allow for questions, but they should be able to answer at least a few tonight."

"Thanks, Wyatt." He hung up and set his phone on the table, finding both Britton and Tucker watching him expectantly. "They found the girls."

"Fuck, yes." Tucker ignored the look of reproach Britton sent him. "It's about time for some good news."

But Vic wasn't looking at Tucker; he was looking at his boss. "They'd set a signal fire, and one of the last sweeps of the area saw them."

"Take some time to build up a fire of any size."

Time spent in one place when they were being hunted. Vic frowned. "They couldn't have been moving fast, either. Wyatt said they were pretty banged up—which is to be expected—and that one of them has a nasty infection." He needed to know how she'd gotten that infection, but those answers would have to wait until they got to the hospital.

"That'd slow them down for sure." Tucker sobered. "You think the other one is the unsub?"

"I don't know what I think."

Vic started to reach for his wallet, but Britton waved him off. "On me."

It wasn't until they were outside in the brisk evening air that Vic spoke the words he'd had ringing around in the back of his head since Wyatt called. "If they got out, then one of them is the unsub—and whichever one of them *isn't* the killer is potentially the next victim."

CHAPTER
TWENTY-ONE

Thursday, June 22
7:17 p.m.

Maggie woke up to the sound of activity. She didn't know how else to term it. There were more footsteps in the hallway than she'd heard up to this point, and there were voices that weren't quite raised but managed to convey urgency despite that. She lay there for a full five minutes, which was long enough for the sounds to die down, but curiosity had gotten the better of her.

That and the need to use the bathroom.

Once she'd taken care of the latter, she padded to her door and peeked out. A pair of women spoke in quiet tones at the nurses' station twenty feet down the hallway, but there was nothing else to see. That didn't stop her, though. She was up—she might as well take a little walk. *At least they gave me a pair of pants to wear so I'm not bare-assed.* She walked toward the nurses' station, trying to look casual.

She failed miserably.

The older nurse saw her first. She had enough wrinkles to convey that she was past middle age, but her body wasn't frail by any definition of the word. She looked like she could bench-press Maggie if she put her mind to it. Her brows dropped, though her tone was polite enough. "Is there something I can help you with?"

"I heard sounds." She realized how silly that sounded and forced a laugh. "I guess I'm being nosy, but I was kind of restless."

The nurse—Jamie, according to her name tag—pressed her lips together, but the younger one, Nicole, smiled. "I can understand. You're the park ranger, right? Must be hard to hold still for so long."

"It is." Sensing a sympathetic soul, she smiled. "I'm not used to being laid up."

"I don't blame you." Nicole leaned forward and lowered her voice. "They just brought in two girls from Glacier. I think they said something about being missing hikers."

"Nicole!" Jamie propped her hands on her hips.

"What? If she's a park ranger, she knows when there are missing hikers, and the fact that she has an injury from an *arrow* means that she's involved." Nicole waved a hand down the hall, presumably in the direction of the girls. "It's not like this hospital can keep a secret to save its life. Besides, their families have already been notified."

Maggie listened with half an ear as they argued, but her mind was already on the case. She didn't realize that she hadn't actually expected to find any of the missing hikers alive. "Do you know how they were found?"

Jamie answered. "The EMTs who brought them in said they lit a signal fire up on Kootenai Peak."

Kootenai Peak. She and Vic had been *so close* to them yesterday. Kootenai Peak overlooked Bench Lake. It was a pretty intense hike to get to the top from that direction, but it was more than doable.

She closed her eyes, trying to picture the area. Depending on where they had set up the fire, the light would be visible for miles. While that didn't mean a damn thing in the grand scheme, it *should* have been visible from Bench Lake, which was the area the unsub had been in just hours previous.

If the unsub was close enough to see the fire, how the hell did those girls get rescued before he could get to them?

Because one of them is the unsub.

Maggie turned for her room. Every instinct she had was screaming that some shit was about to go down, and she wasn't going to be able to do anything about it while dressed in scrubs and a hospital gown. Ava had stopped by and brought her clothing earlier—and yelled at her again for almost getting herself killed.

Back in her room, she stripped, all too aware of the way every single move pulled at her back. It wouldn't take much to rip open the stitches. She didn't think she'd be in danger of bleeding out, but the thought of ripping the stitches was enough to turn her stomach. She wasn't even close to 100 percent at this point.

She'd just buttoned her jeans—with difficulty—when her door opened. "One second."

"Maggie."

Just like that, her entire world stood still. She turned to Vic, torn between smiling just from seeing him and demanding to know why he hadn't called her and told her about the girls being found. But his gray eyes were fastened to her chest when she faced him, which made her acutely aware that she hadn't made it as far as a shirt yet. Her tank top covered everything, but that didn't change the fact that she felt stripped bare without a bra on.

Even injured and tired, her body responded to that look.

He took a sharp breath, as if he knew, and made an obvious effort to drag his gaze north to her face. "I have news."

"Madison and Ashleigh were found." Alive. It was more than she had dared hope for, even if she hadn't been able to admit it to herself.

"Tucker and I are going to talk to them as soon as the doctor gives the okay. It looks like Ashleigh was shot with an arrow on that first night, and the wound has become infected, but no one is worried that there will be permanent damage."

"Not that anyone can see." Her being shot answered the question of why the girls had fled deeper into the forest instead of back toward the campsite that first night. It was the *only* question answered so far.

He nodded. "Not that anyone can see."

Being chased through the woods for days on end, living in a state of terror the entire time, left a mark on a person. If the girls were strong enough to keep going, they'd be okay, but it wouldn't be easy. Their lives were forever changed, and it made Maggie sad to think about.

What was she thinking? One of those girls was, in all probability, the person responsible for all those deaths. Feeling sorry for them didn't change that, and she'd do well to remember it.

She made an effort to set her feelings aside. "Can you help me get into this shirt?" Ava had thought ahead enough to bring a button-up, but Maggie didn't relish the thought of wrestling with it, especially now that Vic was witnessing her weakness.

He grabbed it and helped her shrug into it. "I'd feel better if you weren't in this hospital while they're here—especially on the same damn floor."

"Because we think the same thing—that one of those girls is the unsub." It warmed her that he wanted her protected, but she'd never been content to live her life in a bubble. Even when she was reeling from life knocking her down, she kept fighting. This situation wouldn't be any different.

"Yes, we do." He went to one knee in front of her, carefully buttoning her shirt up as if it were the most important thing in the world. His fingers brushed her stomach, the thin cotton the only barrier between them. The room seemed to heat a good ten degrees, and Maggie had a hard time drawing a full breath as he finished up. "You're checking yourself out of the hospital."

"Yes." She might not be worth much when it came to the investigation, but she couldn't lie in that bed another hour, let alone while there was so much going on here on the same floor. "I'll stay out of the way."

"Did you get much sleep today?"

It was such an odd question that she took a step back so she could see his face better. "I napped. Why?"

Vic smiled, a playful look coming into his eyes. "Because Britton co-opted you for the remainder of this investigation."

"*What?* When?"

"As soon as he landed, apparently. Wyatt wasn't having it, but he promised that it'd be a glorified desk job and that Tucker would sit on you if you tried to exert yourself too much."

She shook her head, still trying to catch up. Of all the things she'd expected him to say, that didn't even make the list. And then the timing dawned on her. "That bastard. He already knew that this had been approved when he came to see me." It put their conversation in an entirely new light. He'd been feeling her out to see if she'd be interested.

Vic's smile faded. "If you're tired or think it's too much, you don't have to do it. Wyatt would probably be relieved if you turned it down."

"Hell, no, I'm not turning it down." She moved carefully, gauging her range of motion. Not great, but it would have to be good enough.

"We're going to interview the girls, and then I'll be back." He brushed a quick kiss across her lips and walked away before she could do something stupid like drag him to bed. The case was winding down, for better or worse, and it would be over soon. She might not be certain of anything else, but she was certain of *that*.

It was just a matter of figuring out what the unsub's next move was.

◆ ◆ ◆

Thursday, June 22
8:23 p.m.

Vic met Tucker outside the girls' room. He jerked a chin at the door. "They both in there?"

"Yeah." Tucker had none of the easygoing swagger that he was known for. He looked tense and worried. "They tried to separate them, but Ashleigh freaked the fuck out. She kept saying, 'It's not over,' which is creepy on a whole different level."

"She's not wrong." No matter which way Vic turned the situation, it didn't fit. Ashleigh had an arrow wound, which indicated they *had* had a run-in with the unsub, but aside from that, the girls were about as well off as if they'd been lost only a few days. Following the logical line of their investigation, one of those girls was responsible for killing six people. But if they were together the whole time . . .

They were missing something—something important.

Could be that the girls are partners . . .

But if that was the case, there had to be a different way they'd go about it. Unless Ashleigh Marcinko was a master actress who had managed to hide her outdoors skills from every single person in her life, if she was part of this, he couldn't help but think that these murders would've happened in an urban setting.

He couldn't rule it out completely, but it seemed improbable.

"No, I don't suppose she is." Tucker rocked back on his heels and slid his hands into his pockets. "Ready?"

"Yeah." It would have been better to separate them and do these interviews at the police station where they could secure both of them, but the hospital wouldn't release them until they were seen to. It was possible that the girls being in a weakened state would make them more likely to slip up and tell the truth, but Vic didn't think he'd get that lucky.

He knocked on the door as he opened it, earning a sharp look from one of the nurses—Jamie, he thought her name was—but this couldn't wait any more than it already had. "Madison. Ashleigh. I'm Agent Sutherland. This is my partner, Agent Kendrick."

The nurse glared. "You have ten minutes, tops. These girls need to get some rest."

"Of course."

Seemingly satisfied, she turned to the girls. "If you get too tired or need anything, just hit the 'Call' button and I'll be back." When they nodded, she left the room, shooting one last glare at Vic and Tucker.

Vic turned his attention to the girls. They'd pushed their beds close enough that it'd be a squeeze to get between them. The blonde had started out her trip thin, but now she had tipped over the edge, her cheeks hollowed out. Her eyes were a little glassy, which indicated she'd had some kind of pain meds already.

The other girl, Madison, was more alert. Her thick, dark hair was tangled and dirty, but she seemed like she'd fared better overall. *Just like she would if she was the unsub.* Her brown eyes were alert, her posture attentive. "You're going to catch the person who killed that guy." She looked away, and then back. "Where are our friends?"

Vic couldn't decide if she was nervous or if she was intentionally trying to steer the interview. Either way, he wasn't about to play along. "Why don't you walk us through everything you've seen and done. Then we can talk about your friends."

From the expression she gave him, she didn't believe for one second that they were getting a happy ending, but since she was right, he ignored it. Finally, Madison sighed. "We had heard that there was a murder in the park, but no one really thought anything of it. We'd scheduled our trip months ago, and trying to get everyone's schedules to align again was going to be nearly impossible." She made a face.

"Take me through that first day." It was the night that everything had gone wrong, but there might be clues in the interactions that peppered the hike up to Fifty Mountain. Plus, starting her off like this was designed to put her at ease and maximize the chance that she'd slip up.

They were so close.

Madison took a tiny sip of water and set the cup aside with shaking hands. "It was a good day. We made decent time, though the group spread out a bit as the afternoon went on." She shot a look at Ashleigh. "Ash and Josh used to date, so there's some unresolved issues there, and they got to sniping at each other. Ethan and I ended up a bit ahead of everyone else, but they all caught up to us once we hit the camping spot." She looked from Vic to Tucker. "We used to hike out there all the time in high school—nearly every single weekend where the weather wasn't terrible. I know that trail like the back of my hand, but we're not cocky about it. The park needs to be respected, and just because something is safe one trip doesn't mean it will be the next time."

Maggie had said something similar. He'd gotten the impression that she had liked Madison—at least the little they'd interacted when they'd all set off together from the ranger station. It would hurt her if she had gotten this close to a serial killer and not known, but he just didn't see how it could be anyone else.

Unless we are missing something . . .

No, that was wishful thinking. Despite twelve years in the BAU teaching him that anyone was capable of murder with the right pressure, he didn't want this fresh-faced girl to be responsible for the horror show they'd seen over the last few days.

He nodded, because that's what was expected of him, and Tucker had apparently decided to take a back seat in this conversation. "You set up camp at Fifty Mountain."

"Yeah. We got the tents up first because they're a pain to wrestle once it gets dark. Ashleigh needed a break, and I was trying to be supportive, so we hiked down a bit to where one of the huckleberry patches used to be. It's too early in the season for them to be ripe, but it was mostly an excuse to get away for a little bit." She hesitated, paling. "That's where we saw the body. I think I screamed. It scared me." She shook her head. "We calmed down a few seconds later, because obviously this guy wasn't a danger to anyone, and he'd been dead for . . . a while."

"He was. Quite a bit of time before your group showed up." He watched her face. She still looked a little like she was in shock, because she was talking about finding a dead person like it'd happened to someone else. *Or she's very good at lying.* "Did any of the others come to find why you were screaming?"

"No . . ." She frowned. "I don't think it was very long from the time I screamed to when the attack came."

He'd known there was an attack—the arrow wound in Ashleigh's arm said as much—but he sat back and let her work her way through it. For her part, the blonde seemed content to let her friend narrate. Her eyes were barely open, and her entire body had relaxed. Vic exchanged a glance with Tucker. While Madison seemed to be coping well enough with the trauma of their experience, the same couldn't be said for Ashleigh. Between her injury and what appeared to be a nasty case of shock, she wasn't going to be much use tonight.

"Someone . . . someone shot Ashleigh through the arm. I think I heard the guys shouting and Lauren scream." Madison shook her head. "We were scared, so we ran. By the time dawn came around, I wasn't really sure where we were, and Ashleigh was pretty messed up. We found a creek and started following it, but we were moving really slow. It took us a couple days to find Bench Lake, which should have taken more than a couple hours normally." She frowned. "At one point, we saw someone with a bow, but they didn't see us."

The unsub—at least theoretically. Most of the SAR people carried some kind of gun or bear spray, but no one would have a bow. Vic leaned forward, just a little. "Can you describe the person?" He asked the question because it was expected of him. The hospital was hardly secured, and if Madison was the unsub, he didn't want to tip her off.

"Dark coat with the hood pulled up, though I couldn't tell you the brand. Same with the pants and boots—dark with no blatant markings. The bow was expensive."

"How do you know that?" Tucker asked.

"I grew up hunting. My dad got me into bow hunting for a little while, but I didn't really like it. But he's kind of a research freak when it comes to new hobbies. He had printouts and reviews of every bow he was considering. He ended up going middle-of-the-road for cost, but I still remember the Spyder. That thing was beautiful—and costs roughly a thousand dollars."

Lot of money, but they already knew the unsub was an obsessive hunter. Only the best would do. It stood to reason that this applied to her weapon of choice. "That . . . What did you say it was called?"

"Spyder." She gave a wistful smile. "Hoyt Archery Carbon Spyder. I couldn't tell you the exact measurements from a distance, but I'd know that bow anywhere."

Interesting. "Those common around here?"

"God, no. Who has that kind of money to blow on a *bow*?" She seemed to realize what she'd said and shuddered. "But if he was using it as a murder weapon, I guess that's a whole different kind of hunter."

"You said *he*. Did you see enough of the person to verify it was a man?"

Madison blinked, opened her mouth, and then frowned. "You know, my first instinct was that it was a man, but now that I think about it, I can't be one hundred percent sure. Like I said, the person was far enough away that I couldn't get a good read on height—and I was trying to keep Ashleigh and myself hidden at the time, so I wasn't exactly standing there measuring the person."

If she was lying, she was extremely convincing. "Try. Please."

She blew out a breath and closed her eyes. "I really don't know. Average height—either a little short for a man or a little tall for a woman. That's not helpful, is it?"

"It's very helpful." It wasn't, other than ruling out anyone shorter than five foot six or taller than six foot. That still left them with every one of the hikers that they'd found so far.

He glanced at the blonde. She was passed out cold, her body relaxed in sleep. They needed to talk to her when Madison wasn't around, but it was obvious they wouldn't get anything out of her tonight.

As if on cue, Nurse Jamie strode back into the room. "That's enough for now."

Vic stood without another word, still watching Madison. "Pretty smart thing you did, hiking up to Kootenai Peak and lighting that fire. Risky, but smart."

"Thanks." She gave a faint smile. "I couldn't think of anything else."

From all accounts, she'd kept both herself and her friend alive and out of the unsub's sights. But that was the problem—from all accounts. "You see Josh at any point after the party split up? Or Ethan, for that matter?"

"No. Other than whoever that was with the bow, we didn't see anyone until the helicopter showed up."

It didn't line up. If she was the unsub, why not just finish the job with Ashleigh and then melt away into the forest? Either they'd assume she was responsible and potentially never find her, or they'd assume she had fallen victim to Glacier and become one of its unrecoverable bodies. Lighting a signal fire and getting herself and Ashleigh brought in—potentially for questioning—didn't fit. "How long did you have the fire going before the rescue crew showed up?"

"Agent, *please.*" Nurse Jamie glared. "There will be plenty of time for questions in the morning. With all due respect, get out."

Madison shrugged. "I got it going around noon. It took us longer than I thought to get to a good spot." She glanced at the sleeping Ashleigh and whispered. "I'm glad we got there in time."

"Thank you. We'll be by in the morning." He followed Tucker into the hall. Tucker started to say something, but Vic shook his head sharply. "This way." He headed down the hall to Maggie's room. They found her just lacing up her boots, her face a grimace of pain that melted away the second she saw him. Vic shook his head again, this time resigned, and went to his knees in front of her. "You're going to hurt yourself." He finished lacing up her boots and stood.

"Uh, thanks." She blushed and frowned. "What are you doing here? I thought you were questioning the girls."

"We were."

"For all the good it did." Tucker threw himself into the spare chair with the grace of a sulky teenager. "It's going to take a bit for Ashleigh's shock and exhaustion to wear off, and she won't be able to either contradict or corroborate Madison's story until that happens. Madison doesn't know shit. Or she's lying. Or some combination of the two. This doesn't make sense. Ethan Conlon couldn't have killed Josh or shot you, because he was in Kalispell at the time. That leaves Madison and Ashleigh, but Ashleigh has an infection nasty enough to limit her ability to get around, so that really leaves Madison."

Maggie sat on the edge of her bed. "If the unsub is one of those girls, don't you think the *other* one would find it a little strange that her friend kept disappearing? Even if it were possible, Lauren and Josh were killed miles apart. The sheer amount of ground the girl—whichever one you're looking at—would have to cover would leave the other alone for hours on end. Hard not to be suspicious."

"There was that person that Madison saw," Tucker mused. "If she was telling the truth. Fuck, I hate going in circles."

"If Madison was telling the truth—something we can't verify before we talk to Ashleigh." That was the problem—they didn't have a reliable witness, *and* every witness was a suspect. Madison had said they were together the entire time, but until they talked to Ashleigh, they couldn't verify it. Vic rubbed his eyes. "Fuck."

"That about sums it up." Tucker stretched his arms over his head. "What say you, Ranger Gaines? Do you have any brilliance to add to the clusterfuck that is this case?"

Maggie pressed her lips together. She was still too pale, and the circles beneath her eyes too dark, but she was alert. "Until we—or, rather, *you*—can talk to Ashleigh, I don't think there's a lot to be done at the moment. But I think you should put a police detail on the girls' room."

"Already called it in." Vic nodded. "We need to get them into separate rooms." Just because Madison might have orchestrated this rescue didn't mean she was finished. Putting them in different rooms would at least protect Ashleigh for the time being until they could get to the bottom of this.

"This isn't over." Maggie sat on the edge of her bed.

"My gut agrees with you." Tucker scrubbed his hands over his face. "Whatever the reasoning behind the girls ending up here, the unsub isn't through. That next move is going to be soon."

CHAPTER
TWENTY-TWO

Thursday, June 22
11:15 p.m.

Maggie's plan to check out of the hospital hit a snag the second she declared her intentions to the nurses on staff. The older of the two—Jamie—gave her a look like she was crazy. "No, honey, you're not." The nurse pointed a finger at Vic and Tucker. "You two are nothing but trouble. You upset those girls, and now you're inciting my other patient to rebellion."

"Ma'am, we had nothing to do with this."

She wasn't interested in listening. "It's nearly midnight. Whatever you have going can wait until morning. And *you*." Her finger moved to point at Maggie. "You can't check out until a doctor signs off on it, and he won't be in again until seven. Before you start talking about waking up the poor on-call doctor, think about what you're saying. It's going to take you nearly an hour to make your way home, and then you're going to toss and turn and not sleep. Go back to your room, do your best to rest, and leave in the morning."

Maggie didn't want to leave in the morning. She wanted to leave right that moment. Rationally, she knew she was letting her emotions get the best of her, but the lure of home was nearly overwhelming. "But—"

"Maggie." Vic didn't say anything else, but it was enough.

She sagged, though she couldn't say for sure herself if it was in disappointment or relief. She lifted her chin out of sheer stubbornness. "The second the doctor gets in, he signs me out."

"I wouldn't dream of stopping him." Jamie eyed her clothing. "I won't make you change, but you might consider removing the boots so you can be more comfortable." It was as much of a concession as she was going to get, and everyone in the room knew it.

"Thank you."

Jamie sighed and left the room. After that, there wasn't much else to say. Tucker bolted like he had places to be—probably his hotel room—which left her and Vic alone. With only him to witness it, she allowed disappointment to take hold, just for a moment. "I just want my bed."

"I know." He sat next to her and carefully wrapped his arm around her. "It's almost over."

Maggie leaned her head on his shoulder, too tired to ask the questions that had been pestering her all day. She wasn't the type of person who did well with inactivity, but she had better get used to it, because her injury was going to hold her back, at least for a little bit. Pushing herself too hard, too fast, would make everything worse.

No matter how restless she felt.

She let herself enjoy the feel of Vic next to her for far too long before she finally straightened. "You need sleep as much as I do, and I can attest that this hospital bed is uncomfortable in the extreme." She squeezed his hand and let it go. "Get some rest, Vic. The case will be here in a few hours. *I* will be here in a few hours. We're reaching the critical point, and a misstep because you're too tired to think straight is going to provoke Britton to give you one of *those* looks."

He chuckled. "If that's not motivation, I'm not sure what is." He pressed a kiss to her forehead. "I'll see you in the morning."

"Okay." There was nothing else to say, and she had no right to the disappointment she felt once she was alone in her room once more. Maggie looked at her boots—the effort required to bend over and unlace them too much for her to even contemplate. She could call in one of the nurses, but she'd be sentencing herself to yet another lecture. Compared to that, the slight discomfort of keeping her boots on was a small price to pay.

She scooted fully onto the bed and leaned back. *I'll just close my eyes for a few minutes . . .*

Maggie shot upright so fast her back spasmed. She froze, blinking into the darkness, her disorientation only made worse by the red numbers glaring from the clock. *Three?* She must have fallen asleep. She blinked and rubbed the back of her hand across her face, trying to figure out what had woken her.

It took several long seconds for realization to set in. Silence. Complete and utter silence.

The hairs on the back of her neck rose, and she went on high alert. Hospitals were often hushed, especially at this hour, but *silence* was unnatural, even for a small place like this. She slipped out of bed, feeling ungainly and loud, but the reality was that the only sound was the soft scrape of her jeans across the sheets. It shouldn't have felt like she'd just blared a bullhorn, but it did. She pocketed her phone out of instinct and sent a silent thank-you into the universe that she'd been too tired to mess with her boots when she'd lain down. Having to wrestle them on now would have been a nightmare.

She padded to her door and eased it open, feeling foolish for sneaking around. She was going to peek out into the hall, see the nurses at their station, and realize it was all in her head.

But when she peered down the hall, the nurses' station was empty.

Maggie froze. Okay, that was weird. She started to try to convince herself that there was a reasonable explanation, but stopped. There was a serial killer on the loose—maybe in a room just down the hallway from her. At this point, assuming innocence was the wrong choice.

She slipped her phone out of her pocket, made sure it was on silent, and sent a quick text to Vic. If it was a false alarm, she'd send a follow-up. If he was sleeping, he probably wouldn't even get the texts until morning. If it *wasn't* a false alarm, she'd call.

Simple. Easy. Nothing to be concerned about.

Not feeling the least bit reassured, she slipped out of her room and started down the hallway, sticking close to the wall. Maggie had never missed her service weapon—she didn't hate guns and could take them or leave them—until this point.

She reached the nurses' station. There, a half-drunk cup of coffee sitting next to the computer. Maggie touched it. Cold. She couldn't see the girls' doors from here, and she had the insane urge to go back into her room and close the door and pretend that none of this was happening. She wasn't an FBI agent anymore. It wasn't her job to investigate.

Coward.

She couldn't walk away.

She looked around for a potential weapon, finally settling on a metal fountain pen that had probably been a gift for one of the nurses, because it was too fancy to have been provided by the hospital. As weapons went, it was pathetic, but it was still better than nothing. She took a fortifying breath and headed around the corner.

An empty chair sat outside a room, innocuous as such things went, but she knew for a fact Vic had called in a local deputy to stand watch until morning. He or she should have been sitting in that chair. *Crap.* Ashleigh's door was closed, and she didn't wait for a chance to talk herself out of it. Maggie opened the door, squinting into the darkness.

It shouldn't have been that dark.

She reached blindly for the light switch and had to bite back a cry of surprise when she found it. The bright clinical light made the room look like a child had finger-painted the entire room in red. No child was responsible for this, though, and that *wasn't* paint. She took in the arterial spray across the walls and finally the source—the blonde girl lying in the middle of the floor, her throat cut in a vicious slash. There was no coming back from that. She was dead. Maggie didn't need to measure the wound to know that it had most likely been made with the same knife that had stabbed Joshua Conlon to death after he'd been shot.

She desperately didn't want to walk into that room, but the bathroom door was shut, and she needed to know if there were more bodies to report before she texted Vic again.

Sidestepping the blood as best she could, she made her way to the bathroom, a hysterical voice deep inside her chanting the old children's rhyme.

Step on a crack and break your mother's back.
Step on a line, and break your mother's spine.
Step on a . . .

She stopped in front of the door. The handle was coated in blood, so the unsub had closed it after killing Ashleigh. Either she was going to find Madison in this room, also dead, or Madison was the unsub. *Should have cuffed them to the beds. Don't know what we were thinking.* It didn't matter that no one had asked her recommendation or that she wouldn't have considered it before now—she still felt responsible.

Maggie took a careful breath, all too aware of how close she was to hysteria. She hadn't dealt with murder in so long, and to have so many bodies piling up in such a short time was too much. She hadn't been prepared, hadn't shored up her walls and taken the necessary step back, both emotionally and mentally. There were training tricks to ensure that her reactions didn't get the best of her, but they weren't second nature now like they used to be.

But too much or not, she couldn't hide from this.

She opened the door, her mind clicking into a cold and clinical place she'd thought was long gone. Three bodies. Two nurses—one stripped of her scrubs—and one cop, their hands and feet zip-tied.

She rushed to the nearest one—Jamie, though she was barely recognizable with her face already swelling from some kind of blunt trauma. Maggie touched her shoulder and startled when she opened her eyes and tried to lurch up. "Help them!"

"Jamie, Jamie, calm down. I need you to tell me what happened." She looked around for something to cut the zip ties with, but the bathroom was void of anything even remotely resembling a weapon. "Take a deep breath."

Jamie struggled onto her back, her brown eyes clearing of some of their panic. Some. "There's a pair of scissors at the nurses' station. Cut me free and I'll take care of the others. Hurry."

She couldn't leave them like this. Maggie nodded and hurried back to the nurses' station, doing her best not to look too closely at the body in the middle of the room. She found the scissors quickly and returned to cut Jamie free. "Now tell me what happened."

"It was that girl." She rubbed her wrists and then her ankles. "Didn't see much. I heard a scuffle and rushed in there, thinking . . . well, I don't know what I was thinking. The policeman they sent to watch the girls wasn't at the door, and I was worried. I walked into the room, saw the blood, and someone hit me from behind. She must have hit me a few more times, with how much my face hurts." She gingerly touched her head right behind her left ear. "I don't think I have a concussion, but she knocked me out cold, so who knows."

"She. You keep saying *she*. Was it Madison?" She needed to get moving, because either it *was* Madison or the unsub *had* Madison. *Too much evidence for the former. Unless Ethan slipped his leash and came to the hospital, it* has *to be Madison.*

Jamie took the scissors from her and cut through the cop's zip ties. "Who else could it be?"

Maggie nodded, because there was nothing else to do. She motioned to the two unconscious people. "Can you take care of them? I'm going to call in reinforcements."

"Yes."

She didn't ask again. She strode back into the room, grabbed a pair of gloves from the container on the wall, and moved straight to the body. For all the blood on the walls, the unsub must have dropped Ashleigh almost immediately, because a pool had collected beneath her. Maggie pulled on a glove and pressed two fingers to the pool of blood. It wasn't warm, but it hadn't started to dry, either.

Not much time had passed since Ashleigh's death.

She sent a silent apology to the dead girl and rose. The unsub would need transportation, so she'd have to steal a car. That took time, even for experienced car thieves.

Maggie ran.

It hurt. A lot. But she didn't slow down, and she didn't stop. If it was already too late, then it was already too late, but she wouldn't miss her chance because she babied her back. She took the stairs, already slipping into Madison's point of view. She wouldn't take the elevator—too public, even dressed as a nurse—and she wouldn't walk out the front door for fear of getting stopped. It was possible she'd go out the back and try one of the other buildings on the medical campus, but most of those parking lots would be empty at this time of night.

Staff parking. That was definitely where she was headed.

Maggie picked up her pace, making it down to the main floor in record time and then heading for the back of the building. She grabbed the first nurse she saw on the main floor, a guy who looked about twelve. "Upstairs. Someone's been killed. Call the cops." To his credit, he rushed to obey, barking out orders with a command that belied his youthful appearance. She didn't wait to see them obeyed.

He called after her as she rushed down the hallway, but she ignored him. Time was ticking, and if she missed her in the parking lot, Madison would be gone for good.

The staff parking lot was sparsely filled, which she'd expected, but her gaze landed on a nondescript black van idling just out of the circle of lamplight.

Don't be stupid. Do not rush out there to the suspicious-looking van.

She moved into the shadows next to the hospital door and pulled out her phone to text Vic a quick update. Now really was the time to call in backup personally with the information she had that the nurse didn't, but that van was idling, and she couldn't risk it getting away from her. She had no vehicle, and even if she did, the chance of keeping up with someone who knew the roads around here was slim to none. Maggie knew them, of course. But there were logging roads that could take a person all the way to Canada if they knew the way, and she didn't.

She checked her phone one last time and then started for the van. There was no way to approach unseen, but she still kept to where she figured the driver's blind spot would be. It wasn't until she was nearly on top of the damn thing that she realized the back door was cracked open. *Trap. Definitely a trap. She might as well have rolled out the welcome mat.*

Maggie readjusted her grip on the pen she'd slipped into her pocket and pulled open the door. It took her eyes several seconds to adjust to the darkness within the van. It looked like something someone had been living out of—there were two sleeping bags, a pile of what she thought were clothes, and a box of . . . canned food.

Her hand brushed something hard inside the sleeping back on the left, and she froze, feeling around blindly. That was definitely a foot. After looking behind her to make sure the parking lot was still empty of people, she climbed into the back of the van, the rational voice in her head screaming at her to get the hell out of there.

I have to know.

She crawled to the top of the sleeping bag and unzipped it a little. That was definitely hair. She felt down farther, still calling herself seven different kinds of a fool, until she touched a face.

Breath ghosted against her palm—alive—but whoever it was didn't move. Judging from the hair and slight build, she'd guess woman, but there was only one way to tell for sure. Maggie slipped her phone out of her pocket, cast another quick look around, and lifted it up enough so that the light of the screen shined on the person in the sleeping bag.

She froze. She knew that face, though her being *here* and unconscious sent all Maggie's previous assumptions into a tailspin.

Madison.

The van door clicked shut behind her, and she moved out of instinct, slithering down and back to the pile of clothes, burrowing under it as best she could. She went still as the driver's door opened and the van shifted with the weight of a new addition. She couldn't see anything more than the silhouette of a head, though the black hood covered any kind of distinguishing features that she could use to figure out who it was.

Not that it mattered. She knew who it was, even she didn't know who it was.

The unsub.

And she'd just broken safety rule number one—never let yourself be taken to a secondary location.

Crap.

◆ ◆ ◆

Friday, June 23
3:29 a.m.

Vic woke to the sound of a text message. He blinked into the darkness, already reaching for his phone before he was fully coherent. He thumbed it on and frowned. He'd missed *five* messages from Maggie.

Heard something weird. Going to investigate. Think it's the girls.
Ashleigh is dead. Madison is missing. Found nurses and cop unconscious but okay.
Heading to parking lot. Unsub is either Madison or has taken Madison.
Dodge cargo van. Don't know the year. Black. License plate 3P 8768P.
SOS. Im backlog of van. Unsub friring. Madison there.

It took him three tries to decipher the last, and once he did, he shot up in bed. She was in the back of the goddamn unsub's van, and if she was able to text, the unsub might not know she was there. "Fuck." Vic threw on his pants and dressed faster than he ever had in his life. He called Tucker, but his partner didn't answer, so he called Britton.

"Yes." From the calm answer, one wouldn't know that it was three thirty in the morning.

"The unsub got to the girls at the hospital. I think Ashleigh's dead, and Maggie and Madison are in the back of the unsub's van. I don't know if he knows Maggie is there, because she was able to get a text out. I have the make, model, and the plates." They could send a BOLO on it, but that wouldn't help them if the unsub was going where he suspected. "He's taking them to the park."

"That would be my guess as well." There was movement on the other end of the line and the jingle of keys. "Tucker will take the hospital. I'll be at your hotel in five minutes, and we'll head for the park."

The sheer helplessness of the situation made him sick to his stomach. "We don't even know where he's taking them."

"When was the last text sent?"

"Minutes ago."

"Then we have time."

He forced himself to slow down enough to acknowledge that truth. It took time to get to the park, especially if the unsub was attempting to get them deep enough where he could play his game without fear that they'd make it back to civilization. "We still need to call in a BOLO."

"I'll do that. If Tucker isn't answering his phone, go to his door."

"Yes, sir." Vic hung up. He looked at his phone for a long moment, the temptation to call Maggie nearly overwhelming. Doing so would put her in danger, even if her phone was silenced. He wouldn't do that, not even to reassure himself. He had to trust that she could take care of herself long enough for him to reach her . . . wherever she was.

They'd find her.

They had to.

He called the ranger station as he left his room and headed for Tucker's. There was only so much the rangers could do, but he still had to call it in. They might not know beyond a shadow of a doubt that the unsub was taking Maggie and Madison to Glacier, but they had his past actions to use as foundation to anticipate his future actions. Every one of his kills had been in a national park.

No, that wasn't true anymore. He'd killed Ashleigh in the hospital. Killed Ashleigh but apparently left the nurses and cop alive.

Vic would think about that later. Right now he had more important things on his mind.

An unfamiliar woman answered. "Glacier National Park."

"Who is this?"

"What the hell? Who is *this*? You're the one calling at three thirty in the damn morning."

Just like that, he knew. "Ava. It's Agent Sutherland. I need your help." He detailed what little they knew.

"Shit." She sounded shaken for the first time since he'd met her. "Okay, give me a second. I need to think." She didn't make him wait long. "If he's driving in, there are only so many pull-off spots. It's the middle of the night, so Going-to-the-Sun Road will be all but empty.

He'll take them there. Or that would be my guess. There are a ton of turnoff points where he could park and haul them farther into the park. People leave their cars at trailheads all the time, so it wouldn't be out of the norm unless you were looking for it."

"That makes sense." It was as good a theory as any. And if he was taking the women into Glacier like they suspected, it would narrow the places to look for the turnoff point. But it would still take *time*. "Can we get the park rangers on this?"

"We don't have many on shift at the moment, but I'll send the ones out that I do have."

"We're coming in from Kalispell, so we'll start on that side."

"That helps."

By this point, he'd reached Tucker's door and lifted a fist to pound on it. "I'll have my phone on me. Keep me updated."

"We'll find her."

"Yes, we will." Neither one of them mentioned what was at stake if they didn't get there in time. Maggie was resourceful, and she knew that park as well as the unsub did.

But she was injured and trapped in the back of the unsub's van, whether he knew she was there or not. She wouldn't be able to keep hiding once he went to pull Madison out, and if she tried to fight him . . .

Who the hell is the unsub? All the suspects are either dead or in custody.

Vic swallowed hard and pounded harder on Tucker's door. A good thirty seconds later, his partner opened the door, shirtless and looking like he'd been sleeping hard. "What's going on?" He took in Vic's clothing, and his gaze sharpened. "What happened?"

"You need to get to the hospital. The unsub was there."

"Fuck."

A nondescript SUV in generic gray pulled into the parking lot. Britton. "There's at least one person dead there, and we need every bit of information the survivors have," Vic said.

"I'm on it." Tucker frowned. "Where are you headed?"

"The unsub has Maggie." Saying the words aloud made the terror that Vic was barely holding at bay all the stronger. He'd just found her again. Even if he hadn't, she still had a life here—passions, hopes, dreams. The thought of such a vibrant life cut off too soon made him sick to his stomach.

Vic had never been more afraid than he was in that moment.

Tucker stilled. "You'll find her." He burst back into motion, heading for his suitcase. "Go. I'll take care of things on this end."

He went.

CHAPTER
TWENTY-THREE

Friday, June 23
4:40 a.m.

Maggie couldn't believe she'd gotten herself into this mess. Well, actually, she could, since she was the one who'd climbed into the back of a suspicious van and gotten herself trapped there. She wanted to check her phone to see if Vic had gotten her messages, but she was afraid to take it out and reveal herself.

She wouldn't have much of a choice before too long.

The lights had dimmed to only the random passing headlights, which was all the confirmation she needed to know where they were going—Glacier. The unsub was going to finish what he started. Or she. Maggie wasn't sure. The silhouette wasn't particularly tall—the top of the head about even with the back of the headrest—and the figure was mostly hidden by the bulky coat. She'd caught a glimpse of the unsub's hand when he'd adjusted the heat, but the light was too low to pick up any detail. The unsub could be anyone.

Anyone except Madison.

The girl hadn't stirred in the time they'd been driving, which was worrisome. Maggie didn't know if she'd been hit on the head like the nurse or if she was drugged, but she wasn't rousing. She hoped the unsub hadn't accidentally killed her—if he was going to do it on purpose, he would have finished it in the hospital the same way he had with Ashleigh.

Though that didn't make a whole lot of sense from where she was sitting. Why kill one girl in the hospital and go through the effort of hauling the other one back into the park? It was riskier to take two, but this unsub had proven himself to be a planner of the highest degree. He'd incapacitated both nurses and a cop. He stole one of the nurses' uniforms . . . for Madison? But why? That didn't make any sense.

Unless the unsub stole the scrubs for himself.

The hospital was quiet at night. Even as small as this one was, people saw what they wanted to see. If they saw a nurse rolling someone on a cot or in a wheelchair, would they question it?

I bet that's how he got her out.

That still didn't explain why he killed one and took the other. There wasn't anyone else who would have stopped him if he'd transported the girls one at a time out of the hospital and into the van. He'd already rendered Madison unconscious, so going back for Ashleigh would have been doable if he wanted to.

So he obviously hadn't wanted to.

The question was: *Why?*

I could get to him now. He might see me in the rearview mirror, but it would be too late.

And it might kill them all when he lost control of the van.

The roads around here weren't like those on the east side of the state. There were too many trees, sudden drop-offs, and mountains to run into if someone lost control. Add in the sheer lack of man-made light, and if they went over the side, someone might not find them for days. It had happened before, and it would no doubt happen again.

If it was just her and the unsub, she might risk it. But there was Madison to consider. The girl was still unconscious or too scared to move. Either way, her position in the sleeping bag would restrict her movements and prevent her from bracing if they crashed. She'd be help-less, and more likely to get hurt or killed as a result.

Maggie hadn't gotten herself into this mess to end up dead—or killing what might be the last hiker alive.

Except for Ethan.

She frowned at the back of the unsub's head. Last she'd heard, Ethan Conlon was still occupying space in the local police station. Who else *was* there?

Damn it, she was going to have to take her chances. The farther they drove, the less chance there was of anyone finding them in time. She couldn't trust that her phone would have service to get a call or text out, and trying to hike back to civilization while injured, with an exhausted and possibly injured girl and a hunter on their heels . . .

Maggie didn't like their odds.

She shifted, trying to get some traction so she could burst from her hiding spot, but the van slowed, stalling her intentions. Would it be better to go for him now or when he opened the back door? Neither would be spots he'd expect resistance, but the van's interior would limit both their movements. That might be a blessing, but if he was bigger than Maggie—stronger—it would give him the advantage. If she wasn't injured, she'd say to hell with it, but she had that to consider. It would slow her down, weaken her.

And then the van was stopped and the engine turned off, and her opportunity to choose had passed.

The unsub climbed out of the van, and she shifted toward the door. It was tempting to check on Madison, but there was no time. The back door cracked open, and she used both her feet to kick it with all her might. A surprised grunt was her only reward, and she sprang to her feet and rushed out into the night.

She got two steps before she realized the unsub wasn't on the ground like she expected. A soft laugh had her turning around to find him on the side of the van, well out of range of the door. The gun in his hand shined dully in the weak moonlight.

"Nice try, Ranger."

Maggie frowned. That wasn't a man's voice. She narrowed her eyes, seeing the lean form in new light. Normal height, petite but not thin, the coat cloaking all signs of gender. She'd assumed male in error because she'd fallen back on the old FBI studies that most serial killers were male. The percentages held up to that belief, even in recent years, but apparently Maggie was looking at one of the exceptions. She didn't immediately recognize the voice, though, and the hood of the coat hid the woman's features from her.

They'd thought the unsub was one of the hikers, but how could that be? There were no women left except for Madison, and she was currently in the back of the van. "Who are you?"

"Haven't you guessed?" The unsub reached up and took down her hood.

Maggie stared. "But . . . that's impossible."

"Turns out reports of my death have been exaggerated." Lauren Rosario laughed and motioned with the handgun. "Now, get that bitch up. We have work to do."

◆ ◆ ◆

Friday, June 23
5:09 a.m.

"They found the van." Britton hung up his phone.

"Where?" Vic was driving since Britton had been coordinating things with Ava and the park rangers. He could have done it, but he was too damn distracted with his worry for Maggie. Driving was easier. He could focus on the physical and let Britton direct him while he tried very hard not to think about the fact it had been more than an hour since Maggie's last text. His phone was in his lap, screen up in case she called or texted again.

Nothing.

With every minute that passed, he was surer that something had gone wrong—something beyond Maggie being in the back of that fucking van in the first place. It only took about forty-five minutes to get from the hospital to a midpoint within the roads that ran through the park. He and Britton were on Going-to-the-Sun, and he chafed at how slow he was forced to go. None of the sights were there at this hour, but once dawn hit, the glory that was Glacier would be there for the viewing.

He could give a fuck.

Britton cleared his throat. "We're almost there. The van is at one of the viewing spots that leads into the Loop."

Though he wanted to accelerate, he forced himself to maintain a reasonable speed. Getting into a wreck now would only distract from the most important thing—getting Maggie and Madison out of there alive.

Two minutes later, they found the van. A park-ranger vehicle sat next to it. David, pale and shaken, but determined. And Wyatt, who had aged decades in the last few days. "Agents." Wyatt led the way to the van. "This matched the description you provided." He shined his flashlight into the back. "We found it like this—the back door was ajar. There weren't any signs of a struggle, but . . ."

But it was hard to tell. The back of the van held necessary items one would need if going camping, but it didn't have the arsenal he'd expected. "He's got a secondary location where he keeps his gear," Vic said. Possibly the same location that he suspected the Haglunds had stumbled onto.

"I would expect there are trophies there as well."

He hadn't heard Britton approach, but Vic wasn't surprised. Even when he wasn't distracted, the man moved like a cat. Vic nodded. "They didn't find anything missing, but with the way the bodies were found, it was possible Dr. Huxley missed something." Cold to talk like this while Maggie was somewhere in the park, possibly fighting for her life. He swallowed hard, fighting for distance. "He's got her."

"Yes," Britton said.

Wyatt shifted, drawing their attention. "The trailhead leads north for about a third of a mile before it branches. One branch heads toward Granite Park, and the other toward Flattop and then Fifty Mountain."

"Fifty Mountain. That's the one he's taking them to." Vic was sure of it. The unsub wouldn't bother to make it all the way to Fifty Mountain unless there was some kind of significance there that Vic still didn't understand. Most of the other deaths had been in the immediate area surrounding that campsite, but forcing two people to hike ten-ish miles in the dark was going to be next to impossible. Even if Madison was incapacitated, the unsub had to know Maggie would fight him every step of the way.

Unless he killed her.

Vic's stomach lurched. "We have to go."

"Keep it together." Britton was there instantly, his body a shield between Vic and the park rangers, his voice low enough not to carry. "If they think you're compromised, they won't let you go with them."

"They can't stop me."

"They can and they will." Britton nodded at the trail. "It will be full light soon, and that's when the unsub will start his hunt. There's time."

"You can't know that." Vic was afraid to hope. The unsub's plans hadn't included Maggie, and so there was no way to know if his desire for a challenge would push him to kill Maggie outright like he had Ashleigh, or if he'd include her in the hunt.

Vic shook his head. "Why did he kill Ashleigh in the hospital? It doesn't fit with his MO." All the other deaths fit, at least to some extent. There were slight discrepancies, but that made sense in the larger picture because all those people meant something to the unsub, though they still didn't know what.

Either Ashleigh wasn't meant to be on that trip . . . but no, that didn't make sense, either. It would have been easy enough to leave her unharmed, the way he'd left the hospital staff. He'd wanted to kill her up close and personally—and hadn't cared that her death wasn't in the park.

The pieces clicked into place. "Why do people kill? Love, sex, jealousy, hate."

"All shades of the same color."

"Exactly." Vic stared into the darkness, as if he could will Maggie into view. "This group of friends was quite the incestuous bunch. Different pairs dating, most of them cheating with others in the group. Ashleigh and Joshua dated through most of high school, but he traded her in for Lauren when she left—before she left, if our information was accurate." He looked at Britton. "What do you want to bet she and Joshua had a little reunion in the meantime?"

"Once you cross that line, it's easy enough to cross again," Britton mused.

"Exactly. They're all linked that way, which plays into the order of killings." Understanding that small part of the unsub led the way to more potential revelations. It kept coming back to those kids and this park. He'd originally thought that something bad happened here, some event that stuck in the unsub's mind until he either built it up to be something it wasn't or let it poison his mind. Now it didn't seem that that was the case.

If he was right, the motive here was one of the most common when it came to murder. It was just the method that was unique.

In the end, it didn't matter.

Wyatt finally hung up his phone and approached. "There's no good way to do this. It's dangerous as hell to hike down in the dark, not least because we'll need lights to make the initial descent, and we're chasing a psychopath. But he's got one of ours, and I've made the executive call not to wait." He checked his watch. "There are more park rangers on their way, but we're going in first. I'm assuming that you're joining us?"

"Just Agent Sutherland." Britton motioned to his phone. "I'm going to continue to coordinate efforts from here and stay in contact with Agent Kendrick."

And use his influence to ensure the search rolled out the way he preferred. Vic didn't say it. They were all control freaks in their own ways, and Britton's tendencies benefited his team 99 percent of the time. This wouldn't be an exception.

Britton motioned to his rental. "I have gear in there for you."

Of course he did. Vic nodded and went to get it. He heard Wyatt and Britton speaking softly, figuring out the game plan, but he was more concerned with double-checking his pack. He trusted his boss, but there were maybe two people in the entire world he'd accept a pack from without doing a quick once-over. Satisfied everything was in order, he shrugged the backpack on and adjusted the straps.

Wyatt and David did the same. Wyatt took a long look at him. "This isn't going to be easy, but you need to follow instructions. We're all worried about Maggie and the girl. Trust me on that. You get yourself hurt or killed because you're rushing this, and it's going to distract from the ones who need our help. Got it?"

Vic wanted to rage at him, to tell him that *he*, of all people, knew exactly what was at stake. But Wyatt was right. He was dangerously close to losing control, and all that would do was put Maggie more firmly in danger. He couldn't let it happen. He *wouldn't*.

So he just nodded.

And that was that. They hiked down into the darkness, and Vic couldn't shake the feeling that he was willingly hiking into hell.

CHAPTER
TWENTY-FOUR

Friday, June 23
5:34 a.m.

Maggie's back burned, and it wasn't just from the glare of the woman behind her. Lauren Rosario. The woman she'd thought was dead and mauled by a bear. The unsub, responsible for killing at least seven people. There'd been no opportunity to fight, despite Lauren's smaller size. She'd never once lowered her gun, even when she'd hauled Madison out onto the ground and roused the girl with a kick to the ribs.

The opportunity to gang up on her never arose. Madison could barely walk, and Lauren had zip-tied their hands in front of them. Instead of trying to figure out how to attack, Maggie was forced to be a moving leaning post for the girl. Madison had taken one look at her friend, and her face had frozen over. She hadn't spoken since, and her expression hadn't thawed.

Shock. It had to be.

As understandable as that reaction was, Maggie couldn't count on help from that quarter. So she'd allowed Lauren to prod them down the trail from the Loop, turning south and then north toward Fifty Mountain.

Always Fifty Mountain.

What the hell happened there that brought on the fixation with it?

She had so many questions, but after that initial dramatic reveal, Lauren hadn't said more than one-word commands. Was the woman working alone? Or was she a pawn in someone else's plan? It was possible. Stranger things had happened.

Or maybe Maggie was suffering from her own version of shock. The short interaction she'd had with Lauren previously—the exception being when the woman *shot* her—had given her the impression of a sweet and shy girl. There was none of that now. Just a cold mask and a look in her dark eyes that didn't bode well for their chances of getting out of this alive.

So she stopped thinking about the why and started thinking about a way to survive long enough either to turn the tables on the hunter or for rescue to arrive. Knowing what Maggie did about search and rescue in the park, she wasn't optimistic they'd be found in time. There was just too much ground to cover, even if someone found the van quickly.

Next to her, Madison climbed mechanically, never looking to either side. Their chances would rise considerably if they could work together against Lauren, but it didn't appear as if that was going to be an option.

With nothing left to do, Maggie started planning. They wouldn't make it to Fifty Mountain. There was no way that was Lauren's plan. Even with the trail closed, people still ignored the warning. They always did. The chance of running into someone was lower than it would be normally this year, but it was still there. If Lauren was as good as her crimes made it appear, she'd know that.

Besides, it's no fun to hunt on the trail.

Lauren had no bow, no other weapons beyond the gun she had casually pointed in their direction every time Maggie looked back. No one had the strength to keep the gun up at all times, but she wouldn't have to because she was behind them.

The lack of a bow bothered her. They'd known the unsub had a place somewhere in the park, but if Lauren didn't have anything on her, it meant it was *close. If we knew where it was, we might get back some of the advantage in this game.* It would take time for Lauren to get there, time for her to gear up. Not enough—never enough—but it might give them an edge.

"Whatever you're thinking, it won't work."

Maggie startled but recovered quickly. If the woman wanted to talk, she would happily oblige her. "Nice morning for a hike." Dawn had already started to eat away at the sky surrounding the mountains, but it would take longer to get to their point.

"It is." There was quiet reverence in Lauren's voice, but Maggie couldn't say what put it there—the park or the anticipation of their deaths. "Have you ever climbed Grinnel Point and just looked out? Even the stars can't stand against the mountains here."

Maggie dodged a branch before her foot caught on it. "I have. It's very beautiful."

Something snapped in the girl next to her. Madison spun, her expression terrible in its fear and grief. "That's what you have to say? Talking about how amazing this park is? You *killed* Ashleigh."

"I also killed Josh, the Haglunds, two other idiots, and a girl who looks a whole lot like me." She laughed, light and free. "Oops. Did I say that out loud? Guess the cat's out of the bag."

"Lot of people." Maggie kept her tone indifferent.

"Can't say they didn't deserve it." Lauren shrugged, her but attention was on Madison. "Can't say *you* don't deserve it."

"What the hell are you talking about? None of them ever did anything to you. *You* are the one who broke Ethan's heart and screwed over Josh and—"

"Shut up." Lauren lifted the handgun again. "Get back to hiking."

"The hell I will." Madison took a step forward, her hands fisted at her sides. "Shoot me if you want to, but I'm not doing this. What's your plan, Lauren? Are you going to hunt me? You spent *days* shadowing us? Why not just do it, then?"

Maggie had been wondering the same thing. From all accounts, Lauren had been close enough to finish the kill before the girls had been found. She took a slow, cautious step to the side, putting her closer to Lauren. If they kept up arguing, she might be able to get the drop on the woman.

Lauren glared, her entire body so tense she was almost shaking. "I was looking for Ethan."

"Ethan." Madison's hands came up and then dropped. "You killed him, too."

"No, she didn't." Maggie hating speaking up, but the sheer lack of tone in the girl's voice scared the hell out of her. "Ethan is fine. He went to get help for *you*, Madison." *Even if he did it in the most roundabout way possible and wasted everyone's time in the process.*

"It wasn't supposed to be like this." Lauren's words were so quiet, if they hadn't been standing in near silence, Maggie wouldn't have been able to hear them. She slid another step closer. Lauren didn't seem to notice. "Ethan and I were supposed to be together."

Madison glared at Lauren with such hatred, even Maggie had to fight not to flinch back. "Then maybe you shouldn't have fucked his *brother*."

"You don't know anything about it. If it wasn't for you, he would have taken me back!" Lauren screeched. She swung the gun around and pointed it at Maggie's face. "Take one more step."

Maggie shrugged, even as her stomach dropped. "Can't blame me for trying." She strained her ears, but there was nothing to hear. The world seemed to have ceased to exist outside their little triangle. If rescue was coming, it was too far away to do any good.

She'd only get one chance.

Lauren twisted to keep Madison in her sight, and Maggie moved. She threw herself at the other woman, going for the gun.

◆ ◆ ◆

Friday, June 23
5:46 a.m.

A gunshot echoed through the forest.

Vic started forward, but Wyatt stopped him with a hand on his chest. "You can't go rushing in there." Dawn had sneaked up on them while they were hiking, and he could actually see the man's face without the aid of the flashlights they'd turned off nearly a mile ago.

He knocked the hand away. "Let me go."

"No." To his credit, Wyatt didn't flinch when he cursed up a storm.

It took precious seconds to get ahold of his temper. Vic took a careful step back. He couldn't afford the wasted time dicking around over whether they should run in there or approach cautiously. Getting himself shot—or worse—would detract from his ability to help Maggie. He was better than this. He *had* to be better than this. "I'm fine."

"If you can't handle this, you can wait here."

It wasn't the first time he'd been asked if he could handle things. His commanding officer would kick his ass to Iraq and back for fucking up an already fucked-up situation with his issues. Vic nodded. "I'm fine." He would be. He didn't have a choice. "I'm good."

With one last look at him, Wyatt turned away. "We approach as quietly as we can. There's a switchback up ahead, so we have a chance to get there without anyone seeing us as long as we're careful."

Vic nodded, his body so tense he was damn near vibrating. He held himself still through sheer force of will, nearly exhaling in relief when David and Wyatt started up the path. They kept a decent distance from him, as if they knew exactly how tightly strung he was. For their part, they were tense and silent. Maggie was one of theirs, after all. They'd worked with her longer than he had, and if anything happened to her, it was possible they'd blame themselves as heartily as Vic currently was blaming himself.

He shouldn't have left the hospital. He'd known there was a risk, but he'd comforted himself with the presence of a cop who'd probably never dealt with a threat larger than a domestic dispute. He should have known that if something happened to those girls, Maggie—who was just down the hallway—would hear it and go to investigate.

No one could have anticipated her climbing into the back of the unsub's goddamn van. When he caught up to her, he was going to rip her a new one over such a stupid choice. They could have found the van without her in the back of it.

But there was Madison to consider . . .

Fuck. He was going to drive himself crazy pursuing this line of thought.

Focus on the here and now. The rest of it can wait.

They rounded a corner, and Wyatt held up his hand. Vic stopped, slowing his breathing even as his heart picked up, trying to listen for any indication that the unsub and the women were close.

Nothing.

Less than nothing—even the whisper-soft nature noises that had accompanied them to this point had gone silent.

Wyatt gave a soft curse, and then they were all moving, striding up the last switchback and to a small flat spot situated on the incline.

It didn't look like much in the growing light, but David immediately crouched and pointed. "Blood."

Not a lot—just a couple of drops that could indicate anything from a broken nose to a stab wound. It might not be serious . . . or it might be serious enough that the wounded person hadn't started to bleed in earnest until they were away from this spot. No way to tell whose blood, either, but it was shiny and fresh. *Fresh.*

Vic scanned the trees, but there wasn't much to see. There was no convenient blood trail to follow, aside from these few drops. Had the unsub started his hunt from here? He stood and turned a slow circle. "Doesn't make sense. Why not wait until they got to the high point?"

"Flattop Mountain is ringed by Livingston Range and Lewis Range. Plenty of places to run in between those taller mountains, but it's contained, to a certain extent."

That didn't help them any. They hadn't seen or heard anything except that single gunshot on their way up, so it made sense that the women and the unsub had cut away from the trail, either to the east or west. *Were they together? Or did he already start his hunt?* It didn't make sense. From what he understood, Flattop would be a better place to start.

But there was that gunshot to consider—and the blood.

Damn it, Maggie, you jumped him, didn't you?

She wouldn't go quietly, not when she had a chance to fight. Having Madison there would only heighten her protective instincts.

They had to find them. *Now.*

◆ ◆ ◆

Friday, June 23
5:59 a.m.

Madison ran. She shouldn't have. She should have stayed and fought like the park-ranger lady, but the gun had gone off, and all she could see was Ashleigh's blue eyes going wide as Lauren held her by her hair and slit her throat. It hadn't been like the movies. It had been so, so, so much worse.

She sobbed and ran faster. Instinct demanded she run downhill, but Lauren would be expecting that. Her bare feet were cut to shreds, and her arm burned from where Lauren's bullet had nicked her, but she didn't feel the pain anymore. *Adrenaline.* It didn't matter. All that mattered was getting as far away from Lauren as she could.

A rock shifted when she put her weight on it, sending her flying. She hit the ground with a bone-jarring thud, knocking the breath from her lungs. Momentum and gravity took over, sending her rolling down the incline until a tree stopped her.

Madison lay there, staring at the tree canopy, trying to relearn how to inhale. Her lungs weren't working, were frozen in her chest, and she couldn't force them to do their job.

All at once, the imaginary band around her chest released, and she gasped in a breath. She closed her eyes and tried to calm the terrified beating of her heart. If she kept running like this, she'd wear herself out and then she'd be easy pickings. She wouldn't go out like that. She *refused* to.

Biting back a cry, she sat up and took a look at her surroundings. She might not know the exact spot, but she knew where she was—just west of Mountain Trail. It wasn't as widely traveled as Highline Trail, but she'd hiked it more times than she could count.

Granted, every other time she'd done it, she'd had the appropriate gear and *shoes.*

Didn't matter. She was getting the hell out of here.

Madison climbed to her feet and winced. No matter how good her pep talk, she wasn't getting far like this. *What would Ethan do if he were here?*

A small sound brought her head up, and she dropped into a crouch, scanning the slope she'd just fallen down. Her descent would have made a ton of noise, so if Lauren was close, she'd be on her way here.

Madison could almost hear Ethan's voice in her head. *Move. Just keep moving, no matter how much you want to curl into a ball and cry.*

But the person who emerged from between two trees wasn't Lauren. It was the park ranger. Madison had one horribly selfish moment where she seriously considered hiding and hoping the woman drew Lauren away from her. Instead, she raised a hand, the small move catching the park ranger's eye.

She rushed down the slope, taking more care than Madison did, and helped her stand. "We have to move."

"I can't run."

The park ranger looked at her feet and nodded. "Then we hide."

It sounded like the stupidest thing in the world, but Madison couldn't come up with a better idea. She limped after the park ranger until they finally found a spot where a tree had fallen against another one. The brush had started to overtake it, and if she curled up, she'd fit.

They both wouldn't, though.

Madison turned, but the park ranger shook her head. *God, why can't I remember her name?*

She motioned, her voice so soft, Madison could barely hear it.

"You can't run. I can. I'll draw her away from you."

"But—" Madison froze.

Lauren's voice drifted to them. "Come out, come out, wherever you are!"

Madison shuddered. She'd known Lauren was messed up—she had to be to stay with Josh all this time—but being okay with a guy who was borderline abusive didn't mean she was justified in *murder*. "Be careful."

"I will." The park ranger helped her get into the spot and pulled some more brush over her. "Don't move, okay? For as long as you can hold out."

"Okay." Madison spoke through dry lips, fear making her voice thick. She watched the park ranger move away until the woman was lost from sight, and Madison couldn't shake the feeling that she'd just made her a human sacrifice so she could live.

CHAPTER
TWENTY-FIVE

Friday, June 23
6:05 a.m.

Maggie didn't run. She wanted to—God, how she wanted to, with that damned taunting voice that seemed to be everywhere and nowhere—but she knew better. If she ran, she'd either run herself into the ground or she'd misstep, twist her ankle, and might as well offer her throat to Lauren to finish her off.

She had no intention of dying today, but if it was her time, she wasn't going without a fight.

She moved uphill, her thighs burning from the climb, her back in constant pain she had no solution for. Lauren would expect her to head downhill, since it was easier. She'd had to leave some sign of her passing so she could actually draw the woman away from Madison. Lauren was too smart to believe her if she started making noise, so she'd been forced to be subtle. A broken tree branch here, a deliberate footprint in the soft soil there. It was more difficult than just blazing a trail, but she had to make it believable.

It wasn't believable that she *wanted* Lauren to catch her.

She touched the metal pen still in her pocket. Her phone had been taken, but the woman had missed the pen. She laughed softly. A pen wasn't any better a weapon now than it had been when she was in the hospital, but it'd have to do. She didn't have time to try to find a decent stick, and even if she found one, she had no knife to carve it to her needs.

No, there was just the pen and, hopefully, the element of surprise.

She stopped. She'd reached the peak of the ridge. It was all downhill from here—literally. It also meant she'd have high ground. Maggie searched the surrounding trees. There were two that would fit her needs, and only one of them had a branch low enough for her to reach. She checked to make sure Lauren hadn't magically appeared . . . which was the exact moment she realized the taunting had stopped. She cursed silently and then cursed again when the move to pull herself into the tree resulted in what felt like her back being torn in two. *There go the stitches.*

There was no time to waste. She shinnied up the tree, sending a silent prayer of thanks to the universe for the fact that most of the clothing she owned naturally blended into the forest. The items Ava had brought her were no exception—a long-sleeve green T-shirt with brown cargo pants that she seemed to remember her friend claiming belonged in the nineties. Maggie had laughed at the time, but they might save her ass today, because they gave her a better range of motion than even her most comfortable jeans. She climbed onto another branch and pressed herself against the trunk of the tree.

Lauren didn't make her wait long. The woman slid out of the nearby trees as if she was part of the forest itself. She still had the pistol, which meant they hadn't reached the spot where she'd stashed her gear.

It wouldn't make a bit of difference if the woman was as good with a gun as she was with the bow.

And I just stranded myself up a tree.

She was roughly ten feet off the ground, and Maggie had never been all that accomplished at springing out and surprising someone. Strangely enough, that wasn't an action covered by either the FBI or the park ranger training.

She held her breath as Lauren moved closer. *What is she . . .* Her heart actually skipped a beat when she realized what the woman was doing. Her gaze was on the ground, her entire body tense with anticipation.

She's tracking me.

Lauren reached the spot where Maggie had climbed up the tree and started to straighten. In another second, she'd see Maggie, and then it'd be like shooting fish in a barrel. Maggie shot forward before she could think too hard about how much this would hurt. She hit Lauren square on, taking them both to the ground with a bone-jarring impact.

"Bitch," Lauren wheezed.

Maggie rolled onto her back, fighting through the feeling of her lungs trying to collapse. *Just knocked the breath out of me. Don't stop.* When she hit Lauren, the gun had flown, and she had to be the first one to get to it. She crawled across the ground, each move sending a flare of pain through her back.

Nurse Colleen is going to kick my ass if I live through this. She almost looked forward to it.

Weight hit her square in the back, and she found the breath to scream. Lauren's fingers wrapped around her throat. *"Bitch."*

"Get a new insult," she ground out. She scrambled for Lauren's fingers, trying to loosen the grip choking the life out her. It was hard, so hard. Her eyes wanted to close. *Fuck that.* She snapped her head back, making contact with Lauren's face. It startled the woman enough that she loosened her grip.

But only for a moment.

Lauren slammed her head into the ground once, twice. By the third time, Maggie saw stars, and her body stopped obeying her commands to fight. Her fingers dug into the dirt, a futile attempt to lift herself, but that was as far as the move got.

And then Lauren's weight was gone, and a shriek of fury echoed through the forest. Maggie lay there, unable to focus enough to even roll over and see what had happened. She took a breath and then another, distantly noting that her face was wet with what was probably blood. Sounds reached her next, staggered breathing and grunts like there was a struggle going on behind her.

Have to see. Need to know.

She dug deep and flopped onto her back to the sight of Madison punching Lauren in the face. It was a solid right hook, and the other woman staggered back but didn't go down. Lauren made a sound approximating a roar and charged her, hitting her in the stomach with her shoulder and taking them both to the ground.

Maggie wasn't stupid enough to get in the middle of a brawl in her current condition, even if she was capable of running over there. Instead, she turned and crawled inch by agonizing inch in the direction she'd seen the gun fly. If she could get to it, she could put a stop to the beating she could hear going on behind her.

It was the *only* way she could do any good.

She caught a glint of metal in the brush and headed for it, trying not to listen too closely to the pained noise Madison was making. Her fingers closed around the butt of the gun, and she gritted her teeth and threw the last of her reserves into sitting up.

Maggie lifted the gun, only to find Lauren smirking at her. The woman had Madison facedown on the ground, one arm wrenched between her shoulder blades in a move Maggie had used more than a few times to subdue reckless idiots.

Lauren's lip was bleeding, and she'd have a wicked black eye if she lived through the day, but she had the upper hand. "Put that gun down before you shoot yourself with it."

Maggie clenched her jaw and tried to steady the shaking in her arms—tried and failed. "Move away from her. Now."

"You pull that trigger, and you might hit her instead of me." Lauren twisted a little harder, drawing another cry from Madison. "Or I could just sit here until your strength fails you."

It would happen sooner or later. Maggie had always been taught never to draw a gun on a person unless she was willing to pull the trigger. She was. Lauren had killed so many people and would kill both her and Madison if she wasn't stopped.

Her arm spasmed, and she dropped the gun without meaning to. Lauren laughed. "That didn't take long."

Maggie reached for the gun again, but her vision grayed alarmingly. She was so beyond tapped out right now, she was worse than useless. She glared at the woman and froze when she caught movement in the trees behind Lauren. Even with exhaustion and pain hazing her vision and making her weave while sitting down, she'd recognize Vic. He was too far away to get to Lauren before Lauren got to the gun, so she lifted her chin. "Anyone tell you that you have serious abandonment issues? I mean . . . fuck." If she could keep her distracted, Vic could remove the threat.

"Shut up."

As if that was going to happen. She'd obviously hit a nerve, so she just kept poking at it. "That's what this is about, isn't it? Poor little Lauren, left behind by everyone she loves." Vic moved closer, almost within reach of the woman. Madison hadn't moved in the last minute or so, which was worrying, but there was a list as long as Maggie's arm of things that were worrying right now. She hitched up her chin. "Guess you weren't as important to them as they were to you. Weird how they wouldn't want a crazy psychopath hanging around."

"*Shut up!* You don't know the first thing about it. They ruined everything."

"God forbid."

Lauren drew a knife from her boot. "Keep talking, bitch. I'll finish Madison and then I'll come for you." She leaned down, going for Madison's exposed throat.

Vic *moved*. He crossed the remaining distance in two bounding strides and took Lauren down to the ground in a tackle that had Maggie wincing. Before she could decide if she was supposed to try to help, he had the woman facedown on the ground and was cuffing her hands behind her. "Lauren Rosario, you're under arrest for the murders of Ashleigh Marcinko and six others. Anything you say can and will be used against you in a court of law."

Wyatt and David approached cautiously, shooting incredulous looks at Vic and Lauren. Maggie couldn't blame them. If she'd been asked before today, she would have put Lauren Rosario at the very bottom of the suspect pool—and that was before the girl had turned up dead.

But to their credit, they didn't waste time. David went to Madison, and then Wyatt was blocking Maggie's line of sight as he crouched in front of her. "You've seen better days."

"You say the nicest things." Her adrenaline started to fade, bringing with it a wave of pain that she hadn't noticed until now.

"You want to tell me what's wrong, or do I need to do a check myself?" Wyatt said.

Mortification at the thought of Wyatt going over her body had her speaking up despite the fact she just wanted to lie there in the dirt and rest awhile. "Ripped my stitches. Bruises, nothing broken." She touched her throat and then her face. "She got some good hits in. Possible concussion."

His gaze went to the gun lying on the ground near her foot. "I'd say you got off lucky."

"Yeah." She didn't feel lucky. There was so much she could have done differently from the time she saw that van and realized that it belonged to the unsub.

"You did good, Maggie." Wyatt touched her shoulder awkwardly. "Pretty sure that agent of yours is going to take off my head if I don't let him be the one to carry you out of here. Unless you think you need a chopper?"

"No." She licked her dry lips and winced. "Not unless Madison does. She's the important one."

"Mmm-hmm." Wyatt stood and moved over to Lauren.

Maggie didn't catch what he said to Vic, but he took over watching Lauren, and then Vic was in front of her.

His gaze raked over her, and he turned to David. "How is she?"

"Banged up, but she'll be okay. She wants to hike out." The thin line of David's mouth said all anyone needed to hear about what he thought of *that*.

Vic just nodded. "Let's get the fuck out of here, then." He crouched next to Maggie and lowered his voice. "Anything I'm going to hurt if I pick you up?"

Her pride demanded she tell him that she was more than capable of walking, but the truth was that she wouldn't make it ten feet before she collapsed. "I'll be okay."

"You had damn well better." He carefully picked her up, tucking her in against his chest. "Fuck, Maggie, you scared the shit out of me."

She was sorry, but . . . she also wasn't. "We got her. She won't hurt anyone else."

"Yes." He didn't say anything else.

Maggie tried to stay awake, but the events of the last twenty-four hours were too much. Exhaustion pulled her under on a dark tide.

Friday, June 23
10:09 a.m.

It didn't take long for Vic to get the information he wanted out of Lauren. She was spitting mad and knew that she wasn't getting out of this without going to prison. There was too much evidence, and the testimonies of Madison and a park ranger were the final nails in her coffin.

Plus, the woman liked to brag.

She confessed with little prompting, every inch the proud sociopath who wanted credit for being clever. As he'd suspected, the Haglunds had stumbled onto the camp she'd set up in preparation for murdering her former friends, and she'd gone after Bill's eyes in response. The only part he couldn't quite figure out was why she'd let Madison and Ashleigh light the signal fire to be rescued. Lauren claimed it was so she could frame Madison, but it read like a mistake to Vic.

Lauren would be going to prison for a very long time, and it was entirely possible she'd get the death sentence, since the crimes were committed on federal land. It left the case wrapped up in as neat a bow as possible, but that didn't change the fact that Lauren was responsible for the deaths of seven people.

Interrogating her left him feeling off center and sick to his stomach. All he wanted was to see Maggie and reassure himself again that she was actually okay.

He didn't expect to run into Britton in the hallway outside her hospital room, but he should have. "Now's not a good time."

"On the contrary. It's as good a time as any." Britton eyed the door to her room. "I'm offering her a spot back in the BAU. There's no hard feelings if she turns me down, of course, but I have a feeling she won't." His lips quirked up in what was almost a smile. "Don't you think, Vic?"

A position in the BAU would put them in close quarters again. It would mean that they wouldn't have to try to juggle a long-distance relationship while they figured things out between them—or after. He swallowed hard, recognizing the gift Britton was giving him. "You'd do that for me."

Britton frowned. "No. Of course not. I'm pleased that you and Maggie are figuring things out, but we lost one of the best up-and-coming agents when she left. I'm keen to have her back."

Of course. Vic should have known that, as in touch as Britton was with his people, he wouldn't do something as permanent as offering them a job without a legitimate reason. "Have you asked her?"

"I thought I'd leave that up to you." Britton checked his watch. "I have a plane to catch. Let me know how it goes."

"Of course." He didn't wait for Britton to disappear down the hallway before he walked into Maggie's room. She lay in the hospital bed, looking tired and grumpy. It was all he could do not to pull her into his arms and never let go. That hellish hike down to the road, the only thing that had kept him going was her breathing and his being able to hold her.

She managed a smile. "Hey."

"Hey." He considered the chair next to her bed, but it was too far away, so he took a spot on the bed and held her hand. "You scared the shit out of me."

"Sorry." She looked at their intertwined hands. "We got her. She's going away for life."

"Yes, she is." It wouldn't change the fact that seven people wouldn't be going home because of her. Their families would have closure, but it was a small comfort in the grand scheme of things.

As much as he wanted to let Maggie rest, there were things still hanging unsaid between them. If this case had done nothing else, it had convinced Vic that he had to fight for what he wanted.

What he wanted was Maggie.

"Maggie, I love you."

"*What?*" She stared at him as if he'd just pulled a gun on her. "How can you . . . It's so soon . . ."

He didn't let her shock deter him. "Britton's offered you a job back at the BAU. I know you love your park, and I'd never ask you to leave your job here if you don't want to. Whatever you decide, I support you. If you want me—if you choose me—we'll make this work one way or another. Distance is a small thing compared with what we've faced in the last few days."

She laughed softly. "Yeah, I guess it is." Her smile faded. "I do love you, Vic. It might have started as a schoolgirl crush, but it's the truth. I . . . I'll think about the job offer."

"Okay." It was more than he'd thought she'd do. Vic lifted her hand and kissed her bruised knuckles. "I choose you, Maggie. The rest will figure itself out."

ACKNOWLEDGMENTS

I am forever grateful to God for putting me in the position to do what I love for a living. The Hidden Sins books are definitely a walk on the dark side, and I'm enjoying every second of it.

Huge thank-you to Krista Stroever for helping me whip this book into shape and make it the best version of itself. You are my people! Thank you to Christopher Werner and Kim Cowser and the rest of the team at Montlake for making this a truly outstanding experience across the board. I wouldn't know what to do without you!

This book wouldn't have gotten off the ground without Matthew Beckerleg. Thank you for recommending a ton of amazing park ranger books—and then answering my questions while I figured out what kind of story I was telling. I would happily share another vodka flight with you and Piper!

Big hugs and thanks to every member of the Rabble who lent me their surnames—Samantha Marcinko, Ginny Rosario, Jackie Conlon, Brandy Thornton, and Erica Haglund. And thank you to Elizabeth Neal for being the one to pick Maggie's name. It's perfect!

This book wouldn't exist—because I would have had a nervous breakdown—if not for Piper J. Drake. Thank you for being there to talk me through plot snags, characters behaving badly, and the inevitable deadline insanity. You are the absolute best!

Thank you to Tim. Yes, you knew you were going to be on this list. Thank you for answering some seriously worrisome questions about field dressing and then sitting down with me to plot out the best way to murder people in a national park. I love you like whoa, and I wouldn't have anyone else at my side to battle serial killers, zombies, and people in general. Kisses!

ABOUT THE AUTHOR

New York Times and *USA Today* bestselling author Katee Robert learned to tell her stories at her grandpa's knee. Her 2015 book, *The Marriage Contract*, was a RITA Award finalist, and *RT Book Reviews* called it "a compulsively readable book with just the right amount of suspense and tension." When not writing sexy contemporary and romantic suspense, she spends her time playing imaginative games with her children, driving her husband batty with what-if questions, and planning for the inevitable zombie apocalypse. *The Hunting Grounds* is the second book in Katee's Hidden Sins series following *The Devil's Daughter*. Visit her online at www.kateerobert.com.